The DIAMOND
INHERITANCE

The DIAMOND INHERITANCE

PIPPA ROSCOE

MILLS & BOON

THE DIAMOND INHERITANCE © 2024 by Harlequin Books S.A.

The publisher acknowledges the copyright holders of the individual works as follows:
TERMS OF THEIR COSTA RICAN TEMPTATION
© 2021 by Pippa Roscoe   First Published 2021
Philippine Copyright 2021   Second Australian Paperback Edition 2024
Australian Copyright 2021   ISBN 978 1 038 90862 9
New Zealand Copyright 2021

FROM ONE NIGHT TO DESERT QUEEN
© 2021 by Pippa Roscoe   First Published 2021
Philippine Copyright 2021   Second Australian Paperback Edition 2024
Australian Copyright 2021   ISBN 978 1 038 90862 9
New Zealand Copyright 2021

THE GREEK SECRET SHE CARRIES
© 2021 by Pippa Roscoe   First Published 2021
Philippine Copyright 2021   Second Australian Paperback Edition 2024
Australian Copyright 2021   ISBN 978 1 038 90862 9
New Zealand Copyright 2021

MIX
Paper | Supporting
responsible forestry
FSC
www.fsc.org   FSC® C001695

Published by
Harlequin Mills & Boon
An imprint of Harlequin Enterprises (Australia) Pty Limited
(ABN 47 001 180 918), a subsidiary of HarperCollins
Publishers Australia Pty Limited
(ABN 36 009 913 517)
Level 19, 201 Elizabeth Street
SYDNEY NSW 2000 AUSTRALIA

Printed and bound in Australia by McPherson's Printing Group

CONTENTS

Pippa Roscoe lives in Norfolk near her family and makes daily promises to herself that this is the day she'll leave the computer to take a long walk in the countryside. She can't remember a time when she wasn't dreaming about handsome heroes and innocent heroines. Totally her mother's fault, of course—she gave Pippa her first romance to read at the age of seven! She is inconceivably happy that she gets to share those daydreams with you all. Follow her on Twitter, @pipparoscoe.

Terms Of Their
Costa Rican Temptation

MILLS & BOON

DEDICATION

For Rani.

Because sometimes all you need is friendship and laughter to put the world right again.

Xx

PROLOGUE

Skye Soames took a deep breath that quivered at the back of her throat for a moment before she drew it into her lungs, hoping that her sisters hadn't noticed. Not for the first time she wondered what the three of them were doing in Norfolk on an unseasonably cold, grey miserable day, standing beside the coffin of a man they had never met.

She clenched her jaw against the cutting wind as it hit her like a slap. They'd been picked up from their small home on the outskirts of the New Forest by a limousine—neighbours frowning and whispering into their hands as they peered through white lace curtains, as if they hadn't had a lifetime of gossip already. But four hours in a car that glided over concrete had co-cooned her and her sisters in a warm, contented state of confusion until they had caught sight of the stone church and the Gothic graveyard beside it.

They were here to…what? Pay their respects? To a man who had kicked out his only daughter at the age of seventeen and cut her off without a penny or word ever since? Because until today that was all they had ever known about their grandfather, Elias Soames.

Summer, her youngest sister, shifted on her feet and drew her dark wool coat around her middle, her face strangely pale against the blonde hair she'd pulled back into a messy ponytail. So very different from Skye's own brown hair, carefully wrapped into a neat bun, and just as different from the long vibrant, fiery red strands the wind whipped across Star's cheeks. A difference that came from each sister's father. Some might have called them half-sisters, but to Skye, Summer and Star there was nothing half about the bond between them. Star's hand came up to brush her Titian hair back, revealing startling green eyes sparkling with a sheen that looked suspiciously like tears.

'Star?'

'It's just so sad,' she said.

'We never met him. He abandoned our—'

'Ashes to ashes, dust to dust...' The words spoken by the priest cut through Summer's response as if in admonishment and another blast of icy-cold air trickled down Skye's spine. She shivered, not for the grandfather she had never known, but for another funeral, one yet to come. One that threatened to rock the very foundations of Skye and her sisters' lives.

Mariam Soames hadn't been able to attend the funeral because of her treatment schedule—if you could call sipping on herbal teas and CBD tablets treatment. Thanks to the postcode lottery that determined access to specific treatments on the NHS, they'd lost out. Big time. And it had only encouraged their alternative life-style living mother further into 'natural treatments'.

Skye had spent more midnight hours than she could count trying to work out how to fund the life-saving health care privately, or even a very costly move into another area where Mariam stood a better chance of treatment. But the housing costs in the nearest health region where that might happen were four times more expensive than what they paid now and, no matter the calculations, they just couldn't make it work. Besides, Mariam didn't want to move, she was focused on quality of life not quantity. Skye's heart twisted that she couldn't find a way to achieve both for her mother.

She looked up at the large house in the distance. Her mother had insisted that even had she been well enough she wouldn't have come. Mariam Soames had said all she needed to her father the night she had left Norfolk thirty-seven years ago.

Elias's lawyer nodded, announcing the end of the small service that marked the end of a man's life. No one else had been in attendance. Clearly Elias Soames had not been a popular figure in the community, leaving the mourners to number five, including the priest.

The lawyer walked them back to the limousine and chose to sit up front with the driver, effectively preventing any conversation until they reached the estate. Skye felt sick at the thought of her grandfather having enough money to fund his daughter's treatment and then some, and felt shame knowing her primary motivation for being here—the will.

Barely five minutes later the car pulled into a grand

sweeping drive that took them towards their grandfather's home and Skye's jaw wasn't the only one in the car to drop.

It might not have had the grandeur of the estate from *Downton Abbey*—Summer's favourite TV show—but it wasn't far off. The sprawling ancient building revealed itself in glimpses as the car took the large twists and turns of the drive towards an impressive set of steps at the main entrance, which finally revealed the house in its entirety.

'Holy—' Star's curse was cut short by a not-so-gentle shoulder-shove from Skye, who had no wish to incur any further disdain from Elias's lawyer, Mr Beamish. But it had managed to draw a spark of something to Summer's grey eyes—a spark that had been absent for the last few weeks.

Skye stepped out of the car and was forced to crane her neck to look up at the glorious building. This was... unimaginable. Her mother had walked away from this? There had to be...

'There are over twenty rooms in the main section of the house, but though the east and west wings have been closed off for quite some time now, they also boast a modest fifteen apiece. I'm afraid we have to hurry things along a bit,' he claimed, barely stopping for breath. 'You'll understand why shortly. Follow me.'

With that, he turned on his heel and disappeared into the bowels of the house. Skye and her sisters followed him down dark hallways with moth-eaten carpets, various pieces of antique furniture, sideboards on which sat china bowls of scentless aged potpourri and walls covered in old dusty paintings of ancestors Skye couldn't even begin to imagine. She saw her sisters' heads sweeping from side to side as if to take it all in. But Skye focused only on Mr Beamish as he led them into what was clearly the estate office. One of them had to keep their head on straight and focus on the situation. And, as always, it would be her.

He gestured for them to sit in the three chairs provided, facing the beautiful and clearly ancient wooden desk. Only when they had done so did Mr Beamish take his place opposite them. Skye watched as he pulled a raft of papers from his briefcase and began the formalities of the reading of the will. Whether it was exhaustion from the day's early start or the particular pitch of his monotone voice, she couldn't keep his words in her head for long and her mind wandered as freely as her eyes around the room. They caught on a large oil painting just behind Mr Beamish.

The image was quite startling, and she knew without a shadow of a doubt that she was staring at a portrait of her grandfather. He looked...mean. And miserable. And nothing like his daughter, who had more laughter, more love in her than she could contain, both traits often trailing in her wake. Skye's mother might be flighty, might have little to no thought of practicalities and necessities, but she loved greatly.

So different from the malicious intent in the eyes of Elias Soames looming up behind Mr Beamish as he delivered his last will and testament. And then her mind snagged on what the lawyer had just said.

'I'm sorry...what?' she asked. Shock cut through

her, as if her body had reacted before comprehending what the words had meant.

'As I said, Ms Soames. The entire estate will be yours, on certain conditions. For five generations the entail known as the Soames diamonds have been missing. Much like his father, and his father's father before him and so on, Elias had been desperately trying to recover them. The specifics of his search are in this folder here,' he said, pushing the folder only halfway towards the women. 'Before his death, my client made the stipulation that you will inherit the entire estate—to do with as you will—on the condition that you are able to retrieve the Soames diamonds within two months of his death.'

Skye was speechless, her mind hurtling at the speed of light through the possibilities this might mean. For them. For their mother.

'So we could sell the estate?' Star demanded.

Mr Beamish nodded. 'If you find the diamonds, yes.'

'Is this even legal?' Skye asked, even while her mind screamed, *I don't care!*

Mr Beamish had the grace to look embarrassed, but not to answer the question. 'Should you fail to discover their whereabouts, then the estate and the entire entail will revert to the National Trust. I believe the deadline set by the will fails to allow for enough time to contest the will. Furthermore, a legal battle would be costly and time-consuming and the two-month deadline is immovable.'

'But—'

Mr Beamish cleared his throat over Summer's protest and pushed on. 'A provision has been set aside for any expenses needed for your endeavours—expenses that I will be able to approve and release as requested. The last stipulation is that one of you must remain in residence at the estate for the entire two months.'

Mr Beamish sucked in a discreet lungful of air as if he'd had to force the words out in one go, no matter how distasteful he had found them.

'You can, of course, choose to refuse the terms, upon which the entire estate and entail will revert immediately to the National Trust. It is clearly a lot to think on. Rooms have been made available for your use this evening, and we will meet again in the morning to hear your final decision.'

With another firm nod, the man left with barely a goodbye—running for the hills, Skye thought. The room was silent until a gasp of horrified laughter erupted from Summer.

'Missing diamonds! How romantic,' Star said on a dramatic sigh.

'That's what you took from all this?' Skye demanded of her whimsical middle sister. 'Romance?'

'Yes! It's *so* romantic,' she insisted, even as Skye shook her head.

Summer had already pulled the thick file which promised to contain details of Elias's attempts to uncover the location of the Soames diamonds towards her from across the table.

'I can't take two months off. I have a job,' Skye insisted, already torn between practicalities and the possibility of what the terms of the will meant.

'A job from which you've never taken a holiday,' Summer said absently, already scanning through the pages of the file. 'Rob would give you anything you asked, and you know it. You just don't ask.'

'Well, it's not long until school's out for the summer,' Star pressed on, covering the need for Skye to respond to Summer's unusually blunt observation. 'I'm sure they'll let me take the rest of the term off. And Summer's just finished her degree so… Oh, this could be so much fun.'

Fun wasn't what Skye was thinking. She was thinking that if they did manage to find the missing jewels, then perhaps they'd be able to cover their mother's medical bills. Pay for even better treatment. And perhaps… But she stopped her mind from going there. Skye had never put much faith in wishes and prayers like Star had.

'If we found them, we could sell the estate…' Summer said. 'Or at least mortgage it?'

'A mortgage we'd never be able to pay back,' replied Skye.

'But how are we supposed to find jewels that have been missing since…?' Star said, ignoring the practicalities as usual.

'1871,' Summer said, glancing up from the folder for the first time.

'And, even if we did, how *would* we sell it?' Skye asked.

Summer looked away, as if considering. 'I might… know someone,' she said with a shrug of her shoulder.

'You might know someone who happens to have…
what? Several hundred million in the bank to buy all
this?' The look in her sister's eyes made Skye feel bad
about her apparent scepticism. 'Summer—'

'I do,' she replied, ignoring the bite of Skye's words.
'It's a long shot, but yeah. And besides, we don't need
several hundred million. We just need enough.'

Skye nodded in return. Just enough to cover Mariam's medical bills.

'Oohh, I love an adventure.'

Skye and Summer shared an eye roll over their sister's excitement.

'So, we're actually doing this?' Skye asked, tem-
pering the unwanted excitement beginning to build in
her stomach. She might have spent her life grounding
her siblings to counter the airy dreams of their mother,
but even she couldn't deny that there was something
thrilling about the idea of going on an actual treasure
hunt. It was a silly feeling, something that was almost
naughty, as if it were a guilty pleasure her heart just
couldn't deny as it thrummed quickly in her body.

When Summer and Star nodded, sharing looks of
excitement and hope, just for once Skye allowed herself to imagine that this could be the start of a thrilling adventure.

CHAPTER ONE

TWO WEEKS LATER, Skye was finishing up her final search of the last room in the west wing and decided, pulling cobwebs from her hair, that there was nothing thrilling about fruitlessly searching through decades of dust. Beamish hadn't been lying when he said the two wings had been closed for years.

By the time she pushed open the door to the library that had become the Soames sisters' base of operations, she found Star hauling a portrait that must have been nearly one hundred and fifty years old across the room.

'Should you be doing that?' Skye queried.

'Why not?' Tug. 'I thought—' tug '—that it would be good inspiration,' tug.

'Because it might be worth a fair bit of money?' Summer replied without looking up from the mounds of paper she had spread out on the table in front of her. Skye winced at the sound of the gilt frame scraping against the wooden floor as Star shoved it up against one of the many bookcases in the room.

'There. The last time the diamonds were seen. Catherine Soames' wedding portrait.'

All three of the girls repressed a shiver at the thought of their great-great-grandmother being forced to marry her cousin. Elias's research had been surprisingly detailed. Then again, four generations of Soames men had been looking for the diamonds ever since they'd gone missing from Duke Anthony Soames's private chambers two nights after the painting had been finished.

'Well, they weren't in the west wing, just like they weren't in the east wing,' Skye said, filling them in on the results of her searches. 'Though, from the damage I've seen, I think Elias thought they were hidden in the walls because there are huge holes knocked into them, dust and plaster and God knows what else all over the place. Honestly, it looks as if Elias went at them with a sledgehammer.'

'Perhaps he was mad and that's why Mum didn't want to talk about him?' Star wondered out loud.

'Perhaps it ran in the family. According to the notes here, after Anthony had his valet arrested and imprisoned for the theft, he then decided that Catherine had hidden them, even if he couldn't prove it, or even understand how she might have done it,' Summer said, looking up from the file that seemed to be permanently glued to her hands.

'I hope she *did* hide them. He sounds like a miserable creature.' Smiling at Star's unique description, Skye flipped on the light switch. Although the library was a great place for them to gather, she didn't like how dark it always was.

Sinking down into one of the leather armchairs, she struggled to remain optimistic. Taking up the terms of the will had given them purpose, a goal, something to work towards for their mother. But two weeks in and it was beginning to seem hopeless. Not that she'd ever say as much to Star and Summer. They relied on her, they needed her to be the one to spur them on.

'I think we should move to another room,' Star said, the floaty material of her wide-armed shirt hanging low as she reached out to touch the old leather spines of the books. 'It makes me feel…hinky.'

'Hinky?' Summer asked with a laugh.

'Yeah…just wonky, somehow.'

Skye frowned. She'd never really noticed it before but, now that Star had said it, she knew what her sister meant. Skye tried to look at the room with fresh eyes, rather than ones that had seen it for more hours than she would have wished. The little library, the women's library, Catherine's library. The room had more names for it than any other in the entire estate and, even though it paled in comparison to the Duke's library, all of the sisters had preferred it here, despite the darkness which, now Skye was looking at it, must have had something to do with the—

'The windows!' Summer exclaimed, at the exact moment Skye had realised the same thing. 'The shelves on the left-hand side… I think…' Her words were cut off as Star ran out of the room into the hallway, peering back into the library, then disappearing off to the next room along and reappearing again.

'The room—it's smaller than it should be!' Star practically screamed and Skye tried to suppress uncharitable frustration at the sister who had most definitely taken after their mother in her sense of both romance and adventure. Skye felt a painfully familiar sense of longing that she was ashamed of. A longing to be more like them, a longing to join in with the fun. But then she would be even less like her father, whose serious, quiet, non-confrontational nature was so very different to Mariam. And she clung to whatever she could of her father because when he'd remarried he'd just seemed to get further and further away from her.

Pushing aside the stab of pain brought by her train of thought, Skye focused on what Summer was doing—pulling out some of the ancient tomes lining the left-hand shelves and piling them up on the floor.

'Skye, can you—'

'Coming,' she said, leaning into the thrill of possibly finding the jewels as a distraction.

'Star, these books are hundreds of years old, please don't just—'

The thwack of another large tome hitting the floor made Summer wince.

'Sorry, it's just so…'

'Exciting, yeah we get it,' Skye mumbled under her breath. Surely if this was the final resting place of the jewels someone would have found them by now?

Two shelves cleared, Summer was running her hand underneath the wooden shelves when all the girls heard a *click*. The central panel of shelves shifted forward. A streak of lightning-quick excitement shot through Skye and she could see it reflected on her sisters' faces.

Had they found them? Could it be that simple?

Pulling hard, the central block of shelves swung

away from the wall to reveal a secret recess illuminated in the light from the window. Dust particles danced and swirled in the air, disturbed by the quick breaths of Skye and her sisters.

Summer reached in to retrieve a large bundle wrapped in an old leather sack, dark with age and slightly moth-eaten. As she carefully placed it on the large table the sisters each took a step back, watching it as if it were an unexploded bomb.

Star and Summer looked to Skye, who released the breath she'd been holding, shifted forward and parted the edges of the leather, revealing the contents concealed within.

Disappointment and guilt hit her hard and fast and Skye was instantly reminded of Christmases when her mother's gifts had seemed to be for anyone other than her. But as she looked at the pile of leather-bound books she was crushed that they weren't the jewels that would have made everything so much easier.

Summer took the top one in her hands, carefully, lovingly opening the cover.

'They're journals,' she said, a trace of awe in her voice.

Pressed into the middle of the pile of journals was a small framed portrait of a young girl who looked about five or six years old, around which was wrapped a chain and pendant, tarnished with age. Star took up the loop of silver chain, carefully unwinding it from the portrait, passing the wooden frame to Skye as she continued to study the unusual pendant. Turning the frame in her hands, Skye read the inscription on the back.

Laura, my love
1876—1881

The girl had been five years old. 'This must have been Catherine's daughter,' Skye whispered, overwhelmed by the emotion of discovering their family history and unable to ignore familiarity in the features of the young girl.

'She looks just like you did, Summer, when you were that age,' Skye said with a sad smile.

Summer blinked at her for a moment before turning back to the book in her hands. She cleared her throat a little and said, 'Look at this,' before offering the book for Skye and Star to read.

June 1864
Today was my coming out and everything and nothing was as expected. I know my duty. The need for me to make a match, given that Father has not a male heir. The risk that I should be married off to my cousin doesn't bear thinking on.

Skye sent Summer what she hoped was a comforting smile just as Star let out a peal of delight, her uncontained energy causing the journal in her hands to look slightly precarious. 'This one is dated 1869 and she's in the Middle East! She's talking about elephants and desert castles...'

'We should put them in date order and read them properly. They might contain information about the jewels,' Summer said.

'Why? They're just journals,' Skye replied, feeling bad for dismissing Catherine's memories.

'Journals that were hidden in a secret hiding place never discovered by any of the subsequent generations,' Summer snapped, before instantly looking so sorry that Skye rubbed her arm, letting her know it was okay.

Star ran the necklace through her fingers, holding the pendant close to her face. 'It's a strange-looking thing for the period.'

'And you know much about jewellery in the eighteen-hundreds?' Skye teased gently.

'No, it's just...so *romantic*.'

'What does the last entry say?' Skye asked Summer. 'It might tell us where the diamonds are.'

Checking the dates on the journals, Summer retrieved the last one and turned to the final page and let out a huff.

> *It has been two days since the wedding portrait and this is where I leave you. There are no shortcuts in life. Already I know that it is the journey, not the destination, that will matter most at the end.*
>
> *As for my life now? That is for history to document. I chose my path and will make the best of it.*
>
> *Go with trust and love, always,*
> *Catherine*

'Well, that's not cryptic at all,' Skye said.
Summer pulled another journal from the stack and

scanned through the pages of neat handwriting—barely a word scratched out, the swirls and loops were pretty on the thin aged paper. Skye frowned when she noticed a letter underlined. Not a whole word, but just a letter. At first she thought it was a mark, a kind of ink blot, but then she noticed another and another.

'Are there any underlined letters on your pages?' she asked Star, who began to flick through the pages.

'Careful! These are over one hundred years old!' Summer scolded.

'See?' Skye said, holding out the journal to show her sisters. 'Here—' she pointed '—and here again. But not every page has them.'

'It's a code. It must be a coded message,' Summer replied with wonder in her voice.

Star sighed. 'This is going to take for ever.'

Hours passed and although admittedly the code was simple, with Summer reading out the individual letters and Star writing them down, there was little for Skye to do other than watch her two younger sisters, who she had almost singlehandedly raised. It had been Skye who had made them dinner and got them to do their homework, got them dressed and to school on time as her mother, more often than not, lost herself to a day-dream, or a commune, or a whim. But in the last few years... Well, they were all older now and their lives were taking them in different directions and sometimes Skye couldn't help but feel a little left behind. A little as if she were no longer needed.

'I think I've got it,' said Summer with no hint of tiredness in her voice. 'Here...'

*If you have discovered my message then I can
assume two things: that you are female, because
no man would wade through the private fripperies of my youth, and that you are clever, to have
found the journals. That alone makes you more
worthy of uncovering the Soames diamonds than
my husband.*

*He has always coveted them. And though so-
ciety deems him worthy of my hand in marriage,
I do not deem him worthy of them. They are the
only part of the estate entailed to the female line
and I will keep it that way.*

*Benoit Chalendar, a familiar name if you have
read my journals, has the map to the secret passageways—the only copy.*

'Chalendar? Why does that name ring a bell?' Skye
asked, turning already to her laptop to put his name
into the search bar.

'He's the guy Catherine's father commissioned to
redesign the house after the fire.'

'What fire?'

'It was pretty bad—it burned down a large part
of the original estate that dated back to the sixteen-
hundreds. I think it happened just before the journals
start. His name came up a few entries into the first
journal,' Summer said, before returning to the message.

*He is the first part of your journey, as he was
the first part of mine. We loved—*

Star squealed, 'I knew it!'

Yet it was as naïve as spring, though I would not have refused it for the world. He has promised to keep the map safe for you, no matter how long it takes.

Good luck, my child. I can almost see you as Laura would have been, brave, loving, intelligent— for you will need all those qualities and more.

Skye hit enter on her laptop, expecting to see the screen filled with pictures of a man from the eighteenth century, which was why she only took in a chiselled jawline, piercing blue eyes and effortlessly styled sandy blond hair. From *this* century.

'Ooh, nice.'

'Star,' Skye scolded, hating the way that her cheeks stung from a blush caused by exactly the same thought. 'This can't be right, though. He's…he's clearly…'

'Hot?' Summer teased.

'Yeah, but look… This says he's the acting CEO of Chalendar Enterprises. Now, I mean. Not then,' Skye replied, trying to regain control of her senses.

'He must be a relative.'

'He could be anyone,' Skye said, exasperated. 'It's been over one hundred and fifty years since Catherine wrote these journals. What are the chances that he— or whoever Benoit's descendants are—still have this map? And what does Catherine mean, "the first part"?'

'I don't know. It's going to take me some time to go

through all these and write out any more messages,'
Summer explained.

'Is that a Victoria's Secret model?' Star said, peering
over Skye's shoulder, looking at the various headlines
proclaiming *this* Benoit as Europe's most notorious
playboy. 'Well, I know her—she's an Oscar-winning
actress,' Star said, pointing to another one of his re-
ported love interests. Well…not *love*, just 'interests'.

Skye turned back to his bio—the company name
rang a bell in her head and then she remembered.
'Chalendar Enterprises—they make high-end building materials. I think Rob's mentioned them a couple
of times,' she said, speaking of her boss, once again
thankful for the construction firm owner's understanding as he'd let her take this time away from the office.
Then again, as her sister had said, she hadn't actually
taken a holiday since…since…had it really been five
years?

'Is there a phone number for him?' Star asked.

'What—we're just going to call him and ask if he
knows anything about a map?' Skye demanded.

'No phone number,' Summer said, looking up from
her own laptop.

'Twitter?'

'You want to tweet him?' Skye asked, incredulous.
'What emoji would you use for map and diamonds?'

'There's a number for his office in Paris,' Summer
said, reaching for the phone.

'Summer! We need to talk about how we're going
to—'

Summer held up her hand, cutting Skye off. 'Hi,

yes. I'd like to speak to Benoit Chalendar, please… Oh. Of course. But it's very important that I… Ah. Well, I have urgent contracts that need his signature.'

Skye felt her eyebrows at her hairline. *What are you doing?* she mouthed to her sister, who shook her concern away.

'I understand, but if these contracts aren't signed by Mr Chalendar, then a massive deal is going to fall through… Which deal?' Summer furiously typed on the laptop, anchoring the mobile between her ear and shoulder, staring at Skye and pointing helplessly at a list of companies Chalendar dealt with. 'Hold on one moment,' she said into the phone. 'What's the most likely "huge deal" that he could be making?'

'Are you insane?' Skye demanded. 'You want me to pick a hypothetical business deal that a man I've never met may or may not be—'

'Just pick one!' her sister hissed.

Skye scanned the list of companies and saw one that did business throughout Europe and America and pointed.

'Hello?' Summer said into the phone. 'Thank you for holding—it's the Stransen Steel contract.' From the loud and clearly panicked reaction from the other end of the phone, it had been a good guess. 'Yes, I'll need an address for the courier… Costa Rica? Two days. Okay. I'll get that done. Thank you,' Summer said, disconnecting the call and tossing her phone on the table as if it had burned her.

'What did you just do?' Skye demanded.

'Found out where Benoit Chalendar is going to be.

But he's only there for two days before he goes "off grid", whatever that means.'

'But shouldn't we find out what the rest of the journals have to say?' Skye asked.

'We don't have time. We have an address for Benoit that expires in two days.'

Star sighed. 'Costa Rica, how rom—'

'Don't,' Summer and Skye said at the same time.

Skye pushed back a strand of hair that had become glued to her temple. The heat was like nothing she'd ever experienced. Perhaps her sisters had been right. She should have dressed more…or, well, actually *less*, given the climate. But she'd wanted to feel in control when she met Benoit Chalendar. So the buttoned-up white shirt and grey blazer, over her jeans and favourite light brown Oxford brogues, had felt like a good idea. Had felt like armour. Until it had been punctured by an eleven-hour flight and a hard dismissal from the man's PA turned bodyguard. He might have looked like a Hoxton hipster but he had been completely immovable. Chalendar would not be seen.

Moisture hung heavily in the air, making it hard to breathe. Her stomach twisted into knots as guilt, shock and desperation clogged her mind. She'd been so stupid. She'd actually thought it might have been that easy. That the man would have agreed to see her. That he would have simply handed over the map.

She searched in her bag for her phone, feeling oddly vulnerable without the luggage she'd left at the airport, having decided to come to find Chalendar first rather than checking in to her hotel. Pulling out her mobile, she bit back the rising sob in her chest and called her sisters.

'What happened?'

Not, *How are you? Did you make it there okay? Was the flight on time?*

'He wouldn't see me. I'm so sorry—'

'Where are you?' Summer demanded.

'I'm outside the hotel, but it's useless.'

'Did you know that Catherine and Benoit had a mad, passionate affair?' demanded Star, as if they hadn't just failed at the first hurdle.

'Yes, I—'

'Skye, you *have* to speak to him,' Summer said, and the urgency in her sister's voice reminded her of exactly what was at stake here. Thoughts of her mother swirled like a mirage in the hateful heat.

'I know, but there's not much I can…' Skye trailed off as she saw a man emerge from the side entrance to the hotel and throw a massive duffel bag in the back of a Jeep. His height was what first drew her gaze. He must have been well over six feet tall but there was a litheness about the way he moved, as if he belonged more in the jungle than a five-star hotel. A honey-blond beard barely concealed chiselled cheeks and a well-defined jaw. It made him look rugged and arrogant, as if he didn't care what people thought. He turned her way and for a second she was caught in the beam of two startlingly blue eyes. An instant jolt ran across her skin and Skye told herself that it was only one of recognition. 'That's him,' she said, forgetting she was on the phone for a moment.

'What's him? He's there?'

'He was…' she replied as she watched him discard her as if she was below his notice and stalk back into the hotel. 'He's putting things in a car.'

'What, now?'

'No, he's gone back inside,' Skye said, exasperated at the running commentary she was having to supply.

'Get in the car.'

'What?' Skye demanded, panic rushing through her. At the thought that she'd miss him, the thought of what her sisters were now screaming down the phone at her.

'Get in the car, get in the car, get in the car!'

'I can't just…' Skye argued even as her feet were taking her towards the Jeep.

'Is it locked?'

'I don't know,' she replied, casting a glance around her to see if anyone was there to see her trying the handle of the door. Her pulse was racing and a sweat that had nothing to do with the heat broke out across her skin. 'No, it's not locked, but I can't just—'

'Skye, I swear, if you don't—'

'Okay, okay,' she hissed into the mouthpiece of her mobile. Cursing herself, and her sisters, she cast one last furtive glance around to make sure no one was looking. 'This is insane,' she hissed as she pulled open the door and slipped into the footwell of the back seat. A bubble of hysteria rose in her chest, threatening to shut off her oxygen supply. She reached towards the large duffel bag and pulled it over her, still firm in the belief that any second the Hoxton Heavy would find her and demand to know just what she thought she was doing. It was a good question. One she genuinely didn't have an answer to.

'Skye?'

'I'm in, I'm in,' she whispered. 'I have to go. I'll call you as soon as I can.' And with that last promise she hung up, wondering if she'd lost her mind.

'Où est elle?' Benoit demanded, looking around the foyer of the hotel. He didn't have time for this. His staff didn't have time for this. Or at least the rest of them anyway, he thought, glaring at his assistant.

'Je ne sais pas. Elle est partie.'

At least his assistant had the good grace to look shamefaced at not knowing where the woman he'd asked to leave had gone. Enough for Benoit to know it wouldn't happen again.

Yesterday one phone call to his assistant had upset the contracts team in two countries as they'd scoured through years' worth of Stransen Steel paperwork to find some apparently unsigned contract. He'd received more phone calls in the last twelve hours than he'd had in the last twelve weeks and he'd had enough. He was meticulous with his paperwork, as were the people he employed. This was Stransen's mess and they could deal with it.

'Alors…' Benoit had given this mystery woman enough of his precious time. *'C'est fait?'*

'Oui.'

He left the foyer without another word to his assistant. Four days. He just needed four days of silence, of nothing. No emails, no demands, no company by-laws that forced him into things he never wanted to do.

He checked his watch. He'd wasted at least twenty minutes looking for this woman. Twenty minutes too long. He wanted to be at his home, the only place where he was truly shut off from the world of Chalendar Enterprises—and the axe that hovered over his head.

He'd given everything to the family company in the last fifteen years, but in the last two... He didn't need his great-aunt's warning ringing in his ears to know that he'd pushed himself and—clearly—the board too far.

Shaking his head and biting back a curse, Benoit simply could not believe that he was in this position. That was why he had to get away. To see if there was any way round the ridiculous by-law the shareholders were threatening to enact that meant he had to marry by his thirty-second birthday. Two weeks. He had two damn weeks.

His Great-Aunt Anaïs had tried to warn him, but the final straw had been when she'd mentioned his father. He was nothing like his father. *Nothing*. Before he'd died of a heart attack, André Chalendar had nearly bankrupted the company that had been in his family for more than one hundred and fifty years. And Benoit had brought it back from the brink, he'd made major deals, and so what if he'd immersed himself in a *little* mindless pleasure in the last two years? He was a healthy adult male in the prime of his life and he had healthy adult *very* male appetites. He was single—and would stay that way, no matter what the board of directors wanted.

Refusing to give in to the streak of fury burning bright, he closed the door to his Jeep gently and, turning the key in the ignition, he put the four-wheeler into gear and took the road out of San José. He needed to get to his house before the sun went down. Although the crime rate was low in Costa Rica, the roads at night were a different matter.

He turned up the volume on the radio and let the music soothe him as he glided the powerful Jeep from the smooth motorways off towards the potholed jagged concrete roads that cut towards the rainforest. Four days of uninterrupted blissful isolation was exactly what he needed.

Thirty minutes into the journey he switched radio stations and almost smiled at the heavy base line pounding through his speakers, letting it ripple across his skin and vibrate deep in his chest, when something shifted on the back seat and, heart in mouth, he watched with horror as a figure appeared in the rearview mirror. Shock caused him to swerve sharply.

He struggled with the steering wheel as it shook in his hands, his muscles tensing against the pull towards danger, and had almost regained control when the car hit a deep pothole which sent it careening off the road and fast towards a tree. He pumped the brakes, desperately trying to slow the car, to lessen the impact, to—

The bonnet smashed into the dense wooden trunk with an angry shriek of screeching metal and something white clouded his vision and exploded—a popping sound cut through his thoughts, pain sliced his temple and from somewhere he could hear the echoes of a high-pitched scream, realising only a moment later that it had come from the woman in the back of his car.

CHAPTER TWO

BENOIT PUT A hand to his head, where the sting of pain was more acute than throbbing and cursed when he saw the traces of blood on his fingertips. Fighting through the haze in his head, he twisted, ignoring the pain in his ribs, to make sure the woman was okay.

'Tu va bien?' he called, hoping that the stowaway in the back of his car would answer.

Nothing, no response. Panic began to build in his chest, outweighing any of his own aches or pains. He was ready to kill her, but first he needed to make sure she was alive.

'Es tu blessée?' His breath only escaped his lungs when he heard her groan. At least she was conscious.

'I don't think so,' came the feminine English-speaking voice from the back. 'I just need to—'

'Stop!' he commanded in English as he saw her reach for the door. 'You may have hurt your neck. Just…just stay there.'

Quickly checking himself over mentally, aside from the cut on his temple, a sore—but thankfully not broken—nose from the airbag and an ache in his side that didn't feel like anything worse than bruising, he wasn't too bad. His blood pressure, though, was a different matter. He was probably going to need statins after this.

He kicked at the door from where it had bent shut in the crash and poured himself out of the Jeep. He opened her door and took in the sight of the dishevelled brunette crumpled in his back seat. Stifling a curse, he ignored the wide stare of startlingly rich brown eyes with a sheen that looked horrifyingly as if it might be tears if given the chance.

'I just want to make sure you're okay.' He leaned in and placed his hands either side of her neck, slender and long, the flutter of her pulse quick but strong beneath his palms. She stiffened but held her tongue as he gently pressed. 'Does it hurt?'

'A little, but I'm okay. Really, I am.' The second statement was stronger and, Benoit noticed, irritated. Casting a glance over the rest of her, not seeing any cuts but a whole lot more clothing than was appropriate for the Costa Rican jungle, the woman seemed to be faring much better than he was.

'Okay,' he said, leaning back out of the car. 'Then would you mind telling me who you are and what the hell you think you're doing in my car?' he demanded hotly.

She flinched and the sight caused him to step back. Adrenaline had spiked pinpricks into his skin but as it receded it left an anger he had to get a grip on.

'I needed to speak to you,' she said as she finally struggled out of the back of the car and onto the forest floor beside him. The woman wasn't tiny but she still had to crane her neck to look up at him. 'It's a matter of great importance,' she insisted, her eyes piercing him with a strange sincerity.

Taking her in with one quick glance, he genuinely didn't know where to start. Usually he wouldn't have given her a first glance, let alone a second one. She was attempting to smooth her shoulder-length brown hair into submission. Her body was entirely hidden by a pair of jeans that were neither skintight nor baggy, their only saving grace that they were a pleasant dark inky blue, a white shirt buttoned up to the collar, over which sat a grey blazer that did absolutely nothing for her skin tone. Then again, it was possible the pallor of her skin could be due to the accident. Or because she was English; it really could go either way at this point. Which drew him to her shoes. He didn't think he'd ever seen a pair of Oxford brogues outside of, well, Oxford. Benoit's lips pressed together against the curse that wanted to be let loose.

'Are you from Stransen? Is this about the contract?'

Her eyes rocketed up to his face and if her cheeks had been flushed before then the blush that rose to her skin was almost painful to see.

'Well?' he demanded.

'About that...'

'Yes?'

'It's not exactly... There is... Mmm...'

He watched as she stumbled over her words, wondering whether perhaps she had hit her head in the crash.

'There-is-no-contract,' she said, the words rushing

out together so quickly that it took him a moment to mentally translate them.

'What do you mean, *no contract*?'

'Stransen. There is no unsigned contract. We needed to speak to you.'

Benoit paused for a beat that served only to fan the flames of his ire. 'Do you mean to tell me that you had nearly thirty members of staff searching through five years of contracts because you *fancied a chat*?' For once he didn't care that his voice had risen to a shout. Only her lips thinned and it was a look that reminded him a lot of Anaïs when she got annoyed at him and he had a sneaking suspicion that he might just have made a grave mistake.

Fire. That was what he saw when she looked at him next, turning her rich, smooth chocolate eyes to molten lava.

'I will not talk to you like this. You're in a mood.'

'Of course I'm in a mood,' he huffed out through an incredulous laugh. 'We're stuck in the middle of the Costa Rican rainforest, a ten-hour walk from civilisation, the sun is setting and the car is a write-off.'

'And when you're over your mantrum I will happily discuss what I came here to speak with you about.'

'Happily discuss? *Tu es folle.*'

'Did you just call me crazy?' she demanded.

He narrowed his eyes in suspicion. 'I thought the English didn't bother with French past GCSE level.'

'That's both a generalisation and offensive,' she replied, her imperious tone ridiculous given the circumstances.

'And true,' he said under his breath, realising quickly that they needed to stop sniping and get moving. Taking a deep breath, he held out his hand. 'Benoit Chalendar.'

'Skye Soames.'

He hadn't expected her handshake to be firm, nor for the touch of her skin to cause a snap of unwanted awareness in him. As she removed her hand from his, using it to shield her eyes from a shaft of sunlight he could see the lithe strength in her body, toned yet not overly, naturally healthy and not paid for like some of the women of his recent acquaintance.

'Do you have a phone?' he asked, even though he'd already calculated the chances of having a signal out here very slim. He looked away when Skye bent back into the car, her blazer and shirt rising a little over her backside, gritting his teeth against the shocking spark of a most definitely unwanted arousal.

'No signal,' came the response from behind him.

'Okay. Then we'd better—'

'And you? Does your phone have any signal?'

'I don't have one,' he said, bracing for her rather obvious and utterly expected response.

'What do you mean, you don't have a phone?' she demanded. 'That's shockingly irresponsible.' It was like getting told off by his elementary school teacher.

'I don't have to, nor will I, explain myself or my decisions to you,' he said, walking round what had been his favourite car and prising open the boot. 'Besides, we don't have time,' he said, reaching for his canvas bag and filling it with what they'd need. 'The roads out here are dangerous at night. Our best and only hope is to go. Now.' First aid kit, water, matches, the food he'd picked up at the market that morning. He eyed the bottle of whisky and decided it was necessary. For medicinal purposes, obviously.

He'd known when he'd started to leave his phone behind on these trips that accidents could happen. While part of the attraction was that he would be completely unreachable—no emails, phone calls or anything to do with Chalendar Enterprises—the other part was that it was a test. Of himself. To prove that he didn't need anyone. To know that he could survive using his own skills and his own mind. Of course it usually wasn't a hardship, with his home fully stocked with all his favourite foods and wines. And if he had to walk ten hours through the jungle to get there? He knew he was more than capable. It was Skye he wasn't so sure about.

He turned back to Skye, taking her in as her eyes swept up and down the road. 'Is that all you have with you?' he asked, nodding to her handbag. 'What's in it? Water?' Her face fell. 'Food?' he asked, and it fell a little more. 'Anything?' he demanded.

'No, I… I left my suitcase at the airport before checking in to the hotel because I wanted to see you before you…left,' she said as if she hadn't just hidden in his car to go off to some unknown destination.

'Okay then. Let's go,' he said, hauling the packed rucksack onto one shoulder.

Skye frowned, feeling distinctly unbalanced and unsure. 'I don't… I don't think I should go anywhere with a stranger,' she said, instantly cringing against her own words. Had she really just said that? Maybe she *had* hit her head.

'So you want to stay out here on the road and just hope that a *different* stranger comes to your aid?'

'I have pepper spray,' she said defiantly and then realised she probably shouldn't have admitted it, if *he* was actually someone to worry about.

'Good for you. But this isn't England, the animals here bite and when they do they're poisonous. And that tightly buttoned shirt isn't going to keep them away.'

She couldn't help but self-consciously play with the button of the collar at her neck. 'What's wrong with my—'

'If you don't lose that blazer and undo a button you're likely to lose at least half your body weight in sweat in the next five minutes alone.'

Skye thrust her shoulders back as if readying herself for a fight. 'I don't know you. For all I know you could be an axe murderer!' She'd definitely hit her head and she definitely needed to stop talking. Because she was in complete agreement with the way Benoit was looking at her right now. She was crazy.

'You have no water, no means of making a fire, you have no means of signalling for help and no *real* means to defend yourself.' Her heart was dropping with each and every failing he found in her situation. 'You're dressed like a nun—'

'I'm sorry, I didn't realise you required a dress code,' she interrupted, glad to find something to be angry with him for because then she might not be so angry with herself for getting into this mess. There was nothing wrong with her clothing, she assured herself. But she *was* beginning to get quite hot. 'Would you have preferred sequins, a skirt that barely covers my behind and a pair of stilettos?'

'Personally? Yes. But for now? I would have preferred not to have a stowaway who caused me to crash my car!'

'It wasn't intentional!'

'Oh, so you *accidentally* fell into my car?'

'Yes! No. Sort of?'

'If you can't decide how you got into this mess, how on earth do you plan to get out of it then?'

'Walk,' she said, hating the way her shoulders raised into a shrug and her voice trembled, making it sound like a question.

Benoit stalked towards her in just two strides, took her by the shoulders and spun her so that she was facing up the road in the direction they had been heading in the car.

'This way, you'll reach the next town in about one hundred and fifty kilometres.' He spun her to face the opposite direction and she tried to focus on the road rather than the way his hands felt on her shoulders. 'That way, you'll reach the next town in about eighty kilometres. Good luck!' he said and stalked off the road and into the jungle.

'Where are you going?' she called after him, feeling for the first time a real sense of fear swirling in her stomach.

'Home,' she heard him growl over his shoulder.

She bit her lip to stop herself from calling him back.
Think, think, think.

She could feel panic beginning to build within her.
If she stayed she could be waiting for hours before
someone found her. But if she followed Benoit into the
jungle it would take her further away from…from…
She shook her head. He had the map. He was the key
to her mother's treatment. Her stomach twisted as if
it had been punched, something she felt almost every
single time her mother crossed her mind. He was the
only choice.

'Wait.'

He stopped walking, turned slowly and pierced
her with his bright blue eyes. 'Which one is it, Miss
Soames? Am I an axe murderer or your salvation?'

She bit her tongue for the first time since she'd got
out of the car and he seemed to nod as if he approved
of her silence.

'Leave the blazer in the car. You won't need it,' he
called out as he set off into the jungle.

Skye threw her blazer in the back of the car, mum-
bling to herself that if he wanted to have a Bear Grylls
moment then he could at least have thought about
bringing a satellite phone. But she instantly felt better
once the thick layer of her blazer was no longer trapping so much body heat against her skin.

This wasn't who she was, she thought to herself
as she followed Benoit through the thick jungle. She
didn't get on planes and fly to unknown places, let
alone follow strangers into jungles. She was a secretary, for God's sake. She had responsibilities—to her

mother, to her sisters. She'd been responsible for them long before her mother had got ill. And would… She couldn't finish that thought.

She almost wished that they hadn't found the journals, that Rob hadn't given her the time off work. Because then she wouldn't be here, so far from everything that was even remotely familiar. Her stomach swirled and she felt a little nauseous. She didn't know what the rules were here, how to act…who to be. Alone with Benoit Chalendar, world-renowned businessman, a supposedly charming international playboy and a man who seemed as at home forging his way through the rainforest as he might be in a boardroom.

He was in front of her, forcing his way through the forest, and she couldn't help but watch the push and pull of his arm muscles rippling beneath his T-shirt as he sliced through another hapless branch. His movements were swift and efficient, his powerful body gliding ahead as if he was in his natural habitat rather than off the beaten path. All the while, heat and humidity pooled in her socks, causing her feet to slip and her shoes to rub. She was being eaten alive by mosquitoes and the sounds of her hand slapping against her skin punctuated the air as much as the thwack of the machete Benoit used to cut back branches from their path.

Hot, Star had said when they'd looked him up on the internet. *Yes*, her inner voice replied assuredly and accusingly—as if Skye had done nothing to feed her body's carnal appetites for far too long… *If ever*, it asserted scathingly.

Benoit Chalendar had been impressive online, but

in person? Once the shock of the accident had worn off, and the minutes in the forest trickled into hours, she'd had time to really consider him...or at least the back of him, which was enough. He was wearing khaki cargo pants, which she'd never expected a French billionaire to wear, but they most definitely suited the situation. Strangely, having seen him like this, she just couldn't imagine him wearing some bespoke handmade suit and leather shoes. The idea seemed so absurd she nearly laughed.

The sound she'd made must have caught his attention as he turned back to her, a query painted clearly in those stunning blue eyes. And for a moment she just stared. His sandy blond hair was just a little longer than necessary, curling at the ends enough to make her want to reach out for them. He had a beard, closely trimmed to his cheeks but more than the designer stubble she saw on the backs of magazines at the office. More... masculine.

His nose was a little on the long side but it was challenging, daring the observer to find fault with it, when there was so much beauty in the rest of his features. She shrugged away the unspoken question and he went back to thrashing the foliage, and she went back to...

She hauled her gaze away from his backside and blushed. She barely recognised herself and blamed it on the situation. Because she hadn't actually checked out a guy in... Oh, she thought on a sad sigh, had it really been that long? And the sting of pain as she thought of Alistair, of how he had left, reminded Skye exactly why she had avoided men for so long.

When the first drop of water hit her arm Skye was genuinely concerned that it might have been a tear. But soon there were far too many to count. The heavens opened and in an instant she was drenched. She looked up to where Benoit was standing, beckoning her on with fast movements of his arm.

'Hurry,' he commanded, and this time she obeyed without question. Jogging along the path as best she could, she stumbled slightly when she caught up with him. The rain drowned out the sounds of her harsh breaths as he pulled her deeper into the forest. The huge deep green leaves did little to protect them from the downpour and as she chanced a glance at Benoit she saw that his hair had turned dark with huge drops of water falling from the curling ends.

Her feet were now squelching deep into the mud, her legs having to work even harder to fight the suction beneath her. Her jeans were clinging to her skin, the material stiff and rubbing painfully. A thin branch whipped out and caught her on the arm and she couldn't help the shocked gasp that fell from her lips.

He shouldn't have turned around, he told himself, trying to focus on the thick, rain-soaked foliage in front of him instead of what he saw in his mind's eye. Mud-covered, jeans-clad thigh and white, nearly see-through, shirt slick against a flat, toned stomach. It had taken a lot more than he'd care to admit to drag his eyes up to her face, but that hadn't been much better. She'd just swept her dark hair back, her eyes a little unfocused, mouth open just a little... *Dieu*. All he'd thought was that this was what she must look like when she'd been thoroughly ravished.

He ignored the rush of blood to his cheeks and other areas. It was the heat and the rain and the pace he was having to set. He cast a look back at her to see if she was following. He was surprised to find her keeping pace. Her head was down, concentrating on her steps, only a slight stress on one leg over the other.

He frowned. She hadn't complained once. She'd fought him, accused him of having a...what was it she'd said? He rolled the English word around on his tongue. *Mantrum?* He almost huffed out a laugh. Almost.

He thought fleetingly of what any one of the number of beautiful women to have graced his bed recently would have done in this situation. There would have likely been tears. No. *Definitely* there would have been tears. Maybe even some screams and not the good kind. He'd bet his life on a tantrum or two. But Skye Soames? She was nothing like those women. Not even in looks.

He'd not realised he had a type. Or at least he'd developed one since Camilla, now he thought of it. Just the mental use of his ex-fiancée's name left a bitter taste in his mouth. There was a good reason he'd taken up a penchant for statuesque blondes and his tastes would stay exclusively on those.

'Talk.' He didn't mean it to come out so harshly but she didn't seem offended.

'About?'

'What do you do? Where are you from? How you learned French,' he said as he slashed another branch with the machete. He needed a distraction. Clearly his mind wasn't to be trusted. There was a pause in which the sounds of the squelching mud beneath them and the roaring rain around them became a symphony and he nearly turned his head again but she started talking.

'I… I picked up a bit of French helping my sisters with their homework. And yes, it was GCSE homework,' she said, the confession lifting the corner of his lips. 'And I'm an office manager for a construction firm.'

'Which one?'

She huffed out a laugh. 'You won't have heard of it.'

'Try me.'

'R. Cole Builders.'

In that instant he realised that she'd been right. It was probably…

'It's a small company in the New Forest area.'

'That's where you're from?'

'Mmm-hmm.'

'What's it like?'

'Very different to this.'

'In what way?'

'Do you really want to hear about my childhood growing up in a two-bedroom rented house just outside of Salisbury with two half-sisters, a single mum whose greatest regret was missing Woodstock and an absentee father who started another family as quickly as was humanly possible?'

His feet had slowed, partly because he was consuming all the information she had just disseminated and partly because no one could have missed the echo of pain in her voice. He knew what that was like. Not wanting to talk about the past, parents or childhood. And he had no intention of pressing on that wound. Hers or his.

'I didn't think so,' she answered, misunderstanding his silence. Which was probably just as well. She'd be out of his hair and out of his life as soon as they got back to his house and she could call for help.

He gripped the machete in a tight fist, refocusing on the pathway in front and the sneaking suspicion that they might have gone off route.

Slash, slash, sweep. Slash, slash, sweep.

They couldn't be lost. He wouldn't allow it.

After five minutes of silence Skye was beginning to wonder if Benoit was lost. It wasn't that they'd passed the same tree exactly, but his movements had become a little…urgent. But perhaps that was a preferable thing to consider rather than to question why she'd just revealed painfully personal details to a complete stranger who was probably not used to more from women than a 'Yes, thank you, more please.'

She exhaled a long breath. She shouldn't have been so defensive. She *should* be trying to get him on side. But suddenly it had all felt too much—getting to safety, to a phone where she could call her sisters, to convince Benoit to give her access to the map, if there even was a map after all this time. She bit down hard against the urge to give in to tears. She wouldn't quit. Couldn't.

She followed Benoit into a clearing and came to

a sudden stop, the sight before her cutting off her thoughts.

'Don't be deceived. It has a five-star rating on Trip-Advisor,' Benoit replied cynically.

CHAPTER THREE

BENOIT STUDIED THE old plane wreck, relief thrumming through his veins. He was soaked through and he wasn't the only one. He'd seen the crash site when out walking on his previous visits and knew that it was too far away from the road to attract unwanted attention.

'Just let me go first.' He didn't mention that there might be things like snakes or poisonous spiders, but they were a real risk. He pulled a torch from his bag and ducked through the jagged hole in the side of the plane where the door had once been. Hitting the torch against the ceiling to scare off any animals, he checked behind what was left of some of the seating of the twin-engine Jetstream and scoured any other possible hiding places he could think of.

Satisfied they were gone, he tossed down the bag and assessed the situation. A fire would be possible—hard, but possible. Though he'd have to be careful what they burned because some of the plane's detritus could have chemicals in it. But there was enough dead wood scattered about for a good few hours of fire, hopefully long enough for them to at least dry off. Nights were dark and cooler than the days, but it would still be warm enough.

But it wasn't really the heat he was worried about. He had to get Skye Soames out of those wet clothes. The way the rain had plastered her clothes to her body was messing with his head and he couldn't afford to be distracted. He cast a look to where she stood outside, her hand at her forehead sheltering her eyes, waiting for his permission to enter, clearly trying to hide the shivers racking her body. Whether it was the cold from the rain, or fear finally kicking in after the crash and the thought of having to spend a night in the rainforest with a complete stranger, he suddenly felt guilty. And Benoit did *not* like feeling guilty.

He called her inside and set about making a fire, not missing the way she perched on the edge of a seat as if ready to flee at any sign of danger. Good. She was learning then.

The smoke from the damp wood wasn't pleasant, but trails of it were finding their way outside through the cracks in the broken windows. Once the fire took hold and the smoke began to clear, he saw Skye shift closer to the heat. The light caught on fascinating strands of red gold in the slowly drying tangles of her brown hair. Hair that rested just above the V in her white shirt, open enough for him to see a tantalising glimpse of...

Scratches. Little angry red lines and an alarming number of bites were already beginning to swell along her slender arms. He stood, not quite to his full height—the angle of the plane's cabin too low for him to straighten fully—and took her in properly, looking past the flare of his unwanted awareness of her to assess the damage the trek through the rainforest and the crash had done to her.

He cursed himself for not realising sooner and reached for the first aid kit in his bag. Opening it, he reached for the one addition he'd made to the small kit a year ago: a bottle of witch hazel. His Great-Aunt Anaïs had instilled a deep respect for the stuff since he and Xander had been kids getting into scrapes at the chateau in the Dordogne. Pushing back the dark thoughts that always followed memories of his brother, he turned back to see Skye twisting her hair in her hand and wringing out drops of water.

He had absolutely no idea why the image of her hair wrapped around her fist shot fire through his body, and if it hadn't been for her cuts and bruises he would have turned his back on her, walked out of the plane wreck and kept on walking all night if he'd had to.

'Here. You need to clean those scratches.'

She looked up at him, her mouth curved into a tight smile. 'And the bites,' she replied. 'I really am sorry about what happened. I must have fallen asleep in the car because I had planned to let you know I was there much sooner. But that's no excuse.'

She'd held his gaze the entire time and he was impressed. The few people he encountered who were inept enough to make mistakes and needed to apologise never met his eyes—instead scurrying to find someone else to blame.

'Let's just make it through tonight and we can figure out everything later,' he said, mentally counting down the hours until they could get to his home and she could phone for…for whatever or whoever would get her back home. He was still determined to rescue some of what would remain of his time in Costa Rica. Alone.

He pulled out a spare T-shirt from his rucksack and threw it to her.

'Change into that,' he said, immediately noticing the steel lengthen her spine at his command.

'What about you?' she asked, her eyes raking over the wet T-shirt plastered to his body.

His jaw clenched, one hundred per cent convinced that she genuinely didn't know what effect that was having on him. 'I guess I'll have to grin and Bear Grylls it.'

The swift intake of breath that followed him out of the wreck spoke of embarrassment and outrage. Good. Much better that than she have any softer feelings towards him. He placed their empty water bottles in secure places to catch the rainwater, while swearing to find out what she wanted as quickly as possible so that when they returned to the house she could leave.

Mortification heated her skin far more efficiently than the fire. The man must have hearing like a bat. He was the perfect predator. Eyesight, hearing, power, looks. Silently growling, she yanked her shirt down her arms and flinched when she heard a tear. She clamped her jaw together, just like she'd done as a child when she'd felt the threat of tears. She wouldn't cry. Not here. Not now.

She was fine. Her sisters were safe. Her mother was

happy for the moment and things would look different in the morning. It was only a few hours. Nothing bad could happen in a few hours.

Peeling herself out of the wet jeans, Skye cast a glance around the wreckage of the plane, wondering who it had belonged to and whether anyone had made it out alive. She shivered at the thought. The thin shards of sky she could make out through the cracked window-panes in the cockpit showed a deepening inky blue. The rain had eased off, but she could still hear the patter of it hitting the body of the plane, which was oddly comforting. Familiar. Unlike every single other aspect of this situation.

The fire had begun to give out some heat and if she hadn't been so hungry she might have fallen asleep. Instead, she hung her jeans, socks and shirt out to dry on various seats and twisted metal and was safely attired in his T-shirt when Benoit returned. Thankfully it was long enough to come halfway down her thighs. If she pulled it down by the hem.

She felt bad as she took in his rain-soaked clothes… until he pulled off his T-shirt and then… All thought stopped. Seriously. He was rich. Clearly defined abs spoke of hours at the gym. This was no lazy billion-aire playboy. The dips and grooves expanded and retracted as he reached for something from his bag and when she saw the protein bars in his hand she wasn't sure whether it was her stomach growling or her inner voice purring.

Purring? She *never* purred.

She slapped a cotton pad doused in witch hazel on

the bite on her elbow and hoped that the sting would bring her back to her senses. He was digging in his bag with his back to her and for just a moment she indulged in watching the play of muscles in the shadows of the fire. He turned to her with something in his hand and she gasped.

'You're bleeding!'

He frowned, touching his hairline and pulling his hand away with fresh blood on his fingertips. 'It's nothing.'

'It's a head wound.'

'It's hardly a—'

'Sit down,' she commanded, channelling her feelings into anger at him for not saying anything. She swallowed her surprise when he actually did as she'd asked and ignored the wry raising of a single eyebrow.

She came around in front of the seat he had chosen, eyeing the cut that bordered his hairline, leaning and stepping forward slightly to get a better look. He tensed. 'I'm not going to hurt you,' she said, sounding as exasperated as she felt until she reached down to pick up the witch hazel and realised that she'd somehow stepped right in between his legs. Trying to ignore the sudden awareness of...*him*, his chest, his maleness, the heat coming off *all that*, she poured the clear liquid onto a cotton pad before reaching to lift a wave of hair, dark and slick with rain, away from the cut.

She squinted through the dim lighting in the cabin and saw a cut about two centimetres long but thankfully not wide. Cuts to the head always bled profusely, as she'd discovered early on with Summer, whose mind was always on a daydream rather than what was in front of her. And as her mother had a very different idea of what a medicine cabinet consisted of, Skye had become well versed in the use of herbal remedies, even if she'd always longed for proper painkillers and antiseptic cream.

'This is going to—'

'I'm not a—'

The word 'child' that would have come out of Benoit's mouth was cut off as she whacked the cotton pad onto the cut and instead she heard a deeply satisfying hiss. Only then did she realise she was close enough to feel it on her cheek, and somehow on the hairs on her arms and shivering down her spine and shockingly deep within her core.

'I'm surprised to find witch hazel in your first aid kit,' she said, trying to ignore the pull she felt to him.

'My great-aunt,' Benoit said. He continued to look straight ahead with an odd determined glint in his eye. 'She swears by it.'

Skye inspected the wound she'd been pressing on to see if it had stopped bleeding. It was definitely slowing. She took a slightly deeper breath and spoke to the air above his head. 'I'm sorry you got hurt in the crash and I'm sorry about all this.'

'You already apologised. No need for more.' His tone was clipped, but when he glanced up at her something sparked low, igniting quick and hard, rushing every inch of her body in one powerful wave. She'd never felt anything like it and when he lifted his hand upwards she thought for a crazy moment he was going to touch her, until he reached past her to retrieve the T-shirt hung up behind her and all that spark and energy turned harsh, biting and hot, twisting into embarrassment.

As Skye retreated, hiding behind a curtain of gently drying shoulder-length hair, Benoit cursed himself to hell and back. He had more finesse than that. But he'd needed to put some space between them before either of them did something they'd regret.

But for that moment, when she'd stood between his legs with nothing but his T-shirt separating them, his hands had fisted on his knees to stop himself reaching for the backs of her thighs, from running his hands up under the hem of the cotton top and palming—

Dieu, he felt as if his heart was about to explode in his chest. He hadn't been like this since he was a teenager. *It's just the situation*, he told himself. He needed food. And whisky. Not necessarily in that order. He reached for the apple he'd been trying to give her when she'd noticed the cut on his head.

'Here,' he said, catching Skye's attention before throwing her the apple. 'It's not the steak I was supposed to be having tonight, but it's better than nothing.' Leaning over and exhaling through the ache in his side, he retrieved the rest of the bag with the food he'd bought at the market this morning. It already felt like a lifetime ago.

He'd not bought anything substantial, knowing that his housekeeper would have stocked the fridge for his arrival, and certainly nothing that would have been affected by the heat and the journey. So really all they had were some nuts, savoury biscuits, bananas, apples and a few protein bars. It was hardly a feast, but it would get them through.

He divided the rations between them and turned to Skye, who now had one foot on the seat, her arm resting on the knee while the other long, smooth leg, shapely calf muscle and tiny ankle caught the firelight and his attention simultaneously.

Biting down on the apple, she was either the most skilled temptress he'd ever met or completely innocent and Benoit honestly didn't know which would be worse. He'd come to Costa Rica to get his thoughts in order. To figure out a way round the by-law. He honestly hadn't thought he'd need to, sure that the board would eventually back down. But they hadn't. And if he didn't find a wife within two weeks the CEO position would pass to his brother because he *was* married. Reflexively, Benoit gripped his fist, knuckles turning bone-white. No. He'd *never* let that happen. Not after Xander's betrayal.

Benoit had given everything and more to Chalendar Enterprises. When he was a child his great-aunt's words had sunk in and sunk deep. *'We have a duty to the past. A responsibility to bear for future generations to come.'* Benoit had felt the weight of responsibility of a company that had been in his family for over one hundred and fifty years. His whole life had revolved around it, studying applied science, mathematics as well as business, working through summer holidays while at university. He'd worked in every single department they had, learning from the ground up, understanding each part of the organisation. He'd brought the entire company back from the brink of bankruptcy. And the board wanted to enforce the by-law that meant he must marry because he'd had a bit of fun for two years?

But it wasn't just the board, was it?

The crunch of an apple being bitten cracked through thoughts of his great-aunt and brought Skye into focus. Just one day, he told himself. He just had to get through one more day with her.

He passed Skye her portion of the food before reaching for the whisky. He spun the lid from the top and took a large mouthful, swallowing the amber liquid with relish. It hit his near empty stomach like Greek fire and warmed him from the inside out within seconds. He put the bottle down and picked up the nuts, catching Skye's eyes gazing at the bottle on the floor.

'Would you like some?' he offered.

She tucked her bottom lip beneath her teeth.

Temptress.

'I've never actually had whisky before.'

Innocent.

She was giving him whiplash. She'd never had whisky? Who *was* this woman? 'Now probably isn't the best—'

She cut him off with an outstretched arm and a look in her eyes that made Benoit try not to laugh. She had the stubbornness of a mule and he had a feeling that if he didn't comply with her request she'd finish the whole damn bottle just to spite him. And that *wouldn't* be funny.

He passed her the bottle and watched as she took a conservative mouthful of whisky and then struggled not to cough as the alcohol burned her throat. For a second the memory of raiding Anaïs' alcohol cabinet with his brother as kids rose in his mind like smoke from the fire. Benoit's eleven-year-old self had been focused not on the illicit thrill of his first drink but making sure his little brother didn't get sick from it.

Skye finally coughed, shaking her head and flapping her hand by her cheeks as if to dry the big plump tears that he could see sitting in the corners of her eyes. Laughter rose unbidden in his chest and the attempt to stifle it made his shoulders shake, drawing yet another glare from Skye. He held his hand out for the bottle and she passed it back.

'It's not that funny,' she said when she had finally stopped coughing.

'No. You're right, I'm sorry,' he said so insincerely that she threw her apple core at him. Which he caught one-handed and tossed into the fire.

For a while silence descended as they each practically inhaled the protein bars, nuts and fruit. Benoit stuck his head outside to make sure that their water bottles were filling up. If they did finish the whisky the bottle could be refilled with water if it kept raining. Not that it was a good idea to finish it.

Coming back to his seat by the fire, he reached for the whisky, only to find Skye sneaking another drink. He raised his eyebrow and she passed it back to him. He settled back into his seat, took a sip and said, 'So, Miss Soames. Are you ready to tell me why you stole into the back of my car yet? Am I over my "mantrum"?'

'You're not going to forget that, are you?' she asked, a slight trace of humour glinting gold in her deep brown eyes.

'Not any time soon, no.'

Skye fought to keep hold of that feeling. The gentle mockery had built between them, but reality began to bleed in just as the heat from the whisky burned out. She was torn between throwing herself on his mercy and telling him everything, or paying attention to the little voice in her head that said if she revealed everything then he'd have the power. The power to demand anything he wanted, because Skye and her sisters really needed that map. Her mother needed the map. And she simply couldn't trust him not to betray that.

'My sisters and I are doing some research into our family.'

Skye was glad it was dark and that the flames from the fire didn't give off enough light for Benoit to see that her cheeks were bright red. She didn't need a mirror, she could feel them. She'd always been terrible at lying.

'*Oui?* And?'

'And we thought that as your great-great-grandfather did some work on the estate in Norfolk he might have some…relevant documentation.' Oh, God…oh, God, she was making it worse. Perhaps she should just tell him the truth.

'You came out here for "relevant documentation" on an English estate?'

She reached for the bottle he'd left midway between them and took a rather large mouthful of Dutch courage. It tasted terrible but at least it made things a little…softer? Or was that fuzzier? She wasn't quite sure.

'You should probably take it easy on the—'

'Yes,' Skye said, nodding for emphasis, only that made the ground wobble a little. 'Relevant documentation. Very important. Benoit Chalendar has it.'

'I don't.'

'Not you. The other Benoit. Your great-great-great-whatever.' She could see that he was frowning at her and she groaned. 'He helped redesign the estate after the fire.'

'I know he went to England in the mid-eighteen-hundreds to explore the glass structures at the Crystal Palace before *that* burned down. He was hoping to help develop a stronger, cheaper way of creating reinforced glass. The research he did there laid the way for the future success of Chalendar Enterprises. But I never heard anything about an estate in Norfolk.'

'Of course you didn't.' She waved her hand as if he were an irritating fly, because he was being particularly irritating with all these questions and details. 'It was a *secret*.'

'What was?'

She had the sneaking suspicion that he was laughing at her, but suddenly it wasn't funny. It was important. 'The passageways in between the walls. They were a secret.'

She reached for the whisky, but Benoit moved it before she could take it. She shook her head. Never mind.

'Benoit Chalendar designed secret passageways in an English country estate?'

'Yes. For Catherine.'

'Catherine?'

'My great-great-grandmother. Or my great-great-great… I don't know. There are a lot of greats in there.'

She watched as Benoit ran a hand through his hair, continuing to stare at her. She wasn't explaining this very well. It was just that he was so handsome and it was hard to keep it all in her head. But, no matter what, she absolutely could *not* mention the Soames jewels.

'What are the Soames jewels?'

'Are you a mind-reader?' she whispered in shock.

'No. You said that out loud.'

'I shouldn't have said that!'

'Apparently not. Skye, I know you haven't drunk whisky before, but have you drunk *any* alcohol before?'

'Yes,' she replied indignantly, but perhaps the occasional cider didn't count. 'Anyway, now that you know—'

'About?'

'About the *jewels*,' she clarified, not quite sure why Benoit suddenly seemed not to be so clever at all, 'that Catherine hid in a secret room, locked with a special key, that only the secret passageways can get to. We need the map. Benoit has it. *Had* it? So we thought you had it. *Have* it.'

'You're on a treasure hunt?' The incredulity ringing in his tone jabbed at her.

'Yes. My sister thinks it's *so romantic.*'

'Really? Why?' Benoit seemed to be smiling at her now. With her perhaps? She wasn't quite sure.

'Because they were *lovers.*' She whispered the word as if it were naughty somehow.

Benoit was trying very hard not to laugh. He pressed his fist against his lips to stop himself from making the situation worse because Skye Soames was going to feel all kinds of bad in the morning. But then he was caught by the idea that his ancestor knew hers. Loved hers.

'Catherine's father asked Benoit to review the structural damage at the estate. He believed that a French tradesman would be "of little consequence" to his seventeen-year-old daughter. But he was wrong. Fathers usually are,' she confided.

But, rather than the conspiratorial tone he'd expected, there was more than a hint of sadness and Benoit remembered how she'd circumnavigated his question earlier.

'So Catherine fell in love with Benoit and he her.'

'Skye, he came home and married Adrienne.'

'Because he had to!' she cried. 'Catherine's father wouldn't allow the match and he sent Benoit away without paying him for the work he'd done on the estate. And then, after Catherine returned from the Middle East—'

'The Middle East?'

'She was forced to marry her cousin Anthony, who was horrible. Like, *really* horrible.'

She shivered dramatically and he decided that the unbuttoned Skye was very different to the buttoned-up one and couldn't help but wonder what had caused such a decisive split into the two parts of her character.

'And that's when she hid the jewels. And wrote the coded messages in the journals.'

'There are coded messages?'

'Oh, Benoit, *do* keep up,' she chided.

'And you think they're still there?'

'They have to be. We need them.'

'Why?'

Of all the questions he'd asked, that seemed to sober her instantly. 'I… That's not your concern. But we do need the map. We need you. Is it ringing any bells? Please?'

Alarm bells maybe, Benoit thought. But…actually, somewhere in the distant past there might have been something his Great-Aunt Anaïs had said. The thought remained intangible.

'And if I help you find this map, what do I get out of it?' he asked.

'I…' She seemed stuck on the thought. 'I have nothing to offer,' she said quietly.

Maybe. Maybe not.

'You should try and get some sleep,' he told her, fishing out some painkillers from the first aid kit and putting them close to the water bottle he'd been trying to get her to drink from. 'We've got a long walk ahead of us in the morning.' And doing it on a hangover would not be pleasant, Benoit thought.

Was Skye Soames really on a one-hundred-and-fifty-year-old treasure hunt? *Had* Benoit been in love with Catherine enough to keep the designs of the secret passageways of an estate in England for her? There was only one person who'd know. And the moment he got back to France in five days' time he'd find out. Because if he did have access to the map Skye so desperately wanted, then maybe there was a way to solve the problem of the damn by-law.

CHAPTER FOUR

SKYE SOAMES WAS never drinking again.

She told herself this every single time her stomach rolled or the pounding in her head became particularly acute. What was so great about it anyway? Snippets of her revealing *everything* to Benoit last night crashed through her mind. But, thankfully, she hadn't spoken of her mother's illness. She just couldn't shake the belief that it would put her completely at his mercy.

She was exhausted. She'd always thought that drunk people just passed out, but she couldn't even do that right. Oh, no. Instead of slamming into complete oblivion, her mind had kept racing with Technicolor fantasies of Benoit without his shirt on. In fact, he might not have had anything on in some of the more explicit moments where he'd—

'Are you okay?'

Skye squeaked in surprise, causing him to smirk, which just made her feel worse.

'No, I didn't sleep well.'

'Because of the alcohol?'

'Because you *snore*.'

The sound of Benoit slashing and sweeping through the rainforest came to a sudden halt and she looked up to find him staring at her in horror.

'I do not snore,' he said, sounding so indignant she couldn't help but laugh.

'Oh. You snore.'

'No one's told me—'

'You stick around long enough to have that discussion?' The words took her by surprise as much as Benoit from the look on his face and the racing heartbeat in her chest. Apparently, this was another symptom of the hangover. Or him. She still wasn't sure. Either way, he chose to ignore her question.

Skye flinched as she caught her already ruined shirt on a branch and heard another tear. Back in the plane Benoit had given her privacy to change back into her clothes from the day before and she now hated the pair of jeans that had once been her favourite. They were still covered in mud from yesterday. She'd have given anything for a clean top but that, along with a lot of other things, had been left at the airport with her luggage.

They'd been walking for three hours now and she hoped that there wasn't much more to go. At first she'd been fascinated by the steam rising from the ground of the rainforest, watching it dissipate in the heat of the morning sun. The strange bird calls, feathers fluttering high above them. But the swishing sound of Benoit's machete had now become commonplace and she was sweaty and uncomfortable. It couldn't be too much longer until they reached his home, could it?

She wondered what it would be like and imagined industrial steel and masculine chrome, so very different from her and her sisters' little place in the New Forest. There was space enough for Mum to stay there when she visited, but since Skye had been able to rent a place for herself and her sisters Mariam hadn't liked to be held down by the constraints of a home. She spent her time drifting between friends she'd met on the festival circuits, or other friends with alternative lifestyles. Mum had always been into alternative medicine, but her latest venture was candle magic. Skye loved her desperately, but couldn't see how a candle was going to magic her back to health.

But if she found the map in time, if they found the jewels in time, if the estate could be sold in time…

A branch slapped against her cheek, shock ricocheting through her, and she wondered if Benoit had done it on purpose. For a moment she'd thought things might have thawed between them, and she'd relished the exchange of whole sentences rather than the monosyllabic sparring of their first encounter. But there was a silence between them now that made her uncomfortable. It was so different from the constant noise of her sisters, or the irregular eruptions of the machinery on the building site where her office was in Rob's construction firm.

'So what are you doing out here?' she called out to Benoit.

'You have to ask?'

She sighed. 'No, I mean in Costa Rica. Why have you gone all…*mancenary*?'

'Okay, you're just making words up now.'

'No, it's like mercenary, but without the training.'

'Is this some new form of misandry? Putting "man" in front of a word and making it a term of abuse?' he replied, surprising her, from the look on her face. 'Because I don't particularly care for it. Having never disliked, mistreated or misspoken to, or about, women I'm not sure why you're directing this at me.'

'Did you say all that to get out of explaining why you're in Costa Rica?'

'Did you answer a question with a question to avoid providing an answer?' he fired back, despite the shock sparking in his chest that she'd called him on it. Because no one did that any more. He'd imagined her getting outraged, storming off in a huff and leaving him—as usual—not having to explain himself. Skye Soames, he was beginning to see, rarely did as he expected. But, from the look in her eyes, she wasn't going to answer so eventually he conceded, 'I'm not good in the morning without coffee.'

'You have coffee at the house?'

'Coffee, food, a shower.'

She groaned out loud, the sound making the hairs on the back of his neck stand to attention.

'I'll have the coffee, while eating a sandwich *in* the shower. So…you're here to…?'

Benoit wanted to growl, and not just because she was refusing to give up the interrogation. The thought of her in his shower… He purposefully shut the door on that mental image. She was completely off-limits. If not because of her obvious innocence, then most definitely because of the idea turning in his mind like a screw.

Map. Marriage. Skye. Map. Marriage…

Perhaps he could use her interrogation to at least test the waters slightly.

'To think,' he answered, shrugging a shoulder as if it was nothing. As if the weight of a multi-billion-dollar company and generations of Chalendar men didn't rest upon them. Easing into the subject, he pressed on. 'To get away. The shareholders of Chalendar Enterprises are threatening to enact a by-law regarding the CEO position.'

'Why?'

The simply delivered, innocent questions were beginning to grate. Partly because he knew where they were going.

'Because they don't like the way I conduct my personal life.'

'But if you're not hurting anyone…'

'There is concern about the more salacious headlines being attached to the company name,' he growled.

'It's none of my business,' Skye said, holding her hands up as if warding off any more details or more anger.

'It would be nice if the board saw it that way.'

'How do they see it?'

Benoit clenched his fist around the machete and slashed unnecessarily at the foliage either side of the path.

It wasn't really a case of 'they'. Benoit was one hundred per cent sure the board would have lost the game of chicken he'd been playing with them for the last two years. They knew they were onto a good thing with him as CEO and wouldn't really depose him and risk losing the obscene amount of money he brought to their bank accounts.

'The concern is that negative headlines could affect stock prices.'

You're becoming just like your father.

His great-aunt's words had been like a sucker punch. He hadn't seen it coming. It had dropped him to his knees. He felt it even now.

'Are they right?'

'What?'

For a moment he feared she was asking him if he *was* becoming just like his father.

'No. I don't think they're right to be concerned about stock prices. But what I think doesn't matter. They are going to vote on it at the next meeting.'

A meeting that Anaïs had called. The reality of it simply blanked his mind. It stopped all thought. As if Benoit simply couldn't comprehend how she, of *all* people, could do that to him—could betray him like that, could threaten to take away the one thing—

'And what is this by-law?'

'It requires me to get married or step down as CEO.'

'That's crazy,' she replied.

'No more crazy than searching for a one-hundred-and-fifty-year-old map of secret passageways and hunting for missing jewels,' he bit back angrily, mentally at war with the need to defend his great-aunt whilst also cursing her. He was the only one who could do that.

'No, I mean what's crazy is the assumption that marriage would suddenly stop you being a philanderer.'

'Philanderer?'

'Would you prefer another description? Playboy, womaniser, Lothario, rake, libertine—'

'You're having too much fun with that,' he growled again. 'You'd think they'd have learned their lesson last time. It's not as if it worked with my fath—' He bit off the word, clenching his jaw, shocked that he'd even half said such a thing.

After a pause, he heard Skye ask, 'So when does this marriage have to happen by?'

'My thirty-second birthday.'

'Which is…?'

'Two weeks.'

'And if you're not married by then?'

'The company goes to my brother, who *is* married. And I'd rather see the whole lot burn in hell before I let that happen.'

Once again silence descended, occasionally punctuated by the thrash and thwack of Benoit's machete. Skye had been surprised by the anger in his voice when he'd spoken of his brother. No matter what had happened with her sisters, no matter how hard she'd had to push them to do their homework or go to school, no matter what she'd given up for that to happen, she could never imagine feeling that much anger or…*hatred* towards either of them.

She checked her watch and realised that it had been twenty-four hours since she'd last spoken to them.

Without a signal she hadn't been able to contact them last night, and this morning her phone's battery had died. The thought of being out of contact with them, with her mum…it was like a thousand spiders crawling all over her.

Were they worried about her? Would they try to call the hotel that she hadn't checked into? Would they try to contact the Costa Rican consulate? She thought of Summer, probably nose-deep in one of Catherine's journals. Of Star, daydreaming about exotic far-flung places. Of her mother, who knew nothing about the journey they were on. They'd decided against telling Mariam any more than that they were stuck in Norfolk sorting out the terms of the will, not wanting to get her hopes up, or remind her of painful encounters with her father. But, beneath the rambling roll of her thoughts, Skye had buried deep the fear that they weren't worried about her. That perhaps they weren't even thinking about her at all.

Benoit began to cut off to the left and soon Skye realised why. She felt an inconceivable amount of excitement when she saw a crumbled concrete road through the dense foliage and jogged to meet him. They shared a victorious smile as they reached the tarmac and pressed on. Without the protection of the rainforest the sun's heat was unbearable but the prospect of his home spurred them on. He pointed out the glimpse of a dark roof off to the left, but it wasn't until they rounded the last twist in the road that Skye finally saw the house.

Wow.

Nestled into the side of a hill within the rainforest, the building sprawled in deep mahogany lines and large planes of glass reflected nothing but the shapes of leaves and trees. It had two tiers perching along the hill's gradient, framed above by a large flat square of concrete that looked suspiciously like a helipad, the shape mirrored harmoniously below by an azure blue pool lined with trees to provide shelter and seclusion.

It took her the final fifteen minutes of their walk just to take it all in. It was the most beautiful construction she'd ever seen. The use of materials perfectly blended with the setting, but not just that…it was the detail. The finish. It was flawless. Rob would have probably dropped to his knees and wept to have seen such a thing. She was on the verge herself with the prospect of finally getting to a phone and speaking with her sisters. Once she knew they were okay, that Mum was okay, then she could talk to Benoit about the map.

She followed him through the front door, her eyes wide, expecting magnificence. She wasn't disappointed. She took in everything—the incredible mezzanine floor book-ended by the most breathtaking floor-to-ceiling window she'd ever seen, creating a wall of green trees, leaves, plants and wildlife. The ground floor was large and open-plan; the kitchen and dining area were along one side and the sitting area was set at a slightly lower level. Skye couldn't help but spin in a slow circle, trying not to feel overwhelmed by its opulence.

The furnishings were modern classic with touches of industrial materials mixing well with the natural wood and glass. Somehow the monotone shades suited the bright rich greens from the rainforest surrounding the house, ensuring that the natural artistry of the location was displayed to its fullest. Skye was drawn to the side wall of the sitting area—the entire length and breadth covered in rows and rows of book-covered shelves all the way to the ceiling. A stair ladder hung from rungs along the very top shelf. She had so many questions. But there was only really one to ask.

'Can I use your phone?'

Benoit stilled just as he was putting his bag on the kitchen countertop, his whole body taking on the solidity of the concrete beneath her feet.

'You cannot use yours?' he asked.

'My phone died last night, and my charger is in my suitcase back at the airport. Look, if you don't want me using your phone, that's fine. I'll just borrow your charger.'

She frowned as she realised that he was looking at her oddly.

'You don't have a charger,' he repeated slowly.

'No,' she said, unsure why he suddenly seemed so... weird.

'When I said I come here to get away, I meant to Get Away. From everything.'

'And?' she demanded, beginning to feel a little irritated.

'Everything includes phones, mobiles, internet... and phone chargers.'

'What are you trying to say?'

'I'm not trying. I'm saying. There is no way for anyone to contact me here. No way for you to call—'

'We're stuck here?' she demanded, the realisation finally sinking in.

'Until the helicopter arrives in four days' time to pick me up? Yes. We're stuck with each other.'

Forty-five minutes later and Benoit's ears were still ringing. He must have told her one hundred times that it couldn't be kidnapping if *she* was the one who'd got in his car. And the suggestion that her panic might be down to hunger had apparently been akin to saying that she was hormonal. She'd screamed. Actually, it had been more like a growl. Though, Benoit thought, that must be an English thing because he was starving and it was making him as angry as she appeared to be and he had no problem admitting that.

He winced as he heard the slam of one of the bedroom doors as she tore through his house, refusing to believe that his house was 'off-grid', as she had taken to calling it, or that he was that 'irresponsible', as she had taken to calling *him*.

'What if there was an emergency and your family needed to contact you?' she'd demanded.

His reply that they would send a helicopter hadn't appeased her.

'What if *you* had an emergency and needed help?'

His suggestion that he'd deal with it had been met with scathing disapproval.

'What if you fell down the stairs and couldn't move and were unconscious?'

He hadn't liked the way she'd looked at the long set of stairs to the first floor—as if she'd like to push him all the way down and test her theory.

He watched Skye come down the staircase and without a word pass through the large glass door that led out to the patio. And then he sighed. Because he did feel a bit bad for her; he wasn't a complete monster. She'd survived a car accident, a night in the Costa Rican rainforest, himself in the morning without coffee, only to arrive at their destination and discover there was no escape.

He picked up the cafetière cups and took them out to the table on the patio. He sat, trying to focus on the peace his garden usually brought him, but his attention snagged on the hunched shoulders of Skye Soames.

'I don't have time for this,' she said, facing away from him.

'I know the feeling,' he said grimly, thinking of the days counting down until his birthday.

'No, I mean I really... I can't be here right now. I need to be back home. I was supposed to be back home by now.'

Once again, Benoit couldn't quite shake the feeling that there was something that she wasn't telling him. Usually he wouldn't care, but there was something about her tone, something that snagged in his chest.

'What back home is so important?'

Everything. But Skye couldn't tell him that.

'Your sisters?' he asked.

She nodded, knowing that it was only half the reason she felt so panicked. She turned and joined him at the table. He tentatively pushed a cup of coffee in her direction, as if worried she might throw it over him. But she gratefully scooped up the china in her hands, her mouth watering at the rich scent and hopeful that it might help stimulate a few more neurons so that she could find a way out of here. She'd been surprised to find that Benoit had been telling the truth.

No phone. No internet. Nothing.

Her heartbeat thudded heavily in her chest as she battled with the panic in her mind. She couldn't be stuck here. They didn't have the time. Her mum didn't have the time. Each hour, minute even that she didn't have the map, that they weren't closer to finding the key, or the passageways, felt like a minute stolen from her mother's life—and that thought was paralysing.

'How old are they?'

'Twenty-four and twenty-two.'

He huffed out an incredulous breath. 'From the way you were speaking, I thought they'd be much younger. They'll be fine,' he said, instantly dismissing her concerns.

'It's a lot for them to deal with—' she tried to justify herself '—and Star? Well, she'll probably fall into some romantic notion about whatever the next step is to find the Soames diamonds and Summer will probably forget to eat because she'll be lost in Catherine's journals.'

'Skye, Star and Summer?'

'Mum's choice.'

'Not your father's then?'

Skye shrugged, ignoring the ache suddenly blooming in her chest, blotting out some of the panic, not quite sure which was the lesser of two evils. She drew her coffee cup to her chest as if it could ward off the question.

'Mum left him when I was about thirteen months old. She didn't like his normal, mainstream lifestyle.'

'And he just let you all go?'

'Well, he let me go. Star was born after an affair and Summer doesn't know who her father is. Don't get the wrong idea—it's not that Mum was...like that.'

He frowned. 'I'm not judging,' he said, raising his hands in defence.

'Everyone judges,' Skye assured him. 'I learned that pretty quickly.' Teachers, parents, school friends.

I don't want her playing with my child.

But Margaret, she's my daughter.

And that's fine. For you. But she runs around here like a wild thing, with barely any clothes or care, and it's not the way I will raise my son.

Skye hadn't thought about the conversation she'd overheard between her father and stepmother for years. It sent a shiver down her spine, despite the thick damp heat of the forest around her.

She'd stopped talking about her childhood and her sisters when she realised a woman with three children by different men was called names. And the children? Her and her sisters? They didn't escape either. But with Benoit she genuinely hadn't felt such censure and it was an odd feeling.

'Look, why don't you have a shower? I'll leave a towel and some clothes out—they'll be mine, but better than what you have with you. I'll stay inside until you're done,' he offered, standing up from the table.

A shower sounded amazing. She was contemplating the opportunity to get out of her two-day-old, sweat-soaked, muddied clothes, when she registered his words fully. 'Stay inside? Where's the shower?'

He nodded over to the corner of the patio. Of course this man would have an outdoor shower. *Of course* he would.

She heard him disappear into the house while her mind registered the implications of showering outside, naked amongst the elements where anyone—or Benoit—could see her.

It's just a shower, Skye, she told herself sternly, disliking the way even the thought of it made her feel exposed, vulnerable...but hating the way it also sent a thrill rushing through her. As if it were something illicit, guiltily pleasurable. A thrill that she welcomed for blocking out all thoughts of her father, of her mother, her sisters...

She cut a glance to the shower and slowly pushed back her chair and made her way towards it, staring at it as if it were a challenge to her 'conservative' lifestyle—something her mother always bemoaned. Mariam Soames would have loved it.

Benoit returned with a towel and the clothing he'd promised before leaving again, but Skye waited for a good few minutes before she made her way across the decking towards the stunning outdoor shower surrounded by huge green leaves offering a sense of privacy. Small mosaic stones and turquoise-coloured tiles covered the floor in a beautiful pattern.

Toeing her shoes from her feet, her heart was racing to a different rhythm, a lighter one, faster. The idea that Benoit could—at any moment—catch a glimpse of her naked under the jets of water made her feel...*alive*.

She peeled her jeans from her legs, half fearful, half desperate to get rid of the clinging denim. Now that he wasn't in front of her, her mind raked over and indulged in memories of Benoit by the fire without his T-shirt on. The way his shoulders had seemed like organic boulders, large and powerful, the sandy blond trail of hair dipping below the waistline of his trousers.

The blush that rose to her cheeks stung in its intensity and she doused her heated skin with an icy blast of water from the shower. Only instead of soothing her fevered imagination, it inflamed. As she ran her hands over her body, in her mind they belonged to Benoit and it was making her want things she never had before. Certainly not with Alistair, her one and only boyfriend.

She turned beneath the spray, the sight of something glinting in the forest further down the hill cutting off the direction of her thoughts. She frowned. That couldn't be right. Benoit had said there was no one around here for miles. But then again, he hadn't mentioned the motorbike she'd found in the garage either.

Had he lied to her?

Skye turned back to the rooftop she'd seen glinting in the distance. It was definitely a house. Surely they would have a phone. Knowing there was no way she could stay here for four more days, she reached for the towel and fresh clothes before she could change her mind.

* * *

Benoit was hiding in the house from the temptation that was Skye Soames. The house wasn't very big but it was definitely clever. His ears strained for the sounds of the shower and he realised he hadn't heard it running for a while. In fact, he hadn't heard anything for a while now.

Frowning, he risked a glance outside his bedroom window and couldn't see her. Unease stirring in his chest, he scanned the spare rooms on the mezzanine floor and made his way downstairs. Not seeing her on the lower floor, he went out into the garden towards the shower, where the floor was still wet from use.

He looked about and, catching sight of the roof of his neighbour's house, he ran to the garage. His motorbike was gone.

He cursed out loud. She was going to get herself killed.

Or worse—ruin his damn bike.

CHAPTER FIVE

THE WHEELS SPUN on the hot tarmac and Skye grappled with the evil machine as it threatened to shoot off once again without her. She was shaking with fear and it wasn't helping her control the bike, but she was determined to master the thing.

She'd made it at least two miles before she'd had to wobble to a stop when she'd hit one of the many cracks in the road and nearly toppled the whole thing over. It had been half that distance since she'd last seen the roof of the neighbour's house but the road kept twisting her in the wrong direction and she was beginning to worry now.

How on earth did people ride these things? Underneath the shower she'd felt rejuvenated and determined but the road was dusty and having a go on Alistair's moped seven years ago hadn't seemed to have given her any real ability to handle Benoit's motorbike.

She took in a shaky breath and told herself that she could get control of this blasted machine, of this damned situation. She had to. She desperately wanted to speak to her sisters but, more importantly, she didn't want to turn back, humiliated and shame-faced, and see that *I told you so* look on Benoit's face.

With trembling hands, she twisted the bike's handle, her heart momentarily soaring as the engine spluttered into life, only for it to buck and stall beneath her, knocking her off balance. The weight of the machine pulled her downwards and she and the bike crashed to the ground, hot metal digging into her calf muscles and pressing her skin into the gravel on the road.

She slammed the floor with her free hand and let loose a curse. 'What am I doing?' she demanded of herself.

'I was about to ask you the same question.'

She gasped out loud as she saw Benoit bearing down on her, his body so imposing it blocked out the sun. How could she be both relieved and terrified at the same time? Except she couldn't quite put a name to what she was scared of.

Benoit hauled the bike off her, righted it and, putting it on its stand, checked it over for damage. He remained silent but she could see the way he clenched his jaw, the muscle flaring again and again. She didn't have to justify herself or her actions to him, she thought defensively. Only...she had stolen his motorbike, probably damaged it, just like she'd damaged the Jeep.

Oh, God, the repair costs! She hadn't even thought of that. She was barely covering rent, let alone the contributions to Summer's university expenses. If they didn't find the map and the diamonds she'd be in debt to Benoit up to her eyeballs, and her mother...

Skye bit back the sob that was about to rise in her chest.

'I'm sorry,' she said, to Benoit and to her sisters. She'd let everyone down. She felt the hot press of tears behind her eyes and blinked desperately, hoping they wouldn't fall. 'I'm sorry,' she said again. 'I don't know what—'

'You saw the neighbour's house and the bike and thought I'd been keeping it from you. *Chérie*,' he said, finally turning to pin her with a gaze the colour of frost, 'do you think I want you here? Do you think I like the idea of sharing these four precious days—the *only* days in my whole calendar year that I'm not at the beck and call of emails or meetings or contracts?'

She bit her lip to stop it from trembling. Benoit spun around but barely spared her a glance before pacing back and forth with clenched fists.

'If I'd thought my neighbour was there I'd have taken you. If I thought there was enough gas in the tank of the bike to get us anywhere near a phone or civilisation I would have taken you. If there was any way I could have got rid of you, Ms Soames, I swear to you I would have taken it.'

Benoit was furious. But he was also relieved not to have found her in any serious trouble. The fear and anger he'd felt when he'd found the house empty... A shiver worked its way up his spine, and only now was the tension beginning to ease. Scouring the house for any sign of her had reminded him of the way his brother had run through the house the morning after his mother had left them. The slicing pain in his heart as he'd seen the moment Xander had realised that their mother had gone and left them behind.

Something Benoit had already known since the night before.

'Are you sure they're not at the house?' she whispered, making him feel bad. Which made him feel angry all over again.

'He's never at the house. But I can see that you don't trust me, so come on,' he said, ignoring the twist in his gut as he realised it was true. 'Let's go.'

She frowned, casting a glance over his sweat-soaked shirt and the rapid rise and fall of his chest. 'How did you—?'

'I ran,' he growled forcefully, slowing his breathing, its rapid pace having nothing to do with exercise or his anger. The moment he'd seen the bike on top of her... It just didn't bear thinking about. She ignored his hand and got up by herself, so he turned and swung a leg over the seat of the bike, pulling it to standing. 'Get on.'

'What?'

'Get on. We're wasting daylight hours and I don't fancy another three-hour walk in the rainforest, do you?' he asked pointedly.

Benoit held the bike in place as she tentatively stepped towards the machine she'd nearly destroyed. She was dressed in the clothes that he'd laid out for her. She'd rolled up the sleeves of the white linen shirt; the smallest one he could find was still large on her. It was tucked into the tan cargo shorts, which were cinched at the waist by the belt she'd worn previously, but the legs hung so low that they looked like culottes on her. There were a few inches of creamy, delectable calf and slender ankle on show before her tan Oxford brogues. How on earth she'd made the outfit look even remotely stylish was lost on him.

He felt her settle into the seat behind him and couldn't help but roll his eyes as he waited until her hands were around his waist. Finally, when she'd exhausted every other option, he felt them, but she'd pushed herself as far back as she could get, which would topple them the moment they took the first corner. He reached behind him, hooked a hand behind each of her knees and tugged her against him, holding back a curse as he felt her slender thighs encase his own, the press of her breasts against his back. It wouldn't be for long. He could control himself in the less than ten-minute ride to his neighbour's. He had to.

He glanced at the fuel tank and prayed that they'd make it back home. He was done with trekking roads and jungle with this woman, especially when there was no whisky to make it at least a little enjoyable.

The thought reminded him of her missing jewels. The search for a map that had brought her out here in the first place. Last night it had seemed amusing, like a campfire fairy tale. But now, with the sun beating down on them and Skye's desperation as clear as day...

Something strong and sure told him that if the map existed then Anaïs would have it, would have kept it all these years. He could recite the words she often said by heart. *We have a duty to the past. A responsibility to bear for future generations to come.* He felt them as if they were written on his soul, had always been.

He hadn't worked eighty-hour weeks for nearly fifteen years just because he wanted to prove himself better than his father, or to fill the devastating sinkhole he'd made in the company's finances. He'd done it because he'd felt the weight of the ancestors *before* his father. The ones who had given blood, sweat and tears for Chalendar Enterprises. Because they deserved more than his father. He'd done it for Anaïs and even now, when she was threatening to take it from him, he'd do it all over again. Because Chalendar Enterprises was the only thing in this world that—unlike people—wouldn't let him down.

The company that in two weeks he'd have to hand over to the brother who'd betrayed him because Anaïs no longer trusted him. Benoit revved the engine, momentarily forgetting his purpose until he felt Skye shift slightly behind him.

Skye, who was so desperate she had flown halfway across the world, stowed away in a stranger's car, stolen a motorbike she clearly didn't know how to ride…

A desperation he could use to his advantage.

Skye shielded her eyes against the rays of the sun as if that would suddenly allow her to see signs of life in a home that looked more like a prison. It was a foreboding concrete block of a house, so different to Benoit's. Instead of sympathetically echoing the surrounding nature, it stood out like a sore thumb. Angry and out of place.

As Benoit leaned the bike on its stand she rested her hands on his shoulders to lever herself from the seat and wobbled unsteadily on aching legs before finally coming to stand on her own. No. A second look did not reveal any more signs of life, other than a red blinking light next to what looked like a security camera. Perhaps...

'Don't even think about it.'

'What?' she asked innocently, as if she wasn't considering criminal action to get what she needed. Maybe she *was* going crazy. That, or she'd inherited a little more of Catherine Soames' adventurous nature than she'd realised. But there was a thin line between adventurous and reckless.

'If you do that you'll end up in jail for breaking and entering—which, I assume, was the next stage of your plan. And as much as I resent your presence here, I don't think I'd like to see you in a Costa Rican jail cell. Because that's what will happen. And then you and your sisters really will be in trouble.'

Anger spiked through her then. 'Don't use them against me.'

'Why? It seems to be the only thing that will get through to you.'

'It's just that I'm... I'm...'

'Feeling out of control and hating the fact that there's nothing you can do about it,' he cut in.

'Would you not finish the end of my sentences?' Her shout was consumed by the dense concrete and live green foliage surrounding it.

'Fine,' he replied, tight-lipped and grim-faced.

She knew that he was right. She couldn't break into someone's house to see if they had a phone. She might have ticked reckless behaviour, theft and destruction of private property off her criminal to-do list, but she couldn't add breaking and entering to the list. Even for her sisters.

Benoit was right; the neighbour wasn't at home and he really hadn't exaggerated the situation. There was no way out. Not until his helicopter arrived in four days' time.

'It is only four days,' he said, his tone for the first time neither mocking nor angry.

Four days.

Just four days. Skye knew that in the grand scheme of things it wasn't a lot of time. Even with her mum sick, it wasn't long. And really, what could Summer and Star get up to in ninety-six hours? She couldn't fight it, couldn't carry on like this. It was exhausting and damaging. She had to trust that they would all be okay. She *had* to.

'Are you done?' Benoit asked Skye the moment the resolute energy holding her up seemed to drop away and she sagged in defeat.

'Yes,' she replied as a wave of exhaustion threatened to pull her under and she dropped onto the seat behind him. This time she put her arms around Benoit's waist without a second thought, her body sinking against his as the speed of the bike picked up and the air rushed through her hair.

She allowed her mind to completely blank, to simply relish the sensations around her. The cool rushing air against her skin, the feel of Benoit's torso beneath her fingers, the shift and sway of the muscles of his back against her chest, her thighs reflexively tightening around his as they turned a corner... She closed her eyes and leaned a cheek against his shoulder blades, losing herself to the sensations of the bike's movement, rather than those of her fevered imagination. When she next opened them, Benoit was slowing the bike at the gate to his home.

He walked the bike into the courtyard and leaned it on the stand. He waited for her to slither off the seat before he gracefully swung his leg over and stalked off into the house. His silence was beginning to really eat away at her and she hurried after him, having gone from wanting to flee to feeling as if the only safety she had was when she was with him.

'Where are you—'

Her question stopped short as she watched, eyebrows at her hairline, as he started to strip off his T-shirt.

'Shower,' he growled, looking at her as if daring her to comment.

She bit her lip and watched as he stalked through the French windows, grabbing a towel he must have left there earlier. She pulled her eyes away the moment his hands reached for his waistband.

Instead she turned to the kitchen and, with her back firmly to the garden, she focused on the contents of the fridge and not what was happening outside. In the shower. Where, in the gathering dusk, stood a very naked Benoit.

Food. They both needed to eat. And although she wasn't completely comfortable rummaging around in a man's fridge, it was the least she could do. The list of debts she was accruing with Benoit was getting longer and longer by the minute.

As she marinated steak and chopped cucumber, lettuce, tomatoes and whatever else she could find to go in a salad, the twist and turn of embarrassment that gripped her like bindweed wouldn't quit. She was embarrassed by her actions, by the train of her thoughts. By the way she'd reacted to the feel of her hands wrapped around his waist. A low thrum at her core reminded her that it hadn't just been the vibrations from the bike she'd felt, that the heat hadn't just been from *his* body, and...

And then Benoit walked through the French windows, emerging from the shower with just a towel around his waist and water droplets darkening the sandy blond hair curling around his head. She nearly dropped the knife she was using to cut the tomatoes.

Her eyes drank in the sight of him, the ripple of his muscles as he stalked towards her, her mind thankful for the barrier of the breakfast bar between them, her body crying out in frustration. The power of him, the predatory look in his gaze as he allowed her to take her fill of him unabashed, unashamed. Her skin sizzled in response; the thin flame of need turned into a wildfire storming through her body. She yanked in a jagged breath.

'You should not look at me like that unless you have every intention of finishing what you're starting.'

His words hung between them, the challenge ringing loud, clear and utterly undeniable.

Skye looked away, pretty sure she heard him say, 'I thought so,' as he made his way up the staircase to the second floor.

By the time Benoit was dressed he told himself he was back in command of his libido. She'd clearly had no idea what that look had done to him and he wished *he* didn't. Because it was interfering with the now fully formed plan in his mind. The one that said Skye Soames was the answer to his problems. And the reason that she was perfect was not just because she desperately needed the map that he was convinced his great-aunt had hidden away, but also because nice girls like Skye Soames didn't go for bad boys like him. In fact, he fully expected her to find his proposal so outrageous it would cut that attraction dead. Which was good, because he had absolutely no intention of messing up the only decent solution he'd found to this entire situation with something as fleeting as sexual desire.

Feeling a familiar sense of complete self-belief in his plan and its success, he snagged a bottle of wine before heading out into the garden where Skye had laid the table and placed the steaks.

She had waited for him but when he took a seat she barely met his eye.

'Would you like a glass of wine?' he asked.

'I don't think—'

'Not that I want to pressure you into drinking, but

it's a light wine and you can stop at one glass. You'd be drinking with food so…'

'The effects won't be as potent as the whisky?'

'Pretty much, *oui*.' He smiled, hoping to put her at ease, and to completely ignore the passing comment he'd made on his return from the shower earlier, even though the words still burned his tongue. 'This looks delicious, thank you.'

After he took his first bite she seemed to gingerly approach the steak and spear the smallest piece with her fork. She stared at it a long time before putting it in her mouth.

'Is something wrong?' he asked. She shook her head, slowly chewing and eventually swallowing.

'No, it's just… I…haven't eaten meat in five years.'

Benoit nearly spat out his wine. 'What? You're vegetarian?' he demanded.

'It's not that shocking.'

'I'm not shocked by the vegetarianism, but that you'd suddenly decide to eat steak!'

'Well, it's not me that's the vegetarian. Summer became vegetarian five years ago and Mum's been vegan for years, so it just seemed easier if we all did.'

'Skye, there are plenty of vegetables in the fridge!'

'I know. But you missed out on your steak last night. You said so… And, given how much trouble I've been…the Jeep, the bike… I can't even imagine how much I owe you,' she said, still not meeting his eye.

'You don't owe me anything,' he said sincerely, not once having given thought to charging her for the damage. Instead, he was searching Skye's face for traces of the determined, no-nonsense woman who'd trekked through the jungle covered in scratches and bites. He rubbed his forehead, appalled that she had just broken her principles to appease him.

'Please, Skye, don't eat any more of it,' he said, the small bite he'd already managed sitting heavy in his gut.

She looked up then, gold flecks flickering in her brown eyes. 'Actually,' she whispered as if confiding a secret, 'I really like it.' And she took another mouthful of succulent meat. And another. And another.

She groaned in appreciation and Benoit fisted his cutlery in his hands, trying to shake off the realisation that this woman had spent years denying herself pleasure when he never refused it.

'I'm sorry. I genuinely support vegetarianism. I wholeheartedly believe that it's both better for our digestion as well as the environment,' she explained, eyeing up another forkful.

'These were sustainably sourced, I assure you.'

'Thank you. I appreciate it, I really do. But every once in a while…it makes you appreciate and value the meat you do have.'

'Will you regret it tomorrow?' Benoit asked, genuinely curious. Rather than fobbing him off with an answer she seemed to give the matter some thought. She looked into the distance over his shoulder, squinting a little as if working through possible consequences. Once again, he was struggling to fathom how she had put her own wants—something as simple as the occasional piece of meat—aside for her sisters. As a man who had luxuriated in giving into his every selfish want in the last two years it was a strange notion.

'No. I don't think so. It doesn't mean that I'll call my sisters and tell...' She trailed off, clearly remembering that she couldn't just pick up the phone and call them. 'But I knew what I was doing when I chose the steaks for dinner,' she pressed on.

'So the vegetarianism was...?'

'My mum,' she supplied. Benoit couldn't be sure but there was something in her eyes...as if she both wanted and didn't want to carry on the conversation. 'Mum's lifestyle is...*alternative*. It's a wonder we all survived childhood.'

Benoit was thinking that it probably had more to do with Skye than a wonder.

'What's she like?' He was clearly tired as usually he would never have allowed himself to voice such a personal question. But he couldn't deny that he was curious. Something about this woman was niggling at him. Like a puzzle that he wanted to solve.

Skye smiled but again that smile... It was...sad?

'She's loving and enthusiastic and creative, but not the most down-to-earth. She is truly a free spirit.'

'And you're not?'

'No, it's just that when you're a child, school and homework and clothing are actually mandatory, not just *governmental interventions on parenting and free will.*'

'She's a nudist?' he asked, the image of the self-contained, conforming Skye in front of him and the free-living and loving picture she was painting jarring in his mind.

'No—' Skye laughed '—not really. She just values her freedom to be how nature intended, freedom to love who she wants, be how she wants. But in reality that doesn't quite work when you have three children to drag into adulthood.'

Or two. Because Benoit had the distinct impression that it wasn't her mother who had nurtured her children into adulthood but Skye.

Anger ignited in his gut and it took Benoit a second to get a hold on his feelings. The power of them had taken him by surprise while Skye seemed oblivious. In his mind's eye he saw his mother, the look on her face as he had caught her packing her bag that last night.

'Is it cooked okay?'

'Yes. Very okay,' he said, forcing an answer to numb lips as he returned to the present. He smiled belatedly and she cocked her head ever so slightly as if sensing something was wrong.

'I've been thinking about your map,' he said, forcing a change in subject and his mind onto the goal he should not have strayed from. 'The only person who might be able to help is my Great-Aunt Anaïs.' Even if their last parting had been heated, Benoit knew her love for him was as undeniable as his love of her and not even Chalendar Enterprises would change that. Especially if he found a way to keep it, despite her attempts. 'Anaïs is all about family duty, honouring the past to secure the future. She's also devious enough to have kept something like that a secret from me this long,' he said, a smile pulling at his lips.

'You love her,' Skye noted.

'You sound surprised? Of course I do. Anaïs took care of us after our father's death. Two orphaned teenage boys, as wilful as we were wayward.'

'Were?' she said sceptically.

'You think I'm wayward?' he replied, trying to avoid the truth of his past but knowing he couldn't. 'Our childhood was different to yours. My father might not have left, but sometimes I wonder if we would have been better off if he had.'

'Don't say that.'

She was right. He shouldn't have said that. Shouldn't have revealed as much. If there had been a thought that she might have understood…it disappeared like smoke.

'When the helicopter arrives,' he said, getting himself back on track, 'it will take me back to France, to the Dordogne where Anaïs lives.'

'And you'll take me?' The hope shining in her eyes was startling. For a moment he didn't want to douse that hope. But he had a company to save.

'That's up to you.'

'Why?'

'Because I have a proposition. One that you'll need to think seriously about before agreeing,' he said, his eyes locking with hers, confirming the seriousness of what he was about to say.

'What proposition? You know I have nothing to give you,' she said, frowning. 'And I doubt you need money.'

'Not money. I don't need that. But I do need a wife.'

CHAPTER SIX

SKYE STARED AT Benoit, waiting for him to laugh and tell her it was all a joke.

'You can't be serious,' were the only words to escape her lips.

'I am,' he said, his blue eyes hardening like ice. 'I have something you want—' the dismissive shrug of his shoulders just plain irritated her '—and you could be something I need. It's a simple exchange.'

'Exchange? It's not an exchange, it's a *marriage*,' she couldn't help but cry, her mind scrambling to process everything, her mind racing as he offered the one thing she needed and then pulled it from her reach. 'You're barbaric.'

'No, it would be barbaric to kidnap you and force you to marry me, but I'm not. I'm offering you a deal—'

'A deal?' she demanded, horrified at how quickly Benoit had turned from someone sharing confidences to contracts.

'You don't have to take it.'

'But we need the map,' she insisted.

'And I need a wife,' he said determinedly.

'Find someone else,' she begged.

'I don't have time.'

'But you *did* have,' she accused.

'Honestly, marriage is the last thing I ever wanted, and I truly thought I'd find a way to manipulate the board.'

'And instead you manipulate me?'

'It's easier,' he said as if he really didn't care.

She'd been about to tell him about her mother. To explain why it was he shouldn't have wished his father had left, no matter what. To try and share how precious life was, even if that relationship was flawed... And now? There was no way. This was not a man whose mercy you could hope for.

Her heartbeat pulsed in her ears.

Thud, thud, thud.

It felt like the seconds marked by a clock. Time running out. For the jewels, for her mother. And, horrifyingly, she could already feel herself wavering— her mind running over the possibilities, the steps that could be taken.

'This is crazy.'

'You want a way to control the situation—well, this is it. I'm offering you a way to take back that control.'

'By handing it over to you?'

'I wouldn't be that kind of husband.'

'And I refuse to be that kind of wife,' she said mulishly.

'Then the helicopter will drop you back at the airport, where you can get a flight home and you can explain to your sisters why you will never have access to the map.'

'Now that definitely sounds like blackmail,' she said, pushing back from the table, her half-eaten plate easily discarded now that her stomach was in turmoil. She stood and walked to the edge of the pool, casting a look about the dark shadows of the rainforest but not seeing it. Instead, she imagined her sisters in the library at the Soames estate, poring over Catherine's journals, trying to find the next clue in the search. She saw her mother in her friend's back garden looking over the New Forest, counting down sunsets that she had left. All the while Benoit waited. Waited for her to come to the same conclusion he had. That there was no other option.

She shook her head as if trying to deny what she knew she had to do. There must be another way, she thought. 'Why do you want the company so badly?' she asked in the hope that his answer might offer one. 'Surely it can't be the worst thing for your brother to—'

'I'll never let him have it. He's taken too much from me already.'

Once again Skye registered the darkness behind his words when he spoke of his brother. And for the first time since he'd dropped this shocking proposal like a bomb between them he wouldn't meet her gaze. This time *she* felt like the predator, waiting and watching, looking for signs of weakness. He had used hers against her and she was determined to repay the favour.

'Explain,' she demanded.

'No,' he scoffed.

'It clearly has something to do with this "deal" of yours and I would like to consider all angles—'

'There are none,' he growled.

'I'm sorry if this dents your ego, but if there's a way I don't have to marry you I'll take it,' she returned angrily.

His eyes turned even more frosty and a chill ran down her spine as if it had been touched by an icy finger.

He glared at her one last time before looking out at the rainforest over her shoulder. 'I was engaged once before,' he said, his voice grim and his jaw tight. 'Camilla was the daughter of a business associate. We met five years ago and within weeks it seemed like the perfect match. She was impeccable, poised, understood my need to focus on the company. Or…that's what I thought at the time. For three years we courted, Camilla reluctant to move in with me until we were married. I had proposed, but I was holding out on the wedding—I wanted everything in place, everything perfect. Xander and I were selling off one of the subsidiary companies to focus on the research and development side of things.

'Research and development was something I'd always wanted to do. My father had no head for science, nor finances, and under his tenure the company had gone to the brink. I wanted the company to get back on track, to work on building a foundation that was more than just about supply and demand of building materials. I wanted us to be *leading* the demand. There is so much that can still be done, different ways to make the materials. Cheaper ones that could be of benefit to the world as well as the environment, instead of mindlessly using what's already there despite now knowing the impact and the harm.'

She heard the pride and ambition in his voice. The passion. In some ways she felt it was the truest thing she'd heard him say. Felt it call to her because it met a yearning within her that she'd never been able to fulfil. Not while looking out for Star and Summer. And when he returned to the story of what had happened in the past, the light went out of his eyes.

'I'd been distracted by a big new contract and Xander had been distracted by something else. He'd grown withdrawn and uncharacteristically antagonistic. I was relieved when a trip to Hong Kong had been cancelled at the last minute so that I could see him and get to the bottom of what was going on. I wanted to make sure he was okay.'

Benoit huffed out a bitter laugh. 'I went to his apartment…' His words conjured memories he hadn't allowed himself to examine for two years and in his mind he retraced the steps up towards his brother's door. He watched himself retrieve the spare key to the apartment from his pocket, knowing that he should knock, perhaps even then sensing unconsciously that something was wrong.

As he'd walked down the hallway he'd known, he thought now. Because why else would he have pressed on, why else would he have rounded the corner to his brother's bedroom, when any sane person would have turned back? He'd ignored the signs in the kitchen and dining room—the glasses, the empty bottles of red wine...

'I found them. In bed.'

Even now bile rose to the back of his throat. The sight of Camilla in a red lacy body suit dressed for seduction churned his stomach. He remembered how she'd shifted, leaning back, and the moment that he'd locked eyes with Xander. The pain, guilt and anguish he'd seen there lost to the horror and outrage exhibited by Camilla.

'Rather than owning any sense of shame, she became a harpy, screaming and accusing.' For some reason all Benoit could call to mind was the flash of her bright red nails—the colour matching her lingerie— nails that had seemed more like talons that night. 'She told me it was my fault. That I had taken too long to get married. That Xander was everything that I wasn't.'

'And your brother?' he heard Skye ask, her voice filtering from the present into the past.

'He didn't say a thing. He didn't have to. He knew. I knew.'

Knew that the trust had been broken. And they would never get it back. Even now Benoit hated that the anger was mixed with an agony he daren't name, let alone acknowledge. And he would certainly not dig deep enough to investigate why it also made him feel a little less guilty.

Turning his back on the past, he looked at his future. Skye.

'I'm truly sorry that happened to you. I can't imagine what that kind of betrayal would be like,' Skye said. 'But is marriage really the right way to ensure the company stays with you?'

'I didn't tell you this for your sympathy,' he bit out. 'I told you to make you understand that there is no alternative. My hand has been forced by my family—something I believe you are familiar with—and I will not let you near the map unless you agree to be my wife. Now, it's getting late and I, for one, am looking forward to sleeping in a bed tonight.'

Skye looked around as if she'd only just noticed that the sun had set, the stars had risen and the day had turned to night.

'I don't have an answer for you, but I won't forget that you twisted my arm into this.'

'Good. You shouldn't. Don't forget, *never* forget, the one thing that can be trusted in life is that when everything is on the line, selfishness will always win out.'

Skye woke to the sound of Benoit's words on a loop in her mind, his accent and the softly spoken words at complete odds with the sentiment.

Selfishness will always win out.

And then she remembered his other words. *I need a wife.*

And I need the map, she thought.

She couldn't see a way round it. Benoit was the only person who could give her access to Anaïs, who *had* to have the map. And they needed the map to find the jewels to sell the estate if they were to have any hope of raising the money for the treatment Mariam needed so badly. For just a moment she had considered telling him about Mariam. About the cancer that was ravaging her body and how the only treatment they could get was freely given to others but would cost them the earth.

Or her hand in marriage.

Selfishness will always win out.

She just couldn't trust him not to use it against her. So no. She would *never* tell him about her mother.

She pulled back the covers of a bed so comfortable it had been like sleeping on a cloud. She went to stand in front of the window that formed the entire wall of the bedroom, just as it did below. The night before, the view had been a dark velvet cloak punctuated with silver sequins. Now the sight of the rainforest was magnificent, an endless stretch of green, making her feel like the only person on the planet.

She found her bag in the corner of the room where she'd dropped it yesterday, beside another shirt and a pair of lightweight trousers she *hadn't* seen yesterday. She'd have expected to feel outraged at the idea of Benoit in her room while she slept, but the image of him looking down on her while she'd been unaware… She shut down her errant thoughts.

This was a man who was trying to coerce her into a marriage she didn't want.

As she showered, she realised it didn't matter. Even if he wanted her to stay with him in France and never set foot back in England, even if she never saw her sisters again, Skye knew without a shadow of a doubt that she would do *anything* if it meant her mother would get the treatment she needed. If it helped the girls to find the jewels that would also secure their futures.

Even marry a complete stranger.

Only Benoit didn't *really* feel like a stranger. The only thing that had seemed strange about him was how cold he had become the night before. It was as if telling her about his ex-fiancée, about his brother, had drawn all the warmth from him. And she couldn't help the part of her that wanted to give him the benefit of the doubt. Because he was the man who had dismissed thousands of pounds in damages, who had been worried about her when she'd disappeared with his bike, who had been almost distraught at the idea she might have eaten meat on his account. And he was also a man who was clearly devastated by the hurt caused by his brother two years ago.

Dressed in the clothes that Benoit had left and the set of clean underwear she always carried in her hand luggage whenever she travelled, Skye followed the scent of coffee all the way to the patio outside.

Benoit was sitting in the same chair as the night before and if he wasn't wearing different clothes she might have thought he hadn't moved. His eyes were closed, his face turned up towards the sky and the sun. He seemed truly relaxed for the first time since she'd met him. There were slight crinkles around his eyes, but not as if he spent a lot of time laughing; rather that he spent a lot of time squinting—as if suspicious, or calculating.

The short beard was getting a little thicker, tempting her to wonder what it would feel like beneath her fingers. Soft? Rough? The way it framed his bottom lip, the full flesh casting a shadow from where it crested seemed carelessly sensual.

'Do you want some coffee?'

Skye jumped and couldn't help the cry of laughter that escaped at her own silly reaction. Her heart pounded in her chest and she felt tingles running all over her skin in relief as the spike of adrenaline crashed out of her system.

'You scared me,' she accused, taking the seat opposite Benoit, who still hadn't opened his eyes.

'You shouldn't sneak up on people.'

'*I* wasn't the one sneaking around.'

He opened one eye and peered at her. She gestured to her clothing, which she instantly regretted because the heat that burned beneath the places where his gaze raked was indecent.

'Would you rather have gone about naked? Or, worse, in yesterday's clothes?' he queried.

'I'm not sure you have that in the right order.'

He shrugged as if he didn't agree with her.

Despite having rolled up the dark blue linen trousers, the material kept unwinding to fall about her feet. But they were cool in this humid heat and, as Benoit pointed out, clean. She'd used her belt again to hold them in place, but somehow doing so had made her think about him, about the way his torso tapered down...

'Terms,' she said out loud, startling them both. 'We need terms,' she reaffirmed.

'So you agree? To the deal?'

'On one condition.'

'Yes?'

* * *

He'd nearly said, *Name it*, but that would have told her how much he needed her to agree. He hadn't realised how unsure he'd been of her answer. The night before, memories of the past had made him overly harsh and some alien inner voice told him to stop now before it was too late. But a darker one was already relishing victory.

Skye Soames was too sweet for this. She'd probably already rationalised his behaviour, finding some reason to justify his ruthlessness. But he had given her fair warning. *Selfishness will always win out.*

'I get the map first.' Skye's demand cut through his thoughts.

'No.'

'Yes. I have time constraints.'

'Which are…?'

'Immediate,' she replied, not answering his question as he'd have liked, nor meeting his eye. She clearly didn't like being evasive. He could use that.

'How immediate?'

'More immediate than your birthday.' This time she was looking straight at him. In her eyes he could see a firm line. This, she wouldn't budge on.

'*D'accord*. When we return to France I'll take you to Anaïs and we will attempt to find this map of yours. Then we will marry.'

'Wait? France? No. I have to get back to England.'

'Not until after we are married.'

'Hold on—'

'Skye, let me make this incredibly, painstakingly

clear to you. There is no way I'm going to let you have the map, should it exist, and leave, just trusting that you'll come back.'

'But I give you my word.' Her insistence was sweet, but definitely naïve.

'Sadly for you, that is not enough,' he said. 'For all I know you could be an axe murderer,' he replied, throwing her once hotly issued words back at her with a shrug of his shoulders. 'So. You can have the map, photograph it and send it to your sisters. You can courier the thing for all I care. But you will not leave France until we're married.'

He could tell she was buying time. She managed to stretch out pouring a single cup of coffee. Then she spent an inordinate amount of time picking her breakfast from the feast of fruits, pastries and yogurts he'd assembled before she'd come down from her room.

He watched her hand sway over a *pain au chocolat*. It went back and forth and, curiously, eventually back to her lap, leaving the pastry where it was. There was something about that he didn't like. It frustrated him that she would refuse to allow herself something she clearly wanted. It angered him, he realised, as he reached across the table, picked up the *pain au chocolat* and put it decidedly on her plate.

'I—'

Benoit cast her such a look—he might even have growled—that she immediately stopped what she'd been about to say. 'If this is another thing, like the vegetarianism, I don't want to hear it,' he commanded.

Skye folded her lips between her teeth and picked

the corner of the flaky pastry, popping it into her mouth. She chewed slowly at first and then reached for another piece, then another until finally she picked up the whole pastry and started to take proper mouthfuls.

He picked up his coffee and looked out into the distance, away from where Skye's slender throat was working, clenching his jaw *again* against her gentle groan of pleasure that sent sparks down his spine and made his stomach curl. He cleared his throat, trying to block out the sound and restore his equilibrium.

'I have terms of my own,' he managed to bite out. As she was still enjoying the croissant, he took her raised eyebrow as an invitation to continue. 'This,' he said, gesturing between them, 'will not evolve beyond this deal.'

She blinked. Then she swallowed. Then she squinted. 'You mean...?'

'No romantic notions, no daydreams of a happy ever after, no—'

'I get it,' she interrupted before he could say any more. 'That won't be a problem,' she went on as she removed a flake of pastry from the corner of her mouth with her thumb. He watched every single second of her doing so. 'So what would this actually look like?'

'Real,' he replied more quickly than he'd have liked.

She locked her gaze onto his. She seemed to bite back a sigh. 'How do you see it working?'

In all honesty, Benoit wasn't sure he *had* seen it working. He'd fully expected her to tell him to go to hell.

'I need to be married before my birthday, which is two weeks away. I know that you have business to attend to, so afterwards I wouldn't expect you to be chained to my side,' he said, his vivid imagination stumbling over the image of metal loops and wrists and… 'But the board would need to believe that the marriage is real. And my family are the board of Chalendar Enterprises so it will have to look good. There is, however, not a length of time stipulated by the by-law. Perhaps because it was written when marriages were expected to last.'

'So we would divorce?'

No, he thought, but couldn't quite explain to himself where that had come from, so instead replied, 'Yes.'

'How long?'

Benoit shrugged, aiming for a nonchalance he really didn't feel. 'Three years.' He'd meant to say two.

Skye choked on her coffee. And not just a pretty throat-clearing for effect. Flakes of pastry and coffee caught in parts of her throat they shouldn't have been in, produced a considerably violent outburst.

Three years seemed impossible. She didn't even—

The thought stuttered to a halt, but Skye forced herself to face it. She didn't even know if her mother would be here in three years. The almost constant sob caught in her chest, throbbed. But if Mariam Soames wasn't alive in three years, then did it really matter what Skye's world looked like then?

'Water?' Benoit offered as if he didn't know that he had been the cause of her choking.

'No,' she said, clearing her throat. 'No, thank you. Three years…' she said, turning over what that might mean in her mind. 'You'd be celibate for three years? Really?' she said, her errant thought escaping before she could stop it.

Now it was Benoit's turn to look shocked.

'Explain,' he demanded.

'It might not be a real marriage, but I'm assuming there will be a fair amount of public scrutiny at the news that a well-known international playboy...' she pushed on past the scoffing sound he made '...is getting married. And I have absolutely no intention of being humiliated while you are repeatedly photographed with your latest plaything.'

'Plaything?' he repeated.

'*Not* the point, Benoit,' Skye replied, knowing that she would stand firm on this.

'And you?'

'What about me?'

'All things being equal, you would also be celibate for three years.'

'That...that's fine,' she said, suddenly not liking the way the focus of this conversation had turned back on her.

'There's nothing *fine* about it,' Benoit returned hotly. Honestly, Skye really didn't know what he was getting so worked up about. The one time that she'd had sex with Alistair had been...had been...well, *fine* and she just didn't really know what all the fuss was about.

He was staring at her now as if there was something wrong with her and she didn't like it. It was the same way she'd felt when she'd overheard women talking about sex as if it was something incredible—as if she

were missing something. Life was so busy that she'd
not really had a chance to make close friends and there
was *no way* she was talking to her sisters or mother
about it. Her mother, who thought that sex was a divine
right, that bodies should be worshipped and that love
was something that was better shared with as many
people as possible.

Oh, God. She wanted to put her head in her hands.
She was a twenty-six-year-old prude.

'We can talk about this later,' she said evasively.

'Oh, no. We're talking about this now. We'll have
other things to talk about later,' he warned.

'Why—are you going to demand that I share your
bed if you're not allowed to find others to do so?'

'Don't be crass. I wouldn't do that to an innocent.'

He said the word with such distaste that it took her
a moment to realise what he was saying.

'Wait—you think I'm a virgin?'

'You're not?' he asked, just as shocked.

'No!'

Skye didn't know why she was so offended. There
was absolutely nothing wrong with being a virgin; it
was just that she wasn't and she didn't like him thinking that she was. Was that really how she came across?
But now he was looking at her as if he couldn't quite
work her out.

'Who was he?'

'No one important.'

'Clearly.'

'I didn't mean it like that. And I have no intention
of sharing that with you.'

'Skye, we're going to have to get to know each other *very* well if we're going to fool my family and the Chalendar board that we're in love and getting married. And if you can't even tell me about a boyfriend then—'

'Fine, but not now.'

'You have something better to do?' he asked, as if amused.

'Yes.' *No.* She just had to get away from him. She didn't like the way she felt when he looked at her like that. As if he saw...*into* her. She pushed the chair back from the table, stood and nearly tripped right back into it when her foot caught on the long hemline of Benoit's trousers.

He reached out an arm to steady her, the muscles of his forearm corded and powerful; she looked from there to his face and his eyes...frosty blue shards flaring in the sun. She pulled herself back upright, rubbing at the spot on her arm that prickled from where he'd held her.

He'd let her off. She knew it and he knew that she knew it too.

CHAPTER SEVEN

IT SHOULD HAVE been easy to get lost in a house several times the size of the one that Skye shared with her sisters, but it wasn't. She was acutely aware of Benoit the entire day she tried to hide from him. First, she'd gone back to her room but there was absolutely no chance of her falling back to sleep again. Then she'd wanted to go for a shower but Benoit was still outside, having been for a swim, just soaking up the sun like a seal. Sleek and wet and...

Stop it!

Then, when she'd ventured downstairs to the bookcase that stretched all the way up to the ceiling and ran the entire breadth of the house, she'd been overwhelmed by choice. There were thousands of books. She ran her fingers along the spines, awed by the sheer number of crime novels, biographies and architecture and design books. She found a thriller she hadn't read and turned to go back upstairs but Benoit was cutting through the open living area so she dropped, sinking into the plush sofa, hoping that she hadn't been seen.

She lost herself in the story of a misanthropic British secret agent two years from retirement, stalking his arch nemesis through Westminster and London to Moscow and eventually Paris. She missed the sounds of Benoit making lunch in the kitchen, missed the sounds of her stomach growling as she turned each page. She couldn't remember the last time she'd had the luxury of getting lost in a book, without worrying for her sisters or her mother.

An ache she'd been ignoring for far too long rose within her. Usually she was too busy with work, with the house, with checking on Star and Summer and her mother to pay any attention to it. But here in the stillness of Benoit's Costa Rican paradise, with no distractions, it was getting harder and harder to ignore.

The suspicion that she hid behind all those things swirled like steam within her, thick, damp and sad. Sister, daughter, secretary, *parent*... The suspicion that she hid in those roles because they gave her purpose. They gave her a sense of identity, something she had lost when she had been torn between two vastly different households and ended up feeling as if she quite fitted into either of them.

She'd been so young she'd barely even had a sense of who she might be when it had seemed far easier just to be something else. The perfect, well-dressed daughter for her non-confrontational father, the stand-in parent for her half-sisters, the sensible, practical daughter for her mother—the mother who did exactly what she wanted, was exactly who she wanted to be, not having to conform to the rules because Skye was there to do it for her.

But who did Skye want to be?

'It's a good book, Skye, but it's not *that* good,' Benoit announced, cutting through her thoughts and the sob that had half risen in her chest. He placed a glass of wine on the table in front of her that looked red and rich and her mouth watered.

She looked up, startled. Night—it was night again?

'You've been reading for about eight hours.'

'Eight?'

'Yes. Hungry?'

'All I do here is eat and sleep and—' She broke off, looking at Benoit's broad, encouraging smile. 'What?'

'That is the point.'

'Of your escape here?'

He gave a deep sigh as he sank into the corner of the large L-shaped sofa, the breath expanding a chest clearly defined by a lightweight dark wool sweater over a white linen shirt. 'Yes. To completely switch off and recharge. There isn't always time in France.'

'Why Costa Rica? Why not the Caribbean or Monaco or…?' she asked, genuinely curious.

'Some other generic playboy destination?'

'Yes! That, exactly,' she replied, enthusiastically warming to the teasing, perhaps too much, desperate for a distraction from her thoughts.

Benoit leant his head back against the high arm of the sofa so that he was looking up at the ceiling. She hadn't meant it to be a probing question, but she realised in an instant that she had pushed his thoughts to a part of his past that he didn't want to go.

'My brother and I used to play forts. Anaïs would

pack us lunch and we'd run off to the woods for the entire day, building fires, exploring. I loved it. I thought I'd be an explorer one day. But every time I'd ask where Xander wanted to explore next. It was always the same—'

'Costa Rica,' they said together, Skye smiling at the sweet story.

But it was a sad smile he offered her in return. 'I think even then we were making ourselves scarce from our father. He was...' Benoit struggled to find the right words to describe him. 'You never knew what mood he'd be in. He was charming and irrepressible when he was in a good mood, but most of those good moods were spent with other women, outside the home. And when it was bad he would rage through the house, berating us or our mother for some imagined slight.' The memories of those times rose up around him. His father's spiteful shouts, red-faced rage and fury were something he rarely dwelt on. 'He could be paranoid and furious. It's partly why he was so dangerous as CEO. The board thought that a wife and family would settle him, but I think we only made it worse. He had a marriage of convenience with my mother. I'm sure that she didn't know what she was getting into, which is why she chose to run away.'

He had spent so much of his childhood protecting Xander from his father, from his mother's absence. So yes, he knew something of what Skye felt towards her sisters. But he also knew what it had felt like when all that sacrifice, all that protection was turned against him, betrayed. Since the night his mother had left he'd always tried to protect Xander, to look out for him, to bear the brunt of his father's fury. Only for him to sleep with Camilla.

'What happened to your mother?' Skye asked.

'She died about two months after she left—a car accident in Italy.'

'I'm sorry.'

'Don't be—the family will expect us to know things like this about each other.' He knew that wasn't what she had been apologising for, but it made it easier to circumnavigate the solid ache in his chest. 'It's good; we need to know more about each other, so keep asking.'

He looked up at her. She had her feet tucked under her and a light throw over her lap. She seemed to fit, as if she'd always been here at the house. The reds in her hair blended with the dark wood and the paleness of her skin echoed the pale walls. She was a thousand textures. Smooth, soft, sharp, strong...

'Why did you think I was a virgin?'

His eyes snapped to hers in surprise. That was *not* what he'd expected her to ask. Her fingers were playing with the throw and it was clear she found the question deeply uncomfortable. He could lie to her. It would have been easier, for her and for him. Less...dangerous. But that wasn't his style.

'You don't seem that in touch with your sensual side,' he said, wondering if it was a trick of the light that made her cheeks seem to flush. 'You don't seem very aware of that part of you. You dress like a secretary.'

'I *am* a secretary. Well, office manager, but...'

He smiled. 'But you weren't working when you came out to Costa Rica to meet me. It's more than the clothes though. It's...' he waved his hand towards her and shrugged '...it's the way you are,' he said, avoiding the simple truth he felt to his soul.

'What is it? Just tell me,' she said, finally meeting his gaze.

He clenched his jaw. 'You don't behave as if someone has given you pleasure.'

Skye clamped her teeth together to prevent whatever reaction was welling up within her from escaping. Because she didn't know what would come out. Embarrassment, anger, hurt, arousal, cries, screams, sobs. She felt it all.

She might as well have been a virgin.

'Alistair was...we were young.' Why was she defending him? Because they had been young. They hadn't known better. Not really.

'How young?' Benoit demanded hotly.

'Not *that* young,' Skye said with a small smile at the strange kind of protectiveness that seemed to be on display. 'He just...'

'You were pressured?' Benoit had gone very still.

'No. Not in the way you think. We'd been together for the last two years of school. I don't even know what he was doing with me, even now. We hardly saw each other; I was so busy with Summer and Star and school. And he'd been patient and kind and understanding.' Sweet. It had felt sweet. 'But when it came time to leave school, to move onto the next stage in our lives, he thought I was going with him to London.'

'You didn't want to?'

'I did. But Summer was starting GCSEs, Star her A-levels. I couldn't go. He was hurt, sad. And…' She shrugged, unable to find the words as an adult, the ache in her chest, the awkwardness clogging her mind.

'You slept with him because you couldn't go with him to London?'

'I wanted him to have something that he wanted,' she said, heat in her cheeks. It seemed wrong, looking back over the distance of time.

'But did you want to?'

'Yes,' she replied. She'd wanted *him* to have that.

'You shouldn't make a gift of yourself like that. Your sexuality, your pleasure—that's not something to give away. You can share it, but you must have it for your-self at the same time.'

'Do you need to know anything else about him or are we done?' Skye forced the words out.

'You can ask me anything you like,' he said, his tone immediately lighter, for which she was eternally thankful. Because what he'd said had made her warm, ache, hurt and happy all at the same time.

'Your girlfriends? No, thanks.'

'Really? You don't want to ask me *anything*?'

'Not particularly. Though…the headline about the sisters… No. Actually, I don't want to know,' she said, laughing as she reached for the glass of wine on the table. It tasted dry but fruity on her tongue and she

wondered whether it was just because he had an exquisite wine collection or he'd chosen it for her.

'What about your parents?' Benoit asked, studying
her gently over the rim of his own wine glass. 'You
said your mum is a free spirit?'

'Yes. The full package—tie-dye flowing skirts,
flowers in her hair, the festival circuit. Her head is in
the clouds but her heart is bigger than anyone's I've
known,' she said, smiling at the memory of Mariam
Soames dragging them out of school to play with them
in a wildflower field, but feeling sad that she hadn't
been able to fully enjoy it because she'd been too worried. About what the teachers would think. About what
her father's new wife would think. She had been so
torn. She ached to think of what she had missed. If
only she'd been able to fit in with her mother and sisters just a little more.

'And your father?'

'A professor.'

'Of…?'

He clearly wasn't going to let her get away with
one-word answers.

'English Literature. They met at university in London and had a passionate affair before Mum decided
that "university education was riddled with the not
always unconscious bias of male upper-class oppres-
sion".'

'She too doesn't like the patriarchy?' Benoit teased.

'Etymologically, patriarchy means a structure of
rulership distributed unequally in favour of fathers,'
Skye explained, slightly wincing at the tone of her own

voice, but unable to stop. 'So I'm with Mum on this; universities are not skewed in favour of fathers, so I didn't mean patriarchal.'

His smile at her response hit her square in her chest. 'Where did you go to university?'

'I didn't,' Skye said, frowning and pulling at the thread on the beautiful throw covering her lap. She really shouldn't, she told herself. It might completely unravel.

'Really? Why not?' The surprise in Benoit's voice stung as much as it pleased. She liked that he'd thought she'd gone to university.

'We didn't have the money.'

'A university professor couldn't put his daughter through school?' He sounded half confused, half outraged.

'Dad remarried and he and his wife wanted to…decided that…' She hated that she was stumbling over words. It shouldn't be this hard just to say it. 'They put their money towards their son's education.'

'What?'

'It's fine,' she said to him in the same way she'd said to her mother, and to her father when he'd told her that he wasn't able to help. Even though he was able to; he and his wife had just chosen not to.

'It's not. What kind of mother is she?'

'Good, from what I can tell,' Skye replied honestly. 'She's a loving, perfect, stay-at-home mum who was on the PTA. The kind of mother who packed her son's bag the night before school, never forgot lunch, helped him with his homework and always remembered indoor shoes as well as outdoor ones.'

'Did you spend much time with them, growing up?'

'Some,' she said, remembering the way it would make her feel when she would leave home to spend the weekend with her father and then the way it would make her feel to come back home. Awful, awkward and not fitting in at either house. 'I didn't exactly make the best first impression. I was a bit of a wild child, running around naked, making a mess and ruining things. Margaret, Dad's wife, couldn't handle it and, no matter how much I tried to be the kind of daughter she might have in her house, it didn't seem to help.'

'Why bother?' Benoit demanded arrogantly, full of the self-assured confidence she'd never possessed.

'Because I wanted to spend time with my father?' she replied hotly. 'Because I would have liked to have got to know my brother? Because there's half a family out there that is mine and I'm cut off from them? It's not as simple as not caring what other people think, Benoit,' she said, fearing that the tears she felt pressing against the back of her eyes might escape.

She could feel the weight of his gaze on her face, on her skin, warming it, and then it cooled, as if he'd looked away.

'So is that what you'll do with the money?' Benoit asked, purposely changing the subject. They might need to get to know each other, but he didn't want to press any further than he had already. Because there was something about the way she had described being cut off from her family, the hurt there that called to his own, to the way he felt without Xander in his life.

'From the jewels?' she asked, as if needing clarification at the giant shift in conversation. 'No. I think I'm too old to go to university.'

'Oh, I didn't realise that they refused to allow people to attend university after the age of what, twenty-five?'

'Twenty-six.'

He rolled his eyes. 'So young.'

'And you're positively ancient,' she mocked. 'I wouldn't know what to study,' she said, not quite sure that was true.

He laughed. 'Really? I'd have thought it would be obvious.'

She frowned at him and Benoit wondered that she couldn't see it, how intelligent she was. Her mind was quick and she absorbed information like a sponge. And she was most definitely opinionated. That beat half of the people Chalendar employed and he employed some of the best.

'Sociology or politics. Definitely something to do with gender studies, though you really will have to stop using words like mansplaining and—'

He dodged the pillow she threw at him and laughed while rescuing the glass of wine before it could spill.

'No, university is for Summer. She has the brains; she's applying for her Masters as we speak.'

'And that stops you how?' Benoit asked, unsure as to why she would think any less of herself than her sisters.

'I just…it's not something I'm willing to get into debt over.'

'But we're talking about what happens if you find the jewels. Surely money won't be an issue then and you can spend it on whatever you like.'

'Yes. Of course,' she replied blankly and Benoit had the distinct impression that Skye wouldn't put herself first even if she had all the money in the world. It would go somewhere else, to someone else. And suddenly he was angry with the parents who had made her feel that she was not worthy of wanting such things for herself.

'It's late, so…' she said, unfurling herself from the sofa with an unconscious elegance that drew his gaze. Until she nearly tripped on the hem of his trousers again. She was going to hurt herself in those. He sighed. He'd liked those trousers.

'Come here,' he said, gesturing to her and hauling himself into a more seated position. He patted his pockets for the miniature Swiss army knife on his key chain. In the shadowed room, Skye looked at him with watchful eyes.

He glared up at her and she came close enough for him to snag her hip and pull her in between his legs. He didn't miss the way she flinched, nor the way she had bitten her lip between her teeth as if to stop herself from asking what he was doing. And he was thankful because for a second his mind went blank. He could feel the heat of her cresting over him like the gentlest of waves. His palms itched to feel the back of her thighs, her skin beneath his palm. His pulse jerked and he held his breath so that he couldn't be tantalised by the simple scent of her. No perfume or hair products, or gels or lotions. Just pure Skye.

He made the mistake of looking up. She was watching him, her neck bent so that her hair fell over her face like a waterfall. It reminded him of the plane, of her standing between his legs then, but this was different—*more*, somehow. Large brown eyes with golden flecks watching him, embers flaring, just waiting for a spark to ignite, to burn them both. He heard it, the hitch in her breathing, and warned himself to stop this, but seemed unable to.

He clenched his hand to prevent himself from pulling her towards him and felt the heavy ridged metal shape of the army knife in his palm. He broke the connection of their gaze and knew that he wouldn't look back at her again. Instead, he pulled out the scissor attachment, picked up one loose leg of the trousers at her mid-thigh and snipped.

'What are you—?'

Rip.

The tearing sound cut through the quiet of the room like a scream. He pulled the two edges of the material wide. She started and almost stepped back but, because he still held the material in his hands, couldn't.

'You were going to fall and break something, constantly tripping over the ends of these,' he said, turning his attention to snipping where the material had refused to tear on the inner seem. It had sounded like a growl. Like anger, as if it were her fault his trousers didn't fit her. He had to bend his head to see where to slip the scissors, only he felt a tremor in his hand. And that had nothing to do with anger, but it did have something to do with heat. It was spreading thick and fast over every inch of his skin. Invisible vibrations rattled him. He was always in control, but this? It was testing him.

Finally, he freed the first trouser leg and turned his attention to the other. She took another breath, as if she'd been about to say something, but he focused on the trousers. He felt her relax; the hands that she'd held up at her chest as if to protect herself dropped to her sides and he wished they hadn't. She needed to be on guard around him. She needed to protect herself.

He lined up the shortened leg with the hemline of the second and snipped. Skye's body swayed slightly as he tore the linen, the sound making him think of tearing other clothes from her body, and he made the mistake of looking down at her long shapely legs. The skin so smooth, and barely inches from his mouth, his tongue, his teeth.

'Go to bed,' he commanded without looking up.

She stayed for a moment, as if intending to defy him, but thankfully thought better of it. He sat there for a long time after she went to bed, wrestling with the bindings of the terms he had placed on their agreement.

Skye just didn't know what she was going to find when she came down to breakfast the next day—the charming, at ease playboy or the dark, brooding ruthless magnate. Both felt like an extreme of his personality and she couldn't help but feel that naturally he lay somewhere in the middle. But she was surprised to find him packing a bag when she rounded the corner.

'Going somewhere?' she asked.

'Oui,' he said, tight-lipped.

'Without me?' she asked, instantly wishing she could eat her words.

He paused ever so slightly before pressing a towel into his rucksack. That he'd planned to leave her alone made her feel…something she didn't want to examine too much. But, as much as she didn't like the idea, she wasn't going to force herself even more on a man who'd come here to be completely alone.

'Have fun. I'll…see you when I see you,' she said, cringing as she stuttered over the words that made it clear she didn't want to be left alone.

He sighed and she felt even worse.

'Get yourself a towel,' he threw over his shoulder. Only now she really didn't want to go, but couldn't say so because he'd have to insist that she came and it would be even worse.

Ten minutes later they had left the house and, rather than following the road, they'd cut down a worn path through the rainforest. Unlike before, their footsteps were meandering and the hacking of the machete was not as regular. Bathed in shadows and beams of light, she couldn't stop looking upwards at the way the impossibly tall trees stretched into a canopy high above them. Every single different shade of green she could imagine cocooned them, making her feel oddly safe in this huge expanse. A warmth that was faintly damp and the smell of the rich earth was so very different from the sprawling English forests she was used to. Skye felt alive and present in a way she had never done before.

Benoit looked back at her for a moment, and she

wondered what he could see. She knew that the information they'd shared last night had been necessary to fool his family that they were engaged.

Engaged.

The word hit a wall in her mind and fell to the ground with a *thunk*. It still didn't feel real. Neither had last night.

You shouldn't make a gift of yourself like that.

Was that what she'd been doing? Offering herself to Alistair as some kind of thank you for his relationship with her? So desperate for affection or attention because of her parents, so *thankful* that she'd…

Benoit had stopped and she had to pull herself up short to prevent herself from running into the back of him. When she looked up over his shoulder she couldn't help the gasp that fell from her lips. How she'd missed the sound of the stunning waterfall before her she had no idea, until she realised that the dense foliage must have protected them from the gentle roar of the cascade.

A jagged rocky outcrop reached high above them, covered in moss and spindly trees that clung to the stone. Water poured off the edge of the cliff and rushed headlong into a clear blue pool at the base of what must have been a twenty-foot drop. The pool was surrounded by flat rocks, joining the forest floor. It was like something out of a fairy tale.

'It's incredible.'

She felt the heat of his gaze against her cheek, but when she turned to look he was staring at the waterfall.

'I come out here as many times as I can when I'm

in Costa Rica. It's so far off the beaten track that only my neighbour and I can access it. But, as we've established, my neighbour is away,' he said, stalking off down the path before she could respond.

'I don't have a swimsuit,' she called after him, mildly frustrated.

'Neither do I,' he growled.

CHAPTER EIGHT

BENOIT HAD STOPPED on a grassy outcrop beside the pool and dropped his bag. He pulled off his shirt and toed off his shoes and socks, his fingers going to his waistband before his hands fisted at his sides.

She forced air into her lungs as she took in the powerful shoulders and sculpted chest that tapered into Benoit's lean hips. Good God, did people really look like that? Alistair had been a young tangle of limbs and the majority of the men working at the construction site had beer bellies that they joked were 'bought and paid for'. In the blink of an eye, Benoit dived into the pool, plunging beneath the surface, not emerging until he was far on the other side, as if he was desperate to put some distance between them.

He was pushing her away. The realisation hurt, tapped into deeper issues that she'd long covered over with roles and duties and responsibilities. But it also unlocked something within her, because if he *was* pushing her away then it meant she had come too close. It meant she wasn't the only one feeling...feeling...

She looked back to the other side of the pool,

shocked to find Benoît half walking and half climbing up a pathway that she couldn't quite make out. The way the muscles on his back moved, rippling over strong shoulder blades, the powerful width of his arms looking as if he might tear the jagged cliff face down rather than scale it was hypnotic.

By the time he reached the top, Skye had to shield her eyes from the sun and the blush of her cheeks from his gaze because, standing atop the jagged outcrop beside the edge of the waterfall, he looked...like a conqueror—proud, exhilarated. And for just a moment she saw it—*felt* it—the entire weight of his gaze, his focus, his attention bearing down on her like a physical thing. Her heart stopped, her breath caught in her lungs, and then he soared into the air, his perfect dive slicing into the crystal blue pool below. It was over in a matter of seconds, but her quick mind had captured every detail, every movement his body made, her ears barely hearing the break of the water beneath him.

She didn't release her breath until he emerged from the water, shaking dark golden tendrils of hair from his face, sending droplets scattering across the surface of the pool. His mouth was still a thin line, but his eyes...they were electric. Zipping and zapping sparks of adrenaline and excitement that were so tempting.

'Your turn,' he said. He didn't have to shout, to project his voice. She heard it as clearly as if he were standing next to her.

'I don't think so,' she replied, only the words felt like a lie on her tongue.

He stayed where he was in the pool, just staring at

her, holding his gaze on her as if he could tell, as if he knew that she wanted to take that leap as much as she needed her next breath.

'I have no intention of repeating myself,' he warned.

Skye looked up at the waterfall, the pathway that Benoit had made look easy, and she wanted it. Wanted to know what he'd felt, what he'd experienced that had made him look so *alive*. The yearning in her stomach reminded her of how she had felt last night, standing between his legs, so close to him. The thrill, the fear, the excitement rippling from her core outwards over her body.

An ache formed in her chest, one of pure want, like nothing she'd ever experienced before. As if she were building towards something that only leaping from the top of the waterfall could satisfy.

Without another word, she pulled her shirt over her head and Benoit turned away as if it had nothing to do with her modesty and more to do with a lack of interest. And it stung. It stung because she couldn't deny how much she wanted him any more. But the hurt didn't stop the aching need; it simply made it more obvious.

She kicked off her shoes and the shorts, ignoring the embarrassment she felt about being in her soon-to-be wet underwear. She dived into the water and reached the other side before she could change her mind. She dragged herself out onto the rocky outcrop, where Benoit was already standing. He barely looked at her and it only made her more determined.

'Follow where I put my feet and hands.'

She didn't bother replying. If he was going to be a monosyllabic brute then so be it.

She had expected the climb to be much harder, to hurt her feet, but the stone had been worn away by years and years of people doing exactly what they were about to do. As they got higher, the roar of the water was deafening and the spray flicked against her skin, making her feel hyperaware.

They reached the top and for a second the sudden absence of sound and spray was disorientating, but not as much as the view. The pool at the bottom looked a million miles away and she backed away from the edge, right into Benoit's chest.

The adrenaline in her body turned to fear, her legs trembled and her stomach twisted. She'd been wrong; she couldn't do this. She suddenly wanted to go home. Not back to his house or the estate in Norfolk, but to her little house in the New Forest. To life before Costa Rica, Benoit and the search for the jewels. She wanted to live in the bubble that she'd been happy with until she'd exposed her life to Benoit and found it wanting.

His hand was on her shoulder, steadying her but also keeping her literally at arm's length.

'I can't do this,' she said, the trembling in her legs getting worse.

'Why not?'

'It's not who I am. I don't do this kind of thing,' she said, leaning forward a little to peer down at the pool below and wondering how difficult it would be to climb back down. Gently, he pulled her back and turned her to face him. The way his eyes bored into hers, the icy blue depths glinting not with charm but determination struck her to her core.

'I don't want you to be something you're not. I want you to embrace who you are.'

Skye had to work so hard to keep the sob that rose in her chest from escaping. It felt as if in three days Benoit had unearthed the cornerstone of her entire being and it hurt. It hurt because she knew that he was right. That she needed to heal that part of herself that was always trying to be whatever other people needed her to be and not what she needed for herself.

'What do you see when you look at me?' she asked, unable to prevent the question falling from her lips and unwilling to meet his eyes.

'That's the point, Skye. It's not about what *I* see, but what *you* see.'

And with that he stepped past her and jumped, soaring into the sky and over the edge of the waterfall. Skye counted the rapid heartbeats fluttering in her chest until she heard the splash of water and knew that he was safe.

She expected her pulse to slow, but it didn't. Because it was her turn. She knew she could climb back down. After all, it was up to her and that was just as much a part of the point he was making. But she didn't want to. She remembered the thrill in his eyes just after he'd jumped the first time, the excitement stirring in her own body, the desire to feel that for herself. She approached the area where Benoit had jumped from. What was the worst that could happen? She could fall and break her heart. Arm, she corrected; she'd meant arm, obviously.

Before she could change her mind, she bent her legs and launched herself away from the grassy bank at the edge of the waterfall, shaping her body into a dive. It was as if everything she felt rushed through her in less than a second. Fear, happiness, excitement, pleasure. She was pretty sure she screamed, but by the time she rose from the depths of the water below she knew one thing about herself for certain.

She was someone who jumped off waterfalls and loved it.

Now she wanted to know what would happen if she took a different kind of leap.

Benoit let the spray from the shower clean away the sweat and traces of dirt from the return journey through the rainforest. It pummelled his skin but it wasn't enough. He switched the temperature to cold, then freezing. Anything to shock his system into clearing the kaleidoscope of erotic images of Skye from his mind. Skye in her wet underwear, climbing up the side of the waterfall like a sprite, emerging from the water and sweeping her hair from her face, her strong legs and arms holding her steady in the water.

Just like he'd dreamed the night before. At first his dreams had been intense and mouth-wateringly erotic; he could have slept for ever with dreams like that. But then, just before dawn, they'd changed. In his bedroom, in his *bed*, he'd found Skye in a red negligee with a faceless man and he'd woken with his heart pounding and a cold sweat over his entire body.

Was it a warning? Not about Skye—he didn't think for a second she would do such a thing. But for himself. He, of all people, knew that his judgement was unsound around women. Camilla, his mother—he should never forget that. So that morning he'd planned to go to the waterfall alone to get his head straight. But the way she'd looked at him at breakfast... And then, at the waterfall, the diamonds in her eyes after she'd jumped... It was as if he felt what she did—the adrenaline rush, that power. She'd jumped the very first time. Her strength was something he'd never questioned about her, but she seemed not to realise it about herself and that was a tragedy.

It had been getting dark by the time they'd returned to the house and now the patio was lit by the moon and stars overhead. He wrapped a towel around his waist and stalked back into the house, feeling angry. Angry at Skye, angry at himself. No, he corrected, not one for self-deceit, it wasn't anger—it was frustration. He wanted Skye with an intensity that he'd not experienced before, even with Camilla. And he had been stupid enough to make a deal that involved keeping her in his life for another three years. Once they were married he'd let her return to England. He simply couldn't be this close to temptation all the time. Because he was certain that he would destroy her. As he'd nearly destroyed his brother the night his mother had left.

He walked through the house and up the stairs, seeing no sign of Skye as he made his way to the bedroom.

But he couldn't shake the feeling that she hadn't gone to bed. In his room, he threw the towel into the basket in the corner and pulled on a pair of loose black cotton trousers, the material for the first time awkward against his skin. Something was tearing at his insides to get out, something he'd not wanted to face for years.

The door to his room opened, drawing his gaze from the window to where Skye stood outlined in a halo of light. He ground his teeth together. She was wearing his shirt. Nothing else. The image was seared into his brain in the time it took to realise that Skye was unaware of what the light behind her revealed. He could see the shape of her hips against the thin linen material, the dip of her waist, the slight shadow of the curve of her breast and the seemingly endless expanse of the smooth pale skin of her thighs.

He clenched his hand to stop himself from reaching for her.

'You haven't spoken a word to me since we left the waterfall.'

'And you think coming here, now, you'll find what you're looking for?'

'Yes.'

He turned his back on her, on the temptation that she presented, and looked out across the dark shadow of forest beyond the windows. He shouldn't have pushed her at the waterfall. He just… He'd just wanted her to know. How amazing she could be if she stopped letting other people dictate who she was.

He heard her take another step into the room and closed his eyes. This could ruin everything. They had a perfect deal. Each would get what they wanted and walk away.

'Why do you cut yourself off from everything here?' she asked, her English accent so clear and unwavering.

It wasn't the question he'd been expecting so it took him a moment to shift mental gears. A moment in which she took another step forward. He felt it.

'Because it's completely cut off from the rest of my life.'

She nodded as if she not only understood but had expected the answer. 'It's contained.'

He frowned, but yes—it was contained.

'As if,' she said, coming another step towards him, 'what happens here doesn't affect what happens there.'

He stilled, realising where she was going with this but not sure he wanted to follow.

'Does it work the other way round?' she asked, and her simple question raised the hairs on his forearms. She was asking too much.

'No one else has ever been here to find out,' he said. He was losing the fight because he wanted something in his mouth other than the taste of guilt and regret. He wanted her.

Skye stood by his side and as she looked out through the window she let him study her, take her in; she felt his gaze against her skin, where his eyes roamed across her face and back.

'We have a deal,' he snarled, not scaring her in the least. She knew he was struggling with this. Knew that he wanted her as much as she wanted him. 'You've agreed to be my wife—for three years. If this gets—'

'You think because I'm inexperienced I won't be able to separate this night from our deal? Or do you think because I'm a woman I won't be able to separate my emotions from—?'

'It's not you,' he growled. 'It's me. It's me because I know, deep down, I am my parents' child—selfish and always one step away from doing whatever the hell I want. And, believe me, I want you. But it can't happen.'

He finally turned to face her and the look in his eyes stole her breath. She could see he was fighting it and it made her angry.

'Really? You spent all day pushing me, probing my emotions and hurts, demanding that I accept myself just as I am. You tell me to go for what I want and then tell me I can't have it?'

His eyes flared in the dark room, the moon shooting stars across his icy blue irises.

'One night? You just want one night?'

'Yes,' she breathed, not caring about the longing in her voice.

'It will never be enough, Skye.'

'Your arrogance is astounding,' she breathed, outraged.

'I didn't mean for you.' His voice was dark, angry with warning. It matched the fire he'd started within her and there was only one way forward now—to let it burn.

'It will have to be,' she said on a shaky breath. Because she wasn't ready for more. She wasn't sure she'd ever be ready for more.

She looked up at him to see if he'd heard, or even understood. He watched her for so long she was ready to turn and leave, when finally he nodded. Once.

And that was all the warning she had before his lips crashed down on hers, his hands coming to frame her face, pressing against her hair and anchoring her to him, angling her to him in a way that she couldn't resist. She opened up for him, his tongue plunging deep within her, filling her in a way that she felt she'd missed her entire life.

Her hands flew to his shoulders, holding on as he feasted upon her, but also taking something for herself. His smooth, hot skin was perfect beneath her palms, her fingers flying over his collarbone to the stretch of his powerful traps, around his shoulders and down his sides. She felt like a sculptress, learning the figure she wanted to create by touch.

Each inch of skin she discovered was incredible but not enough. *More, more, more.* It was like a mantra turning over again and again in her mind. She wanted absolutely everything he could give her. He walked her back a step and she felt the coolness of the glass at her back through the thin linen shirt covering her fevered skin. He left her lips swollen and ravished as he bent his mouth to her neck, pressing open-mouthed kisses beneath her jawline down to her shoulder, where he gently bit down on her flesh. Her core clenched in reaction, desire and heat pooling low and throbbing.

Unable to help herself, she arched her chest to his, needing to feel him against her body. Benoit threaded an arm behind her in the space she had created, hauling her against him, and she lifted her leg, shamelessly hooking it around his hip and pressing into his erection.

The feel of it, of him, between her legs was indescribable. Her head fell back in pleasure as he continued to kiss, suck, lick, bite his way across her shoulder. His free arm came up in between them, his hand angling her head back so that he could lavish attention on her body. His fingers traced downwards, finding the central notch with his index finger, then her sternum, following the motion with his tongue until he veered off as his fingers found one nipple and his mouth the other.

She cried out. She couldn't help it. Never had she felt so utterly devoured and sure. Sure that there was even more pleasure to be had. An impatience was building within her, a need that she couldn't control. She curved into the hardness of his arousal and he growled against her breast, clenching the hand now fisting her bottom.

Nothing. She'd felt *nothing* like this before. Thoughts flitted through her mind at lightning speed. Benoit's dark glare…showering outside in the garden…swimming in the pool beneath the waterfall… Benoit hauling himself out onto the rocky outcrop…

You don't behave as if someone has given you pleasure.

Standing between his legs as he tore the linen trousers…

I want you to embrace who you are.

Jumping off the cliff…

Each thought merged with the way he touched her, the way he pulled desire and cries of pleasure from her soul. He pursed his lips around her nipple and she bucked away from the pleasure, pressing back against the glass. At the release of her breast she looked up and met eyes that were glistening like freshly formed frost beneath the moon. Intent, dark and devastating, he didn't take his eyes from her once as he tore at the button of the shorts and thrust them down her thighs. He was daring her, challenging her to stop him.

In that moment she knew she never would.

Still without taking his eyes from hers, he hooked his thumb beneath the waistband of her briefs, giving her a chance to stop him every step of the way. The power that hummed beneath her skin, the complete assurance that she was in control, that she could stop this at any point, the knowledge that he would stop, was intoxicating.

He seemed angry that she didn't. A look of resignation crossed his features for a second before desire blotted out everything and, finally, he broke their gaze as he turned his attention to where his thumb was pulling down the thin material of her briefs.

Benoit cursed. He cursed himself, cursed her, and cursed the fact that she looked, smelt, felt, tasted like everything he'd ever wanted. Slowly, inch by inch, he removed her panties, teasing her, teasing himself, he just didn't know any more.

You don't behave as if someone has given you pleasure.

He wished he'd never said it to her, because now it was all he could think of—giving her so much pleasure it overflowed. The delicate cross-hatching of curls at the apex of her legs was perfect to him and he anchored his hands at her hips, coming down onto his knees. She wriggled in his grasp and he couldn't help the spike of pleasure that flared, knowing that she was just as affected by this as he was—affected, tested, delighted. There were such fine lines between the range of feelings surging through him.

He brought his hands down around the curve of her bottom, cupping and tilting her pelvis, causing her legs to splay slightly—enough. Enough for him to bend his head, to press his mouth to her core. He ran his tongue the entire length of her, loving the way she parted for him, thrilled by the taste of her, delighted by the sobs of sheer pleasure that fell from her mouth into the air about them.

He found the soft nub of her clitoris and she trembled in his hands, her pleasure heightening his to an ache, throbbing and hardening and roaring for release. The shakes cascading through her body edged her closer and then further from his mouth. And it wasn't enough. He wanted her completely at his mercy, just as he felt at hers.

He released one hand from the back of her thigh, bringing it round to lift just behind her knee and place it over his shoulder, giving him greater access. His tongue fastened against her clitoris, he pressed a finger to her core and heard the sound of her back hitting the glass; faster and faster he heard her inhale, filling her lungs with air as he continued to fill her with his hands and mouth.

Until that moment—the moment where everything stopped…breath, thought, heartbeat…and he felt her come apart against his fingers and tongue. He consumed it all, everything she had to give and more. He held her through it all.

When the trembling in her body finally stopped, he picked her up and took her to the bed, laying her gently down on the mattress, her skin flushed and eyes closed.

'You were right,' she whispered. He wouldn't do her the disservice of asking what she meant. He knew. No one had given her pleasure before.

He stayed at the end of the bed, looking down on her. No matter how much he wanted to move, to lean over her, to touch her everywhere, to taste, to fill her completely, he wouldn't move until he was completely sure.

'We can stop now,' he said, even though he knew what her answer would be.

'More.'

'What?' He wasn't sure he'd heard the word that had escaped her mouth; her eyes were still closed in bliss.

She slowly opened them, leant back on her elbows, levelled him with a stare and said, 'More.' Her voice was strong and clear, her cheeks were flushed; he could tell that it took a lot for her to say it, but he knew she meant it.

Skye watched him climb onto the bed, over her, surrounding her completely, with an anticipation that rivalled any she'd ever experienced. Her heart was still beating a wild tattoo from an orgasm that had felt as if it had been trapped within her for years. Benoit came so far up the bed she had to crane her neck to look back at him, arching her back, feeling utterly surrounded by him. He smiled down at her, but it was one of pure wickedness and she loved it.

He leaned back on his haunches, bringing his lips to hers and kissed her like she'd never been kissed before. It wasn't forceful, desperate or even lazy; it was… consuming. Her hands went to his head, to hold him there, but he reached for them and pushed them above her head, holding them there with his free hand while the other trailed an open palm down her neck, sternum and over her breast.

'If you keep touching me, Skye, I won't last,' he said but, rather than sounding weak, it only made her feel strong. She moaned into his mouth and he took it. He took everything.

His hand dipped lower, around her hip and to her inner thigh, gently moving it so that he could come between them. He broke the kiss and locked his eyes with hers. There was no challenge this time, no warning, no anger. This time she felt…assurance. Once again he was giving her power, only this time it felt as if he were trusting her with it.

He entered her slowly and she gasped for air as the length and width of him gently pushed at her muscles, filling her bit by bit but so completely. He never broke eye contact the entire time. Her eyes drifted closed as she got used to the incredible feeling of him within her. And when he pushed further, closer to that indefinable place that she both craved and wanted to delay, her eyes burst open to see him watching her in wonder.

He hadn't been talking about an orgasm, she realised—what Benoit had said about pleasure. It wasn't about an end goal, some point to achieve, but the feeling of luxuriating in ongoing pleasure—*that* was what he'd been talking about and *that* was what he was doing now. Unfurling a seemingly endless wave of pleasure and delight, filling her, overwhelming her, building within her until it poured over and out of her.

For what felt like hours Benoit moved within her, slowly, deeply, incredibly. Sweat slicked their bodies, the air was heated with cries and moans of delight, building a fire within them both. Her hand slid down the side of his body, around the curve of his ass, his hip, and a thread of excitement lit within her as she found where they were joined together.

Her only warning was his growl and then all she could do was hold on in utter glory as he thrust into her again and again, deeper, faster, harder, and her mind could barely register the pleasure that was raining down over her. Her panting met his growls, her fingers flew to his shoulders and her nails dug into his skin; his grip on her hips became an anchor until her breathing began to stutter as she got closer and closer...

'Skye—'

'Oh, God.' She couldn't help the words falling from her mouth. Encouragements, pleas, demands, threats... all were uttered as he drove them off a cliff face into bliss.

CHAPTER NINE

THUD, THUD, THUD, THUD...

At first Skye thought the sound was coming from her body, her heartbeat still erratic from her night with Benoit. But when she lifted herself onto her hands, his plush mattress cushioning her wrists, she realised it was something else. She was about to ask Benoit what was going on when she saw the door to his bedroom swing closed.

The rhythmic sound continued for a little longer before slowing to a stop. The sun had risen and soft beams of light were filtered through the thick foliage outside the windows.

She sat and turned, bringing the high thread count sheets to her chest, the motion making her aware of a pleasurable ache between her legs and she felt...amazing. A flush rose to her cheeks at the memory of what they had shared the night before—the way Benoit had held her as she had come apart in his arms more than once. Even thinking of it brought echoes of the pleasure she had experienced and she fisted her hands against the memories.

One night... It will never be enough.

She had been so sure of herself when she'd only had Alistair as a reference. But now she knew. She knew better. He'd been right. One night was not enough.

Benoit pushed into the room, the door bouncing back against the wall, and she sat further up in the bed.

'What's going on?' she asked, shocked at the sudden transformation.

'The helicopter. It's here. Apparently someone found the car, contacted the police, who alerted my great-aunt. I have to—' He stopped himself. Took a breath. '*We* are going back to France. Now.'

The helicopter ride was incredible. Much like the jump from the waterfall, it was over in what seemed like even half a second and she couldn't shake the feeling that she was hurtling towards an ending she wasn't prepared for. Even though, surely, if she was marrying Benoit then she had another three years? But the speed with which she found herself being led up the ramp of a private plane at Limón Airport made her feel slightly nauseous.

She frowned as she saw Benoit handing over a key. It was the key for the locker where she had left her bags and, more importantly, her phone charger. Her sisters. The map. She was horrified that she'd almost forgotten them.

A flight attendant, picture perfect with bright red lipstick and an immaculately clean pressed uniform, asked if she would like a drink. Skye shook her head, feeling completely out of her depth. She must have

looked a fright in torn linen shorts and a clearly Ben-
oit-sized white shirt. She was led to a seat she was
afraid to use in case her clothes were too dirty or that
she would damage it. She had known that Benoit was
rich, but this? She shook her head.

'Ça va?' he asked.

She leaned her head to one side, not quite sure how
to answer the question.

'My clothes; they're…'

'You're worried about your clothes?' he asked as if
he too was finally considering all the things that they
did have to worry about.

A gentle laugh fell from her lips. 'I'm not sure that
even my luggage contains clothing suitable for…' *what
is about to happen*, she finished silently. She wasn't
sure *she* was suitable for what was about to happen.

'I'll arrange for you to have suitable clothes upon
arrival in France.'

'You know my size?' Skye instantly regretted the
way her voice squeaked at an unreasonably high pitch
on the last word.

He simply looked at her. The old arrogant, monosyllabic Benoit was back, but this time she saw memories
of last night dance across the icy blue depths.

Benoit went to check in with the pilot and complete
the necessary paperwork, and all Skye was left with
was a sense of foreboding. As if soon being able to
turn on her phone had conjured the fear that something
awful had happened, that her sisters had been trying
desperately to contact her, that everything had gone
wrong in her absence. So by the time Benoit's assis-

tant rolled her luggage along the jet's small gangway she was ready to burst.

'*Mademoiselle?*' he offered.

'*Merci, merci.*' She batted the small man aside and dragged the case onto the table in front of her, unzipped the hardened top and thrust in a hand to retrieve her charger. She plugged it into the socket she had already identified and scrabbled for her phone in her handbag. She probably looked like a madwoman but Skye didn't care. She had to wait another infuriating two minutes while her completely dead phone registered enough charge to turn on, but finally the flashing green battery image appeared and it sprang to life in her hands. She quickly turned down the volume, expecting a barrage of twenty or more beeps from a series of increasingly worried messages from her sisters… But there was nothing.

She checked the socket, and the input port for the cable. Frowning, she turned her attention back to the screen as it vibrated just once.

Hey sis, hope you're having FUN! :) Have sent you an email with latest journal info and relevant sections. Catherine travelled to Arabia! After scandalous rel with Benoit forced her out of England. Long story! All in email. Love S&S

And that was it.

Skye had disappeared from the face of the planet for more than three days. And nothing. Her sisters hadn't worried—hadn't contacted the British Embassy, the coastguard or anyone else. They'd hoped she was *having fun.*

She fell back against the seat and stared out of the window. It hurt, she realised. Hurt that they hadn't worried about her in the same way that she worried about them. Guilt sliced through her. Of course she hadn't wanted anything bad to have happened to them, but…but it was clear that they didn't need her. All this time, for as long as she could remember, that was what had driven her—the conviction that without her they wouldn't be okay. She had made almost her entire life about them and she couldn't blame them for not having the same focus on her, because that was what she'd intended when she'd decided to step up to the role that her mother had stood back from. She'd *wanted* them to have their lives and live them. But…

'Are you not going to call them?' Benoit asked from where he stood at the top of the walkway in front of the cockpit.

Skye forced a smile to her lips. 'We're so close to finding the map, I thought I'd wait until I know where I…where *we* stand.'

Instead, fighting back the sting of tears, she fired off a text.

Lots of fun. Will tell you all about it soon. Just off to France (!) to see if the map is still with the Chalendars. Will take a look at email asap. Love S

Given just how desperately she had tried to escape in Costa Rica, Benoit was a little surprised that Skye had barely touched her phone. He couldn't take his eyes off her as she put her phone down and looked out of the window. His fiancée...

A fiancée he'd spent the entire night before thoroughly ravishing. In an instant he was hard and was forced to pull his laptop closer so as not to embarrass the flight attendant. He took a deep breath to calm himself, deeply resentful of the way even just the thought of her raised his pulse and blood pressure. He was thankful that she'd had the presence of mind to insist on only one night. Because even just one more night and Benoit was almost one hundred per cent sure that he'd never be able to let her go, let alone out of his bed. Never had he experienced anything like it. In the past, his tastes had been wide, varied and thoroughly investigated. But Skye...seeing her fall apart, feeling it in his hands, against his mouth...

He cursed out loud, drawing a frown from Skye before she resumed her watchful gaze at the window. He needed the flight back to the Dordogne to get himself under control. Because if he didn't he could lose everything.

Just over eleven hours later the jet taxied on the small private landing strip near the chateau in the Dordogne. He'd spent the entire flight furiously countering demands, threats and coercive emails from the family board members about the upcoming meeting in two days, tight-lipped and grim-faced while Skye slept and drifted to her phone during her waking moments, reading, frowning, smiling…her face so expressive as she reacted to whatever she was reading.

As the jet finally came to a stop, he stood and walked over to where Skye was, once again, asleep. Just before rousing her, he saw the petite frame of his great-aunt through the small circular window, swathed in layers of silk tugged about her on the wind, holding an impossibly tiny creature in her arms. He bit back a curse. The chihuahua had hated him on first sight and ever since had made numerous attempts to destroy any kind of footwear he possessed.

'Benoit?'

He looked down at Skye, who was slowly blinking her eyes open in a way that he'd missed that morning in Costa Rica before the helicopter arrived. He felt an urge to smile, to soften the edge of concern he saw in her gaze—which was precisely why he didn't. 'We're here.'

'The map,' she exclaimed eagerly.

He was thankful that at least one of them had some last thread of common sense.

'We have a welcoming party.' He gestured to where Skye would be able to see Anaïs through the window, hoping that she was ready. Because he sure as hell wasn't.

The wind that whipped about her took Skye by surprise. But not as much as the look on the older woman's face the moment she locked gazes with Skye. A sharp, high pitched *yap* drew Skye's attention to Anaïs' folded arms where something struggled within the swathes of pink and cream silk covering the woman's diminutive frame. With a sigh, Anaïs bent to the floor and released a tiny dog, straining at its lead as if the small animal was determined to break free and ravage… Benoit? Yes. Most definitely the chihuahua's focus was fixed on the man behind her on the steps leading down from the small jet.

Clearly, he and the little dog had history. But when Skye's gaze met with Anaïs, once again she felt an unusual sense that the woman was pleased to see her. There was an unaccountable look of recognition in her eyes but Skye wasn't quite sure how that could possibly be.

'Benoit Chalendar, the first thing you are going to do is get rid of that beard,' Anaïs said in English as he hugged her, her hand reaching for the jawline Skye now knew intimately.

'It is lovely to see you too, Anaïs,' he said, leaning into her hand and pressing a kiss into the palm. 'I am well, thank you for asking,' he said, somehow managing to dodge the chihuahua without inflicting damage on the small dog trying to devour his leather shoes. When Anaïs bent to pick up the yapping dog, Skye was sure she heard Benoit chide her for encouraging 'the little beast'.

'And your hair needs a trim. You look like a hippy,' Anaïs stated firmly whilst managing to convey a heart full of love within the words.

Benoit cast a look to Skye before replying. 'I promise to address the situation, once we've had refreshments and time to catch up.'

Anaïs followed Benoit's look and nodded. 'In the library, I think.'

'We don't usually meet in the library.' Benoit frowned.

'This time we will,' she said assuredly, leaning past Benoit and holding out an exquisitely jewelled hand. 'Anaïs Chalendar. It is nice to finally meet you.'

As Anaïs led them back through the jaw-dropping grounds of a chateau that looked as if it had come straight out of the fairy tales she used to read to Summer and Star when they were young, Skye turned over Anaïs' words in her mind, trying to make them fit. *Finally?* Did Anaïs already know that she was to marry her great-nephew?

Finding no sensible answer, Skye turned her attention to the surroundings. The chateau was beautiful and in a way, cast in the soft setting sun, it seemed everything that the dark, downtrodden Soames estate in Norfolk was not. Gorgeous light blond-coloured stones made up the brickwork of the large two-storey chateau. Little balconies wrapped around tall double-fronted windows, some of which were open, and glimpses of expensive curtains billowing in the breeze made the building feel lived-in and welcoming.

But Anaïs, despite her small stature and what must have been considerable age, was leading them along at a brisk clip. It might have been less ostentatious than the Soames estate, but this building felt more welcoming and loved. As Anaïs led them into the cooler, darker interior, Skye barely had time to take note of the hallways and corridors she found herself in.

'You grew up here?' she asked Benoit in awe.

He nodded. 'My father and mother had the east wing, and after he died...well, Anaïs moved us to the west wing, nearer to her living quarters.'

It was imposing and impossibly grand, but every now and then she thought she could see traces of similarities to the Soames estate. Neither, of course, was anything like the little house that she, her sisters and her mother had shared when they were younger.

Anaïs held the door to the library open and the moment that Skye stepped into the room the air whooshed from her lungs on a sudden, *'Oh!'*

Skye turned to see a large smile across Anaïs' lovely features.

'I thought as much,' the older woman said with a satisfied nod.

'Thought what? Anaïs, what is going on?' Benoit asked from behind Skye, clearly out of the loop of the unspoken back and forth between her and Skye.

It was an exact replica of the library at the Soames estate. There were slight differences in the décor, but essentially it was the same layout. Skye's eyes flew to the window on the left-hand side and she didn't need to go into the hallway to know that the room was the same mis-sized shape as Catherine's library.

'Ms Soames, I have been waiting quite some time to meet you,' Anaïs said, holding out her hand. Skye took the warm delicate hand in her own, channelling as much of her emotions as she could into the simple gesture. 'I believe you know where to find it?' the older woman said with a smile.

'May I?' she asked, permission the only thing holding her back.

'Of course.'

'What is going on?' Skye heard Benoit demand as she went to the shelves to find the hidden release she knew would be there. As Skye retrieved the package contained in the recess, Anaïs began her story.

'Years ago, my grandfather, Benoit, entrusted me with a secret, a responsibility that I have had for nearly my entire life. He told me about Catherine and their relationship in England,' she said, smiling towards Skye, 'always ensuring that I knew he loved his wife and children. But Catherine had been his first love. She had written to him just before her marriage to her cousin and explained that she needed him to keep the map a secret. That one day someone from her lineage would come looking for it and that he was the only person she trusted to keep the map of the secret passageways and rooms of her English estate safe. She swore to burn her copy and leave the rest to fate.'

'But how did you know that was Skye?' Benoit asked.

'My dear boy, do you really think I would just sit around and wait for some stranger to turn up? You're not the only one able to hire a private investigator, you know.'

Thankfully, his great-aunt turned back to Skye before she could see or hear him choking on his tea.

'You're the oldest, are you not?'

'Yes, Madame Chalendar.'

'Mademoiselle,' Anaïs corrected. 'I traced your

mother to the south of England and when I discovered that she had three daughters I hoped that you might be the ones to finally follow the path that Catherine laid out all those years ago.'

Benoit frowned, the suspicion growing that *this* was the family duty that Anaïs had often referred to throughout his childhood—not the family business— shaking him to his core.

'Had not Ms Soames arrived within my lifetime, then I would have passed the responsibility to you,' she said to him.

Benoit was distracted from further thought as Skye took a seat beside his great-aunt with the cloth bundle in her lap. Fingers trembling, she reached for the strings that bound the package and began to release the contents.

There was a thickly bound old-fashioned map which could only have been the plans for her grandfather's estate, something that looked like a letter bearing the name Soames in strong handwriting and a ring. He watched as she held it up to the light, three citrine stones sparkling and set within a gold band.

'Is that one of the Soames jewels?' Benoit asked.

'*Non, chéri.* My grandfather gave Catherine this ring, but she returned it with the map and letter,' Anaïs explained. It was beautiful and he was surprised to see Skye so easily discard it. Instead, she turned her attention to the map and began to unfold it. It looked ancient, the paper having aged into a beautiful golden colour over the hundred plus years it had remained hidden. The map was a study in fine detail, clearly outlining the design of a sprawling estate with secondary passages and chambers within the walls.

'There are so many of them. Surely they can't all be intact?'

'It would take a long time to search them all,' Benoit realised.

'Time we don't have. The will stipulates only two months before the entire estate is given over to the National Trust.'

Benoit watched as Skye snapped a few pictures of the map with her phone, then she was lost in attaching them to a message to her sisters.

Both Benoit and Anaïs were quiet as she did so, but he couldn't shake the watchful eyes of his great-aunt. There was something she wasn't telling him. But whether that was connected with Skye or not he couldn't quite tell.

'My sister emailed me transcriptions of Catherine's journals. I wondered if you might like to read them,' Skye asked Anaïs.

The older woman's face melted into a smile. 'I'd like that very much. I only had Benoit's part of the story all these years and have often wondered about Catherine.'

'I think she loved him greatly, even though she knew it would never be possible for them to be together.'

Anaïs patted Skye's hand. 'Now, my dear, I'm sorry to ask, but there are a few things I need to discuss with my great-nephew. Perhaps you would like to freshen up? I'll have someone show you to a room.'

Benoit registered Skye's response and intention to

update her sisters despite the discomfort that had entered his chest.

'"We have a duty to the past. A responsibility to bear for future generations to come." I always thought you meant Chalendar Enterprises, but *this* is what you really meant, isn't it?' he said when Skye had left.

'Yes, I'm sorry that you misunderstood,' Anaïs replied, the pity in her eyes too much.

'You've kept secrets,' he accused.

'As have you. What's going on with the girl?'

'She's not a girl, Anaïs. She's my fiancée.'

Benoit tried to hold her gaze as it felt as if Anaïs peered into his soul. He fought the anger in him that cried that she had forced this on him. That the board would have given up the by-law without her interference.

'Are you sure? She seems like a lovely young woman.'

'She is and I am.' He couldn't quite understand why Anaïs seemed a little sad. Surely this was what she wanted? Disappointment hung heavily in the air between them.

'This is what you wanted, isn't it?' he demanded.

'Not like this,' she said, cupping his jaw with her delicate hand.

'I'm not like him,' he said to himself as much as her.

'In so many wonderful ways you are not like him, *mon coeur.*'

'Then why?' he asked, his voice barely above a whisper, not quite sure he was ready to hear the answer.

'Because I do not have many years left and when I'm gone I don't want the company to be all you have left. And that *would be* like your father. He cut himself off emotionally from everyone and I don't like to see you do the same.'

Something cracked in Benoit's chest—a tendril of grief and loneliness bleeding out at the thought of it.

'But actually,' Anaïs pressed on in a voice stronger and more determined than a woman half her age, 'I wanted to talk to you about another matter. Xander is coming to the family gathering tomorrow and you should know that he has filed for divorce from Camilla.'

Benoit spent an hour walking around the grounds of the chateau with a bottle of whisky as his only companion. He'd failed to notice how the sky had darkened into night, how the seconds had slipped into minutes, which had crept towards an hour. He knew that he should get back to Skye, but couldn't quite bring himself to do so yet.

Too much was swirling around in his mind. That he'd taken on the mantle of the company because he'd misunderstood Anaïs' cryptic words about duty to the past. That she had forced the vote on the board because she wanted more than the company for him? And more, the argument he'd had with her about Xander still rang in his ears. The first thought he'd had—and had the misfortune to voice—was to wonder whether Xander's divorce would rule him out of the running for CEO.

Enough, Anaïs had commanded. *When did you start to lose your human decency?*

Camilla is a viper, he'd replied.

*Yes, one who chose to bite Xander instead of you—
and have you given no thought to the effects of the
poison?*

No, he hadn't. For two years Benoit had refused to
allow his thoughts to settle anywhere near his brother
and his ex-girlfriend. He was well practised in shifting his mind away from the painful betrayal and now,
when he might have wanted to look slightly closer at
it, his mind would still not allow it.

Unthinking, his feet had turned in the direction of
the chateau, had led him down hallways and up stair-
cases that led to the room he knew his great-aunt had
put Skye in. The entire time, the small object in his
pocket had found its way into his palm, then onto the
tip of his finger. He pulled his hand from his pocket
now to knock on the door, inexplicably desperate to see
her, unbelievably hopeful that somehow she'd soothe
the raging beast within him.

When he heard no answer Benoit turned the handle and opened the door, but his mind couldn't quite
work out what he was seeing. Skye's travel case was
on the bed but, rather than her taking clothes out of it,
she seemed to be in the middle of putting them back
in. The rage he'd only just managed to suppress built
within him.

'What are you doing?'

Skye looked up, shocked to see him standing in the
doorway, filling it completely. She wanted to curse, to
scream and cry out. She hadn't wanted him to catch
her running away. She hadn't even wanted to run away.

Not really. She had given him her word and that meant something to her. But her sisters came first. They always did and they always would.

The moment she'd got to the room, excitement coursing through her veins at finally having found the map, she couldn't wait to speak to her sisters. It was as if she'd jumped from the top of the waterfall all over again. She'd called them instantly and Summer had been just as excited, squealing in delight.

But when Skye had asked about Star, Summer had gone very quiet…

'It's not what you think. I came back to my room and called my sisters and… I can't stay,' she said. 'I *have* to go. Star has run off to some desert kingdom in the Middle East, chasing down the key to the room where the jewels are hidden, and she's just not equipped to handle that. She's too innocent, naïve. I can't let her…' There were no words left. She couldn't put them up fast enough as a barrier between herself and the man staring at her with an intensity and emotion she didn't want to name. 'It's only for a few days.'

'Really? A few days? Come on, Skye,' he said as if he really wondered whether she was lying to herself as much as him. Perhaps she was. 'Once you're there you'll find a way to convince yourself that your sisters need your help, that they're unable to do what needs to be done. Because for some reason you don't think that they're capable of coping without you. You're going to rush back to England so that you can…what? Fly off to the Middle East instead of Star? Arrange for the sale of the house instead of Summer?'

Every single one of his words hurt, sliced into the thin excuses she had drawn about herself like a cloak.

'No! I just need to find out what's going on. And then I'll come back,' she said, her voice weak to her own ears.

'We both know that's a lie.'

He let the accusation stand between them and finally she tossed the shirt she had gripped and scrunched in her hands into the travel case.

'Were you even going to say goodbye?' he demanded.

'Of course I was,' Skye replied, barely managing to choke past the lie that fell so easily from her lips.

'There's no *of course* about it. My mother didn't.'

CHAPTER TEN

THERE WAS AN awful matter-of-factness about his tone that pulled Skye up short.

'Benoit—'

'I saw her that night,' he said, staring at some distant point in time just over her shoulder. 'I was eight when she left. I'd gone to her room because there had been a horrible storm and I'd woken up from a nightmare. I just didn't realise that I'd gone from one to another.'

Skye's heart lurched in her chest. She knew that there was only one way this story ended but she wasn't sure that she was ready to hear it. But Benoit pressed on.

'Usually her door was locked, which was why I was so surprised, why I entered the room.' Benoit shook his head against the memory, as if wondering at his own actions that night.

'Just like I came into this room just now,' he scoffed angrily. 'She looked almost exactly as you did. A half-packed suitcase on the bed, something in her hands and a guilty-as-sin look on her face.' He couldn't stem the tide of acidic bitterness.

'I knew, even as I asked my mother the question, I knew. That she was leaving my father, leaving us. I begged her, *begged* to take me with her. Pleaded and cried like the little child I was. And do you know what the worst thing was? In that moment I would have left Xander behind. I would have abandoned *my brother*,' Benoit spat, hating the memories of that night, how cowardly he had been, how desperately he had begged his mother to take him with her, to love him enough to want to.

'I told her that I hated my father, and that I just wanted to be with her. That I didn't care about Xander. But she kept shaking her head. Kept saying that it was something *she* had to do. That she couldn't take me with her. And then she made me promise not to tell anyone that I'd seen her. Not to say a word to anyone—my father, Xander or Anaïs. Not to cry in case it alerted one of the staff. I was to show no sign that I'd seen her that evening at all.'

Skye's heart was breaking for the little boy who'd not only watched his mother leave, but asked, begged her to take him with her and been refused. She felt fury on his behalf, even knowing that she had nearly done the same thing to him.

'She had no right to ask you to make that promise,' she said to Benoit.

'But I did. And it was the last time I saw her. I went back to my room and waited for the sun to come up, I waited for someone else to make the same discovery I had, but if I'd known that it would have been Xander I...

'I heard him calling for her when he couldn't find

her.' He'd watched as Xander tore through the whole house looking for someone who wasn't there any more. He'd watched as Xander's heart had broken. Their father hadn't even looked up from his morning newspaper and coffee, but Xander? He'd cried for two whole weeks.

'I'm so sorry, Benoit.'

'I'm not. It taught me a very valuable lesson. That when it comes down to it, Skye, we *all* become selfish. We all take what it is that we need. So believe me when I say I'm not surprised by your actions. You have the map and you might even be able to find the jewels and do whatever the hell you want with them. But for me? The company is all I have left. And I'm going to make damn sure that I get it.

'Perhaps you think, because of the intimacies we've shared, that I'm someone whose finer feelings can be played upon. Well, don't. Let me be clear—all intimacies are over but the agreement is not. So you'd better still be here tomorrow, because we *will* be announcing our engagement at the party.'

Benoit speared her with a stare, as if to make sure that Skye understood his warning, before throwing something onto the bed beside her case and stalking from the room.

Skye felt as if the earth was shifting beneath her feet. She hurt for the little boy whose mother had abandoned him, who made him make a promise not to cry. A boy who grew into a man who was betrayed again by his girlfriend with his brother. And then by her.

She had done exactly as all those people who had

hurt him had—taken what they wanted and left. Or planned to.

As much as she wanted to deny it, she *had* been about to run away.

Because, if she was honest, she'd never thought she'd actually find the map. Yes, she'd desperately hoped and prayed for her mother's sake. But the reality of it? Actually finding it? It had been inconceivable. Because that would mean not only that they might be able to find those jewels, but that she would actually have to marry Benoit.

And in some ways *not* finding the map had made that easier. It had been her get-out clause. It meant that she'd never have to face the fact that she'd marry a man who would never love her. So no, Benoit was wrong. She wasn't running away because of her sisters. She was running from her feelings for him. Because they terrified her. More than anything.

She crossed the room to her bed and picked up the object he had thrown there earlier. It was the ring they had found with the map. The citrine crystal that Benoit had given to Catherine before he'd left England all those years ago glinted in the low lighting of the room.

It had been meant to be her engagement ring Skye now realised as she sank onto the bed, the strange synchronicity touching her heart and breaking it at the same time. Tears gathered at the corners of her eyes and as she leaned back against the headboard she felt paper crumple in her back pocket.

The letter from Benoit's great-great-grandfather. As

carefully as she could, she retrieved the aged envelope and with shaking hands began to read.

Dear Ms Soames
Please forgive the assumption of the address. I can only assume that Catherine is right in her faith and belief—as she has been in so many things—that it will be a female member of her family who will eventually unearth what she has hoped to have hidden. It is a hope we both share.

How does one explain such a thing to someone who is not yet born, and may not be for some years? It is almost unimaginable. But safe to say that this hope is one born of love. For Catherine, love of her future family, and for me... Love of her.

I have been truly blessed with my wife and family and would not change a single step on the path that led me to them. But Catherine— her strength, her determination, and the joy that shines through those two qualities... She was an incredible person and I feel lucky to have known her.

Ours was an impossible love. We knew it before we acted on it, during and most acutely after we were forced to part ways. Perhaps in the future, society's decrees will be less rigid, marriages will be less confined by duty and class, and love will be less judged. I hope that will be the case, so very much.

For Catherine, the Soames jewels have been

a heavy weight to bear. They have brought only cruel, desperate men to her door. Her wish—our wish—is that you find the jewels that are rightfully yours and that they bring you great peace and true love.

You are our hopes and our dreams.

Always,
BC

Noticing the use of the same code that she and her sisters had seen in Catherine's diaries, she traced her fingers over the underlined letters on the page. And the message ran over and over in her mind as she put aside the letter and retrieved the ring. She was humbled and overwhelmed by a message over one hundred and fifty years old that was full of love, compassion and understanding.

And as her heart was torn between what she felt she should do for her sisters and what she wanted to do for Benoit, it broke a little. He was right. Her sisters would be fine. They would *always* be fine because she had done that for them, given them a security she had never felt herself. A small part of her realised then that the instinct to go to them was learned, was ingrained and habitual. She thought of the way Benoit had drawn her out in Costa Rica. Just one day, and over five thousand miles ago.

She slipped the citrine ring onto her engagement finger, a surprised sigh escaping her lips as it fitted perfectly. Her sisters had the map; they had what they needed to take the next step to finding the Soames jewels. It was Benoit who needed her now.

As she shifted back onto the bed, the message from Benoit's letter settled into her heart.

Go with love.

Skye hadn't seen Benoit all day. She'd slept late, grabbed some lunch and wandered the garden, looking for traces of Benoit's childhood and not quite finding any. Wandering through the beautiful chateau had only made her feel more in the way and uncomfortable as uniformed staff members hustled and bustled about in preparation for what looked to be a spectacular event. So eventually she'd retreated to her rooms and pored over the pages of Catherine's diaries that Summer had typed up and emailed.

Her heart ached for her ancestor, who'd loved a man she would never have been allowed to marry. And here Skye was, about to marry a man who might never love her. To marry a man she was beginning to fear that she really did love. Because the Benoit she had seen in Costa Rica, the incredible man who had drawn her out and shown her what she could be, the man who only hurt here at the chateau, a man convinced that selfishness was at the root of everything, yet he had only given to her...*that* man deserved her love.

Skye cast a glance at the dresses magically procured by Benoit's assistant, and she frowned. They were all perfectly fine, gorgeous even, but not quite...

A knock sounded at the door and her heartbeat picked up.

Benoit.

But as she opened the door to find Anaïs standing there Skye forced down the disappointment and hoped that it didn't show on her face. The little dog yapped a greeting from where he was nestled in her arms and, with an amused eye roll, Anaïs released him to explore Skye's room, dotingly watching as he raced about searching for invisible treats.

'I wanted to see how you were.' Anaïs looked beyond her to the selection of dresses hung in a row across the top of the dresser and scoffed. 'Benoit's assistant is a man with no taste. Business acumen, yes, but absolutely no taste. Trust me, Benoit would *never* have chosen any of these.'

Skye couldn't help but smile at the thought that Anaïs wanted to assure her that her great-nephew had better taste in clothing. But when the older woman's eyes turned back to her, taking her in from head to foot and then narrowing suspiciously, the first stirrings of excitement began to spread in Skye's chest. Because she wanted this evening to be perfect for Benoit. Wanted him to have a fiancée he would not only stand by but be proud of. And she had a feeling that Anaïs wanted that too.

Pulling at the neck of his shirt, Benoit wondered for the hundredth time how the ballroom had managed to get so hot. For nearly twenty minutes now, his frustration with Skye's absence had grown into a physical thing. He'd barely been able to utter a few civil words to his extended family, resenting each and every one of them for putting him in this situation.

A small rise in volume near the entrance alerted him to a new arrival and he bit back the familiar bitterness that coated his tongue when he finally saw his brother. It took a moment for the image he'd held in his mind and the actual reality of Xander to merge into one. Over the last two years he'd allowed betrayal to morph his brother into a monstrous presence at the back of his mind. But now that Xander was here, greeting members of his family, Benoit was struck dumb. Shocking sentiment clashed against hurt and he didn't know which one would win out. Xander, nearly as tall as his own six foot three inches, bent to greet some of the older generation before casting a glance directly towards him, as if he'd always known where Benoit was in the room.

A set of blue eyes pierced the isolation he had found himself in. Xander's familiar jawline, angular and as determined as his own, clenched as if ready for a confrontation. The murmurs in the room rose once again as the expectation of a showdown increased. Benoit bit off a bitter laugh. As if he'd give them the satisfaction.

The moment his brother made a move in his direction, Benoit purposely turned his back on him, scanning the crowds for any sign of Skye. But he couldn't ignore that he'd felt…not angry, but actually happy to see Xander. For a moment he'd forgotten everything and relief had spread through him at the sight of him. Was it the memories that he'd shared with Skye that had conjured this strange disjointed feeling? He'd admitted to Skye that he would have turned his back on Xander and gone with his mother without a second thought all those years ago, and with it had come the realisation that he'd actually been thankful for Xander's betrayal. Because it had—for the briefest time—overshadowed the years of guilt Benoit had felt. Finally, they were once again equal in their betrayal of each other.

But the ache forming at this thought overshadowed the night. Instead of the guests in the ballroom, he saw trees and branches. Instead of murmured conversations and gentle music, he heard the sounds of boyish laughter. Instead of the rich heady scent of perfume, damp, peaty forest earth filled his nose. Memories of building forts with Xander consumed him, the thoughtless ease and love of their bond stretched through him. The way they had stood together, side by side, with cardboard swords and tea-towel capes, as they faced down imaginary armies. And suddenly what rose up from the last two years wasn't betrayal or bitterness, but loneliness without his brother by his side. The brother he had consulted with each and every business deal, the confidante he had discussed almost every thought and feeling with.

As if pulled up by his own realisation, he was about to turn back to Xander when he noticed each of the guests turning towards the grand circular staircase at the head of the room. Expecting to see his great-aunt, his breath caught in his lungs unexpectedly and his chest seized.

If Anaïs hadn't been holding onto her arm as they rounded the balcony that looked over the huge ballroom, dotted with round tables as if it were a wedding reception, Skye would have stopped in her tracks. A soiree, Anaïs had called it. She was pretty sure Benoit had called it a gathering. This was something *entirely* different.

It reminded her of a ball described in Catherine's diary and, for just a moment, Skye felt the past and present merge. The notion was most definitely helped by the incredible dress that Anaïs had found for her. It had taken her breath away when she'd first seen it. The oyster-coloured silk was floor-length with a small silver waist detail at the front which closed in a ribbon at the back. From the shoulders, two drapes of chiffon veed down to the centre of her waist over the lace detail of the bodice beneath. Skye was thankful for the cap sleeves that left her arms bare in this heat. The lace at her back, exquisitely detailed, crossed her shoulder blades and met at the waist, but it was the skirt that Skye loved most. The silky chiffon fell away from the waist to the floor in thousands of tiny layers, making her look and feel like a princess. The easy glide of it against her skin took her by surprise each time she took a step and it made her feel feminine and sensual in a way she never could have imagined.

As if Anaïs was her fairy godmother and had planned it all, Skye's dress matched the ballroom filled with tables covered in creamy linen tablecloths and pale-coloured dinner sets, the room lit with white candles that hung in wall sconces and from the largest chandeliers she had ever seen.

Everywhere she looked, gold and diamonds twinkled. Music played by a real quartet at one end of the room softened the hum of the quietly spoken conversations rising up from the floor below. Some of the older guests were using fans to cool them from the surprising heat and Skye half expected a footman to be waiting at the top of the stairs that led down to the ballroom to announce her and Anaïs' arrival.

As she scanned the ballroom, looking for Benoit, her eyes snagged on a tall, sandy blond-haired man—the jawline familiar. But while her mind hooked onto the man, her heart knew that this wasn't Benoit and she paused, studying the person who could only be Xander, Benoit's brother.

In an instant Skye wanted to be beside Benoit because she knew that this would be difficult for him. And no matter Benoit's machinations, excuses even, for demanding that she wear his ring…it wasn't about the company. It wasn't about what was rightfully his. Beneath that, Skye had seen the hurt and anger swirling beneath the surface and, no matter how painful his parents' betrayal, Skye knew, *knew*, that the deepest hurt, the deepest guilt, had focused around his feelings for his brother. So she pushed aside the nervousness she felt within her chest and answered Anaïs' shrewd assessing gaze as they stepped towards the top of the staircase with a firm smile. She was ready.

She picked up the skirts of the dress so as not to trip on them or catch them with her heels, casting a look down the stairs to where they were heading. From the corner of her eye, the citrine ring caught the light and sparkled, as if to remind her, *Go with love*.

As they began to descend the staircase, finally her eyes found Benoit and her chest constricted as if she needed his permission to breathe. He was…marvellous. She swore she could feel the power resonating from him. The tuxedo he wore clung to his broad shoulders, dropping to a narrow V just above his waist. The starched white shirt clashed beautifully with the bronze tan of his skin and she couldn't take her eyes off his jaw. Clean shaven, he was even more handsome. As if the beard had softened his impact, it was now painfully clear that he was almost insolently sexy.

Desire shivered across her skin as she refused to drop her gaze, her eyes locked with his with each step that brought her closer and closer to him, with each glide of her silk skirts against her skin, wishing fervently that it was his hands rather than the material of her dress that covered her body.

A blush rose to her cheeks, she could feel the heat of it, not because every single one of the guests had fallen silent at their approach, but because of the sensual magic weaving between them. He stalked towards the bottom of the stairs, the look in his eyes as intense as she felt.

'Thank you for lending Skye to me for the day, but I feel it's time that I returned your fiancée to you.'

Skye registered the few gasps and murmurs that greeted Anaïs' decree, absently wondering if perhaps this was the first time that Benoit's family had heard the news. But everything paled into insignificance as Anaïs moved Skye's arm from hers to his. It felt…ritualistic—as if she were being presented to him as an offering. As a prize.

Anaïs disappeared and all Skye could see, could think of, could feel was him.

'I didn't think you would still be here.'

'I am. But not because you told me to be, but because I want to be.'

She kept her eyes on his, trying as much as possible to express her meaning, to imprint it upon him so that he would understand the truth behind her words. There was so much she desperately wanted to tell him—her feelings for him, why she had done what she'd done, about her mother—but the guests had now turned to crowd around them, questions on their lips and suspicion in their eyes. So she stayed silent as he led her towards the head table.

As she sat in the chair he pulled out for her, staring down at the sheer number of knives, forks, plates, side plates, first and second course plates, the four glasses—*four*—she tried not to flinch as a uniformed man poured champagne into the flute beside her.

It was only when she felt Benoit stiffen beside her that she realised Xander Chalendar had taken a seat opposite. For a moment the guests around the table seemed to take a collective breath until Anaïs launched into a topic of conversation Skye tried very hard to keep up with.

Noticing that Benoit had barely touched his starter, Skye couldn't help but sneak out a hand beneath the tablecloth, to reach for the clenched fist he held against his thigh. The fierce stretch of skin over knuckles told her how difficult he was finding this and she smoothed her palm over his fist and hoped that it would somehow relax him. She hadn't realised that she was holding her breath until slowly his hand unfurled and his fingers gently threaded through hers. A small smile pulled at her lips and finally she turned her attention back to the delicious food, enjoying the one-handed eating style that they were now both engaged in.

The easy conversation that covered the first and second courses, all the way to dessert, had lulled her into a false sense of security. So it took her a moment to realise that she was being pinned by a stare from Benoit's brother, as if he were waiting for her to make eye contact, demanding it even. When she finally did raise her gaze, she purposely left it open. She wasn't quite sure what she'd expected—suspicion, anger? But instead…truly? She thought she saw some kind of protectiveness in his eyes, recognising it as something she felt for her sisters. And that kind of protectiveness? It was dangerous and she was immediately on edge.

'So, Miss Soames,' Xander said, as if it weren't the first thing he'd ever uttered in her direction, 'how long have you known my brother?'

Skye wasn't quite sure what angle he was playing here, because she didn't really know enough about Xander to assume anything. She knew how Benoit felt about him and she didn't need the way he had clenched her hand in his to tell her that he was suspicious of his brother's motivations. Perhaps Xander wanted to disprove their relationship to the family so Benoit wouldn't be able to secure the CEO position permanently, perhaps not. She could hardly ignore the question, but neither was she going to leave Benoit open to any kind of suspicion or doubt.

'It feels like years,' she simply replied.

'I'm sure you could forgive us for thinking that this engagement is oddly fortuitous.'

So he was trying to undermine Benoit. Everything in her rose to his defence and she wouldn't let this go quietly. She didn't know these people, she didn't care about these people, but she did know Benoit. He had shown her time and time again that, despite his hurts, he wanted the best for his company, his family. He didn't want to make the same mistakes as his father or his mother, and not only had he led her to the map, he had shown her a part of herself she had long forgotten.

'I could forgive you for thinking that, but perhaps not for saying it,' she replied.

Xander nodded, accepting the criticism. 'But, with so much at stake, I'm sure that you can understand the family's concern. We would all love to hear how your relationship came into being.'

'Well, you could say that we crashed into each other's lives quite suddenly,' she said, a small smile pulling at her lips. 'And now I couldn't imagine mine without him in it,' she pressed on, surprised at how the sentiment rang true within her.

'I'm presuming the engagement will be short?'

'There's certainly no need to wait,' she fired back, finding strength in the way Anaïs' smile warmed her, while she tried to ignore the brooding anger vibrating from where she touched Benoit.

'I just find it hard to believe that you know each other well enough in such a short space of time,' Xander replied, his eyes flicking between her and Benoit.

Skye let loose a small laugh. 'Ask me anything,' she said, relishing the feeling of power that glowed within her. Because she did, she realised. She did know Benoit. And, for just a moment, she saw doubt spread across Xander's features.

Holding his gaze now, and refusing to look towards Benoit, she pressed on. 'How he likes his coffee? Black, strong and he doesn't stop until he's had three cups—and please, don't try and talk to him before then, he's impossible.' A small laugh rose from the other guests at the table. 'Benoit likes a very rich red wine, but prefers whisky after dinner. He's proud and hates to admit he's wrong, which, admittedly, is rare but does happen on certain occasions. He has a penchant for crime fiction and autobiographies, likes print books instead of E-readers, and once a year travels to Costa Rica to switch off from the world. No phones, no internet, no neighbours and, more importantly, no contact from the company that every other day of the year he gives one hundred and ten per cent to.'

She saw the moment that surprise entered Xander's gaze, didn't miss the way that Benoit's hand had fallen slightly slack beneath hers and knew that she was about to cross a boundary, but she also knew instinctively that what she was about to say needed to be said. For Benoit and, yes, even for Xander.

'As a child he wanted to be an explorer, but gave it up for family duty. He still misses the forts that he once built with you in the forest here and, although he probably wouldn't admit to it on pain of death, he bitterly regrets the distance between both of you now. Something that may be undermined by your rather uncouth assertions that my relationship with him is built on nothing more than a desire to control the family company.'

Silence met her declaration until Anaïs shifted beside her, a sheen of tears glistening in the older woman's gaze.

'You love him,' she stated rather than asked. 'Why?'

'Because he saw me when I couldn't yet see myself,' she answered simply and honestly while her heartbeat raged within her chest. 'Now, if you'll excuse me, I think I'll retire for the night.'

CHAPTER ELEVEN

NEARLY AN HOUR later and fury still roiled within Benoit's chest. Just when he had been softening towards his brother, Xander had gone on the attack. He cursed as he stalked back to his room.

For the first time he'd actually wanted to strike his brother. Camilla's betrayal hadn't even affected him like this. The only thing that had prevented him from launching across the table at Xander had been Skye. Her words. Her declaration.

And that had floored him. She'd left not only him but the entire table in shocked silence as she'd regally retreated from the ballroom. But, once the shock had faded, the fury he felt towards his brother was nothing.

You love him.

Even Anaïs had been able to see it. Clear as day. And Benoit knew that Skye wasn't that good a liar.

She had shown her vulnerability. And he knew himself. He would take it and use it. His selfishness meant he would bend her to his will. His mind showed a kaleidoscope of his misdeeds, countless broken hearts, his brother... Even before, when he'd been fighting his selfish nature, he could hardly pretend that he had offered Camilla a proper relationship. He'd not been there at all, working all hours for his company, selfish even then. And he would ruin Skye. He simply couldn't let that happen.

The betrayal this time was not Xander's—it never had been. It had been his own.

He pulled up in front of his bedroom door, knowing that she would be there, needing to steady himself. To push down the roiling emotions that were making him nauseous. It was all her fault.

He found her perched on the end of his bed, waiting for him. The smooth silks of her cream dress presented her as the perfect package. But Benoit knew there was no such thing as perfect.

'I've arranged for the jet to take you anywhere you want to go,' he announced, his tone bland and completely emotionless.

'And why would I want to go anywhere?' Her tone matched his and it infuriated him.

'Because our deal is done,' he growled, unable to keep the leash on his feelings he'd been so proud of only moments ago.

'What do you mean? We aren't married, the company—'

'The company is a family matter and you are not family.'

He could see that his words had struck home and hard, exactly as intended, but it didn't make the slash of guilt slicing into his heart any easier to bear. But bear it he would, because he was going to have earned it by the end of this night.

'So they're just going to change their minds?' she asked, suspicion shining up from the dark depths of her brown eyes.

'I'm done with being manipulated from beyond the grave by my own ancestors. Aren't you?'

'I don't have much choice,' Skye said, this time something unreadable passing across her gaze. He ignored it, he had to focus. 'I—'

'You have what you need. You have the map, so you can go.'

'What if I want to stay? You might not be ready to hear it, but will you let me show you?' she asked. He knew what she wanted—wanted it himself—but he couldn't let her touch him. He knew that if she did that he'd be lost. And he'd already lost too damn much.

'I said that this part of our relationship was at an end.'

'I know what you said, and I understand why you said it—' sympathy and desire warring in her eyes. 'You were right when you accused me of running away, but not about the reason why,' she said, standing up and stepping towards him. 'And I think that you are also hiding from the very same thing, trying to control it, by denying this.'

She pressed a kiss against his lips—lips he refused to move, no matter how every single cell in his body rioted with the need to take her in his arms.

'Because this is terrifying,' she said, pressing yet another kiss against his lips, her hand coming up to claim his clean-shaven jaw. 'Because it makes us both feel out of control,' she stated, pressing her chest against his, firing need and desire deep within him. He feared that the internal tremors shaking him would be seen, the fierce battle between his desire for her and his need to reject what Skye was saying, reject what she was feeling, raging in his chest.

The softness of her lips met the firm, immovable line of his own. 'But, with you, I find that I like it. I want it. And I want you. Because I…'

And then it was too much. He had to stop her before she said it again, before she could claim him as hers, as she had done at the dinner. Because he didn't think he could survive it. He didn't think he'd be able to let her go.

His lips opened to hers, cutting her off mid-sentence and, as if he'd opened the floodgates, she poured into him, his mouth, his lungs, his veins, all he could sense was her. It blocked out all thought, all of the chaos in an instant; all he knew was her touch, her scent…*her*.

His hand flew to the back of her neck, cradling her head at an angle where he could feast upon her. His fingers tightened in the silken strands of her hair as she moaned her desire into his mouth. Her hands went to his chest, pulling, pushing, grasping him to her as he was pulling her to him. Every thrust of her tongue met the demands of his, as if suddenly all the power they both contained was coming together in a clash of thunder and lightning.

It wasn't enough. This kiss, this raw, feral thing within him, wasn't easing, wasn't satiated; it demanded more—*he* needed more. But more was absolutely impossible. He would ruin them both.

He broke the kiss and turned away, but not before he'd seen the shock and hurt across her painfully expressive eyes. It was something he would never forget for the rest of his life.

'Repeating past mistakes, Skye? Making a gift of yourself? Thanking me for the map?'

She reared back as if she had been slapped. 'Don't say that. Don't do that.'

But he couldn't stop. The words were like ash on his tongue, the pain in her eyes burning his heart, but it was the only way he could make sure that he didn't destroy her completely.

'Then don't belittle yourself by thinking that one night and one sexual awakening means you should beg to be with me.'

He watched her clench her jaw against the numerous terms of abuse she could throw at him, none more colourful or worse than what he was throwing at himself. But still she didn't move. His gut twisted in a knot he thought would never come undone as he forced the words he knew would hurt the most to his lips.

'It's time for you to leave, Skye. I don't need you any more.'

I don't need you any more.

Three weeks, three days ago even, that would have scarred her, scraped at deep hurts that she'd hidden from herself for years. It would have devastated her, would definitely have her running for the hills, no doubt as Benoit intended.

Oh, it hurt. Very much. But not enough to make her leave. Because in the last few days he had opened a door within her. A door that should have been opened years ago. He had made her really look at herself. At what *she* wanted from life. Now and in the future. It wasn't the dependence of her sisters, or approval from her father and his wife. It wasn't the fairy-soft wistfulness of her mother's acceptance either. But neither was it Benoit's money, his Costa Rican holiday home or the vaguely intimidating wealth she saw here in France. It was what she saw in his eyes when he looked at her every time she embraced who she was a bit more. It was the encouragement, the pleasure she saw—*knew*—he got from her being even more of herself each and every day.

No one had ever cared for her like that before. And it was precisely that sense of empowerment that allowed her to see through the walls that Benoit had built up around his heart, causing her to say, 'That's a lie.'

'Really, Skye, all this is making you look a little desperate.'

'And you scared,' she replied quickly before his verbal strike could draw blood. 'Beneath it all, you're just a coward. Because it's not me, Camilla or even Xander that you don't trust. It's yourself. That's why you disappear off to Costa Rica with no access to the outside world. Why you jump from impossibly tall waterfalls. You're seeing if you can trust yourself to be completely self-sufficient, because you're scared of depending on or needing someone again.'

'Don't you dare bring her into this,' he warned, his body physically trembling from the effort it was taking to hold himself in check. No matter. It was all or nothing—Skye knew that the moment she'd told his family that she loved him.

'Benoit, for so long the thing you've clung to from the night your mother ran away is your *almost* betrayal of Xander. You hold it to you as if it's evidence that you're a terrible person. But you were just a child who wanted to stay with his mother, no matter what. Because it was something you could control, the guilt you felt. Rather than what you couldn't—the fact that your mother left. And you've spent so long focusing on that guilt that when Xander betrayed you, *that* became your sole focus.'

'You don't know what you're talking about.'

'You think I don't know how painful it is to be abandoned by a parent and not just once, but again and again? My father chose his new family over me every chance he got. So yes, I do know what I'm talking about.'

She wanted him to see. Not for herself. She had very little hope now that he would relent, that he would keep her with him. But she did want him to see what was shaping the decision he was making. If only to stop him from doing the same in the future.

When she looked into his eyes for a moment she saw unfathomable hurt swirling dark inky streaks into his crystal-blue eyes. Until it passed and she saw...nothing. Complete absence.

'Are you so desperate to forge a connection between

us that you will dig out our deepest hurts to compare them? *Mon Dieu*, Skye, how much more do I have to hurt you before you'll just leave?'

She knew then that she'd lost him. His eyes were dark, his jaw determined. Determined to refuse to see the truth of her words.

'Keep the ring,' he said to her. 'It was always meant for a Soames.'

With her heart trembling in her breast, she asked, 'Do you know why Catherine gave the ring back to Benoit? Despite the fact that she loved him then and always would?'

'Because she knew she had to set him free.'

With that he left and took Skye's heart with him.

Benoit didn't care that the tree stump he sat on was damp and it was seeping into his trousers as he took another swing of whisky from the bottle. It had been three days since Skye had left and it had rained almost constantly since then, as if the heavens were punishing him.

An ache had opened up in his chest the moment she'd accused him of covering over the hurt from his mother's abandonment with guilt, with misdirection, with almost everything other than the realisation of the damage his mother had done that night. It was as if all the years of suppressing it had magnified it, compounded it, and Skye had unlocked a door and it was escaping on one long scream of pain that seemed unending and only grew louder and louder with each passing hour.

All this time he'd been focusing on the pain of betrayal by others, by Camilla and his brother, even his own act of betrayal, and he'd not once thought about the little boy who had promised not to cry. Not to tell anyone. Had he kept that promise all these years? Was he still keeping that promise?

He looked up at the remnants of a fort long ago forgotten by two boys and wondered what on earth he was supposed to do now. His musings were cut short when he heard the soft crunch of wet twigs and he knew, without even having to turn, that Xander had found him.

'Leave,' Benoit said from behind closed eyes. 'Leave now or you'll regret it. It's not an empty threat this time.'

'I'm not going anywhere. I'm not letting you push me away. Not like last time.'

'Are you kidding me? You slept with Camilla! You betrayed me,' he shouted, desperately clinging to a source of anger that pointed outward rather than in. Because, honestly, he feared that this time he'd break.

'Camilla was a monumental mistake. I knew that even before I did it, but she was relentless,' Xander said, sitting opposite him on a fallen tree. 'And I was weak…' The words fell from his lips as if in defeat. 'You were so much to live up to, big brother. *Too* much. For almost my entire life you did everything for me. Looked after me, guided me. Protected me,' he said, the words almost painful for Benoit to hear. Because they were true. Benoit had done almost everything and anything he could, attempting to make up for his unknown betrayal.

'When I said it had to stop she told me she was pregnant.'

'What?' Benoit was yanked out of his introspection with an almost electric shock. Pins and needles dragged along his skin. *They had a child?*

'That's why I married her.'

Confusion spread through Benoit, short-circuiting his brain.

'But she lied. It was *all* a lie,' Xander said bitterly. 'She only wanted to be married to the CEO of Chalendar Enterprises and when I told her that it would never be me she left.'

'What do you mean?'

'I came here to tell you that I'm leaving the company,' Xander said, swiping a hand over his face, that now revealed an incredible amount of exhaustion. But, instead of sympathy, Benoit felt anger.

'Then what the hell was all that about the other night? Interrogating Skye about her feelings for me.'

He was surprised to find the ghost of a smile playing at the edges of his brother's mouth.

'At first I thought your relationship was just a marriage of convenience. And I wanted to ruin it because I didn't want you repeating the same mistakes our father made.' Benoit was pierced by his brother's fierce gaze. 'I didn't want you to sacrifice everything for this damn family company. I wanted to free you from it. Benoit, you've given everything and more for it, but it will never give you what you need and it will never make up for what we lost. And when I realised that she loves you—well, I didn't think you'd be stupid enough to push her away too.'

Benoit felt sick, a nausea that mounted as he scanned over the events of the past. Xander and Camilla, her evil machinations that had severed their connections more easily than his pleas to his mother had done. Meeting Skye, and the times that they had shared, the hurt in her eyes as he had thrown the ring on the bed, the shock on her face as he'd turned to leave. Had he really thought that becoming CEO was worth all she had to offer him?

Finally, he looked at his brother and deeply regretted the years they'd been apart, regretted how he'd let the hurt and betrayal overwhelm him to the point where he'd lost his closest friend. And he'd worn that lone-liness around him like a cloak, as if that would pro-tect him from what was worse…love. And the deepest, greatest pain that love could bring.

A pent-up breath escaped his lungs. 'I had no idea about Camilla. I can't even begin to imagine… lying about pregnancy like that. It's unspeakable.' He watched as Xander shrugged it off, but could only imagine the pain that his brother must have felt when he'd realised how Camilla had lied. 'For so long,' Ben-oit said, finally ready to admit his failing, 'it was eas-ier to blame you, to be furious with you, than to admit the truth.'

'What truth?'

'The guilt I felt because of our mother. For allow-ing her to leave that night. I saw her. I knew what she was doing. I…begged to go with her. I would have left you,' he admitted, shaking his head and unable to look his brother in the eye.

'And, had it been me, I might have done the same,' he heard his brother say as he felt his hand on his shoulder. 'Benoit, our parents made their own decisions and were solely responsible for them. I think that we've spent too long focused on the past and not enough focused on the future. Because you need to get your head on straight if you're going to go after the woman you so clearly love.'

Benoit shook his head. 'I can't...' He gritted his teeth until his jaw ached. Everything ached. 'It's too much.'

Xander reached for the bottle hanging loosely in Benoit's hands and took a long mouthful. 'I'm surprised you haven't figured it out yet,' his brother said. Benoit threw a frown his way in query. 'That the pain of losing someone is absolutely *nothing* compared to hurting someone you love.'

Skye looked out across the stubble of the harvested fields behind the little cottage that Anaïs had taken her to, letting out a jagged breath that caught on the edges of the pain that had speared her chest since leaving Benoit.

She'd done as he'd requested, collected her things and packed a bag—but, as her hand had reached for the door knob, she'd realised that she didn't want to go back to England to see her sisters.

Not until she'd worked out her true feelings. Because there had been a horrible kernel of truth to what Benoit had said that night. So she'd tracked down Anaïs, who had somehow understood the garbled words Skye had managed to form around the lump in her throat and the ache in her chest. The older woman had simply smiled, patted her hand and led her to a car. Skye smiled through the hurt at the memory of Anaïs dismissing her driver, and soon understood the panic in the chauffeur's eyes as she recalled the dangerous driving that had brought the two women to this gorgeous little country cottage.

Anaïs had ensured that the cottage was stocked with enough food and supplies for as long as Skye needed it, and left only once Skye had assured her that she would be okay. It was a lie. She knew it. Anaïs knew it. But they both tacitly agreed to believe it for the moment.

The cottage was surrounded by fields which, aside from the beautiful garden, were the only thing to be seen for miles around. Which was a good thing, because Skye had done nothing but cry for the first two days. She cried for herself, for Benoit, for what they might have had.

She hadn't answered her sisters' calls, texts or emails. How ironic it was that they had begun to worry about her *now*. She'd called each of them two days ago, explaining a little about what had happened, a little of what she had managed to work through and a lot about how much she loved them, saying that she just needed some time and space. She'd promised to be in touch soon.

All the while, Benoit's words rang like accusations in her mind and she knew that he was right. That she had to let her sisters go, to stop focusing on them and live her life. She wondered now at the person who had found her strength with him in Costa Rica. The taste of it had been addictive and truly life-enhancing. But she knew that she needed to find that within herself, rather than borrowing it from Benoit. And that would take time.

When the sun dipped below the horizon Skye had taken to lighting the wood-burner in the small living room of the cottage. She knew it was a luxury—the summer's warmth was still enough to keep the cool nights mild—but each night she looked for the heat from the flames to draw out the cold ache she felt in her heart.

She had been reading the journals that Summer had typed up. This morning a new section had appeared in her inbox, a note reassuring her that her sisters loved her and were there if she needed them. And Skye was beginning to wonder if it might be about time for her to lean on them for a change. It wasn't easy and it wouldn't seem natural, but it was right.

At first, she'd thought she'd find it painful to read about Catherine and her Benoit. And it was. She'd cried with Catherine over the loss of Benoit Chalendar. At how, once Catherine's father had discovered the affair, he'd forced her to let him go. Benoit's family had been no way near a match for a peer of the realm. Skye had found some kind of solidarity with Catherine's feelings of hurt and anguish as they'd echoed her own. And felt the determination ring within her own breast as Catherine had forged a way forward, to the Middle East with her uncle, determined to put the pain behind her. The Middle East, where Star was now searching for the second part of the puzzle—the key to the hidden room.

And yesterday she'd called her mother. Skye knew instinctively that she wasn't yet ready to confront her feelings about her father, the pain was too raw. But her mother…they needed to talk. Skye hated that this was over the phone, but the need to speak to her had become urgent, an almost physical need, so that when her mother asked her if she was okay, the simple relief had her crying nonsensically down the phone for about fifteen minutes, while her beautiful, kind, generous mother poured equally nonsensical words of comfort and love back until Skye's sobs subsided.

Even now, a lump formed in her throat, thinking of the pure unconditional love of that moment and the sadness not only of what she had missed out on as a child by trying to fit in halfway with her father and halfway with her mother, which had made her feel like an outsider in both homes, but of what she was surely to miss out on in the future, even if they did manage to find the jewels.

Mariam Soames had offered to get on a plane and they had both laughed, knowing that neither had the money and that Mariam wasn't well enough to go anywhere. So instead her mother had promised Skye that she had a cup of camomile tea, a large blanket, a comfy chair and was ready for her to start at the very beginning.

And although Skye's story had started at Elias Soames' funeral, jumped to Costa Rica and back to her own childhood, touched on the overheard conversation between her father and his wife, about Skye's wildness and about her university education, moved on to Benoit and Anaïs, Catherine and her Benoit, and finished at Skye's little hideout in France, Mariam Soames was there for every single minute of it, offering comfort, kindness, understanding and sympathy. Not once did she ask why Skye hadn't told her any of this before, or chastise her for secrets and hurts kept hidden. Until Skye had worked herself up to the worst hurt, the worst confession—that she'd been keeping her mother at a distance because she'd been ashamed of her.

The second of silence from her mother was the longest moment of her entire life.

'My love, in my eyes it is the responsibility of a child to form their identity against that of their parents. I did it with Elias. And you did it with me. It doesn't make me shameful, or you boring.'

'And Elias?' Skye half joked.

'Well, he was always a nasty piece of work,' replied her mother sadly. 'Skye, I know that my…lifestyle was difficult on you. Difficult for our neighbours and your teachers and the parents of your friends. I am sorry for that—I'm not apologising for my choices, because I stand by every one of them. But I am sorry for the hurt and confusion it caused you. I don't like speaking for your father, because it has been a very long time since I knew him well enough to do so, but…his character is simply not as strong as yours, mine, and most especially his wife's. He does love you, Skye. He was just never that in touch with his emotions to be able to show it so well.'

Skye let that sink in. Truly sink in to a depth that she hoped might begin to bring acceptance. They'd spoken some more and Skye had promised to call in a few days when she knew what her plans would be. It hadn't been an easy conversation and there would be harder times ahead, especially with her father, but, whatever happened with the jewels—if she and her sisters did somehow manage to find them, and sell the estate to help pay for her mother's medical bills—Skye knew that the healing that had come from their conversation would sustain her throughout her life.

Just before hanging up, her mother had asked why she hadn't told Benoit the truth about what she would use the money for if they found the jewels. There was no censure in her mother's voice, but Skye had felt it all the same. She'd told herself one hundred excuses since that moment, all of which had been both simultaneously true and false. That at first she hadn't trusted him and then later he hadn't trusted her was true…but not reason enough.

And while she had intended to tell him the night of the ball…in some ways it had been a relief not to. Because, deep down, she knew that revealing this would make her the most vulnerable she'd ever been. How he responded to that could break her into a million pieces.

'And it could also give you the support you would need.'

'Mum, please don't talk like that.'

'I don't mean about me. Well, not *just* about me.

You were doing yourself a disservice by not letting him be there for you, by not letting him be the man you believe he is.'

'But what if he's not, Mum?'

'I don't see how that's possible,' Mariam said confidently. 'You wouldn't have fallen in love with him if he wasn't.'

And that was it. As if it were that simple. The thought of the raw vulnerability of telling him about Mariam made Skye's heart quiver in her chest. But the hope that her mother had given her, the fact that she *did* know Benoit, *did* believe him to be good at heart soothed some of her fears and for the first time since leaving the chateau she considered the possibility of seeing him again.

Whether they found the jewels or not, whether they were able to do so in time for her mum's treatment, whether she would actually go to university or not, Skye knew that there were some big changes she wanted to make in her life. And they wouldn't cost a thing.

She would not be torn any more by what people expected or wanted from her. She would work hard to listen to herself, to find what it was she wanted to do or be. And, although everything screamed within her that the answer to that was inextricably linked to Benoit Chalendar, she knew that was something she had no control over.

Skye pulled the shawl around her shoulders as the first bite of the evening's chill edged into the air. She turned to head back into the cottage but pulled up short when she saw the figure standing in front of the back door, believing that she was simply imagining it.

For a second, her eyes drank in the sight of Benoit, as if starved by the lack of it in her life. She thought then that it was one of the most marvellous sights she'd ever seen. Until she looked closer and saw the dark hollows beneath his eyes, the shade of stubble across his jaw.

He took a step towards her and Skye stepped back to keep the distance between them. Because she wasn't sure that she would be able to resist the desperate longing to reach out to him, to touch him, pull him to her.

'What do you want?' she asked instead.

'I would like, very much, for you to hear me out, if you will?'

She nodded, because it was all she could do, her entire body and brain short-circuited by his presence. He gestured towards the old wooden bench beside the rosebush at the edge of the garden and, on stiff legs, she made her way to it. Finally, he sat beside her, leaning his elbows against his knees and looking out across the same field that she had previously been studying.

'Xander and I went to the shareholders' meeting two days ago,' Benoit started to explain, knowing that it was perhaps the wrong place, but the only place he could begin. 'We told them that they could enforce the by-law if they wanted, but that they didn't have to. It was their choice and both Xander and I were willing to abide by that choice. I told them that I should be CEO of Chalendar Enterprises not because I was married, but because I am damn good at it and I want it.' He tried to ignore the way she stiffened beside him and pressed on, hoping that she'd see the truth of his words. 'I do, but not badly enough to bind a kind, loving, amazing woman to me for the sake of it. So I need you to know that I would walk away if needed. Either way, Xander is stepping down from the company and...' he let out a small surprised laugh of his own '...we're going into business together,' he finished, smiling ruefully. If anything good had come out of the awfulness of the last few days it was that he had started to forge the kind of relationship he'd always wanted with his brother, not based on perceived guilt or debt but an honest one. It was interesting and a little like walking through a minefield, but they were getting there.

'I need you to know that before I tell you what I came here to say,' he said, still staring out at the fields as dusk began to draw over them. He clung to that view, a view he'd never seen before but would remember for the rest of his life. 'That you were right. I have spent years throwing distraction after distraction at the hurt my mother caused by leaving. It was so much easier to do that, to blame myself or others, than to recognise that hurt. Which was why I thought it was easier to push others away before they could inflict more of that hurt. But, as someone disturbingly wise pointed out, that pain was nothing compared to what I felt when I hurt you.'

He couldn't look at her. Not yet. He needed to finish what he'd come here to say, otherwise he'd lose it.

'I will never be able to apologise for...' He could barely force the words out through the terrible memory of the words he'd used against her that day. 'What I said was unforgivable. I belittled the time we spent together and I undermined you and everything that is powerful, glorious and incredible about you. Skye, please know that I will bear the scars of that hurt, that pain I caused you, on my heart for the rest of my life,' he promised, for the first time in his life not caring that his vision had become blurred from the threat of tears.

'You were also right when you said I was a coward. Even when I was hurting you, saying cruel things to push you away. I thought I was doing it to protect you from me, but I was wrong. It was because I was scared of the strength of my own feelings for you. You fought against me and *for* me. I was…scared because I've never been as happy as I was in Costa Rica with you, because I love you.'

Finally, he turned to look at her and his heart nearly broke in two when he saw the tears gathered in her eyes. 'I love you,' he said again. He might even have said it another time before she put her fingers to his lips and his heart dropped. He reached for her hands as if to hold her to him, but she pulled back and looked out at the same view he had just been desperately clinging to.

'Thank you,' she said, tucking her hand back under her thigh. 'I…thank you for apologising for what you said that night.'

He felt nauseous all of a sudden, only now realising that he might have truly lost all hope.

Skye hadn't missed the way that he had blanched before she had turned her attention to the horizon. But she'd had to turn away or she would never be able to say what she needed to. Shaking her head, blind to the beauty of the setting sun, she just marvelled.

'How can it only have been eight days?' she whispered, feeling the weight of his eyes on her face, neck, hair. 'In Costa Rica you made me see things about myself that I'd not even thought were possible. You helped me… No, you *made* me confront things about myself that I'd never told anyone. You were also right. I think, because of the way I grew up, I would make myself into what I thought people wanted from me so that they would…' she breathed around the sob welling in her chest '…so that they would keep me.' A tear dropped from where it had grown thick and round at the corner of her eye. She hastily swept it away.

'But you?' she said, a laugh in her voice this time. 'You didn't want me in the first place.'

'Skye—'

She couldn't help but laugh properly now. A sense of joy was building in her.

I love you. I love you. I love you.

She'd remember his words for the rest of her life.

'It's okay. Who would want a complete stranger literally crashing their one and only holiday, where they got to go off and be all—'

'Mancenary?'

'Exactly!' she said, her eyes turning to him, flashing bright with fun and love and everything in between. For the first time she saw a glint of hope shining amongst the icy shards of his blue eyes like a diamond. 'You must have thought me completely crazy, getting drunk and talking about missing jewels and secret passageways.'

'Never,' he said so sincerely she knew he was joking.

'But Benoit,' she said, finally looking at him, all the love she felt for him rising up and pouring out of her, knowing that she was safe, that her love was safe because she could see it shining in him. 'Who knew that, beneath all that mansplaining,' she said, reaching up to cup his jaw, running her thumb against the stubble he'd allowed to grow since the night of the ball, relishing the way he captured her hand in his, holding her to him, 'and all those terse monosyllabic replies, was the only man I would ever truly love?'

He took her hands in his then, his eyes open and expressing every single thing he felt. Pain, guilt, but also hope and love.

'I'm so sorry that I caused you such pain.'

'The pain was always there, you just exposed it to sunlight, allowing it to heal. Allowing me to really embrace my love for you without giving myself away. I *do* love you because you allowed me to have that control in my life, you showed me that I can be strong and powerful and allow others the freedom to love me for who I am and not what I can be for them.'

Skye took a deep breath, her heart full with happiness, sadness, a little bit of grief and a whole lot of love. 'But I also need to talk to you about something before I can say anything else. Because I'm going to need you to love me through this.'

He frowned and took her hand as if sensing the gravity of it. Slowly and with halting words, Skye explained how her mother had been diagnosed with stage three cancer and how they had just missed out on the most successful treatment the NHS had to offer because of where they lived. He held her hand as the tears fell and Skye confessed that the sisters only wanted the diamonds so that they could sell the estate and pay for Mariam's treatment, he held her—shaking in his arms—as she revealed that she'd been scared of telling him because if he did this, if he supported her, loved her through this then she wasn't sure that she would ever be able to let him go.

He told her that she'd never have to let him go as he wiped the tears from her cheeks. He promised her that together they would find either the treatment or the jewels, whatever it took to keep Mariam healthy for as long as possible, as he pressed gentle kisses to her forehead, eyelids, cheeks and mouth. He took her hand and placed it over his heart and told her that it belonged not just to her, now and always, but to her family, her sisters and mother, and that she would never face a hardship alone ever again.

'Then I will marry you tomorrow, or any other day before your birthday if that's what you want,' Skye promised him, feeling as if she were soaring into clouds with the love that she felt within and around her.

Benoit gazed at her, moving so slowly that she almost hauled him to her—and, as if realising that, a smile curved the corner of his lip upwards and she'd never seen him look so devastating as he was in that moment.

'You are so beautiful,' he said, placing a kiss on her cheek. 'So perfect,' he said, kissing her neck. 'So incredible,' he said, his lips gently pressing against hers. 'I have done nothing to deserve you,' he said. 'But I promise to spend the rest of my life trying to do so.'

He kissed her then, a slow building, powerful roll of lips and tongues and heat and love that threatened to take her breath away. They stayed there, kissing like teenagers until the moon came out and the stars twinkled as if laughing with them.

'We should go in,' Skye said reluctantly.

As if suddenly realising that inside there were many more options, like beds, and sofas, Benoit's eyes brightened. 'We should! We definitely should. But,' he said, his eyes growing serious, 'before we do... I won't be marrying you tomorrow.'

Skye pulled up short in confusion as his words seemed to contradict each other.

'I do want to marry you, more than anything I've ever wanted before. But I also want you to know that it's not because of any possible connection to the company. So, Skye Soames, would you do me the honour of waiting until a year from today to marry me on my thirty-third birthday?'

She laughed, shock and a happy sort of surprise soaring in her breast. To know that, no matter what happened with the company, this was his gift to her. To know that he truly did love her, no matter what.

'A year?' she asked.

'Yes.'

'Well, I suppose that will give you plenty of time.'

'Time for what?'

'For you to teach me how to ride a motorbike.'

EPILOGUE

THREE HUNDRED AND sixty-five days later and Skye was standing in front of a floor-length antique gold mirror in the most beautiful wedding dress she'd ever seen. Delicate lace detail smoothed over silk that draped perfectly over and around her incredibly large baby bump, making her smile even more.

'Oh, Skye,' her mum cried from behind her, tears of joy glistening in her eyes. 'I never thought…' Skye watched as Mariam Soames pressed her lips together, holding back the words as Star reached for her mother's hands and Summer placed her head on Mariam's shoulder.

All four women knew the end of that sentence. Knew how close they'd come to not having this moment. So much had happened in the last year, highs, lows, fraught battles and hard-won victories, each one bringing them to a love and happiness that they never could have expected. Skye turned and was instantly wrapped in the loving embrace of the women she shared her life with.

'If you start crying…' Star warned through her own tears.

'It will ruin your eyeliner and that took me almost ten minutes to get right,' finished Summer, with the same sheen of tears as her sister and mother.

'You know weddings are supposed to be happy, right?' Skye chided. 'And that you're not supposed to cry until the end?'

'But it's—'

'So *romantic*,' Skye, Summer and Mariam Soames finished for Star, before they all descended into gentle giggles.

There was a knock on the door and Xander, Benoit's best man, called out the time, alerting the girls to the fact that the ceremony was to start shortly. Skye ushered them all from the room with a smile, just wanting a moment to herself. With promises that she'd be down in a minute, she turned back to the mirror and took in the glow in her cheeks, the shine to her hair—a nice boon from her pregnancy—and the glint of the citrine ring on her finger the most magical of all. In some ways, it was even more special than the diamond necklace that hung from her neck, dropping low into the V of the bodice of her wedding dress. One third of the Soames jewels, the other two with her sisters, making it feel—as it always had done—as if some things were meant to be.

Life had changed so much in the last year. The moment Skye had returned to England with Benoit and been reunited with her sisters, to hear the accounts of their own fantastic journeys, her mother had been rushed into treatments that had dramatically changed everything. It had not been easy and, a year on, the only thing they knew the future held for certain was hope. And that wouldn't have been possible without Catherine Soames.

During that time, Skye had grown in confidence, had let go of the responsibilities she had placed upon herself and started to embrace her inner thrill-seeker, all of which had been down to her future husband— even if he did regret showing her how to ride a motor-bike. She had fallen in love with the Dordogne and her French was improving every day, which was invaluable as they now split their time between England and France. But the love, the certainty and security she had found with Benoit was something she marvelled at the most, never imagining how powerful a thing it was to love and be loved without measure.

And, no matter how long she lived, she would never forget that she wouldn't have met Benoit without the Soames jewels. Wouldn't have rushed headlong into an adventure that—she now knew—had only just begun when she slipped into an unlocked car. And she hadn't been the only one, as Star's part in finding the Soames' jewels had been just as magical and exciting as her own, but that was a story for another time.

Downstairs, more than two hundred guests were taking their seats on the white chairs with large white bows on the beautiful green lawn in front of the wild-flower arbour beneath which she would declare her love for Benoit. She bit down on her bottom lip when she thought on the fact that her father wasn't amongst them. It didn't hurt as much as it would have a year ago, but she wouldn't deny herself the moment to honour that feeling, before letting it go.

Frowning, she felt something draw her to the window and she had learned in the last year to pay attention to her instincts. With a smile already pulling at her lips, she pulled the curtain across her body to cover her dress, conscious of the superstition about wedding gowns and thankful that she had. Down on the grassy bank, as people made their way towards their seats, stood Benoit, staring up as if they'd arranged to meet like this.

He looked at her with wonder, as if he'd never seen anything more beautiful than her, as if he'd never stop looking at her. She watched as he covered his heart with his hand and then pressed it to his mouth. She would swear until her last day that she felt his lips against hers in that moment. But, in truth, they didn't need words, they didn't need touches, or kisses—they were, of course, welcome and wonderful—but unnecessary because she felt more than his kiss. She felt his soul entwine with hers, making her more than just herself, making them greater together. Skye no longer feared being herself, no longer feared past hurts or future pains because, whatever storm would come, they would survive it.

Because they would always *go with love*.

* * * * *

From One Night To Desert Queen

MILLS & BOON

DEDICATION

This was written during the break between coronavirus lockdowns in the UK when, more than ever, I was reminded of the power of reading romance. The power to escape, to hope, to love and to look to a brighter future with a happy ending.

So, this is for all the incredible romance authors, editors, copy editors, cover artists, production staff, admin staff, publishers, retailers, bloggers, reviewers—all the individuals that help make romance available to us readers even in the hardest of times.

Thank you.

PROLOGUE

'I'M NOT SURE that I should go.'

'We don't really have much choice.'

'I don't want to leave you with Star and the rest of it...'

Star Soames's heart thudded painfully in her chest. She knew that her sisters would be absolutely mortified if they knew she was listening, but hated the way she had been lumped in with 'the rest of it'. As if she were a duty, a burden, just like the one the grandfather they'd never met—thankfully, as far as Star was concerned—had placed on them.

Star willed back the tears clouding her vision as she tried to concentrate on what Skye, the eldest, was saying.

'It should only be a couple of days. Fly to Costa Rica, get the map from Benoit Chalendar, come home. Simple as that.'

'Except he's not likely to have the map on him, Skye,' came the gently worded reply from Summer, their youngest sister and the peacekeeper of the family.

'Okay, so add in a day to return via France and I'll be back before you know it.'

Star ran her thumb down the length of the thick gold chain of the necklace that they had found only yesterday, along with their great-great-great-grandmother's journals, in a hidden recess tucked behind a section of shelves that swung open at the flick of a notch in Catherine's library. Star preferred that name to the other names the smaller library had come to be known by, like *the women's library* or *the little library*, and she wasn't surprised that none of the male Soames heirs had ever thought to look there.

If anyone had ever suspected Catherine of spiriting away the family diamonds from her evil husband Anthony, it had never been more than a suspicion as generation after generation went half mad trying to solve the mystery of the missing jewels that must be worth a small fortune. It was as if every single subsequent Soames had let the sprawling Norfolk Estate run to ruin in order to chase a myth, including Elias Soames, the man who had rejected and disowned their mother before she'd even left her teens. Star shivered in memory of the image of his portrait hanging in the estate office, where she and her sisters had first heard the terms of his will. As the lawyer had read the fiendish requirements of the inheritance, Elias Soames had stared down at them like a Dickensian villain, for all that the painting could only have been made twenty years before.

Elias had given them only two months to track down the Soames diamonds. And if they failed? The estate would pass to the National Trust. Star nearly laughed. If it hadn't been for their mother, the girls might have given the estate to the Trust with their blessing, none of them wanting anything to do with such a twisted manipulation. But because of their mother...

'In the meantime, please keep an eye on Star. You know how she gets.'

How she gets? Star mouthed to herself, frowning, shifting away from the door, really not wanting to hear any more but unable to get far before hearing Skye carry on.

'I'm worried that she'll try and go after the next clue herself. Especially as it could be so...'

'Romantic?' both of her sisters chimed together, descending into fits of giggles. Star clenched her jaw. She'd read and loved romances for more than half her life, defended them more times than she could count and would continue to do so while she still had breath in her lungs.

'I just worry that she'd get herself into trouble. And we really can't afford to...we don't have the time to get this wrong.'

A stab of hurt cut through her. While she hated what her sisters were saying, they were right. She looked around at the library, through the window where the stars in the night sky blinked over the land that came with the estate. Land that, had Mariam Soames lived there, might have had the right post-code. A postcode that would have meant she'd have had access to the most successful treatment for her stage three cancer. But her small flat in Salisbury, near the New Forest, was about as far as possible from this sprawling estate with two wings and more than forty rooms and was very much in the wrong postcode. Star couldn't help but shake her head at the injustice of it, at the cruelty that meant life or death was based on income, savings or property location.

'We've already lost two weeks getting this far. But now we have the journals, now that you've decoded the secret message written in them, we have our first real start to finding the Soames diamonds. Benoit Chalendar has the map of the secret passageways in the estate, I'm sure of it.'

'Skye, even if you do get the map, then we still need to find out where on the map they are hidden and how to access it when we do find it. They're not going to be just lying in a corner of the secret passageways. And if we find whatever the next clue is while you're still away, then Star will *have* to go. I need to be here to meet with the potential buyer and you know that the clause insists that one of us stay in residence for the two months we have to track down the missing jewels,' Summer reminded Skye.

'Can you believe this is our life right now? On a treasure hunt for diamonds that have been missing for over one hundred and fifty years?'

'No more than I can believe that all this could be for nothing if we don't find the jewels and the entire estate is handed over to the National Trust. And then we wouldn't be able to help Mum.'

Selling the estate was the *only* way that the sisters would be able to pay for their mother's medical treatment.

'You haven't said how you know this mysterious billionaire…'

Star listened for an answer, but none came from Summer.

'You know you can talk to us if you need to.'

'I know.'

Star listened as the footsteps retreated down the corridor away from the library before sinking into the ancient leather chair. Again, her fingers ran up and down the thick bronze twists of the necklace, the action comforting as the heavy rectangular pendant swung like a pendulum back and forth from where it hung. It hurt that her sisters didn't think she could do her part without getting into trouble. That they doubted her. But, instead of wallowing in self-pity, she saw herself like an Arthurian knight, brandishing her sword, battle cry at the ready, determined to fulfil her quest. Gripping the pendant in her fist, she swore that she would follow the next clue wherever it led and she *would* return proving her sisters wrong, she *would* help to save her mother.

CHAPTER ONE

KHALIF INHALED DEEPLY through his nose and out through his mouth. Repeating the action did nothing to dislodge the tension pounding angrily in his temples. He rubbed at his eyes, squinting against his thumb and forefinger.

Five hours.

Five wasted hours he'd sat in that room, while fifteen people stared back at him as coffee grew cold, sweets grew stale and the room had become so stuffy they'd needed to open a window.

Stalking down the corridor, he told himself that he just needed air. Fresh air. He wasn't running. He just needed a minute to himself. Which was why he was taking the staff routes through the palace, not the main ones. He was *not* hiding from Amin, his brother's—no, his *own*—assistant. He was simply ensuring the longevity of the bespectacled man's life.

Through the window, across the courtyard, Khalif could see the tourists leaving the exhibition housed in the public areas of Duratra's palace. The sound of two boys laughing as they were chased affectionately by their mother cut through Khalif like a knife, transporting him back to a time when he and his brother had run rings around the palace guards.

Grief was like a punch to the gut. Swift, harsh, hot and angry. An emotion he could not allow to be seen now that he was first in line to the throne. Three years on from the terrible accident and he still caught himself noting something to tell his brother, wondering what Faizan would think, would advise. But Khalif wasn't sure what was worse, to do that, or for that to stop.

It was a visceral sense of wrongness. As if that day the world had shifted a few degrees. Grief felt like trying to push the entire world back into place, millimetre by millimetre. And nothing worked. Not even pretending that he didn't feel like an imposter. A substitute for his brother's throne, as if Faizan would just appear from around the corner, laughing at him, telling him it was all a joke and taking back the responsibility that he, unlike Khalif, had been taught to manage. But Khalif knew better than to believe in fairy tales and daydreams.

The urge to find the nearest bar and wash away the acrid taste of resentment and grief with a drink was strong. But he'd not touched alcohol or a woman since he'd received the news about his brother. He might have once been the spare, the Playboy Prince loved internationally and equally by women and newspapers alike, but he was now next in line to the throne. And each and every day had been a battle to prove his worth as he forged himself into a ruler that honoured his brother, his father and his country.

He skirted the corridor that ran parallel to the rooms that housed the large public exhibition on Duratrian history and rounded the corner to where the security suite for the public areas was located and came to a halt. All five security staff, two in uniform and three in plain clothes, were huddled round the monitor as if their lives depended on it. Adrenaline crashed through him, his body preparing for fight.

'What's going on?' he demanded as he entered the room, searching the bank of monitors lining the back wall for any sign of threat or danger to the royal family.

The way the men all started and looked as guilty as schoolboys would have been funny if his heart hadn't still been pounding in his chest, his pulse throbbing painfully in his neck as the adrenaline receded.

'Nothing.'

'Sorry, Your Royal Highness, Sheikh—'

'I know my name, Jamal,' Khalif ground out. 'What is it?'

A few more denials hit the air, too many shaking heads and hands, and even if that hadn't piqued his curiosity a flash of red caught his eye on the central monitor. The one that the men had all been staring at.

'What is...'

A tourist stood in front of one of the large paintings in the Alsayf Hall. Khalif cocked his head to one side as if that would make the image easier to see. The female figure was respectfully dressed, despite the relaxed attitude towards attire in Duratra, with a sage green headscarf that...

Again, there was the flash of red. The scarf had fallen back a little and a long, thick curl of fiery red slipped forward before the woman quickly tucked it back behind the folds of her hair covering. All this was done with an economy of movement and without taking her eyes from the painting. Without the distraction of the bright red hair, Khalif took in the rest of the woman.

The denim jacket she was wearing covered her arms and was folded back at the cuff to reveal a series of gold and bronze bangles that hung around a delicate wrist. The jacket was cropped at the waist so that the white and green striped dress that dropped all the way to the floor should have been perfectly modest had it not hinted at the mouth-watering curves of her—

He forced his eyes from the screen and looked to the men in charge of his family's security.

'Jamal, you're a married man,' he scolded as if he hadn't just been staring at the very same thing. 'I expected more from you.'

'It's not that—' the guard tried to justify.

'No, of course not,' Khalif interrupted with a half laugh, 'because your wife would have your balls if—'

'No, Your Highness, it's really not that... She's been there for an hour.'

'And?' Khalif demanded.

'No, she's been *there*, in front of *that painting*, for an hour,' Jamal clarified.

'Oh.'

Khalif returned his attention to the monitor, where the tourist still stood in front of the painting of Hātem Al Azhar, his great-great-great-grandfather. He frowned, wondering what it was about the painting that had enthralled her for *an hour*. Given that, on average, it took one harassed school teacher to ferry a group of unfocused seven-year-olds a total of fifty-four minutes through the first section of the exhibition on the history of Duratra—a fact he knew only too well since his father had deemed it necessary for him to spend his teenage summers working at the exhibition in an attempt to instil in him a respect for their country's history and an awareness of the importance of tourism. Instead, all it had done was broaden his pick-up lines to include several more international languages. That aside, it *did* seem strange that this tourist had spent so much time in front of one painting.

He felt a prickle of awareness across his skin as he realised that the men had regrouped around the same monitor as if drawn by a siren call. He turned to stare at them until they moved out of his personal space, some clearing throats and others grabbing pens to make useless notes on unnecessary bits of paper.

Khalif gave her one last look, trying to ignore the twinge of disappointment as he took his leave. At one time she would have been just his type.

* * *

Star looked up at the large painting of the man who had ruled Duratra over one hundred and fifty years ago and smiled. The patrician nose was broad and noble, the jaw line masterful. Even allowing for artistic integrity, Star was thrilled to see the handsome image of the man Catherine Soames had met after her doomed love affair with Benoit Chalendar.

She felt as if she could get lost staring into the deep penetrating eyes of her great-great-great-grandmother's second love, until the security guard she'd met when she first entered the exhibition that morning cleared his throat. She turned and saw him gesture slightly to the clock on the wall.

'Wahed, I'm so sorry. I had no idea that so much time had passed!' She was shocked and annoyed with herself for being such an imposition. The exhibition should have closed fifteen minutes ago and Wahed had been so helpful showing her around earlier. She smiled her brightest and most sincere smile, leaving the room just before she could catch the blush that rose to his cheeks, and drifted towards the exit.

Her first day hadn't been a failure *exactly*, she thought as she made her way towards the exit. *Yes*, they were short on time, Star admitted to herself, but the ache in her heart from a sadly now familiar panic would help absolutely no one, certainly not her mother.

The day after Skye had flown to Costa Rica, Summer had decoded the second part of the hidden messages Catherine had left in her private journals to reveal a description of a special key that could be found in Duratra. The key would unlock the room where Catherine had hidden the Soames diamonds.

With Skye tracking down the map of the hidden passageways, Star felt with every ounce of her being that finding the key was the final step in finding the jewels. When they did that they would have met the terms of their grandfather's will and they could finally sell the estate and be able to pay for the treatment that would save their mother's life.

On the plane to Duratra, Star had read and reread the stories of Catherine's adventures in the Middle East while travelling with her uncle and his wife. Catherine's father had been convinced that being a companion to her aunt by marriage would keep her out of harm's way until she was ready to marry someone suitable.

Even now, Star smiled at the thought of what Catherine had managed to get up to under the lazy eye of her aunt, of the poignant relationship that had developed between Catherine and Hātem. A smile that slowly fell as she remembered reading of the heartache of the two lovers as they had been forced apart by duty.

But, despite that, after she had returned to England, when Catherine had reached out to Hātem to ask him to make a key of special design, he had created something marvellous: a key that could be separated into two sections that mirrored each other. When joined, they would open a special lock, but when separate they could each be worn on a neck-

lace. He had sent Catherine one half of the key and
the lock, and he—as Catherine had requested—had
kept the other. To Star, the fact that Hātem would
always have a piece of Catherine with him was, as
her sisters mocked her constantly for saying, *so romantic*.

Her fingers went to the chain around her neck,
patting the thick twist beneath the thin material of
her dress, reassuring herself it was still there. Tomorrow, she would leave it in the safe of her hotel
room. But for this first day she'd wanted it with her,
as if perhaps somehow it would draw out its other
half. She'd had no idea of its significance when she'd
first picked up the necklace from amongst the journals in the hidden recess in the library. Only that she
was drawn to it. And now she couldn't help but feel
a little as if it had been fate.

As Star made her way down the brightly lit corridors of the exhibition halls, weaving around obstacles
with unseeing eyes, even she had to concede that she
might have become a little carried away by the romance of another star-crossed love affair involving
her ancestor, but she would never regret coming to
Duratra, no matter what.

She had already fallen half in love with the bustling, incredible, beautiful city. In the fifteen-minute
walk between her hotel and the palace that morning
she had been surrounded by impossibly tall apartment buildings and office complexes and passed
sprawling open-air markets before reaching the ancient stone structure of the palace in Duratra's capi-

tal, Burami. It was a clash of modern and ancient, as sleek electric cars glided silently down tiny cobbled streets and animals carried food, silks and spices to stalls that also sold the latest mobile phones and music players.

Star marvelled at the feeling that she was walking in both the past and the present—that her steps filled the footprints left behind by Catherine herself. And whether that worked to add a layer of magic and mysticism to the mundane, Star wasn't sure that she minded because of how complete and whole that sense of interconnectivity made her feel. Not that she'd say so out loud, and certainly not to her sisters, who would laugh at her when they didn't think she could hear.

So, despite the fact that she hadn't managed to find any reference to Catherine's necklace, Star wasn't discouraged. Instead, she was looking forward to seeing Burami at night and was even more eager to return tomorrow for the next section of the exhibition.

She was so lost in her train of thought that she walked straight into something tall, broad, not very soft but most definitely clothed. And breathing.

'Oh, I'm so sorry. Really, so—' She started apologising before she looked up, which was probably a good thing because her words were cut short by just one glimpse of the impossibly handsome man staring down at her as if he was more surprised than she was.

Star immediately pulled her eyes from his as if somehow that could stop the searing heat flashing over her skin. She blinked a few times, hoping that would clear whatever had come over her. If she'd been asked in that moment what he looked like, she'd not have been able to answer for all the world. But something instinctual told her that she would have known if he'd been within one hundred feet of her. Even now she felt it, the waves of something more... physical than sight. More visceral.

Still unwilling to meet his gaze, and genuinely concerned about the power he seemed to have over her body, she tried to extract herself from the situation. 'I really am sorry. I genuinely didn't see you there, which does seem a little implausible given...' at this point her hand entered the fray and gestured to the rather large entirety of him '...all that. You see, I get a little lost in my thoughts sometimes,' she tried to explain, finally daring to lift her eyes. 'I'm Star and...' she resisted the need to look away and ignored the burning in her cheeks '...I'm clearly assuming that you speak English, which suddenly feels quite conceited.'

The almost minuscule twitch at the corner of his lips made her think that he might be smiling at her rambling and Star sighed in relief at the indication that he at least seemed to understand what she was saying. 'I hadn't meant to be this late, or get this lost. I was in the exhibition,' she said, looking behind her and frowning, unable to recognise the corridor she was in, 'and time just...' She bit her lip, shrugging, wondering why he hadn't interrupted her yet. Her sisters would have. The teachers she worked with would have smiled vaguely and just pressed on past her. But he was still there. She knew this because she was now staring fixedly at his chest, debating whether Dickens had been onto something with the whole spontaneous combustion thing.

But the longer he stood there, not saying anything, the more aware she became of...*him*. This was silly. Maybe she was overreacting.

'Star...'

Her name on his lips drew her eyes upward like a magnet and she was immediately struck by the sheer force of his gaze.

Nope.

She had *not* been overreacting. He was looking at her as if she had the answer to an unspoken question. She felt as if he were searching for something within her.

She shook her head, severing the strange connection, and slapped him gently on the arm. 'You *do* speak English,' she chided, peering over his shoulder for the exit and missing the look of absolute and complete shock that had entered the man's eyes, which he'd managed to mask by the time she returned her attention to him. 'You had me going there for a moment.'

'Sir—'

Star turned in time to see Wahed, his eyes bright and his cheeks red, rushing towards them, making Star think that she really had overstayed her welcome.

'Wahed, I'm sorry. I took a wrong turn and bumped into...' She turned back towards the man she had bumped into, deciding it was safer to look somewhere around the area of his left shoulder. And then became slightly distracted by the way his suit jacket fitted perfectly to the—

'Kal.'

She jerked her eyes to his briefly, before turning back to Wahed. 'Kal. Yes. Right. As I was saying, I got a bit turned around and couldn't find the exit, but I can see it now,' she said, spotting a green sign with white writing and an arrow that she could only presume to be a sign pointing to the exit.

Looping her arm through the arm of the man mountain she had crashed into, she determinedly dragged him with her as she made her way to the exit. She could *not* afford to get herself barred from the exhibition and, to avoid any more trouble, she was removing herself and this other tourist from the premises ASAP.

'Come on, Kal,' she said, passing Wahed, who looked a little as if he were about to explode.

Khalif was so busy processing the fact that this woman knew the first name of his security guard, whilst simultaneously calculating the number of royal codes of etiquette she had broken simply by touching him, that he did nothing to stop her from marching him halfway towards the fire exit that was for staff use only. But, even if he hadn't been, Khalif could not be one hundred per cent sure that he would have dislodged her tiny pale hand from his elbow. It was so small and delicate he feared he might break it.

He was still staring at it as they drew closer to Wahed, as if by studying the delicate fingers splayed across his forearm a second longer he'd be able to identify just why it was that something so small was sending enough electric currents across his skin to light the city of Burami for a month. And that was when he realised that it was the first physical contact he'd had with another person in nearly six weeks.

Obviously Khalif had not been under the naïve impression that he'd be able to continue his romantic liaisons while being first in line to the throne, but he'd not expected the strange social distancing effect the position would hold. Where once he'd have been able to slap Jamal on the back as he'd mocked him about his wife, now there was the painfully awkward renegotiation of power that still didn't quite sit right with him. And where once he'd have been more than able to remove the tiny pale hand from his elbow, now he seemed entirely incapable.

Wahed hadn't taken his eyes from Khalif, eyes that had grown rounder and wider the closer they came, sweat breaking out on the man's forehead as he clearly tried to figure out how to get his country's Prince out of the hands of this flame-haired pixie-sized bombshell.

'Goodnight, Wahed,' Star said as they drew level. 'I'll see you tomorrow,' she stated.

The look of panic increased on Wahed's features and Khalif had to look away in case he laughed and shamed the man even more.

'Tomorrow?' the guard asked weakly.

'Oh, yes, I've only covered the first part of the exhibition. I have three more parts to explore over the next three days,' she said, throwing the words over her shoulder.

'You're going to explore the exhibition for three more days…?'

Khalif couldn't be sure, but he was half convinced he'd heard an actual whimper from Wahed, who was now staring after them as Star continued to guide him towards the exit.

Unable to help it any more, Khalif allowed the tug on his lips to form a full grin and his chest filled with the need to laugh. It bubbled up, filling his lungs and pushing outwards, and he felt lighter than he had in weeks. Months even. Years… The thought was a pin pressed into a balloon as he realised it was how he had felt before. Before his brother had died.

'Did you like it?' she asked, having turned around, looking up at him and squinting in the late afternoon sun. She'd managed to get them out into the staff courtyard, where he saw Jamal peering at them through the window of the security suite.

'Like what?' he said, shaking his head to Jamal to signal that he didn't need their help.

'The exhibition,' she said, laughing again, as if she were half laughing at him and half with him. That sound, so light, so carefree, caught him like a physical blow. He was almost jealous of it. Her hand was still at the crook of his arm and he knew that he really needed to remove it, but he just couldn't bring himself to yet.

'Well, I don't want to give anything away. You still have quite a bit to cover.'

Rather than being disappointed by his answer, she seemed excited.

'Perfect! Please don't. I like surprises.'

Her face, upturned to the lazy yellow lowering sun, was a picture. Despite the expectation of green suggested by the red hair that was still just about tucked behind her headscarf, her eyes were blue—the dark blue of dusk.

'Star,' he said, understanding dawning on him.

'Yes?'

'No, sorry. I…'

I am never tongue-tied.

Pull. Yourself. Together.

'It's an unusual name,' he clarified.

She looked at him as if she could tell that wasn't what he'd intended to say. As if she could somehow sense things about him that he didn't want to share. That strange dusky blue of her irises seemed almost prescient. The dusting of freckles across her nose fanned out over her cheeks as if she'd been flecked with gold. He found himself leaning down towards her as if subconsciously trying to take a closer look, as if he was trying to count the freckles, as if there was something he was trying to work out about her but didn't know what.

'Yes. Even in England. And Kal?'

'It's…an old nickname.' It had only been used by his brother and Samira. He'd not said it or heard it for three years.

If she'd noticed that he hadn't answered her implied question and revealed the whole of his name she didn't seem offended by it. She turned to look beyond the railings surrounding the staff exit to the palace and frowned.

'I think perhaps this wasn't the exit,' she said as she finally let go of his arm and took a step towards the road that ran the length of the capital city.

'Do you know where you're going?' he asked. There was no way he could leave her in the middle of Burami—she seemed entirely capable of bringing about some kind of massive accident that would be sure to bring his country to a grinding halt for months.

She raised her hand to her eyes and looked out beyond the railings. He followed the direction of her gaze and clenched his jaw. In the distance he could see his father's sleek black motorcade making its way back to the palace and he felt the tightening of the steel bands of duty around his wrists.

'Yes. I can see the café there on the corner. That's the road my hotel is on. It's a...' She turned to look up at him. 'It's a nice café. If you'd...' She shrugged as if hedging her bets as to whether to finish the sentence or not.

He looked away, hiding just how much he wanted to say yes, from both her and himself. He smiled sadly and by the time his gaze had returned to those eyes understanding had dawned in them. 'Please take a car to your hotel. You are safe in Duratra. But perhaps Duratra is not safe from you,' he said. It was meant to be a tease, a light exchange before he left, but it had come out differently. It had been a warning from a man who was the embodiment of his country.

Dusk descended in her eyes and for a moment it was as if she had understood. And then the smile was back in place, the one that had hypnotised all the palace staff she had encountered—and he could see why.

She nodded and he watched her walk away, just as a gust of wind pressed the white-and-green-striped dress against the back of her legs, causing an explosion of erotic thoughts until Khalif's father's car turned the corner and grim reality intruded.

CHAPTER TWO

FOR WHAT FELT like the hundredth time that day, Star forced herself to reread the English translation of the description of how Duratra had been one of the largest academic centres during the height of the Ottoman Empire. But she just couldn't concentrate. Instead of finding clues or traces of Catherine or the necklace within the paintings and history of this beautiful country, she was hoping to see Kal—despite being aware of how unlikely it was.

She'd gone over and over their encounter in minute detail from the moment she'd left him in the courtyard until her latest breath. Although she'd initially thought him a tourist like her, she now thought that perhaps he worked at the palace. While she'd not wanted to give Wahed a reason to ban her from the palace exhibition, she now wondered if Wahed and Kal knew each other. Not that she'd asked the security guard when she'd seen him that morning.

No, sometimes it was better not to know, because this way she could imagine him as the undercover Prince of a neighbouring kingdom, here on a top-secret mission. Perhaps he was trying to correct some great wrong and he would need her help escaping Burami and together they could ride off into the desert and…

And then she laughed out loud at herself, not noticing how she had startled the other people in the very quiet room. She had never ridden a horse and couldn't imagine that riding bareback would be comfortable. But being in his arms? Once again, Star felt herself flush from head to toe. Looking at him had been like looking at the sun. Heat. All-consuming heat that she'd had absolutely no control over whatsoever.

No one had ever had that effect on her. She'd read about it so many times but had honestly thought it just a metaphor. She'd wondered at it, had brought out the memory of him standing there, searching her face, her eyes and *whoomph!* Head to toe. Every time. Even now she felt that pink heat stain her cheeks and, lost in her own world, fanned her face, nearly taking out a large German tourist with her elbow.

As she moved further into the room, golden glints and rich magentas caught her eye and she came to stand before a tapestry that took up nearly the entire length of the room. It was exquisite in detail, despite the clear effects of age, inscriptions flowing beneath the images, and instead of fighting for space at the explanatory plaque, Star wanted to stand back. Take it in, just as it was.

She wondered whether Catherine had ever seen

this, whether she had stood looking at it, searching for meaning the way that Kal seemed to have searched her eyes. She forced her mind away from him and onto the fact that she was on the second day of her search.

Time was running out for Star to prove to her sisters that she could play her part, that she could travel to the other side of the world without needing their support, protection or concern. Why couldn't her sisters trust her when she regularly and successfully managed to take care of a class of thirty seven-year-olds?

She and Summer had decided that if there was no sign of the necklace she would return to Norfolk no matter what. From there, the sisters would decide together what to do next. If any more travel was needed, they would apply to Mr Beamish, the estate's lawyer, and he—as stipulated in the will—would fund whatever expenses were needed during the two-month period. Well, one month and just over one week now, Star thought, doing the maths.

Thirty-eight days. Her heart began to pound in her chest. It was the bass-line that beat beneath the layer of faith and hope she held in her heart. Constant, exhausting. She hated it and needed it. Because while that deep thrum in her heart was there, so was her mother, so was the chance that she'd be able to find the necklace. That she and her sisters would be able to find the diamonds, sell the estate and access the medical treatment Mariam Soames needed…and Star wouldn't lose her only living parent.

A flash went off, slicing through the rising panic in Star's chest, and Wahed crossed the room to speak to the German tourist's wife, who had clearly ignored the sign that said no photography. Before the argument could get heated, Star made her way back out of the room to one of the larger areas, looking for somewhere she could…breathe.

She was trying to find her way out when the hairs on her arms lifted and heat broke out across the back of her neck. She paused, eyes closed, just feeling her way through that moment. Her pulse thudded in her ears for such a different reason than just seconds before, and when she opened her eyes and saw a figure marching down the corridor ahead of her, her heart raced. Instead of continuing down the hallway, he cut to the left and entered the beautiful green courtyard on the other side of the large glass wall that separated the corridor from the exhibition space.

Star placed a hand gently against the glass, the smooth cold surface sucking the heat from her skin. It was one thing to bump into a man and a whole other thing to approach him. She should go back to the public area of the exhibition. She should absolutely do that.

Khalif leaned back against the wooden bench, feeling the sun on his face, eyes closed, remembering the way that Star had done something similar yesterday. Why couldn't he get her out of his head? All the way through the council update with Reza, Duratra's Prime Minister.

'If I didn't know better,' he'd joked, 'I'd ask who she was.'

Khalif's grunted reply had been as non-committal as he got with his oldest friend.

All that morning he'd caught himself looking at his arm where her hand had been, remembering the way that her laugh had cut through him, recalling his last sight of her. It didn't help that he knew she was here. Somewhere in the exhibition. It was as if his body had been in a heightened state ever since he'd reached the lower level of the palace and he bit back a curse. He was worse than an untried school-boy, lusting over his first crush.

Until the last hour, during a meeting with the Secretary of State for His Majesty Sheikh Abbad Al Jabbal. Samira's father had found fault with nearly every suggestion that the team had put to him. Not that Khalif could blame him. He knew they still hadn't come up with the best way to honour their loss. When it came down to it, there certainly wasn't a *right* way. There was nothing right about the deaths of his brother and sister-in-law, so why should their memorial be? Khalif braced himself against a shock-wave of grief that sent out invisible ripples of in-comprehension and pain, refusing to bend to it, to go under.

'Funny meeting you here.'

Khalif's eyes shot open and he stared at Star, standing in the centre of the courtyard as if she'd just magically appeared.

'How did you...?' His words trailed off as he saw

the commotion gathering on the other side of the glass at the corner of the east wing. Several dark-suited guards were reaching for their weapons, ready to storm the courtyard. He threw a glare their way, wondering how on earth this English girl had slipped undetected past his usually highly efficient body-guards. He held his hand out to stop them intruding and turned back to Star, who was still looking up at him, thankfully having missed the exchange.

'I hope that's okay… I just… I saw you and you looked…' She shrugged, not quite finishing her sentence.

She looked around the space, giving him time to take in the dark blue cotton headscarf, grey floor-length skirt and white top she was wearing beneath the same denim jacket, so very different to the glitz and glamour he'd seen throughout Europe's most fashionable destinations. But, instinctively, he knew that hers was the face he would remember in years to come. Her bangles clinked slightly as she moved forward to smell one of the plants in the giant urn in the centre of the courtyard.

As he listened to her inhale, he forced his eyes away from her and instead took in the scene he'd been blind to until she'd appeared. Four separate areas were full of thick green foliage and he would always associate this courtyard with the oasis his family used to visit in the desert.

'…hungry.'

'Excuse me?' he asked, dragging his eyes and awareness back to Star.

'You looked hungry,' she replied with a smile.

'Really?' he asked, surprised.

'Aren't you?'

'Well, yes, but...'

Star sat down beside him and began to unpack the large canvas bag she'd had slung over her shoulder. An impressive glass-bottomed lunch box landed between them on the bench. A flask of something was soon propped up against it, while she passed him a smaller box with the instruction, 'Can you open that?'

He found himself once again staring blankly at her before recovering and doing as she'd asked, the traces of yesterday's smile returning to his lips. It had been so long since someone treated him like an equal, he was determined not to break the spell.

He lifted the lid from the box she'd handed him and the smell of parsley and coriander and rich tomato sauce hit him hard, making his mouth water. He stared at the *mahshi* in wonder.

'Where on earth did you get this?'

'Oh, the chef at my hotel,' she replied, reaching over to take one of the courgettes stuffed with rice and vegetables. 'He promised that he didn't mind making it for me.'

'Of course he didn't,' Khalif replied, thinking that she could probably talk the birds down from the sky as easily as getting a chef to make her whatever she wanted. He bit into the courgette he'd helped himself to and groaned. Hats off to the chef. He really hadn't realised how hungry he was until she'd asked.

'We were talking last night and he was telling me about…'

He let her voice trail over him as he cast an eye back to where the security detail had come up against Amin, who seemed almost apoplectic that he'd taken food from a stranger. Khalif didn't really know what he was so angry about. Amin would probably prefer it if there *was* poison in the food. That way he'd be able to fulfil his royal duties without the hindrance he clearly saw Khalif as being.

He cast an eye back to Star, still talking but looking ahead of her and gesturing expressively with her hands, clearly missing the way that the thick tomato sauce was dripping perilously close to his trousers. Khalif supposed that she could be a spy sent to poison him—if it hadn't been for the fact that there had been no threats to either the country or the royal family in over one hundred years. Faizan's helicopter crash had been investigated by both Duratra and an international investigative team and both had confirmed that a mechanical fault was to blame. Accidental death. Somehow the term seemed cruel, especially for the twin daughters he and Samira had left behind.

'And so, after a few failed attempts, it was decided I should probably leave it to the professionals. But it's so delicious I just couldn't refuse,' she said, handing him a piece of flatbread and the little porcelain pot of hummus. She'd managed to convince the chef to make her a packed lunch with breakable china? He stared between the little pot and the redhead, who seemed utterly oblivious to the impact that she had on those around her. And suddenly he envied her that. No second-guessing and doubting the impact of every single move, look, step, decision or indecision. As he scooped some of the hummus topped with beautiful pink pearls of pomegranate and flecks of paprika onto the flatbread, he saw his assistant throw his hands up in the air and as the taste exploded on his tongue Khalif decided that frustrating his particularly sanctimonious assistant was a small victory in an otherwise complete failure of a day.

'That was the best *mahshi* I've ever had,' she sighed, leaning back against the wooden bench.

Khalif laughed. 'Had a lot of *mahshi*, have you?'

Star nodded, her smile lighting up eyes that were a touch lighter than they had been yesterday. 'Yup. My mum, she's…some would call her *alternative*,' she said in a half whisper, as if confessing some great sin. 'But she travelled a lot when she was younger and that influenced her cooking. We're all vegetarian so we do a lot of cooking ourselves. That, and we didn't have a great deal of money growing up,' she announced without the resentment that usually weighed down such a statement.

'What do they do? Your parents,' he clarified, unable to resist going in for one last mouthful of the hummus.

She should have known it was coming. Usually she could feel it building in a conversation, but with Kal it had taken her by surprise so she hadn't been ready for the swift pain that nicked her heart. 'My father died when I was a few months old, but he was a carpenter.' She rubbed her hands unconsciously, as she often did when she thought about her father, imagining the calluses on his hands that her mother had told her about.

'That must have been very hard. I am sorry for the loss you have felt.'

Rather than shy away, this time she wanted to feel the burn, the flame that was lit when Kal looked at her, even if she felt guilty for welcoming it to avoid that ache, but instead what she found in his eyes... Her heartbeat thumped once heavily in sympathy.

'And I am sorry for yours.'

He frowned, his head already beginning to shake, but she stopped him with her hand on his arm.

'I'm sorry if that was intrusive. I don't know who or...' she trailed off '...but I can tell.'

Kal nodded once. It was an acceptance of her offered comfort, but a definite end to the moment. Seizing the threads of the earlier conversation and definitely not ready for him to leave just yet, she pressed on. 'My mother has done lots over the years, but currently she's into candle magic.'

She folded her lips between her teeth, waiting for the inevitable reaction.

'Wait...candle what?'

'Magic. It keeps her happy and there is harm to none, so...'

'Alternative, huh?' he said, wiping his hands on the napkin she'd found tucked beneath the boxes, and she would have replied had she not been distracted by the way he smoothed the cloth across his skin.

'You're the youngest?'

She turned to him, curious as to how he knew that she had siblings.

'You said "we're all" and you don't strike me as an only child,' he explained.

'I'm the middle. Skye is older, and Summer is younger.'

'And do they all have…?' He waved his hand towards a strand of her hair that had come loose from her headscarf.

Laughing, she tucked it back safely behind the stretchy jersey. 'No, just me. Skye's hair is a dark brown and Summer's is cornfield blonde.' She could see his mind working, trying to do the maths, and took pity on him. 'Technically they're my half-sisters. But I'd never call them that.'

'Different fathers?'

She could tell that he was trying to keep his tone neutral and she appreciated it. Not everyone was that considerate. 'It certainly drew a lot of unwanted attention and judgement when we were younger, and a *lot* of stares.' Her sisters thought she hadn't noticed, but she had. Long before her grandparents had made their feelings known, Star had been aware of the way neighbours and some of the school parents and, in turn, their children had treated them, judged them, excluded them.

'Ahh.'

She cocked her head to look at him, as if the different angle would reveal more than he'd done already. 'You know how that feels?'

'A little,' he admitted. 'Different reason though.'

Star looked him up and down, noticing the sharp cut to his clothes, the thick, heavy gold watch at his wrist, the expensive sunglasses sticking out of his pocket and smiled kindly. 'Rich parents?'

'Something like that.'

'Rich *and* powerful. I *am* impressed,' she assumed. He barked out a laugh and she felt as if she'd won something precious. 'Children can be unintentionally cruel,' she said, thinking of the young charges she loved working with.

She sighed heavily, feeling very far away from her teaching assistant's job in the New Forest, and allowed herself a moment to bask in the sun. The warmth of it on her face, the feeling of contentment was tinged with a little something more. She hadn't realised how much of a relief it was to talk to someone. Okay, so she might have been talking *at* him, but still. Without opening her eyes, she drew his image to her mind, surprised how easily it came after the difficulties of yesterday. She mentally reached out to trace the strong jaw line shadowed with a close-cropped beard, imagining the feeling of him releasing the tension that she had seen when talking about loss. Unable to help the way her thumb stretched out to press against the plush lower lip, fire burning her thumb and core. The skin on her cheeks began to tingle, as if she had been stroked, and she leaned her head into the invisible touch, opening her eyes to find Kal staring at her, sending a jolt of pure lightning to her heart.

But, rather than turn away, embarrassed at being caught staring, he seemed to focus only more intently now that her eyes were open. A moment that she would hold to her as more precious than any romance book and she wondered for just a second if he might kiss her. Then he blinked and the haze of desire was banked.

'Where have you reached in the exhibition?'

She took a breath and grounded herself, taking a second to focus enough to remember where she had been. 'The attempted occupation by the Ottomans.'

'Ah. A Particularly violent and difficult period.'

'I should think so too. His Majesty Sheikh Omar could hardly allow the kidnap of his daughter to go unpunished.'

No, he could not, Khalif echoed silently, wondering what Star would think if she knew that, rather than being kidnapped, the family rumour was that Omar's daughter had run off of her own volition to be with a Turkish prince and unwittingly nearly started a war.

'And tomorrow?' He cursed the question that had fallen from his lips before he'd had time to think it through. He really shouldn't care what she had planned for tomorrow.

Star smiled excitedly and it rivalled the sun. 'Tomorrow is the Fatimid period.'

'History interests you?' he asked, unable to curb his curiosity.

'Yes, I like to see how everything comes together. How one generation impacts another,' she said, the blue in her irises deepening.

'What are you looking for?'

'Who said I was looking for something?' she asked a little too quickly and his eyes narrowed at the shift in her tone. He waited her out and, as expected, she clarified. The English were very predictable. 'Research.'

'For?'

'A family thing.'

And then, before he could stop her, she'd leaned over, clasped his wrist, turned it in her hand and read the time on his watch. It was not sensual, no trace of practised flirtation, it was perfunctory and over in a matter of seconds, but those seconds had branded him like molten metal.

'I have to get back. I need to find out what happened to His Majesty Sheikh Omar's daughter before it closes for the day,' and, before he could say goodbye, she'd slipped through the doorway, passed the seven large suited men, none of whom could take their eyes off her, and disappeared into the exhibition.

That night, Star returned to the hotel after discovering that Omar's daughter had been forced to marry a Turkish prince and felt the sting of injustice of a marriage not born from love. She sighed, thinking of Catherine's marriage to her horrible cousin, a man whose sole interest was property and diamonds.

*He has always coveted them. The estate and
the jewels are almost an obsession for him. And
though society deems him worthy of my hand
in marriage, I do not deem him worthy of them.
They are the only part of the estate entailed
to the female line and I will keep it that way.*

She had read Summer's translations of the coded
messages over and over again since they had first
found them buried within the pages of her journals. For Catherine, Omar's daughter and even
her own mother, marriage had been nothing more
than a shackle. But...for her? Secretly, she'd always
thought that she'd quite like to be married. To have
a wedding and stand beside someone who told the
world how much she was loved. To be claimed pub-
licly, completely. And though she'd never admit it to
her mother, Star couldn't help but wonder if her life
might have been different had her parents married
before he'd died, whether that might have changed
the minds and attitudes of her grandparents, whether
they could have been a positive part of her life rather
than...

Star cut off that train of thought before it could
take hold, turning instead to wonder if she should
call Skye in Costa Rica. She was halfway through
her time in Duratra and she was beginning to lose
the confidence that she'd arrived with. She had only
two days left and it was getting harder and harder to
ignore the inner voice wanting to know what would
happen if she didn't find the necklace, and what that

could mean for her mother. But if she admitted as much to Skye, she would only tell her to go home and Star wasn't ready to hear that. She could call Summer in Norfolk, but she didn't want to hear her sister's gentle voice reassuring her that it was okay, that it had always been a long shot to send her to search for the necklace.

Star drew air into her lungs to cover the hurt and turned in the bed onto her side, closing her eyes to see Kal's staring back at her, eyes crinkled with the hint of that enigmatic smile and the light of… interest? Was that what she saw in his gaze? Was that what made her heart beat faster? What made her feel a little sick in her stomach at the thought of seeing him tomorrow, but feel even worse at the thought of not?

Two days, she reminded herself, she had two days. Though this time when she delved into what it was that made her heart beat like specks of sand dropping through an hour glass, it wasn't thoughts of Kal, but the fear of not finding the necklace.

After lunch in the courtyard, and after thoroughly reprimanding a slightly sceptical security detail, Khalif had surprised himself by managing to make some headway in the afternoon. He'd looked for her as he'd left the palace, but Wahed had informed him that Star had already left. Yet knowing that she'd be there the following day made him feel…as if he had something to look forward to.

So it had been a shock to discover that the depth

of his reaction to *not* seeing her the next day was nothing short of painful. A sense of panic had risen within him. Panic that he'd never see her again, never find out what she was looking for, never see the accidental chaos that seemed to follow in her wake, never feel that sense of inexplicable peace he'd found in her company... He'd caught himself looking down corridors, purposely walking past the security suite to see if the guards were watching her again. Tempted, so very tempted to ask if they had seen her.

By the time he'd reached the afternoon of what he knew to be her last day at the exhibition, he'd convinced himself that such an extreme reaction indicated that it could only be a good thing that she was gone from his life. What did he think he could do if he saw her again anyway? Only that thought sent up a cascade of sensual imagery that he shut down before it could cut him off at the knees. He was no longer able to indulge in such whims. There was a plan. In three years, when he had proved himself the steady hand that would provide for his country until his nieces came of age, then a suitable bride would be found. And that suitable bride would *not* have flame-coloured hair and eyes so dark blue they were almost regal.

So as he left his office that evening he was halfway through congratulating himself for having survived a temptation called Star when he came to an abrupt halt. The gods were either laughing or punishing him.

Things might have been different if he had found

her anywhere else in the palace. But Star had found the one spot that was sure to pack an emotional punch. The three steps looked deeply insignificant, and probably would have been to anyone else. But to Khalif they were painfully familiar.

He had spent just over seven hundred hours waiting for his father and brother on those steps. Despite having been largely excluded from the lessons Faizan had been required to have from their father on matters ranging from governance and international policy to languages and business studies, he'd thought he could wait them out. And his stubborn streak had lasted for two hours, every day for an entire year.

In that moment he knew what he should do—and what he shouldn't. His Highness Sheikh Khalif Al Azhar walked on, past the security suite, through the exit of the palace and towards his evening appointment with Duratra's council.

Kal, however, stood before a beautiful woman and heaved a sigh of relief.

'You know it all turned out okay in the end,' he said as he stood between her and the sun, her body enshrouded by his shadow. She looked up at him with huge ocean-blue eyes. 'That's the problem with looking at the history of a country backwards. Really you should have started with the Umayyad period, it's especially beautiful, given the metalwork and textiles.'

The smile that spread across her features chased the watery sparkle from her eyes. 'Perhaps you should have been my tour guide.'

'I would have been honoured,' he replied, surprised by the sincerity in his tone. 'You are leaving?'

'Tomorrow.'

'And you don't want to go?' he asked, wondering why that seemed to make her sad.

Her smile wavered. 'I want to see my sisters, and my mother, but... I didn't find what I was looking for.'

'Anything I can help with?'

He would have sworn on his crown that he felt the weight of her sigh. 'No, sadly not.' And he would have given it away to lighten that load.

'So, what are you going to do with your last few hours in Duratra?'

The shrug that barely moved her shoulders an inch was enough to drive him to action. He liked the tumble and roll of her words, the way they wound through his mind, treading down a path to wherever they wanted to go.

All Star could think of was the necklace. She had genuinely thought that she'd find it, and to not have found a trace or clue as to where it might be was devastating. She had let her sisters down. And, worse than that, her mother... She felt a wave of hurt crash over her anew, breaking out in a hot sweat on her neck and down her spine. She'd just got off the phone with Summer. And she'd meant to tell her, intended to explain that she would be coming home empty-handed, but Summer had been full of excitement with the news that Skye had found the map.

Star's phone was full of the pictures Summer had forwarded with promises that she would work on the plans to find where on the map the Soames diamonds were located. And at the end she had asked, hopeful for the first time since Star had got on the plane to Duratra, whether she might have located the necklace. A hope that Star had been unable to respond to. She had proved them right—that she couldn't be trusted to locate the necklace. How silly was she, to think that she could have done this alone?

All she wanted to do was stop for a moment. To not have to think, or fear, or worry. And although Kal had extended an offer of sorts, she'd sensed how torn he was. He probably had something to rush off to. And she certainly didn't want another person having to look out for her.

'Is there anything you haven't seen? That you wanted to?'

'Well, I've spent all my time here, so—'

'Wait, you've not seen anything of Burami?' he demanded, full of not *completely* mock outrage that distracted her heart just a little. Perhaps for the evening, rather than being a daughter hoping to save her mother, she could just be a tourist on her last evening in Duratra?

'Not unless it was between the hotel and the exhibition at the palace,' she replied.

'We can't have that.'

She couldn't help but laugh at his conviction. 'My flight is tomorrow—how much can you show me before then?'

'I can show you it all.'

He held out his hand and while she couldn't explain it, was helpless even to resist, Star felt as if she were Alice about to fall down the rabbit hole.

CHAPTER THREE

HAVING BEEN PROMISED the opportunity to see Burami, Star was surprised when, instead of turning out towards the main road, Kal led her back to the palace. The surprise lasted only a moment. She was distracted by the way sparks flew from where his palm pressed against hers, encompassing it, making her feel comforted in a way just seconds ago she'd not thought possible.

They came to a corner and Kal pulled up short before turning back to her, holding a finger to his lips.

Star folded her own lips between her teeth, but still a smile pulled at the edges of her mouth. 'Are we sneaking into the palace?' she whispered to him.

'Yes,' he replied, peering around the corner to see if the coast was clear.

'You do this often?' She couldn't keep the laugh from her voice this time.

He looked at her, eyes blazing with something a little more than humour. 'More than you'd think,' he replied cryptically and drew her back into the hallway.

They'd made it about four feet towards the staircase Kal seemed to be heading for when they heard the hushed voices of two guards. Eyes wide and heart pounding in her chest, Star didn't know whether to laugh or scream in fright. Either way she was pretty sure that she'd squeaked when Kal spun her round, pressing her back against a wall, arms braced either side of her head, and covered her with his body.

Star wasn't laughing now. They were staring at each other as if that alone would keep them invisible from the palace guards. This close, she could see that there were flecks of gold in the rich espresso depths of his eyes, she could almost taste the smoky sweetness of the breath that fanned gently against her skin. She dared herself to inhale the scent of him, woodsy, masculine, brought to her from the heat of his body. In her peripheral vision she could see the flicker of his pulse just beneath his jaw, and shockingly she wanted to place her palm there, to feel it beat in time with her own.

His head dipped ever so slightly towards her, his nostrils flaring ever so slightly, his inhale expanding to close the space between their chests from inches to millimetres. Beneath the voices, she could hear footsteps coming closer and closer. She pressed into the wall as if that would make her and Kal invisible, adrenaline reaching deeper and deeper into her bloodstream. What would happen if they got caught? Her eyes flew to his, her mouth opening just slightly as if ready to ask the question when she felt the pad of his thumb against her lower lip, just as she'd once imagined doing to him. The gesture she was sure was intended to stop her words, not her heart, but that was the effect.

She wanted to bite down on his thumb, to anchor it there before he could remove it and in an instant any fear was completely consumed by exhilaration. She'd never felt like it before. She could just hear the sound of footsteps over the pounding of her pulse in her ears, and she couldn't resist courting danger.

'Are we going to get into trouble?' she whispered against the pad of his thumb, instantly gratified when she saw his pupils flare.

'No,' he whispered back with an arrogance that was utterly devastating.

The footsteps receded, and Khalif waited until there was complete silence in the corridor. Not because he couldn't move, he sternly assured himself, but because he was waiting until the coast was clear.

He walked on into the hallway, leading Star by the hand, his heart racing, half hoping someone would stop him, half hoping they wouldn't. This was ridiculous. And certainly the first time he'd sneaked a woman *into* the palace rather than out of it.

Four feet to the staircase. He could still change his mind. Could still turn back.

Three feet. Her fingers tightened within his hold ever so slightly.

Two feet and he cast one last look up and down the long hallway.

One…

They raced up the stairs as if the guards were still behind them, falling through the door and collapsing on the other side in half relief, half surprise as if they'd not actually expected to get that far.

He watched as Star straightened and turned to look around at the room, wondering what she'd make of the large living space, lined with bookshelves on one side and a large television on the other. The sunken seating area was actually an illusion, the rest of the floor having been built up to allow for the cables and security measures fitted retrospectively to the ancient palace.

'Are we in someone's home?' she asked as she looked between the open-plan kitchenette that he couldn't remember using ever and the glass-fronted sliding doors that led to the balcony.

'It's okay, I know the owner,' he replied, watching her walk towards the view he woke up to every morning.

'I hope they'd be okay with this,' she said as she reached the partly opened door.

'They are,' he assured her, but his answer was lost to her as she slipped through the narrow gap and out onto the stone balcony.

He told himself he was giving her time. That it had nothing to do with having to get himself— who was he kidding?—his *libido* under control. He clenched his fists as if it would erase the feeling of her lip beneath his thumb, her between his arms, the ghost trace of her chest against his... Three years without sex might not kill a man, but one night without Star might just do it.

No. This was for her. He'd seen how devastated she'd looked. Whatever had happened, or not happened, this was about ensuring that she didn't leave with that look haunting her eyes. Instead, he reached for his phone, fired off a message to the palace staff asking for refreshments to be brought to his quarters, and another to Reza cancelling their meeting. He then purposefully put his phone on silent so as not to be subjected to the barrage of queries his oldest friend was sure to launch at him.

Clenching his jaw and ordering himself to behave, Khalif made his way out onto the balcony. He loved the large, deep green palms potted either side of the doors. The ornate, detailed carvings in the red stone balcony were almost as familiar to him as his reflection. Off to the left was a cream awning, under which were a table and chairs, but he knew that Star had seen none of it, her gaze instead glued to the whole of the city stretched out before her, beneath a sky that was turning the beautiful deep blue of early night and littered with stars more dazzling than any diamond.

'Burami?' she asked him without looking away from it.

'A very, *very* large part of it, yes.'

It was absolutely the height of insanity to bring a woman to his palace quarters. It was something the old Khalif had never done. Had he deprived himself of so much that he was at risk of recklessness? And then he remembered the look in her eyes as she'd sat on the steps and knew that he'd have done it all over again just to see her eyes sparkle.

He heard the soft click of his door, movement in the kitchen area that seemed to pass unnoticed by Star and the door closing once again. The last thing Khalif felt was hungry, but somehow it seemed fitting to serve Star food, when she had done the same for him. The memory of her basking in the sun sliced through him, competing with the dusk that surrounded them now and haunted his suite.

He retrieved the platter of food and pitcher of the delicious apricot drink he thought Star would enjoy and returned to the balcony, stopping mid-stride. Star was still looking out at the desert, but her shawl had come loose and now hung from her shoulders, leaving her hair...

Thick streams of long, lazily curling fire danced on the wind, a riot of golds, deep reds and every imaginable shade of umber, flooding his tongue with the taste of turmeric, paprika and cinnamon.

She had removed her denim jacket and the long-sleeved top slashed across her neck, leaving her collarbone and delicate neck exposed to his desire. The blue cotton, regal and powerful, strong and bright enough to stand beside the glory of her hair, made him think of an ancient astrological chart he'd once seen, created from the deepest of blues and golds, rich with circles, lines, arrows and stars, all working to prove some mystical assertion.

Mystical. That was what Star made him feel. And

it hit him like a hammer, as if this moment was something they'd stolen from ancient gods. Something that was just for them.

Star felt him return to the balcony behind her. As if his presence had the power to pull at her like the tide. He was giving her the time she needed. And she *did* need it. She was in the private rooms of a palace looking out at the desert. She'd had to pinch herself *literally*, she thought as she rubbed the pink flesh on her forearm, to know that this wasn't a dream she'd conjured from her imagination.

She knew that she should feel danger, or at least a very real sense of concern. She barely knew Kal, but that felt wrong. She didn't feel as if he were a stranger. He was physically imposing, that was true, but, rather than making her scared, it made her *want*—want in a way that she'd only ever read about before. She had waited all her adult years to find someone who made her feel the things she'd only ever read about and she was leaving tomorrow.

Star might be very used to daydreams, but she wasn't naïve. She knew in reality that there was nothing past tomorrow for her, for them. But did that mean she should walk away from the possibility of what tonight held? She wanted to laugh at herself for being presumptuous, but... Her tongue ran over her lip, where his thumb had pressed so gently to such great effect. A tremor shivered over her skin and down her spine. Surely she wasn't the only one affected by this?

She turned, expecting to find him looking at her, having felt the burn of his gaze across her shoulders and back, but he was busy removing small plates from a tray, two glasses and a pitcher that was rich with condensation from the warm air, despite the dusk falling around them.

'If you'd like something alcoholic…?'

She smiled. 'No, thank you. I'm afraid the Soames women cannot hold their drink.' She reluctantly moved away from the balcony, fearing that she might search the rest of her life for something as beautiful as that view and never find it again.

She slipped behind the table so that she faced the cityscape edged by golden sand that looked like slashes of an abstract painting. He offered her a small glass of the *amar al din* she was going to miss terribly when she returned to England. Her mouth watered in expectation of the sweet, cooling apricot drink, but that was a mere shadow of the explosion of taste that hit her tongue when she drew it to her lips and she was helpless to prevent the moan of sheer delight that fell into the air between them.

'That is *so* good,' she praised unashamedly when she'd finished it. 'I'm going to have to learn how to make it.'

She chanced a look at Kal and veered back to the cityscape before she could be burned further by the heat in eyes heavy-lidded with desire. It scorched the air she breathed, jolted her heartbeat and pulsed and flared through her body.

By the time Star was ready to risk another glance

at him, he had turned towards the desert, staring at the magnificent view as if it were his. Possessively. The way she wanted him to look at her. The way she'd thought, just for a moment, he had.

Blushing, she returned her gaze to the same view, wondering whether Catherine had ever seen it. Star had read over the journals Catherine had written while in Duratra, but she couldn't seem to make the descriptions from then fit with what surrounded her now.

'I wonder what this view would have looked like a hundred years ago,' she half whispered, her voice breaking on the words emerging from a throat half raw from need.

His reply was so long coming she'd begun to wonder whether he'd heard her.

'There was less metal, less chrome and glass, and it was a touch smaller. But one hundred years ago, Burami was still an impressive city.' She watched the way his throat worked as he swallowed, his eyes frowning once again at the view. 'The market you passed on the way to the palace has been there for nearly three hundred years. The skyline would have been not too dissimilar, the silhouette of the minaret and the cross, the turrets of the university. We've always had a mix of cultures, religions—mosques near churches, near synagogues, near temples…all from the very beginning.'

He spoke with a cultural pride that was unfamiliar to her, a sense of personal history she felt that she'd only just begun to experience herself.

'How long has your family been here?'

'Since around then.'

'It must be incredible—that sense of history, that sense of ancestry.'

'That's one way of looking at it. What about you?'

Star sighed. 'We've just discovered a grandfather on our mother's side.'

'And that is what has you upset?'

She resisted the urge to ask how he knew, but it must have been clear on her face. She'd never been very good at hiding her emotions.

'I... I have let my sisters down. My mother,' she said, hating the way that saying it out loud seemed to make it real.

'I know that feeling. With my brother. My father. I wasn't exactly their first choice,' he said before coming to an abrupt halt.

'Choice for what?'

She watched the way his jaw clenched in the darkness of the oncoming night.

'The head of the family business.'

'Really?' she asked, surprised. 'You'd be my choice.'

'You don't know me,' he replied darkly.

It was on the tip of her tongue to deny what he was saying. A half-forgotten song lyric hummed in her head about having loved someone for a thousand years... She shook her head, as if to free the words, but it only sent them scattering. Instead, she caught the words of one of her most loved books.

"It is not time or opportunity that is to determine

*intimacy; it is disposition alone. Seven years would
be insufficient to make some people acquainted with
each other, and seven days are more than enough
for others."'*

He barked a laugh, not *at* her but as if *with* her,
and she felt the appraisal in his eyes even as he made
a joke of it. 'You just happen to have that to hand?'

'It's Austen. She should always be "to hand".'

'Oh, so you're one of those,' he teased.

'If by *"one of those"* you mean someone who
reads romance then yes, I am,' she said with pride.
'And there's absolutely nothing wrong with that.'

He held his hands up in surrender. 'I believe you.'

'No, you're humouring me. That's a very different thing,' she said, not unkindly. 'It's very easy to
be cynical and sharp-edged in this world. It's harder
to have hope, to hold to romance and sentimentality,
to allow the enjoyment of them and the sheer optimism, the faith of it all to sink deep into your bones.'

'Faith?'

'The conviction that love in whatever form con-
quers all.'

'And if I say I don't believe, does it knock a romance reader down dead?'

'No,' she replied, unable to turn to look at him
with the smile on her face. 'But it seriously dimin-
ishes your chances of finding true love.'

There was a beat—of *something*. Something that
passed his eyes and crossed his features before he
barked out another laugh that had both traces of the
humour she sensed in him but also the weight that

pulled at him. And it was that weight she felt partly tied to, as if the deeper it plunged, the more it drew her with it.

She caught herself frowning, not because she was confused by her feelings—she knew what they were, knew that this attraction was something as unique as it was raw. She was confused as to what to do about it. Because, while she didn't need to know the why of it, Kal was holding back and Star just wasn't confident or experienced enough to call it out into the open.

But she didn't want to walk away from it either. She couldn't explain it. But she was sure, more sure than anything she'd ever felt, that if she walked away now, she'd never find this again. This feeling that sank into her skin and delved into her bones, that caught her by the throat and squeezed at her lungs. She wanted to gasp for air, she wanted to gasp for him. Just thinking about the way he made her feel had her pulse quickening, and something deep within her quivering.

The only place he'd ever touched her was the thumbprint he'd left on her bottom lip. She bit down once again, into the soft flesh as if...

'Stop,' he commanded.

'Stop what?' she asked, her words breathless, as she peered at him through the sensual haze that had descended like a fog. The muscle in his clenched jaw flared again and again, as if he was as reluctant as she was to voice this thing between them.

'Stop looking at me like *that*,' he ordered, and

she wondered how she looked at him. She'd thought it was just her who experienced the flashover when their gazes met. The thought that he could feel something similar...

'Tell me,' she whispered, hoping he couldn't detect the begging in her tone, the tremor in her voice as she shuddered under the weight of her attraction to him.

'Tell you what?' he asked, his gaze still clinging to the horizon as if his life depended on it.

'What you see when I look at you like that.'

He bit out something in Arabic that sounded hot and heavy, half-prayer, half-curse. She saw him inhale, drawing oxygen deep into his lungs and expanding his chest, the breadth of it making her palms itch and her fingers tingle. He moved his gaze from the horizon to the table between them, as if having to work his way up to looking at her. And when his eyes finally cut across the space, up to her face to meet her eyes, she felt branded.

'It's not what I see but what I feel,' he said, his voice scraping over her nerves with wicked deliciousness. 'A heat that snags on a spark just begging to catch fire. I see a want so pure, so powerful, so... naïve...as if it would rush headlong into a burning forest and be happy to die in its blaze.' His eyes interrogated hers, leaving nothing unseen, unexamined. 'I see fuel for a flame that lies deep within me and a fire that I'm too tempted by to not get burned.'

His words caught her heart and drew it upwards

into the night sky. Not one book had prepared her for how this felt.

'Which is why you should go,' he said, dragging his gaze from hers, but it was too late. The damage was done. 'You're leaving tomorrow,' he clarified to the question that had yet to leave her lips.

'I know,' she said simply.

'I can't follow you.'

'I didn't ask you to.' She knew that he belonged here as much as she was needed in Norfolk. But she also knew that she would never forgive herself if she walked away from the promise of this night. *One* night.

'Star, you're innocent. You are—'

'A virgin? Yes. I am. Does that mean I don't know what I want?' she replied.

'No, but that doesn't mean I can give you what you need.'

'Oh. Would you not treat me well?' she asked, not thinking for a second that he wouldn't.

'Of course I would.'

'Would you be selfish and only take what you wanted?' She couldn't even imagine it.

'No, I—'

'Would you not be very good?'

The question was a taunt and his response, 'Star...' was a growl on his lips, a warning and an incitement, a call to arms that she felt down to her core, setting her on fire, energising her in a way she could never have imagined.

'So you think I should leave and instead find

someone who I'm less attracted to, who might not be good or treat me well and only be selfish in their wants?'

The thought burned the back of his throat and bruised his palms from clenching his fists too tightly. He couldn't argue with her logic. He had spent years cutting a swathe through Europe's most beautiful women and not a single one of them had caused this…arcane chemistry that burned the air between them—and his willpower to dust.

With his unseeing gaze still on the horizon, he felt her eyes like a brand against his skin, waiting for an answer, a response. His mouth ached to say the words, but he held them knowing he needed to be strong. He felt the subtle shift of her body as the fight left it and he closed his eyes, not wanting to see how giving up haunted her eyes.

Wordlessly she stood and approached the balcony as if the silhouette of his city contained answers that he was unable to give. She bowed her head and for a moment looked defeated. He wasn't arrogant enough to believe it was all him.

'I have let my sisters down.'

'You'd be my choice.'

'"It is not time or opportunity that is to determine intimacy…"'

Snippets from their conversation whispered once again in his ear, threatening to pull him under, the word 'intimacy' like a spell drawing him to her. Before his mind could catch up, his body had taken him to her.

He stood behind her, inches from her, his mind on all the reasons why giving in to this desire would be bad and his body itching to touch all the reasons why it wouldn't be. The glorious river of red had fallen over her shoulder, the delicate curve of her neck exposed. But it was when she moved her head slightly to the side, her pale skin gleaming in the light of the moon, willingly exposing her greatest vulnerability, surrendering to him completely, that he was lost.

He placed his hands against the stone balustrade either side of Star's, encircling her without yet touching her. The roar of blood in his veins, the pounding beat of his heart in his ears—something primal, elemental was taking over, and as he placed his lips against that stretch of the palest, smoothest skin he offered his first prayer in over three years.

The shudder that travelled through him rippled through her and he couldn't tell whether it was her legs shaking or his. He pressed his body into hers, leaning them both gently against the balcony, trapping her, holding her still. Her head fell back against his shoulder, her hair streaming over his forearm, offering him access to more of her. Rough stone was replaced by smooth skin as his hands left the balcony and swept around her petite body. He prised his eyes open to see the valley between breasts that were made to be held in his palms. He was torn, wanting to take this slow and wanting to take it all.

'Please,' she whispered.

And the leash on his restraint was lifted.

His hands swept over her breasts, palming the weight of them and feeling complete. His thumbs brushed her nipples into stiff peaks, ringing a shuddered moan that tightened Khalif's arousal. As if feeling it, Star arched back into his groin, pressing against the length of his erection until it was cradled against her bottom. Desire exploded on his tongue and he gently scraped his teeth against the muscle of her neck. She shivered again—and he felt it against his chest, his hands, his thighs and his calf muscles, questioning why they were still standing.

It seemed inconceivable to him that Star was a virgin and, despite feeling all kinds of selfish, he couldn't bring himself to stop. Unless she wanted him to.

'Star, you need to know that if you want me to stop—'

'Don't stop, please, I—'

He bent his head to hers so that his lips were against her ear. 'Nothing would make me stop. Not the sun falling from the sky, the desert freezing over, floods, locusts, or a third world war. Nothing would make me stop...but one word from you.'

'I don't need—'

'Star. At any point, do you understand? You can stop me at any point.'

CHAPTER FOUR

NOTHING WOULD MAKE me stop. Not the sun falling from the sky... Nothing...but one word from you.

Star couldn't deny that she had been nervous until he'd said those words. Words that had overflowed with the same need, want, *yearning* that she felt deep within her, and the *only* thing she was afraid of was him walking away.

She twisted in his arms, turning to face him, to look up into his eyes so that he knew. So that he believed her when she said, 'Yes. I understand.' She searched his face as if she was seeing it for the first time. Emboldened by his declaration, she was ready to stand in the path of his flame.

'Show me?' she asked, the weight of her desire making her voice shake.

He pulled his gaze from his observation of her face, her body, and dragged—reluctantly, it seemed—his eyes back to hers. 'Show you what?' he asked.

She bit her lip, trying to stop the smile that was

ready to burst against her mouth. 'Just how good you are.'

She watched as the rich brown depths of his eyes were eclipsed by the pitch black of his pupils, his response marked in deep red slashes across his cheekbones. He claimed her then, passionately, possessively, his lips crushed against hers, his tongue slipping into her mouth, tangling with her as deeply and completely as she wanted him.

His hands drew her to him, the soft curves of her chest pressed against the hard ridges of his, but it wasn't enough. For either of them. He drew her up and she felt herself lifted from her tiptoes, her legs instinctively wrapping around his slender hips until she was above him, his neck bent back to kiss her, her hair streaming down around them, curtaining them within red velvet tendrils.

Her hands braced against his shoulders, revelling in the flex of his muscles beneath her fingertips, the power as he held her there, restrained and raw—and all for her. He looked up at her as if she were the most incredible thing he'd seen and she felt it. For the first time she really felt it.

He walked them back from the balcony and into the living area and a thought snagged at her mind. 'Is it okay? That we're here? That we…' She didn't quite know how to finish that sentence, but she read the understanding in his eyes.

'It is. This suite…it's mine.'

It was the first time she had seen him look worried, as if concerned what her reaction would be, or what questions she might ask. 'Okay,' she said simply, her faith and trust in him complete. He looked as if he were about to say something, to qualify or justify. 'It's okay,' she said again, before pressing a kiss to his mouth. Then another. And another. Lips brushed against lips until he opened beneath her and this time it was her tongue that led the dance, and raised a dragon within her. One that breathed fire and clawed skin. He had cast a spell over her and she felt transformed.

She lost herself to the feel of him beneath her, eyes drifting closed to savour the moment, and when they opened there was nothing in his gaze but lust. He turned and walked them through a doorway and into a room that faced the same balcony, the same view. Moonlight poured in through the glass doors, casting a silvery glow on a large bed with pure white sheets. Very slowly he drew her downward, his arms and hands cradling her back, so that she was ready when the back of her thighs hit the surprisingly high mattress. She looked up and saw the net canopy hanging from a hook in the ceiling placed at the centre of the bed and stretching out to the four corners. She felt like a princess and almost said as much, until she caught the look in Kal's eyes as he took her in, leaning back on her hands.

She watched as Kal pulled his shirt from the waist of his trousers, slowly undoing each button and revealing inch after inch of impeccable bronzed skin. Only once he had removed the shirt could her eyes roam as freely across his body as she'd wished.

He removed his trousers while she was distracted and on her next inhale she saw him standing before her, black briefs hugging his skin, revealing the contours of his body, the dip of his abs, the flare of his hip bones and the length of his arousal.

'I will stop at *any* time, Star.'

'I know. But thank you for saying it,' she replied sincerely and, no matter what happened that night, she was thankful. Thankful that she was sharing this with Kal.

He came over her on the bed and covered her with his body. It was only then that she realised she was shaking. But the moment his lips touched her skin that shaking became a shiver, became a well of need rising within her.

His hands slid beneath the hem of her top and lifted it over her head, casting the cotton aside as if the few seconds she was hidden from his sight were too much. Slipping the strap of her bra from her shoulder, he pressed kisses across her shoulder as he slipped his hands beneath her and flicked open the clasp. She gasped into the sudden freedom as he threw her pale pink bra from her body and the bed. The fire in Kal's eyes made her feel glorious as his palms swept up her thighs, rucking the jersey of her skirt into pleats that he bunched in his palms before tugging it gently over her hips and down her legs, from her ankles and onto the floor.

He trailed open-mouthed kisses down her throat, between breasts he cupped, the warmth of his palms reassuring, the thumbs against her nipples sensually unsettling. Her back arched involuntarily, pushing her body upwards against his, wanting more, harder, deeper.

His tongue teased the sensitive skin of her abdomen as his hands moved to her hips, hooking his fingers beneath the small band at her waist and drawing her knickers down, over her thighs, then her knees, gently pushing them away and making room for him between her legs. Her mind was overwhelmed with sensation and she was oblivious to thought or words, but a craving roared to life within her and she felt the echoes of the dragon once again.

She felt herself parted, exposed, but not vulnerable and she relished the groan of pure satisfaction from Kal, just before the world tilted on its axis as he pressed an open-mouthed kiss at her core. She arched against the wild streak of desire that almost lifted her from the bed, thankful for the anchor of his forearms holding her in place as a second sweep of his tongue stole her breath.

And she was lost. To pleasure, to sensation, the sparks of fire racing through her bloodstream that she'd never known before. Kal had set them alight, making her glow from the inside, throb with a pulse of energy that powered both her sense of self and her need.

She heard herself begging for something she couldn't even name and gasped with sheer pleasure as his fingers joined his tongue. The unfamiliar feel of the stretch within her soon gave over to passion

which gave over to frustration. It wasn't enough—
she wanted *him*.

'Please, Kal,' she begged. 'Please.'

Kal reluctantly drew away from her. He had wanted
to feel her come apart on his tongue, to show her the
heights of pleasure before any kind of pain she might
experience for her first time. But that was *his* want
and this was about hers. His tongue swept out across
his bottom lip to taste the raw honey and milk of her,
not wanting to miss a single drop. She was exquisite,
a man's final feast, and the thought that she would
be the last thing on his mind before he gasped his
dying breath stopped him still.

But then her hands reached for him, pulling gently
at his shoulders, and he would have followed her
anywhere. Leaning up over her, bracing himself
on his forearms, he took in the pink path his rough
hands and tongue had traced over such silky skin.
The marks would be gone in the morning, but right
now the primal animal satisfaction he felt at such a
sight made it seem as if she were the royal and he
were a beast. He traced his fingers over the outline
of her hip, watching her shiver and buck beneath the
lightest of touches, across the sweeping hollow of her
waist, and tripped them over rib after rib after rib
to reach the underside of a breast he couldn't resist
cupping in his palm, the weight of it feeling like a
lost pound of his own flesh. A missing part of him,
one that he'd not known of until now.

He looked up at her face to find her watching

him so intently that where he would have smiled, he couldn't. Could barely breathe for the sight of her.

'It may hurt, but I will take that pain away. That, I can give you,' he swore, hoping that she understood all the things that he could not give her. She nodded and he leaned over to his bedside table for a box of condoms that he'd never thought he'd need.

He retrieved the packet, tearing at the foil with his teeth, and felt the searing heat of her gaze as she watched him roll the latex over his length. He felt her shift on the mattress and looked up to find her leaning back on her forearms, her teeth punishing her bottom lip with a bite. He reached out to smooth away a rich red curl that had fallen forward and she leaned into the palm of his hand. Selfishly, he wanted to keep her there. Keep this moment. He could fool himself all he wanted but, while he would do *everything* in his power to make this special for her, he wanted this as much as she did.

'If it gets too much—'

'Then the sun would have fallen from the sky—' she returned his words to him '—the desert would have frozen and I would be myself no more.'

It sounded like a quote from one of her romances, but he didn't recognise it—it felt as if it were just for them. He kissed her back against the mattress and settled between her legs, relishing the way his body covered hers almost completely, fitting together like a puzzle piece.

His pulse began to race, awed by the trust she had placed in him. He leashed himself with more control than he'd thought himself capable of as he cradled her face with his hands and pushed forward gently into her.

Her body tensed, as he knew it would, and she breathed in through the pain he could see she felt. He kissed her neck, the secret spot between her jaw and ear. 'It's okay, Star. Let it go. I've got you,' he whispered, holding himself still, impossibly still, until she was ready. Her deep inhalations pressed her chest into his as he dusted her skin with Arabic, words of comfort, of reassurance, promises that he'd be there to catch her when she fell. Star's body began to relax and he watched as her eyes opened, pain and shock replaced by wonder and desire once again. She nodded at his unspoken question and gently, and so, so slowly, he began to move.

He cursed. He prayed. He'd never felt anything like this. She was everywhere—around him, beneath him. His touch, his tongue, his taste was full of her and the air he breathed was laden with her. As her body undulated beneath him, he moved within her, their bodies joining together as if they were independent of thought and focused solely on pleasure.

Star strained towards him, her hand at the back of his neck pulling him down into a kiss that sent fire racing up from the base of his spine. A fine sheen dusted their skin, slippery and slick, sliding and tantalising, erotic sounds heating the air.

Star moaned into the kiss and he consumed it, the cries of her pleasure feeding his, bringing him closer and closer to orgasm. Each mewl of desire reached a higher pitch than the last and Khalif could tell she was on the brink. And he was torn between drawing out this singularly sublime moment and rushing them headlong into sheer bliss.

But then she tilted her hips downwards, drawing him even deeper within her, to press against a spot that saw Star explode beneath him, thrusting him headlong into an orgasm that stole his breath, his sight and his thought. The moon slipped behind the sun, the ocean poured away, and Khalif was completely and utterly spent.

When Khalif regained awareness it was to the feel of Star's fingers tracing swirls on his shoulders, her small hands slipping over his skin, as if stealing all the moments she could. Then he felt her lips tracing kisses down his spine, her body reaching over his as he had reached over her. He twisted beneath her and pulled her into a kiss as if the sand in their hourglass had already run dry.

Throughout the night they reached for each other almost endlessly and the sun was a curse on the horizon when Khalif finally made his way to the bathroom, running water from the tap—desperate to quench the thirst that hadn't quit even after the first taste of her. He was about to throw the protection they'd used in the bin when he noticed a small tear. And even had he closed his eyes to block out the image, his mind raced at the speed of light and all the while a voice screamed in his mind over and over and over again.

Pregnant.

Star could be pregnant. She could be carrying his child.

Star woke to the feeling of the sun streaming onto her skin, warming her and reigniting memories of the most incredible night of her life. She ran her hand over the sheets of Kal's bed, marvelling that it was his—the bed, the suite, the room in the palace. Sidestepping what that meant, she indulged in the belief that it had made what they'd shared a little more real, more meaningful than if they had been in a hotel room.

She was so glad that she had waited, that she had saved herself for him. He'd been so gentle, so generous, and her cheeks throbbed with blushes from the memory of what they had done the night before.

She turned onto her back, wondering where he was. Then, drawing the pale silk sheet around her, she made her way to the door, hearing the sound of voices beyond too late to stop her opening it.

The tableau that met her stopped her in her tracks. Khalif, dressed in suit trousers and a shirt, stood half turned towards her, his hands fisted at his thighs. A look of immense frustration was painted on his features for the second it took to register her standing in the doorway, before his face went blank. He was mid-conversation with another man, also suited, peering angrily at her through his glasses. A shift of weight drew her gaze to a uniformed security guard positioned in front of the door to the rest of the palace and finally a woman stood in the kitchen with a cup in both hands, gently blowing steam across the rim with a look of sympathy in her eyes.

Star shook her head as if trying to clear the image and pushed the door closed, hoping that the next time it was opened all these strangers would have gone and Kal would be there to tell her it was all a dream.

She was still standing there a minute later when he opened the door—through which she could still see the people staring at her.

'We have to talk,' Kal said, shutting the door behind him and walking forward.

'Mmm.' She wasn't so sure she wanted to talk but she was definitely sure she wanted a bit of breathing space between them so, for every step he took towards her, she took one back until the backs of her knees hit the mattress and she half sat, half fell on the mattress.

She clenched her jaw, trying to block everything out, even sound, but it was impossible as her eyes tracked Kal, pacing back and forth before her, his hands sweeping angrily through his hair. His lips, the perfect, sensual, powerful lips that had worshipped her last night, were bringing words Star could barely process into a room where they'd shared such incredible passion. Words that didn't make any sense at all.

In a daze, she tried to assemble what he'd said.

'I'm sorry, can you repeat that last bit? Just one more time.'

'I am Sheikh Khalif Al Azhar. First in line to the Duratrian throne.'

A sheikh. A prince.

He couldn't be.

But then she thought of the way he had looked to the horizon as if he owned it. The way that she now remembered his interaction with Wahed and the other guards, as if they had known each other. At how he had known his way around the palace.

How had she missed that?

She knew how. She'd been caught up in the romantic history of Hātem and the terrible tragedy of Crown Prince Faizan and his wife, and the loss that would be to their two small children. The tragedy had made the headlines of almost every international newspaper, with images of the twin girls being held by their grandparents and a stony-faced half shadowed brother she now knew was Khalif. There had been a subtle aspect of the exhibition that covered it—Samira's wedding dress, pictures, footage. The loss mourned by a nation had been handled well by the exhibition and there were references to an upcoming memorial to the short-lived ruler and his wife, but nothing had yet been confirmed.

He'd lied to her.

'Star,' he said, as if reading her thoughts in the widening of her eyes. 'You didn't recognise me and I…you were the first person to…'

There was a firm knock on the door.

'Not now,' he growled.

Star looked between the door and Kal. No. Not Kal any more. Khalif. His Royal Highness Sheikh Khalif Al Azhar. Hurt, embarrassment and shame

flooded her as she realised that he had hidden who
he was while she had been absolutely and completely herself. So focused on finding the necklace
she hadn't been able to be anything but plain old
Star Soames.

Rich and powerful. I am *impressed.*

Her shaking fingers pressed against her mouth.
Oh, God. She'd said that.

*It is not time or opportunity that is to determine
intimacy.*

She'd said that too. Had he laughed at her?

No. While she might not have known he was a
prince, she *did* know him well enough that she could
tell he hadn't laughed at her.

'But why all this?' she asked, gesturing to the
door. 'Why tell me now? Did something happen?'
she went on, wondering if it was fanciful to worry
that perhaps a war had broken out, or that something
had happened to a family member.

He came to sit beside her on the bed, their knees
not quite touching, as if something more than his
title had put a distance between them that hadn't
been there the night before.

'This morning, I noticed that the protection we
used had torn.'

She tried to look at him but he was facing straight
ahead, as if confronting some unforeseen future
head-on. She frowned. Torn protection? She couldn't
quite see what he...

'You think I might be...'

'Pregnant.'

A baby.

Could she be?

A flood of pure bright light dipped and soared across her heart, her skin, her mind, before swooping to the floor and scattering like diamonds on marble.

This wasn't how she'd imagined finding out that she might be pregnant. She'd thought that there would be joy and a dizzying happiness as she shared the special moment with her husband, not a sense of confusion and disbelief and the father-to-be looking so...so *forbidding*.

'But it's highly unlikely, isn't it?' she asked him, looking for reassurance.

'That's not really going to work with my advisors.' His voice was heavy and grim in a way she'd not heard before.

'It doesn't have to,' she said, wondering why such a thing would be decided by committee. 'It only has to work with you.' She shrugged. 'I'll catch my flight home and when I can take a test I'll let you know what the results are and we can speak about it then.'

He smiled. It was a firm line of determination. 'There will be no *speaking about it then*, Star.'

She studied him until he finally turned and locked his gaze on hers. 'Oh,' she said, feeling a tremble work its way down her spine.

'What?'

'The sheikh look. Does that actually work on your staff and subjects?' she asked, forcing herself to keep her tone light.

'Usually,' he said, his tone still cold enough to cut stone.

'I spend my days with thirty primary school children who throw much better tantrums than that.'

'That wasn't a tantrum,' he ground out.

'It was about to be,' she said, relishing the heat that had entered his voice. Heat she could deal with, cold...not so much.

'And that would be at Salisbury Primary?'

'Yes, how did you...?' Her words trailed off as she realised that if he *was* the Sheikh, if she *might* be pregnant, then of course his advisors would have looked into her background. As her heart slowly poked and prodded the idea that she might be pregnant, her mind ran like a stream over cobbles and stones. 'I always wondered what that would feel like,' she babbled. 'You know, in romances, when the hero does a "background check"? He usually gets something horribly wrong and so there's a big misunderstanding between them. I read this one—it was actually pretty funny—where...'

'Can we focus here, Star?'

'Of course,' she replied automatically, wondering how on earth she was supposed to focus when her thoughts had been picked up by the wind and scattered across the desert floor.

She looked up, finding one thread of thought to hold onto. 'Is it that bad?'

'That depends on whether you are pregnant with the heir to the throne of Duratra.'

* * *

Khalif left the bedroom while Star showered and dressed. He wished he could ignore the room full of people—the guard, Amin, Maya… No. He'd not ignore Maya. She had made herself as invisible as possible, but the subtle comfort she offered was everything to him right now. He could rely on her confidentiality even if she wasn't married to his best friend.

A best friend who would be calling him every shade of stupid for last night. And he'd be right. What had he been thinking? He'd been selfish. Completely and utterly selfish for wanting her, for acting on it, and now Star was going to pay the price.

This wasn't how it was supposed to be. He was supposed to get to grips with running the throne for a few years and then, after his thirtieth birthday, there would be discreet enquiries as to the availability of a suitable wife who wouldn't challenge him or interfere with his duty. And once the twins were of age, of course, the throne would return to them.

Years ago, he'd imagined something different, *someone* different, to wear his ring and have his children. But then he'd learned. Duty, the throne, family. It all came first.

But this? Star being possibly pregnant? He ran his hand through his hair, ignoring the uneasy glance his assistant sent his way as he stalked through the living area towards the balcony, stopping himself before stepping out onto it, remembering Star in his arms, hair streaming down around them. No one had ever affected him in such a way. Not even the one woman he had loved and lost.

He cursed out loud, uncaring of who heard him, his mind taking him to all the places he didn't want to be that morning.

Pregnant.

Star might be pregnant. And if she was? Then there was no doubt whatsoever. They would marry.

Showered and dressed in the previous day's slightly rumpled clothes, Star was looking out of the window when there was a gentle knock on the door.

The doctor. Star's pulse raced as she realised that she hadn't asked him what kind of examination or questions she was expected to submit to. Expecting a grim-faced old man, she was surprised when a pretty woman a little older than herself came through the door.

'Hello, Star, my name is Maya Mourad,' she said, introducing herself in English lightly flecked with an Arabic accent. Her headscarf was a pretty green and Star was a little distracted by it, which was why it took a moment to connect the name.

'Mourad, like the Prime Minister?'

'Yes, he is my husband,' Maya confirmed, her smile deep and full of the love of a happy wife. 'Khalif has explained that I would be seeing you?'

The gentle way about her was soothing to Star's edgy nerves. 'Perhaps "explained" might be a bit of an exaggeration.'

Maya nodded knowingly. 'I see. So, I am a family

doctor,' she explained. 'A little like your GPs, but I specialise in women's health.'

'I didn't think that you could tell if I was pregnant so soon after...' Star's words were replaced by a fierce blush and suddenly she wanted her sisters. She didn't want to be here, no matter how nice Maya was. She should be talking to Skye and Summer about her first time, about how wonderful it was, not how she might be pregnant and how that meant she couldn't come home.

She could almost hear them now. Skye would immediately be making plans about prams and cradles, nappies and booties, Summer would turn to books and have all kinds of information on birthing styles, baby names and vitamins. Both of them would be completely supportive, with all the kind words of encouragement and soothing she could possibly need.

But there would be that silent *I told you so* in Skye and Summer's shared looks. They had expected her to get into trouble and, while they might not have forecasted just how big that trouble was...they'd clearly been right to worry.

'We can't tell whether you are pregnant yet,' Maya said, answering Star's half formed question from moments before. 'But first I want to see if you're okay. Then we'll talk about the options.'

'I won't have a termination.' The words were immediate and determined, natural and instinctive. They came from a place deep within her, and Star almost heard the growl of the dragon that Kal had called forth within her. 'I'm sorry, I—'

'No. It's good for you to know how you feel about this, even at this early stage,' Maya said, her gentle smile soothing a bit of the shock Star was beginning to feel. 'I meant options in terms of the kinds of tests we can do now, the tests you're *happy* to do now, and any medical information you feel comfortable giving me.'

'You mean giving Khalif?' Star asked, more curious than resentful.

'You are my patient. If there is anything you wish for me not to say, then you have my confidentiality.'

Star thought about it for a moment. 'No,' she said finally and resolutely. 'I have nothing to hide.'

Maya smiled and gestured for her to sit. 'So let's start with the easiest question and then work back a little. When was your last period?'

CHAPTER FIVE

THE MOMENT MAYA emerged from his bedroom, Khalif demanded to know how Star was.

'She is fine,' Maya replied. 'Taking a moment, but she is—'

His assistant stood, snaring Maya's attention. 'Any medical conditions we should know about? Family history of—'

'That's enough, Amin,' Khalif said.

'Your Highness, we need to know if there is any—'

'*If* Star is pregnant, we will get to those kinds of questions. Until then I will *not* invade her privacy in such a way,' he warned.

Amin stared at Khalif until Star opened the door to the bedroom and came out, with a smile only he might be able to tell was nervous.

'As I told Star,' Maya said to the room, 'we will need about eleven days before we can be sure a pregnancy test will be completely accurate.'

'That's the day after the memorial event,' Amin said angrily as if somehow that was Star's fault too.

'Yes,' Maya confirmed as Khalif's head began to spin. Everything seemed to be converging on that one event.

'You can't miss it,' Amin said to Khalif.

'Why would you miss it?' Star asked Khalif in confusion and started a little at the glare his assistant sent her way. Khalif was about to say something when she turned to Amin. 'Are you okay?' she asked, peering at him. 'Do you need some water?'

Amin turned an indelicate shade of puce. Khalif couldn't tell whether Star had been purposely oblivious to Amin's obvious anger or simply unseeing of it.

'You cannot leave, Your Highness. There is still too much work to do—'

'Amin…' he warned.

'She can go,' Amin said, waving an arm in her direction as if she were a baggage to be passed around, 'but you are needed here.'

'Enough!' Khalif barked, his hand slicing through the air and any further objection his infuriating assistant might have. He was done. 'Out. Everyone. Now.'

Amin looked as shocked as if he'd just been told categorically that Santa Claus was real and moved only when the security guard in front of the door opened it and gestured to him to leave. Maya ducked her head—quite possibly concealing the ghost of a smile—but left and was followed by the security guard closing the door behind him.

'Did you want me to…?' Star's question fell short, probably at the look on his face which—if it was anywhere close to his feelings right now—would be a sight to behold. He resisted the urge to run his hands through his hair, aware of how much that would give away.

'Do you want a coffee?'

'If I *am* pregnant, probably not, no.'

'Right. Of course. Really? Already?'

Star shrugged her shoulders and stared at him as if he were an unexploded bomb. He certainly felt like one.

'Herbal tea would be lovely, if you have one.'

That he could do. He went to the kitchenette and retrieved one of the herbal teas he'd always kept for Samira.

His brain stumbled over her name as if, even mentally, he couldn't face it. He glared at the leafy infusion as if it were responsible for creating a link between Star and her at this specific moment.

Pulling himself together, he passed the cup under the heated water tap.

'I know you're a prince and everything, but if you don't know how to boil a kettle...'

He felt a smile soften the grim line of his lips and shifted to the side so that Star could see the steam coming from the boiling water.

'Ah... Fancy.'

'Very,' he confirmed. He turned and passed her the tea. 'How do you feel?'

'Not pregnant, if that's what you're wondering,' she said, gently blowing the steam from her tea across the rim of the cup. She looked up at him and shrugged. 'Kal— Your— Oh, please just tell me what to call you?' she pleaded lightly.

He smiled at her evident fluster. 'Kal when it's just you and me, Khalif in front of the people who just left the room, and Your Highness if there is ever anyone else present.'

If there is ever. Not *when*.

Star gripped the cup tighter to disguise the shaking of her hands caused by the realisation that he had no intention of introducing her to any more people than was strictly necessary. And while that hurt, could she blame him? She had only intended to share one magical night with him before returning to Norfolk. Something that now seemed impossible.

'I get the feeling you're not letting me on my flight,' she said.

'No.'

A dull thud hit her heart and blood rushed to her cheeks. Eleven days, Maya had said. She couldn't stay here for eleven days! Panic flooded her body, adrenaline effervescent in her blood. What about her mother? Every single minute she stayed with Khalif the necklace remained lost to them, as did the chance to save her mother.

She put down the hot tea before she could spill it and burn herself. 'I can't... I can't be here for eleven days, Kal,' she said, her voice almost a whisper.

'You won't be. In half an hour we'll head into the desert.'

'The desert?' Star asked before realising that he

wouldn't want her somewhere she could be found by some unsuspecting staff or family member.

'We have a family residence in the desert.'

'Really?' Star frowned. She'd not heard or seen any reference to it in the exhibition. Maybe, just maybe... She couldn't tell whether the thread of hope winding around her heart at the possibility that she might find the necklace there was fanciful or fated. And then she was horrified at herself for thinking such a thing, for being opportunistic at this time, and her stomach began to hurt as much as her heart.

'I need to call my sisters.' They would know what to do, she thought, rubbing absently at her stomach— a move that Khalif's keen gaze homed in on.

'You can't tell them.'

Her eyes flew to his face.

'You can't,' he repeated. 'If news gets out then...'

'I trust my sisters.'

'I'm glad. But I don't.'

'You are cutting me off from a support that I need right now,' she warned.

'Then allow me to be that support.' His words were at odds with the grim determination on his features.

She turned away from him.

'Star.' She halted without looking back. 'If you are pregnant—'

'We'll cross that bridge when it comes to it,' she interrupted, not wanting to hear the rest of his decla- ration. Because she knew it would erase all the good that they had shared up to that point, all the moments of connection and how she'd felt *seen* by him.

'I need you to understand that while Duratra is a peaceful, inclusive and diverse country, even we balk at unmarried sheikhs with illegitimate heirs. Family is incredibly important to us. It comes first.'

'I appreciate that,' she said, still facing the door to the bedroom.

'Star. I need you to *understand* that if you are carrying my child, we *will* marry.'

No.

This wasn't how it was supposed to be. She was supposed to come to Duratra, find the necklace and return home to Norfolk, where they could find the jewels, sell the estate and get the treatment their mother needed.

Spinning to face him, 'But I can't be what you'd imagined as a wife?' she said.

'No. You're not.'

She pressed her teeth into her lip to stop the hot ache in her throat from escaping.

'But if you are carrying my child that won't matter.'

'So you'd marry me for the sake of our child?' she demanded.

'Yes.'

'But not love. You'd not *want* to marry me.' Star rubbed at her wrists, trying to soothe away the impression of shackles that her mother—that Catherine—had seen marriage as.

'No royal marries for love, Star.'

'That is very sad indeed.'

'It's just the way it is,' he said as if it were a tenet to live by. 'If you are pregnant, we will marry.'

Less than two hours later the Jeep jerked a little to the right as they skirted the base of another impossibly tall sand dune and he cursed. Usually Khalif was a much better driver than this. He loved this drive. Not that he'd taken it in the last three years. No one had been back here since Faizan and Samira's accident— as if distance alone would help stave off their grief.

Khalif was hit by an overwhelming need to speak to his brother right now.

You're a fool, Faizan would have said.

And Samira would have looked at him with her large, deep brown eyes, accepting, understanding and hopeful that he'd found happiness at last.

He braced himself against the wave of loss that hit as inevitably as the tide. *That* was why he didn't like thinking of them. The pain that always followed was too much to bear.

He gripped the steering wheel and turned to check on Star. She had regained a little of the colour in her face. He resisted the urge to lift his sunglasses and rub his eyes, instead pushing forward with focused determination. As if the distance between them and the palace was something to be beaten into submission.

'I'm sorry about your mother's diagnosis,' he said. It had been burning a hole in his conscience since

Maya had told him. He couldn't even begin to imagine what that must feel like.

'Thank you,' she said quietly.

'Is there anything that can be done?'

'We are working on it.'

Star stared at the rich yellow sand, rising and falling as if endless, silently praying for it to distract her. The 'family residence' in the desert was her last hope and she would turn it upside down if she had to.

Because if she didn't find the necklace and they couldn't save their mother then…then…she'd be alone. Her sisters loved her, but her mother *understood* her. And the awful shadow of loss she felt for the father she had never known would be *nothing* in comparison to what life would be like without her mother.

She cleared her throat against the aching burn and Khalif passed her a bottle of water. She refocused her gaze on the miles of golden sand and brilliant blue sky.

'How do you feel?'

'No more pregnant than I did an hour ago,' she said, the concern in his voice a kindness that softened her reply.

If you are carrying my child, we will marry.

It was only now that she might be pregnant that Star realised just how much she'd wanted to marry before having a child. It was in the way her heart quivered at the thought of her baby growing up to experience the same stares and whispers that she and her sisters had. An experience that Khalif had shared in his own way.

'But if I was,' she said hesitantly, picking up the threads of her answer, 'if I *was* pregnant, if we had a child, can you ensure that they wouldn't be judged, or excluded or…?'

'Star, look at me,' he said, removing his sunglasses. Only when she met his gaze did he continue. 'With every ounce of my being I would protect you and our child. Our family has an agreement with the press, both in Duratra and internationally, that protects our children from scrutiny until they turn eighteen. They attend a central city school until they decide whether they want to attend university. We can't protect them from everything, but we do our best.'

Star thought about that for a moment, not immune to the devotion and determination in Khalif's tone. She had grown up sure of her parents' love, even though her father had passed. Their love of her, love of each other, hadn't needed a marriage certificate. But her grandparents' behaviour had made her see through different eyes—ones that were hurt and had caused hurt. And she would never do that to her child.

'If I were pregnant, I would do whatever it took to protect them,' she said, finally turning back to him, knowing that he would understand what she meant.

'As would I.' His words felt like an oath and she felt the stirrings of the connection she'd been drawn to when they'd first met and something tight eased in her heart.

The sound of his phone ringing cut through the Jeep, but he put off answering it until Star returned to look out of the window.

Biting back a curse, he pressed the wireless ear-bud to his ear and pressed a button on the steering wheel to answer the call. 'Yes?' Khalif answered in Arabic.

'Wow. Okay. Nice to speak to you too,' came the sardonic response from Reza.

'I don't have much time. I'm on the way to Al-hafa.'

'Really? Is that…wise?'

Khalif glanced across at Star. Nothing about his decisions had been wise since she'd come crashing into his life.

'There wasn't much choice.'

'The plans for the memorial are barely finalised, let alone—'

'I know, Reza. But what do you want me to do? Abbad will never be happy with the choice of memorial for his youngest daughter. We could have renamed the mountains and it wouldn't be compensation for his loss.'

'If that's what you're trying to achieve, Khalif, then…' Reza's voice trailed off, genuine concern evident.

He cursed. 'I don't know any more, Reza.'

'Well, at this rate, Amin might have a heart attack and be removed from your staff for medical reasons.'

'He's necessary.'

'He was necessary for Faizan. I'm not sure he's necessary for you.'

'Is that what you called me for? To berate me for messing up this memorial *and* my choice of employee?'

'Actually, I called to berate you for possibly impregnating a British tourist, but sure, while we're at it, we might as well—'

'I'm hanging up now.'

'Khalif, it defeats the purpose if you tell me that you're—'

Khalif pulled the earbud from his ear and tossed it into the well near the gearbox, smiling. The moment of relief was, however, quickly dulled by the realisation that Reza was right.

If that's what you're trying to achieve...

'I am sorry,' Star said in the wake of the terminated phone call. He risked a glance towards her. 'For your loss,' she clarified.

He clenched his jaw, only capable of uttering the same two words she had given to his concern about her mother. 'Thank you.'

'Memorials are hard to choose,' she said, and he wondered if she had somehow understood the one-sided conversation. His anger escaped before his mind could catch up, his response a half growl, half scoff, questioning what she'd know about it, until he remembered the loss of her father.

'My father was cremated,' she said, her eyes ahead on the horizon, but clearly seeing some distant past. 'His ashes were scattered in the Solent but Mum wanted me to have somewhere that I could go to, that I could visit if I wanted to. Somewhere just for me and him. She saved a little bit of his ashes for me, so that when I was old enough I could decide where that would be. I...' She trailed off, as if searching for the words. 'It was hard to decide. I didn't know him, I could barely remember him and I felt this...*pressure* to get it right, like I was being tested somehow on some instinctive connection I should have with the father I had never known.

'And then I realised that it wasn't about him, or Mum, or what people expected. This was for me.' She pressed a hand against her heart and his palm itched as if he felt the beat of her heart there. 'There's a forest near to where we live, and I spent days searching for the oldest tree. It's this beautiful old gnarled oak that's been there for hundreds of years. Mum, Skye and Summer came with me and we lit candles and I buried the little vial of ash in its roots so that he'd always be a part of the wood we both loved so much.'

Khalif remembered that she'd said her father was a carpenter and thought that it was perfect. It must have been a beautiful moment for her. For them. And he was struck by a spark of jealousy. Jealous of the privacy and intimacy of the moment.

'It's not that easy,' he said, his voice shockingly hoarse.

'Easy?' she asked, the tone to her voice making him realise how that had come out.

'I'm sorry, I didn't mean it like that. It's just that

this memorial is not just for me, my nieces, my family, my country, but Samira's family, her country…
It's…'

'Big.'

'Yes.'

She nodded. 'So all the more reason to find the one that feels *right*?'

He looked at her for a second longer than he needed to, causing the arousal he felt to sneak beneath his defences and grip him low and hard.

'So, tell me about this family residence,' she said, breaking the moment, a brightness to her tone that hadn't been there moments before. And if it felt just a little forced, he could understand why.

He sighed and cast his mind back through the family history and legends of the old fortress. 'It's been there almost as long, if not longer than the city. It was originally a fortress between our land and the neighbouring countries, but it hasn't been used by the military since the fourteenth century. It was barely even used in the last few hundred years, but my father liked it and started to hold family gatherings there, especially since his friendship with His Majesty Sheikh Abbad.'

'Your sister-in-law's father? His country borders yours?'

'Yes. But, before my father, it was mainly known for being used for…'

He trailed off, as if not wanting to finish the sentence.

'For what?' she prodded.

'For the Sheikh's mistresses.'

'How fitting,' she replied drily.

'You are not a mistress,' he announced.

'No, I suppose being a mistress would require more than one night.'

Silence filled the Jeep as they both descended into a mix of memories and fantasies of what had been and what could be. Star wanted to bite her tongue and Khalif clenched the steering wheel.

They rounded the curve of a road that would have been invisible if he hadn't known where to look, and his pulse started to beat a little harder just as Star gasped in astonishment at the incredible medieval structure that was more beautiful to him than the city palace. The ochre stonework stood proudly against the bright blue sky, beside the rich forest-green slash of the palace gardens.

Despite its military exterior, inside smooth functionality gave way to intricate and ornate carved stone and corridors with rooms that opened up like Russian dolls, and mentally Khalif traced a path towards quarters almost as familiar to him as his own.

'Star, before we get to the residence—'

'That's not a residence, Kal. That's a palace.'

'Yes. Sorry, were you expecting—'

'Something smaller, perhaps? As implied by the word *residence*,' she teased. 'Sorry, you were saying...'

Khalif's stomach tightened, hating himself already for what he was about to say. 'Because of the situation, because we can't risk any word getting out, I have to request that you stay in your room for one

hour in the morning and one hour in the evening.'
She stared at him, those oceanic-blue eyes levelling
him with their eerie calm. 'It is so that the staff can
get what they need to do done, without seeing you.
It's safer for you and them. No matter what happens,
I don't want any hint of impropriety linked to either
of our futures, no matter what they are.'

'Okay.'

'If you need anything at all, you can just leave a
note in your room and they will provide it for you.'

'Okay,' she said again, forcing the word to her
lips. Because the sharp sting of rejection was too familiar. Too tainted already with the feelings of shame
and being unwanted. And right then she promised
herself that if she was pregnant, her child would
never feel the hurt of that.

He hadn't missed how quiet she'd been since his declaration. Yes, he trusted his staff implicitly and yes,
they were all discreet. But he would never put them
in a position that would leave them open to questions from the press, or worse—his father. It was
vital that he kept them and Star apart. She would
understand. One day.

He had shown her the gardens first because they
truly were breathtaking. Thanks to the aquifer that
fed both the nearby oasis and the palace, there was
enough water for the lush greenery that filled the
palace gardens and to allow the natural life in the
surrounding areas to thrive.

It seemed to have a similar effect on Star as a rosy

blush was brought back to features turned stark by the restrictions he had placed on her. He would have wanted to show her more, but he needed to get Star settled so that he could call his father and explain his sudden departure. He drew her back towards the interior of the palace the family affectionately called Alhafa, escaping the searing heat of the desert sun the moment they passed through the doors. The thick outer walls of the palace, deep corridors and open courtyards worked to keep the internal temperature cool and manageable.

'This entire wing has the family suites,' he explained as he led her down the left-hand side of the palace.

'I don't want to take someone's room,' Star announced. It might have been the first thing she'd said since they'd left the Jeep.

'It's just us here.'

She nodded, keeping her head down.

'Thankfully, my father listened to my mother and had the suites fitted with en suite bathrooms when my nieces were born. She refused to have her granddaughters spending time in a military fortress with no decent plumbing.'

As he'd hoped, it drew a gentle laugh from Star and the sound tripped down his back.

'It didn't matter for you and your brother?'

'We were boys. It was different. It was good to toughen us up a little.'

Star looked towards a corridor shrouded in darkness. 'What's down there?'

'Nothing,' he said as icy fingers gripped his heart.
'But—'

'That area is off-limits.'

She turned back without a word and continued in the direction they'd been heading. His gaze was glued to her back because if he looked anywhere else he was terrified of the ghosts he'd see.

By the time they reached the room he'd had prepared for her, Khalif wanted to leave. To return to Burami. He should never have brought her here, where around every corner was a memory of his brother, of Samira. This was where he had first met her…and where he had last seen her. This was where he struggled the most to fit his feelings into a box called grief.

But it was the only place where he and Star would not be seen. And no one could find out about this. If she was pregnant, they'd deal with how and when the news of their engagement was delivered. If not… then they would go their separate ways and never see each other again.

No royal marries for love.

The words echoed in his mind as he watched her take in the room that would be hers for the next ten nights. She went straight to the balcony. The wooden screens had been pulled back to reveal the majesty of the desert. The bed was freshly made, the scent of jasmine hanging on the air from the beautiful blooms of fresh flowers in vases he'd not seen before. Her fingers trailed over her small suitcase as if in surprise and she turned to him, her hair swept over one shoulder, making him long to touch it.

'Your fairies have been at work.'

'I'm not sure how the staff would feel to be called that.'

'Well, they're invisible and do your bidding and don't you dare say you don't believe in fairies,' she warned, a slight tease to a tone that must cast spells over the children she taught.

'So that would make me Peter Pan?' he asked.

'And me Wendy,' she said, the teasing gone.

And suddenly he couldn't explain it, but his heart hurt at the thought of her returning home while he stayed in Neverland.

They both started when the sound of his phone cut through the moment.

'You can go anywhere you like—apart from that wing. I'll meet you here at seven and we can go for dinner.'

'Oh, taking me to the best restaurant in town?' she joked, as if his father's call wasn't important.

'It's *the* place to be,' he assured her with a quirk of his lips. And as he closed the door behind him, his smile flattened into a grim line and he flexed his hand from fist to open three times before retrieving the phone from his pocket.

This was not going to be fun.

Two hours later and the tension that had built across his shoulders and up his neck was as solid as concrete. The conversation with his father had gone about as well as any interaction they'd had in the last three years—terribly.

Have you forgotten your promise to Nadya and Nayla? You were supposed to spend the evening with them.

He had. He'd completely forgotten—but he couldn't reveal to his father why. Bitterly disappointed in himself, guilt and grief swirling thickly in his stomach, he promised his father he'd make it up to them.

But the words were over-familiar to them both. They had been a constant refrain in the weeks, months and first few years following his brother's death. Khalif had returned to Duratra and, even before the earth had settled on the coffins of his brother and sister-in-law, he had thrown himself into his duty. He'd sat up for nearly three straight nights, consuming every single piece of information needed. He'd made state calls, international calls, presenting himself as the first in line to the Duratrian throne. He'd handed over the running of an internationally successful business, stopped drinking, womanising, misbehaving and he'd worked. Hard. But he'd also hidden in that work. Hidden from his father, from his mother and most especially from Nadya and Nayla, who had been distraught not only at the loss of their parents, but also their uncle.

He couldn't face them. Any of them. It hurt too much. To see his own grief reflected in their eyes. He hadn't found solace with them, he'd found judgement, he'd found himself wanting.

Raza had intervened. They'd argued and fought until both were a little beaten and bruised, but Khalif had seen the truth of it. In the last year he'd been better, but he knew deep down he'd just been going through the motions.

Until a woman standing before a painting, with flame red hair, had caught his eye.

He almost growled as he stalked along the hallway towards the steam room in the lower level of the palace. His towel low on his hips and his bare feet slapping against the cool stone, diminishing some of the ire-fuelled heat that sparked across his skin.

He'd wanted one night. Just one. With a beautiful woman who made the weight of the crown lighter because it had been invisible to her. He'd wanted the taste of freedom she was unaware she had…and instead he'd quite possibly bound her to him for ever. Trapped her.

He banged the meaty side of his fist against the stone wall as he rounded the corner, welcoming the wet heat that was reaching out to him from the room beyond. He sent a prayer of thanks that Masoud knew him well enough to ensure the steam room was ready for his stay.

He pushed through the door and was hit by a bank of wet white air. He breathed in deeply, welcoming the mandarin and bergamot scented steam into his body, willing the heat to soak into his skin and relieve the stresses of an almost diabolical day.

He grounded himself, mentally drawing power up from deep beneath the ground, letting it fill his feet, his calf muscles, the base of his spine and up his back. He rolled out his powerful shoulders and flexed his neck from side to side. He just needed a moment. One to himself. He inhaled deeply again when he felt something brush past him.

Adrenaline and shock sliced through him as he reached out his hand and his fingers curled around a slender bicep.

'Star?' he asked, surprised and confused.

'Yes. It's me.' She sounded almost guilty. 'I don't want to intrude.'

He willed his heart to recover from the surprise of there being someone else in here, but his pulse didn't slow. Instead, his sight blocked by the steam, his other senses were heightened. He registered the silky sheen to her skin, his thumb smoothing away a drop of moisture, and found himself pulling her towards him. As he drew her closer and closer, she came through the thick vapour into soft focus. His eyes dropped to her chest, straining against a white towel pulled tight beneath her arms, rising and falling with the quickening of her breath and making him want to lose himself in the exquisite pleasure of her all over again and damn the consequences.

With one hand still wrapped around her slender bicep, he raised the other to cup her jaw. She leaned into his touch as if she craved it as much as he did. His thumb traced down her neck and tripped over a gold chain. He followed the loops of precious metal to the pendant that lay beneath her collarbone and stopped.

He took the pendant in his hand, holding it up to his inspection and clenched it in his palm, rocked by fury, shock and a grief as swift and as powerful as the harshest of desert storms.

'Where the hell did you get this?' he demanded.

CHAPTER SIX

THE MOMENT STAR winced as the necklace pulled against her skin, Khalif dropped his hold on the pendant and stepped away from her as if he'd been burned.

'It's mine,' she said past the pulse pounding in her throat.

'I don't believe you.'

The hairs on the back of her neck lifted.

'You recognise it?' she asked, shocked. While she had known that Hātem had kept the other necklace, she had never imagined that Khalif would be familiar with it.

'That necklace belongs to my family and has been with *my family* for over one hundred and fifty years,' he all but growled.

Despite his obvious anger, Star's heart soared. If Khalif recognised it, he knew it. And if he knew it, then perhaps she finally could hope to retrieve it.

'Not this one. Your family have protected its sister necklace, but this one has been with *my* family for over one hundred and fifty years.'

He frowned, searching first her face and then the pendant as if it could reveal the truth of her words. He reached for the pendant again, but drew his hand back, a guilty red slash across his cheekbones.

Star held the pendant between them for him to inspect.

'There's a slight difference,' he said, turning the embellished gold design from side to side. 'As if it's the exact opposite.' There was something like wonder in his voice, until something dawned on him. 'I thought it was just a story,' he said, his eyes gazing over her shoulder on some distant memory.

Star placed her hand over his and brought the necklace back to her. 'I think we have much to talk about,' she said.

'Starting with why you came to Duratra.' His eyes were now firmly fixed on her, assessing her with an almost hostile gleam.

She opened her mouth to speak, but he shook his head.

'We should both be fully dressed for this conversation.'

All trace of the heavy sensuality that had built between them was now gone and in its wake was the horrible feeling that perhaps Star had an ulterior motive for being in Duratra. Perhaps even there had been some kind of plan behind their night together, a seduction maybe? But as Khalif gestured for her to leave the steam room before him, he knew that this was nothing more than paranoia and confusion.

It was simply the shock of seeing the necklace for the first time in three years. In line with their family's tradition, Samira had inherited the necklace on her marriage to Faizan. It had been on her that he'd last seen it. And where once dark skin had embraced and heated the gold, Star's pale skin and red hair brought the gold to life.

Star cast a look at him before she turned down the corridor that would take her to her room. He could barely look at her, the delicate shoulders, the trailing streams of red hair, the way that the thick white towel wrapped around her slender frame made her look vulnerable now. He pulled his gaze from her before he could once again catch sight of the necklace.

He had never wanted a drink more. But he hadn't touched a drop since Faizan died and he wasn't planning to start now. The last time he'd given into temptation...

Star had taken a quick shower, scrubbing the slick citrus-scented steam from her body as if it could rid her of both her unwanted desire for a man she might never again have and the discomfort she felt every time he saw the necklace.

There had been a moment when she'd felt hope. When she'd thought that perhaps she'd been meant to come to Duratra, to find not just the necklace but *him*.

Now she wasn't so sure.

She dressed in a loose-fitting T-shirt over an ankle-length skirt and left her feet bare. For some reason, she wanted to feel the ground beneath her feet—as if it might be the only thing she could be sure of.

When she knocked on his door a few minutes later she didn't hear him ask her to enter, but she was sure that he was there. Gently, she pushed open the door to the most incredible suite she'd ever seen.

She'd thought the room she was staying in was something from a fantasy. It was almost the entire size of the flat she shared with her sisters, and the impossibly large bed had mosquito nets that had become silks fit for a princess in her mind. The view of the desert was something she would take with her until her last breath. The detail of the carvings, the faded plaster and history pouring from every inch of the walls, was so different from the shabby neglect of the estate in Norfolk. It was as if it were full of pride and strength and love from every generation of this family that had ever stepped across the threshold.

She felt that and so much more as she ventured into Khalif's domain.

He was standing with his back to her, hands clasped behind him. Her eyes scanned the room, surreptitiously and quickly. It wasn't obvious wealth, though that was evidenced by the luxurious pieces of furniture, pristine despite their obvious age. By the gold, silver, precious metals and jewels that were scattered across tables, inlaid across tabletops, shelf-edges, doorframes. Everything was exquisite… everything was priceless.

It was that everything spoke of Khalif. The rich

dark mahogany that was both weathered and strong, the hard edges and sharp angles opulent and eye-catching. The colours were masculine but there were hints of a playfulness that she sometimes felt he was capable of.

But in the centre of the wall that dominated the room was a shelf that was devoted to his family—photos, trinkets that one would collect, memories. *Family comes first*. It was a sentiment that she could both warm to and be warned by.

On the low slung table between them were trays of food, both sweet and savoury from what she could tell. Steam streamed from the spout of a large silver teapot and she told herself *that* was the cause of her mouth watering, not the power of the man in front of her. Her stomach was hungry, not clenched with desire and need. Her pulse was racing because she was unfit, not hoping for more of the man who had taken her innocence and left in its place a wanton woman whose sole focus was pleasure.

She took a step to close the distance between them and just over his shoulder was able to see what he was looking at that had him so absorbed.

It was a black and white picture of a family of four. Even if she hadn't seen pictures of him in the exhibition, Star would have recognised the good-looking man with the same jaw and nose as Khalif. Faizan had his arm around his two young daughters and was leaning into his wife, Samira, who was smiling at the camera as if there was nowhere else in the entire world she'd ever want to be.

Star's eyes were drawn to the gold necklace hanging just below the neckline of her silk top, almost exactly the same as the one Star had removed the moment she had returned to her suite.

He didn't flinch, noticing her presence, she felt it as if it were more of a tightening within him.

'She was very beautiful,' Star said, shocked by the sudden drop in temperature that followed her declaration.

'Tea?'

His question was such purposeful distraction, it was almost as if it were a challenge, or a warning. She nodded, but walked past him towards the view of the desert. Sand swirled in the distance, like her thoughts, shifting, scattering, only to be swept up by the air and thrown down elsewhere. Khalif, Samira, Faizan. Despite what her sisters might think, she wasn't so clueless as to go blundering into a clearly painful area for Khalif. But there was definitely something there.

She could see it as surely as she could see the sky begin to turn to that purple pre-dusk hue that always reminded her of lavender and salt. And home. She felt a sudden pang of homesickness she'd not yet experienced since arriving in Duratra. Suddenly she didn't want to know how Khalif's family had cared for the necklace, why Samira had worn it and how Star might be able to get it for herself.

She wished she'd never heard of the Soames diamonds, of the estate in Norfolk.

And then a swooping wave of guilt and horror

overwhelmed her, knowing that without it her mother would have no hope for recovery. For her mother, for her sisters, she would face Khalif, explain it all and do whatever she had to in order to return to the UK with the key to the missing jewels, whether she was pregnant or not.

She went to sit on the long sofa opposite the chair Khalif had occupied. She took a deep breath and began. 'My grandfather died nearly a month ago.'

'I'm sorry to hear that,' he said, his formality clearly echoing the lack of emotion in her tone.

'We'd never met him. Mum had never spoken about him and I guess we just didn't ask.' There was so much she hadn't asked her mum, so much more she wanted to know. 'We were notified only because he had named us as…sort of beneficiaries of his will.'

'Sort of?'

Star shook her head from side to side. 'His will held a complicated stipulation. If we meet that stipulation, we will inherit his country estate in Norfolk. Which we could then sell.'

Realisation dawned in his tawny eyes. 'And pay for private treatment for your mother?'

Star nodded, breathing a sigh of relief that he understood. That he hadn't immediately assumed she and her sisters were simply out for money. 'It doesn't have to sell for the biggest value—we have no idea what that would even be. It just has to be enough.'

'Star, if you need—'

'We don't,' she said, cutting him off before he

could offer her anything. 'Because we're going to
meet the stipulation and sell the estate.'

And Mum would get her treatment and be fine.

They had a plan, they would stick to it and everything would be okay, she assured herself. It had
become a mantra in the last few weeks. A rhythm
in her mind and her heart like a prayer.

'So the stipulation…it has something to do with
the necklace?' he asked.

'What do you know of it?' she asked, hoping that
might give her some indication of where to start.

'It's been in my family for over five generations
and has been worn by the wife of every Sheikh during that time.'

'Really?'

'Yes, why?'

It made her feel strange that Catherine's necklace
had been worn by the woman who'd married Hātem.
And by the wives that had followed. Perhaps that was
why she had not found a trace of it. She had been
looking for it with the male heirs. And she suddenly
felt a little foolish, remembering the words from the
first part of the coded message her sister Summer
had translated.

*If you have discovered my message then I can
assume two things: that you are female, because no man would wade through the private
fripperies of my youth, and that you are clever,
to have found the journals.*

The pieces of Catherine's mystery had remained secret because they had been protected by women. As, even, had this piece.

'I might have been naïve to assume that Hātem would have kept it with him.'

Khalif shook his head. 'The men in our family do not wear jewellery.'

She nodded in understanding. 'And what do you know of where it came from?'

'I thought you were supposed to be telling me,' he said, half impatient, half grumble, his tone completely familiar to her from the little children she taught when they weren't given what they wanted easily.

'Humour me?' she asked.

He sighed and ran a hand absently through his hair. 'Honestly, even now it feels more like a fairy tale than reality or a part of family history. I used to tease Faizan about it when we were children.'

'About what?'

'That his wife would have to wear the *fairy tale* necklace.'

Star threw a hand-woven tapestry pillow at him without realising that the piece was from the seventeenth century and probably hadn't actually been touched for at least two.

He caught it one-handed and put it down with great care.

'I was a child,' he defended. 'Anyway, we knew that it had been worn by our mother, and our grandmother, and our great-grandmother and so on. Every generation was proud and protective of it, always ensuring that the first in line to the throne would present the necklace to his wife.'

Goosebumps pebbled on his skin and the hairs on the back of his neck lifted as he followed his thought to its natural conclusion.

'But you take it seriously now,' she said, unaware of his thoughts.

'Very,' he replied without hesitation. 'We were told that some day someone would come and claim the necklace. That it would be clear who they were and they would be given it without question or hesitation. Any more than that, I'm afraid I have no idea. My mother might know, but...' He shrugged, his mind still half on the thought that if Star was pregnant it might have found its way to her anyway. Either by becoming his wife, or it being returned to her, Star would end up wearing the same necklace as his grandmother, mother...and Samira.

'My great-great-great-grandmother came here,' Star said, causing Khalif to blink in surprise. 'In the late eighteen-hundreds she was travelling with her uncle as his wife's companion. They were passing through the Middle East and had come to Duratra to meet with His Majesty Sheikh Hātem Al Azhar to discuss Duratra becoming part of the British protectorate. Many other countries in the area had agreed, but Hātem had neither interest or need to do so.'

Khalif raised a sceptical eyebrow. 'And you know this how?' She was right, but it was strange hearing her so certain of the thoughts and feelings of a man who had died over one hundred years before.

'Because Hātem and Catherine grew very close and she wrote about it in her diaries,' she stated, her large blue eyes shining up at him with nothing but sincerity.

'I don't—' He stopped short, his mind incapable of processing what Star was implying. 'This is not possible,' he declared.

Star looked down at the necklace in her hands as if trying to soften the blow of what she was implying. 'Catherine's uncle was called back to Egypt, but his wife refused to travel again so soon. According to Catherine, her aunt had a weak constitution, not suited to the climate, which irritated the husband she was angry with for bringing her to the Middle East in the first place.

'But Catherine was happy to stay behind. She loved it here. She begged Hātem to take her out on horseback so that she could explore as much of the desert as possible.'

'Star, this is all very fanciful but—'

'She spoke of an oasis. Which is what had me confused,' Star said, not noticing the stillness that had come over him. 'I was confused at the palace in Burami because some of her descriptions didn't seem to fit. I just assumed that things had changed in the last hundred years. But when you showed me the gardens here, I realised…*this* is where Catherine met with Hātem. This is where she stayed with her aunt, and spent the night at the oasis with the crossed palms.'

* * *

Khalif's mind screeched to a halt. No one outside the family had visited the oasis. So there was no way that Star could have known about the crossed palms. A sudden memory of him and Faizan digging at the base of the huge ancient trees, convinced there was buried treasure to be found, filled his mind and heart, his ears echoing with the sounds of boys' laughter and the feel of sand against his skin.

'What do the diaries say of Hātem?' he ventured, half hoping she was being truthful and half still disbelieving.

'Quite a lot,' Star replied with a smile. 'That he'd seen what had happened in Egypt and the way it was being torn between Britain and the Europeans, the impossible loan rates and finally the political coup. According to Catherine, Hātem insisted that Duratra had been fine without being under the British protectorate and would continue to be so. He'd been surprised when Catherine had agreed with him though.'

'Why did she?'

Star bit down on her lip, distracting him momentarily. 'Because she knew what it was like to live with a gun to her head.' She turned to look at the desert as if needing to gather her thoughts.

'When Hātem and Catherine returned from the oasis, it was to news that her father had died. Everything that Catherine had, all she had known, would be inherited by her cousin—a man who had made it clear he intended marriage. Would it surprise you to know that Hātem asked Catherine to marry him?'

'Yes,' Khalif barked. And then, 'No. At this point, Star, I don't think anything would surprise me,' he said, reaching for his tea to quench both his thirst and his wonder at all of this...information he'd never known about his ancestor.

'Catherine knew that he was betrothed to Alyah. She thought Alyah would be a good bride for Hātem.'

'Really?' Khalif asked, knowing, of course, that Hātem had married Alyah.

Star leaned towards him with one of the little leather journals she had brought with her gently held open and pointed to the top of one of the pages.

He will be happy with Alyah. Kind, loving and patient... We are too similar, too adventurous, too impatient. But he refuses to see that.

'What did she mean by that? That he refuses to see it?'

'Hātem didn't believe that Catherine had to return to England. She said, *Men think women know nothing of duty. Sometimes it is all we've ever known.* He just couldn't see why she wouldn't stay and they parted on not so great terms.'

'But if they left on such bad terms, how did Alyah end up with the necklace?' He felt like an impatient schoolboy, desperate to hear the end of the story.

'I thought this was fanciful and...?'

He cut her off mid-taunt with a glare.

'Really?' she demanded. 'Does that stare *really* work on your staff?'

'Yes!' he groused. 'Just not with you,' he said through only half reluctant laughter.

'Catherine wrote to Hātem when she got back to England. Her marriage to her cousin Anthony was much worse than she had expected. He was violent and verbally abusive. The journals really only continued for a few years after the marriage and then she had them packed away, so it's a little hard to say. But she'd reached out to ask a favour of Hātem. She hoped that he would make her a key that could be separated into two parts. One part was to be kept by her, and one to be kept by him, guarded until the day someone came to find it.'

'What is it the key to?'

'Catherine wanted somewhere safe to hide things from Anthony. Her diaries, pictures…and the one thing that Anthony wanted most—the Soames diamonds. Catherine left clues and coded messages in her journals for someone worthy of finding them, but the men in the Soames family dismissed or ignored the signs. Ever since Anthony, the Soames men have been driven mad desperately searching for them.'

'Because none were worthy of it,' Khalif realised. 'So, the necklace is actually a key?'

'When the two are joined, yes. They will open the locked room marked on the map of the secret passageways that Skye found the day we…my last day in Burami,' Star stumbled.

Khalif was too caught up in the story to notice, only now making the connection between how down she had been and her desperate need to help her mother. 'That's why you were so sad? Your sister had found the map, but you hadn't found the key?' He nodded to himself. 'And with the diamonds…'

'If we find the diamonds we can inherit the entire estate and then sell it to fund Mum's treatment.'

'I imagine you could do a lot more than that.'

'We don't want anything more than that. Nor do we need it.'

It was said so simply, as if she was genuinely confused as to why they might want to have more than they needed.

'It's just that…' He tried to find the words to explain. 'It would seem that Catherine went to a lot of trouble to keep those diamonds safe for someone worthy to inherit. And to sell them for less than their value…'

'I think Catherine would understand our duty to our mother over the weight of the past,' she said with a finality and firmness that surprised him a little.

Khalif looked out to the balcony and the night sky beyond, his fingers rubbing at the slight stubble on his jaw and chin as he traced the stars with his gaze. He wondered if it was fanciful to think that the historic link between their families might account for the instant impact Star had made on him.

And then she shifted, her hair cascading over her shoulders, down her back and his gut clenched. No. That was all Star. So Hātem had taken Catherine to the oasis… He couldn't help but wonder whether Catherine was the reason Alhafa was known for hiding royal mistresses. Hātem and Alyah had made

Burami their central residence and it had been that way ever since.

'What does it mean, Alhafa?'

His language on her tongue sounded soft and strange but utterly hypnotic. 'I suppose the closest translation in English would be The Edge. You can view the desert from every window and it often feels as if we're at the edge of the world.'

'It's truly beautiful.'

'My brother would have agreed with you. I…don't find it easy being back here,' he admitted. 'Nadya and Nayla loved this palace. Faizan was planning to move them here permanently. When they were younger the twins would run screaming down the corridors, terrifying the staff…' He couldn't help but smile at the memory, but it wobbled as he re-alised how much he'd cut himself off from them. 'Faizan taught them to swim in the pool, just like our father had taught us. It was where we…we met Samira. Her father's family came to visit one summer.' Samira would have been exactly the same age as the twins were now, the realisation catching him by surprise. 'On the first day, she climbed up the tree in the courtyard and refused to come down.'

'What did it take to bring her down?'

Me.

'Food,' he lied, the word burning his tongue. 'Speaking of which…it's getting late. I'm sorry that wasn't a proper meal, just snacks and—'

'It was perfect. I wasn't hugely hungry,' she said

with a smile. 'Though I might be tomorrow,' she warned.

'Then tomorrow we will have a feast,' he assured her.

She stood, but appeared hesitant, worried almost.

'What is it?'

'Khalif, do you know where the necklace is?'

Her large blue eyes were wide with hope. For a selfish moment he wanted to deny that he did. He wanted to refuse her the legacy that was so clearly hers because the necklace was so entangled with his memories. A thread woven through his family that to unpick it, to remove it from them would make Samira the last wearer...

'Yes. I do,' he said gravely.

'Is it here? Can I see it?' For a moment he thought she might clasp his shirt, but instead her hands were entwined before her.

'Star, it's back in Burami, I'm sorry.' She bit her bottom lip again and the sight made him want to soothe away the punishment with his thumb. 'I will speak to my family, but I do believe you, and I believe that it belongs with you.'

'Thank you.'

He gestured for her to go before him and followed her out into the gently lit corridor, realising for the first time that her feet were bare. The sight of them had his fists clenching and he wrestled to get himself under control. He absolutely refused to believe that he had developed a foot fetish in the last twenty-four hours, but he couldn't deny the wicked bent to his thoughts.

He knew that she could feel it too. Hadn't missed the way that her shoulders had tightened, how she'd tilted her head just a little to the side, as she had done only the night before in Burami. He'd pressed his lips and tongue to that spot on her neck...

This time it was he that punished his lip with his teeth, hoping that the short sting would bring him back to his senses. Senses that were almost completely filled with her. She reached the doorway and turned, her hand against the wood, as if anchoring her in place, for which he was thankful. She looked up at him and he was instantly aware of how he towered over her, filled with memories of covering her completely with his body, her pheromones already making him recognise her as his.

She rose onto her tiptoes and he stilled, unsure as to whether he wanted to encourage her or not. Leaning in, she turned her head just slightly and pressed the simplest of kisses against his cheek and it held all the power of a tsunami. While he was trying to navigate his way through the swirling waves, she disappeared into her room and he was left in the dark, clenching his fists, feeling far too much.

CHAPTER SEVEN

KHALIF WOKE FROM a nightmare, heart pounding, skin sweat-soaked, his body tangled in the sheets. The bands of a tension headache pressed against his temple before he'd even opened his eyes, and the cords of his neck ached as if he'd roared his way through the night.

The phone by his bed lit up as it vibrated and he didn't need to check it to see that he had about thirty unread emails and probably at least eight missed calls from his father about the memorial.

He looked at the clock, guessing that it was early as the sun was yet to rise. Five thirty a.m. felt brutal after last night, but there was no way he was going back to bed. The conversations he'd had with Star had felt oppressive and he still hadn't shaken the weight of the past from his shoulders.

He got dressed, choosing loose trousers and shirt, and placed the *kufi* on his head before wrapping the *keffiyeh* into a turban, pressing his palms against the secure familiar material that felt as if it were keeping the pounding in his head contained.

He made his way down dark corridors, not quite ready to let go of his grief, of the images and memories of his brother…of Samira. Of the way she had looked at him just before she'd married his brother.

His heart flared as he stalked towards the stables, looking for his favourite horse. Mavia, a true queen like her namesake was regal, strong, proud and determined, and by far the best in his stable.

She greeted him like a jilted lover and he would have expected nothing less. He really shouldn't have been away from Alhafa for so long. But within moments she was nudging him with her head and demanding the affection he was always willing to give her.

He made short work of her saddle, itching to ride, and he launched himself into the desert just as the sun began to rise and the moon and stars to set. He raced them up a dune and out into the far reaches of the desert—his back to both the oasis, Alhafa and Burami.

He wanted nothing but sand and sky, no past, present or future, just the way his pulse beat to the rhythm set by Mavia. He ignored the sweat on his brow, the fire in his thighs and the ache in his soul as they crested the dune and soared down the other side.

But his mind refused to let up. Doubts, fears, shadows and ghosts rose up around him like a wave of sand before the storm. For three years he'd rode the pain, the grief, the guilt and anger at both Faizan and Samira for their choices, bearing it in silence and in secret. He'd tried to bend and shape himself away from the wanton playboy he'd been and into even half of the leader his brother would have been, and the *one* time he'd slipped, the one weakness he'd given into…

Star.

Her name was like a prayer and a curse.

Only she was the one who would fall fowl of it. That her freedom was the price of his selfishness was nothing short of a tragedy. Everything about her, the bright, effervescent positivity, the gentle soothing babble of words, her enthusiasm, her hope-filled romantic belief…he would have to watch all of those things be dimmed by royal duty and etiquette. He would have to see her denied the freedoms she so clearly took for granted. He would have to see her caged.

How would he ever bear the guilt of doing to her what had been done to him?

As he came to the top of the last dune before returning to the palace he twitched the reins, bringing Mavia to a halt.

He couldn't.

And in that moment, as the sun crested the horizon, he swore an oath that if Star wasn't pregnant he would let her go. No matter what, he would let her go for ever.

Star peered out of her door, holding her breath. Not seeing anyone, she stepped into the corridor and stopped to laugh at herself quietly. She felt like a naughty schoolgirl being caught sneaking out of school grounds. But the hour she'd been asked to stay in her room had come and gone, and she couldn't stay locked up in there any longer.

As she trailed a finger gently across the chalky feel of the corridor wall, she marvelled at how light she felt, knowing that soon she might have the necklace in her hands. Her heart felt as if it had swooped upwards last night and was still soaring high. She'd desperately wanted to call her sisters to let them know all that she had discovered. But the memory of how low she had felt when she'd thought she'd never find it…that shocking disappointment had rocked the ground beneath her feet and she couldn't do that to her sisters. She would wait until she had the necklace in her hands, rather than getting their hopes up.

Star turned right, unable to shake the feeling that she was alone, as if she could sense that Khalif wasn't in the palace.

The silence was rare for her. There was always noise at the school; even outside the classroom children ran down hallways and played in the grounds. There was noise from the busy road she lived on, in the flat she shared with her two sisters. And even when Summer was away at university, Skye was always there, keeping her on track and running like clockwork. Star wondered whether Skye had realised that she'd kept her company almost constantly since the day that Star had met her grandparents.

She wanted to shake that thought off, the low ache she often felt when reminded of them, but there was something in the silence…something about it…that reminded her of Khalif. Not the Kal she had met, though there had been a reservation within him even then. But Khalif the Prince? The man she might have to marry? Unease swirled in her chest and she rubbed her sternum, trying to ease it. She didn't feel as if she knew Khalif as well as Kal who'd she'd spent one magical night with. Because there was hurt and anger that Khalif was holding onto and she couldn't shake the feeling that if she didn't confront it—*him*—then she might never know him completely.

Room after room showed furniture protected by large white sheets, window shutters closed against the damaging rays of the sun. There was not a speck of dust anywhere—unlike the estate in Norfolk. But, despite that, there was the same impenetrable sense of isolation and mourning.

The loss of Faizan and Samira was palpable; it felt as if it were forbidden to utter their names. But that kind of grief could be dangerous. Locked up tight, stoppered, it festered, it wounded, it spread like a poison... And that poison could do very real hurt and damage. She thought of the twin girls, wondered if they were allowed to express their grief, to talk about their parents as her mother had encouraged her to do. Throughout her childhood and into her teens, Star had opened up her feelings, so that difficult became easier and painful became loving. And while there was still an ache, low and constant, deep within her, it was not to be overcome but accepted as evidence of that connection, that love, between her and her father.

Star found her way to the corridor Khalif had

specifically declared off-limits and, despite that, she turned down it anyway. There had been nothing particularly different about it yesterday, just a sense she'd had…until she'd seen his reaction.

Passing through a partially opened door, she came to a stop.

Unlike the others, this room looked as if it had only just been left. Drop cloths on the floor, half-painted walls, rollers stuck to trays with dried, cracked paint next to large tins with the same colours spoke of a half-finished decorating project. Moving further into the room, object by object she saw signs of a home, of life she'd not found elsewhere in the palace. A jumper had been thrown across the end of a sofa in the larger living space. Some nail polish on the side table. Toys scattered on the floor, waiting to be put away.

They were signs of a family.

Faizan and Samira's family. She turned back to the room where she'd seen the most decorating equipment and realised that it must have been the twins' room and an overwhelming cascade of sadness drenched her where she stood.

There was something so incredibly tragic about the half-finished rooms—as if Faizan and Samira's hopes for their children were only half fulfilled. It looked as if the decorators had stopped suddenly, midway through the day. Perhaps to the news of the shocking accident.

She looked at the two tiny beds, now far too small for the twin Princesses, and turned back into the living area, drawn to the warmth and the everydayness of the family photos on the tables and the book lying open at a page.

Star could understand why it had been left, but still…it was such a shame to keep Nadya and Nayla from what was supposed to have been their home, from what their parents had wanted for them. She frowned, looking at the colours chosen for the room, the sweet style of shelving, and she could almost make out how beautiful it would have looked, had it been finished.

She was about to turn back into the corridor when she felt the hairs on her neck lift.

'What are you doing in here?'

She turned to find him full of thunder, heavy dark curls of sweat-soaked hair slicked to his head, his chest heaving as if he'd run here from the desert. His white *thobe* open at the collar, as if he'd been interrupted in the midst of changing it. He looked like an Arabian Darcy having caught her trespassing, but there was no eager welcome in his gaze, no tentative hope in his demeanour. Instead he stood, refusing to cross the threshold, staring at her as if she'd committed a truly heinous crime.

'How dare you?'

Khalif was shaking with rage, grief and shock. He hadn't thought for a minute that Star would betray him in such a way. So when Masoud, awaiting his return in the stables, had informed him where Star was he hadn't believed him.

He tried desperately to keep his eyes only on Star but, not having been in these rooms for three years, his gaze devoured *everything*. It showed him things he wanted to see and things he didn't. Pictures of his brother and his daughters, himself and his nieces... of Samira. Memories hit him thick and fast and he would have sworn he could smell the perfume Samira used to wear drawing him, against his will, across the threshold.

'I was wondering why the memorial was so difficult for you. And then... I think I understand now,' Star said, her eyes watching his every move.

'You understand nothing,' he bit out angrily. Raw, exposed and vulnerable, he did not want to be here.

'I understand loss,' she said, not once breaking that serene stare of hers. 'Loss that has happened... loss that is yet to happen,' she said.

He hated that. He didn't want that for her.

'Whether it is in the past or the future, they are the same emotions, Kal. Grief, anger, resentment, devastation, helplessness. But this?' She looked about the room. 'It's as if you all stopped breathing the moment they died. Do you even talk about them?'

'Of course we do,' he said, spinning away from her, hoping that she'd just stop.

'When was the last time you said their names out loud?'

'With you,' he growled.

'That's not what I mean, and you know it.'

'It's not important,' he said, unable to stop himself from peering through the doorway to the room that would have been for Nadya and Nayla.

I want the two beds facing each other, and the mosquito netting to be pink, and the nightlight to have stars so that it covers the ceiling with the night sky. It's going to be beautiful, Kal.

Samira had been the only other person to call him that.

'It might not be important to you. Or your parents, who must have many memories of Faizan and Samira's life—'

'Don't!'

In that instant he genuinely wasn't sure if it was because Star used her name, or because of what she was saying, but he really didn't want her to continue.

'It's important to Nadya and Nayla. It will be, if it's not already.'

'What's that supposed to mean?' he said, turning, her words ringing in his heart.

'It means that I know what it's like to grow up in the shadow of grief. I know what it's like to want to know who your parent was before they died. You want to know everything about them. Where they came from, what they were like at every birthday you reach. Whether you're like them, whether they would have liked who you are becoming, whether... whether they would have loved you.'

Everything hurt. For Nadya, Nayla, for Star...for himself.

'And if no one talks about them, it's like a denial. A denial that the person existed. And that makes it feel as if the ache in your heart has no real anchor, cutting you adrift in your grief.'

He opened his mouth to ask, but she pressed on before he could.

'And this?' she said, sweeping her arms out wide and spinning in a circle. 'This suite? This palace? It was going to be their *home*. It meant so much to Faizan and Samira that they wanted to *live* here, they wanted to decorate this suite and make it perfect for their children. It's clear from the photos, the memories, the plans...this was where their heart was and their children haven't been back, their family hasn't been back to it and it's just so sad.'

It was an accusation that cut him to the bone.

'We were trying to do what was best for them,' he defended.

'No. You were trying to do what was easiest.'

'Don't push me on this,' he warned, half growl, half plea.

'Why? Someone has to. You can't stay like this,' she warned. 'You're unhappy with the memorial plans—'

'But they're done!' he yelled, no longer caring what effect it caused. 'Three years on from the accident and at least it's done.'

'Really? Then why are you so dissatisfied with them? You keep changing things to fix it, but it's never going to work if you know in your heart it's wrong.'

'You don't know what you're talking about,' he

said, slicing his hand through the air, trying to terminate the conversation.

'At least I'm talking. Really, Kal, is everyone around you so afraid of you that they refuse to tell you what they think?'

'Okay, Star, you tell me. What do you really think?'

'I think you're so afraid of whatever you feel guilty over that it's stopping you from feeling anything real about Faizan and Samira. And because of that you've somehow allowed the memorial to be something not even half worthy of their memory.'

He felt the blood drain from his face. He wanted to fight, to rage, to shout against what she was saying, but he couldn't.

Not even half worthy.

He felt sick. 'It's a disaster,' he admitted through the acidic taste of bile at the back of his throat. 'Everyone knows it. No one wants to admit it. But trying to find something that Samira's father wants, something that my parents would be happy with, not to mention my nieces...'

He felt the weight of her gaze on him, could almost hear the words.

That's not what I mean, and you know it.

He bit the inside of his cheek, torn between wanting to explain everything and wanting to bury it all for ever.

'Samira was six when her family first visited, I was seven and Faizan was eight. We were inseparable, terrorising the palace staff, climbing trees, wreaking havoc…until Faizan had to start taking lessons to prepare for becoming ruler. Then it was just the two of us. It's lonely being royal. Even attending a central city school, it's not that easy to make friends who understand the presence of adult guards, or who don't want to take advantage of who you are or your position. Samira understood it. She understood the constraints of royal life. But where I found it difficult, she seemed to thrive on it. She wanted to use her position to do great things. She would tease me about shirking my responsibilities and I would tease her about taking on too much.'

He missed the sound of her laughter. The way that it had lightened his heart and soothed the ache he felt there. He'd never found it easy being royal, but Samira had borne it with grace and beauty.

'I'd always thought, hoped…' He'd hoped so much. 'Faizan was due to marry the daughter of an ambassador but she ran out just before the announcement, unable to take the weight of public scrutiny. The palace was in an uproar and Abbad… Abbad offered Samira as a replacement. And everyone agreed.'

Without telling him, they had all agreed. Even Samira. Khalif would never forget the moment he'd been told. The sheer incomprehension he'd felt until he'd seen it in her eyes. The sympathy, the silent apology. Even now he felt the wound deep in his heart throb and ache.

'Had you never told them how you felt about her?'

'What do you mean?' he asked.

'That you loved her.' Star's simple words left vibrations in the room that could have cracked the walls.

He could lie and tell her that he hadn't, but it would break something within him, and he wouldn't dishonour either Samira or Star like that.

'I didn't have to tell them,' he replied, like he'd not had to tell Star. 'I did love her—' the words were both bitter and sweet on his tongue '—but the moment she became engaged to Faizan—'

He shook his head, struggling to find the words to describe just how much he'd fought, he'd wrestled and cursed his feelings. 'After she had Nadya and Nayla, my feelings changed completely. Everything changed. She was different…a mother. She had two beautiful babies who were her sole purpose for being and…' Everything really *had* changed.

'It must have been incredibly difficult to watch Faizan and Samira marry,' Star observed.

'She wanted to marry Faizan,' he said, knowing the truth of it. 'She could see how much our parents wanted it. She knew him, *liked* him. He was… better—' Khalif breathed '—he was the better man.'

'He was a *different* man,' Star stated.

'You should have met him,' Khalif replied wryly.

She watched him walk further into the suite, as if somehow dredging up the memories had released the ties holding him back and she was glad. Glad that he'd spoken about Samira. Love should never be something that caused shame or hurt, even if deep down she forced herself to acknowledge a pinprick of jealousy. But it wasn't as much pain as it was sadness for him.

Because he must have felt so incredibly *betrayed*. His family couldn't have missed his feelings for Samira—if *she* could see them still now. She believed him when he said that his feelings had changed towards her when she had Nadya and Nayla. But even so…her heart ached for him and felt now more than ever that he needed this as much as the girls did. They all needed to come home. To where their hearts had once been.

She took a deep breath and crossed her fingers. 'I want to finish what they started.'

He stilled, as if he'd been instantly turned to stone.

'I want to help make this a home for Nadya and Nayla.'

'I'm really not sure about that,' he said, turning to face her. She could see the warring in his eyes.

'I think it would be good for them.'

He nodded reluctantly. 'I'm not sure what you're planning to do,' he said, looking around him as if he wouldn't have a clue where to start.

'That's okay. I have some ideas. Would you like to—?'

'No. Ask for whatever you need from the staff. Just leave the list in your room.'

When Star didn't appear for breakfast the next morning, he had his suspicions. When he reached his brother's suite she was finishing the white undercoat in the hallway that someone had started over three years ago. Her back was to him and every time she reached upward above her head the sleeveless vest she was wearing lifted and he could see a slash of pale skin between the top and the loose linen trousers she wore. And he turned away.

He found an excuse to be at that end of the corridor a few hours later and was surprised by the extent of work she'd achieved. This time he nearly crossed the threshold, but he didn't.

By the time dinner came around, Star looked happy but about to fall asleep in her food. She had tried to keep up with his questions.

'How are you today?' had been met with, *'I still don't feel pregnant,'* which had been delivered with a tired smile. He wondered whether he should just hire a decorator for Star to direct. Even Faizan and Samira had done that. His thoughts flowed with a little more ease than he was used to and he realised then—that had been the first time that he'd thought about them naturally, without that sense of creeping guilt and ache that often accompanied such moments.

The next day he found Masoud hiding in the suite's corridor, looking as if he were about to have a heart attack, periodically peering around the door frame and spinning back to look to the heavens as if in prayer. Khalif was surprised. So far, the staff and Star had managed to stay out of each other's way.

Stepping as quietly as possible up to the man he'd known never to break a sweat under *any* circumstances, Khalif peered over Masoud's shoulder to see what had made him behave in such a way and nearly choked on his own shock.

He clamped his jaw shut firmly.

For there was Star, without a care in the world, humming away as she painted large brushstrokes of admittedly *very* expensive undercoat over a nine-hundred-year-old fresco. Masoud was actually fanning himself and looked almost on the verge of tears.

'We have more, Masoud,' he whispered, reassuring himself as much as the older man.

'I know,' he replied mournfully. 'It's just that this one was particularly beautiful. I just didn't have the heart to tell her…' He trailed off. 'She's doing such a wonderful thing.'

Khalif could only nod, marvelling at the way the head of the palace staff was willing to sacrifice the ancient fresco for Nadya and Nayla, and even for Star.

'I am a little worried about the drill bits, though.'

'Drill bits?' Khalif whispered harshly.

'She's asked for a drill and several sizes of masonry drill bits.' At this, Khalif could completely understand Masoud's concern. He winced himself at the thought of what she might do.

'We can fix whatever needs fixing…if it *needs* fixing,' he promised, hoping that he was right.

The next day, once again, Star had failed to appear for breakfast and this time Khalif took a small collection of pastries with him when he went to the suite he was beginning to think of as Nadya and Nayla's.

Through the door to what had once been the girls'

room, he could see that Star was already painting and yet again her hair was worked up into a large woven cloth turban high on her head. She had finished the hallway and had worked her way around the first corner of the suite and if he wanted to see how she was getting on he would have to cross the threshold.

As if she had been waiting for him to do so, she turned and greeted him with such a beautiful smile that his heart missed a beat.

What would it be like to wake to her each morning?

Not to the blare of an alarm, the flick of the coffee machine or the imperious visage of his brother's acerbic assistant.

'Perfect timing,' she said, looking at him with a gleam in her eye.

'No. Nope,' he said, shaking his head and holding up the pastries.

She looked at the food he was carrying and her eyes rounded with pleasure. 'Thank you! I'm starving. And there's just this little spot...'

He looked over her shoulder to see the stepladder.

'Tell me you weren't just on that,' he demanded, the fury in his tone catching them both by surprise and he bit back a curse.

'Of course. How else was I supposed to—'

'*Khalas!* No. No more,' he said, slashing the air with his hand. 'I'm worried about the paint fumes, I can't trust you not to go up ladders, I'm sure that you'll be trying to move those beds soon enough—'

When her eyes grew wide, he clenched his jaw. 'What did you do?' he bit through clenched teeth.

'I dismantled them before I moved them,' she said, as if that would make it any better.

'How did you—?'

'Well, they're not exactly Ikea, but the principle was the same, and the Allen keys were here, so…'

'Why were Alan's keys here and what does he have to do with…?'

He trailed off because suddenly Star descended into musical peals of laughter. She was almost bent double and sweeping moisture from her eyes.

'I don't understand what is so funny,' he said, trying hard to keep hold of his anger. She made it too easy to breathe sometimes. Too hard not to laugh with her. And for the first time in three years he questioned why that was a bad thing.

'Just take the roller and get into that spot,' she ordered like a military general. He looked down at his clothes. 'Afraid of getting dirty?' she taunted.

'Well, you're clearly not.'

'No,' she said, smiling as she looked down at the splashes of paint across her trousers and forearms. 'They're just clothes that prove how much I'm enjoying myself.'

She had a spatter of paint on her cheek and he itched to smooth it from her skin, but didn't. Instead, he agreed to do the area she indicated, despite the fact that he was already late for a video conference with his staff.

Colour started to appear on the walls over the next

few days and Star now had him completely bent to her will. When he'd asked how she knew about dismantling furniture or checking walls for electrics, let alone the mind-boggling range of fillers, sealants, sandpaper sheets and blocks, she'd said something about a man from her sister's job showing them how to fix certain issues in the flat. And when he'd drilled through the wall and taken out a chunk of plaster he'd been half terrified—not that he would have admitted it on pain of death. But she'd only laughed at him and told him that fixing mistakes was the best and only way to learn.

That evening, Star finally managed to get him to open up about the memorial, but instead of questioning his plans, she asked him more about Faizan and Samira. What they were like, what made them laugh, what made them angry. He was recounting a time when Samira had smoothed over ruffled feathers at an embassy ball, when he remembered the nickname they'd given her that night: *jisr*. Because she'd bridged the gap between ideas, people, countries.

'And what do Nadya and Nayla think?'

He looked at her. 'Think of what?'

'The memorial.'

'They're six years old.'

'Yes. Six—not three, not one. Six-year-olds can even generally feed themselves.'

He glared at her teasing, feeling angry and awkward.

She paused, the teasing tone melting away. 'No one asked them?'

He shook his head, not quite sure why he felt so ashamed.

What do Nadya and Nayla think?

It was now almost midnight and he couldn't get those words to stop spinning in his mind. He hated to think that he might have contributed to a sense that his nieces' grief was something to be denied, or ignored. As if his own, his parents' or the nation's grief was somehow more important than theirs. Unable to shake that sense of overwhelming guilt and shame, he knew that he *had* to return to Burami. He needed to see his nieces. And at the same time he just might be able to retrieve the necklace for Star. The need became so overwhelming, he felt as if demons were chasing at his heels. He had to leave—*now*.

CHAPTER EIGHT

THE FIRST TIME that Star had made a list of things she needed and left it in her room for the invisible staff to collect, she'd been surprised to find that it actually worked… That within twenty-four hours, forty-eight at the absolute most, her exact wishes were fulfilled. Out in the middle of the desert.

She tried to stay awake one night to see if she could hear the sounds of Jeeps or even helicopters bringing the materials she needed, but nothing. They just appeared as if by Christmas magic when she needed them. Which wasn't helping Star's determination not to live in her dream world any more. They were human staff, not fairy godmothers, and she was sure that the spontaneously appearing materials had more to do with Khalif being a prince than the staff having any magical powers.

The fact that Khalif was royalty still didn't feel real. Yes, he behaved like a prince and there were as many glimpses of spoilt stubbornness as there were of grief and loss, but in the last few days she'd felt as if they'd been talking. Really talking. Building something, so that perhaps if she was pregnant it might not be so terrible. That perhaps having a child with Khalif could be her own happy-ever-after?

After her morning shower, Star crossed to the living area, hoping to find the bronze gold paint she wanted to use for the finishing touches across the girls' bathroom ceiling, so when she first saw the note that had been thrust under the door she assumed it was from the staff, apologising for not being able to track it down.

She was already thinking of other ways to achieve the look she was hoping for when she caught sight of the scrawled K at the bottom and her heart leapt.

It was only because she was distracted, she told herself later, that the thought that it might be a love letter crept into her mind. That was where her mind had been so that when she opened the thick cartridge paper she had to read it over three times before she could make out the message.

Which essentially boiled down to a quick apology for having to return to Burami. He'd be back as soon as he could.

Unconsciously she rubbed at the ache in her chest, telling herself that she was silly to have got her hopes up. To be thankful for the reminder that although he was a prince he was made of flesh and blood, not ink and paper and imagination. This wasn't a fairy tale romance. He was important and had been called away, and it wasn't reasonable to expect that he could have woken her up to let her know.

She arrived in Nadya and Nayla's suite to assess

what still needed to be done. The bathroom was beautiful. Star knew it was a silly thing to get excited over, but it really was. This was where she had seen the touches Samira had planned most, the bronze gold taps and the antique glass panels. It was a faded beauty, but regal. There was an enormous roll top bath, only marginally outmatched by a shower unit dotted with pale pink tiles that matched the soft natural plaster that ran through the entire palace. But it was the midnight-blue that called to her. The depth and richness of the paint that had been chosen by Samira seemed as endless as the night sky. And when the bronze gold paint arrived she would cover the ceiling in stars. Large, small and everything in between. She sighed, hoping that it would come soon.

Star left the bathroom and walked back into the central living area to the project she had enjoyed almost as much, knowing that she could work on this until the gold paint arrived. She had kept Khalif away from this part of the room, wanting it to be a surprise. Wanting to see the look on his face when he saw the tree. When the girls saw...

She swallowed. It was quite likely that she wouldn't be there when the girls saw all this. Her throat thickened and she blinked back the damp sheen in her eyes.

No matter. It wasn't about her. It was about them. And they would know and see how much love had gone into this. And knowing that their uncle had helped would make it even more special for them.

She ducked under the sheet protecting the special project from view and picked up her paintbrush, trying to lose herself in the rich browns sweeping up the wall. Despite Khalif's instruction, she *definitely* needed a ladder for this, but she had been very careful.

She only had this to finish, and the stars in the bathroom, which was a good thing because in four days they would be returning to Burami for the memorial and to find out if she were pregnant. After one test, she would know whether her life would irrevocably change or go back to how it had been before. For as close as she and Khalif had become in the last few days, she couldn't deny that he had not spoken of what would happen if she wasn't pregnant. And she couldn't shake the feeling that the answer was…nothing. Nothing would happen. She would return to Norfolk as if they had never met.

But, even if that were the case, she knew instinctively that her life would never be the same again. She felt changed. Not just by Khalif, but by Catherine, by Duratra, all of it. It was as if the desert had seeped into her skin and bones and was part of her now.

But, like Catherine, she also knew her duty waited for her back home. She would return to Norfolk with the necklace, they would find the Soames diamonds, sell the estate, her mother would get the treatment she needed and… And then…

For the first time in her life, the thought of returning to the flat she shared with her sisters, and the job she loved so much with the children…it just didn't seem as exciting as travelling through the desert, or seeing what else was out there in the wide world. Meeting so many different people, all with their own stories.

It struck her then that she hadn't spoken to either of her sisters for nearly a week. She knew she was avoiding them because she didn't want to lie to them about the necklace, or about where she was. But she missed them so much. She retrieved her phone and hit the call button, holding it to her ear with one hand while she painted a rich vein of muddy red upwards towards the ceiling.

But as the phone rang and rang she was transported back to a bus stop nearly ten years before. Cold, wet, she shivered even now. An automated voice announced that she had reached Summer's answering service and the tremor that tripped over her body had her hanging up without leaving a message.

Minutes had turned into hours at that bus stop. She'd sat unseeing, facing the road as it rained, stopped and then rained again. Her mother and sisters hadn't come for her. And the entire time her grandparents' voices ran on a loop in her mind.

We want nothing to do with your mother or you. Do not ever come back here.

And that was when Star had realised that reality was a much harder, darker place than stories ever could be.

Khalif hadn't meant to stay overnight, not that he'd slept for more than three hours, or let his staff sleep much more. But he was anything but exhausted.

Star had been right. He should have spoken to Nadya and Nayla months ago. If his mother had been surprised when he'd asked to see his nieces, she didn't show it. And neither did they. They'd run to him as if he hadn't stood them up only days before, they'd run to him as if he hadn't retreated from them emotionally and physically in the last three years.

He'd spent hours playing with them, building forts from cushions and sheets draped over tables and chairs. He'd smuggled in *ma'amoul*, the semolina cookies that had been a favourite of Samira's, and *ghraybeh*, the shortbread that his brother had preferred. And as dusk had fallen and their bellies had filled with the sweet treats, he'd talked to Nadya and Nayla about their parents. He'd always imagined that they would find it sad and difficult but the moment he'd said their names the twins chatted away happily. And while it had taken a little while to get used to, time for his heart to get over the initial jolt of shock and unfamiliarity, the girls had launched into a list of the things they remembered about their parents as if they recited it every day.

Nadya had wanted birds, Nayla had wanted flowers, and Khalif had managed to sidestep World War Three by promising that the memorial would have both. He couldn't believe he'd forgotten how much Samira had loved birds. He had, in the way only adults could, assured himself that the twins couldn't make a contribution that he hadn't already thought of. He felt as if he were see-sawing between a sense of sadness, happiness, relief and regret for so much wasted time.

He'd gathered his team together and informed them of the changes—the *big* changes—he wanted them to implement. He was done trying to please everyone else. There was no way that could be done. Trying to second-guess what his parents, Samira's father and the people of Duratra wanted had only served to dilute all previous ideas and he would not risk that again. And despite the concerned looks that crossed the table from one side to the other about the timeline they had to accomplish those plans, Khalif was finally completely happy with the memorial.

By the time he'd finished the briefing it had been too late, or rather too early in the morning to track down his mother, so he'd returned to his suite, crashed out on his bed fully clothed and woke a few hours later with a thumping headache. He'd showered, dressed in fresh clothes and was a second mouthful of espresso down when he'd watched his father's cavalcade leave the palace from his balcony. Khalif couldn't say for sure that he'd purposely missed connecting with his father, but it had made the visit easier. Because he knew instinctively that he could not stand before his father—his *King*—and keep Star's possible pregnancy from him. Only when he knew for sure…

Unbidden, the image of himself holding a child—*his* child—left him winded. Because in all the scenarios that had run through his mind—the practicalities of what would need to happen were Star pregnant—he'd not allowed himself to think of what it would be like to hold his baby in his arms. A baby with Star's blue eyes and his dark skin. Someone who trusted and loved him implicitly, without question. The weight of that responsibility heavier than a crown or a country.

In that moment, Star's possible pregnancy morphed from something to be feared to something that he might actually want, might look forward to. And in his mind he saw Star, staring at him with the same trust and love and his heart turned.

His mother had sensed it when he'd sought her out. She'd asked if something had happened and he'd forced his thoughts away from Star herself and instead to the reason she had come to Duratra. When he'd finished explaining what he needed, his mother had seemed surprised and curious, but had done as he'd asked without question.

Now that he turned the last corner on the road to Alhafa, he wondered how Star had been in his absence.

Still not pregnant, he imagined her saying and couldn't help the smile that formed on his lips.

Entering the palace, he went straight to Nadya and Nayla's suite. A quick scan told him that she wasn't there. She wasn't in her rooms either and the tendril of concern that he'd been away too long began to root in his stomach. The palace felt empty. He quickened his pace and went straight to the staff area, hoping that they would know.

He knocked on Masoud's office door, surprised to find the man glaring up at him from behind his desk.

'Your Highness.'

Khalif frowned, the shortness of Masoud's tone unusually censorious.

'Have you seen Star?'

'I might have,' he said, looking down at the paperwork on his desk.

'Masoud.' His tone rich with warning, Khalif glared down at one of his most loyal employees, wondering when Star had enticed him over to her side.

'Sir, with all due respect—'

'Masoud, I'm noticing a distinct *lack* of that due respect,' Khalif prodded.

'You should never have left her alone like that, with no company and no word.'

'Where is she?'

'Have you looked for her?'

'Of course.'

'Have you seen the incredible things she's done in the Princesses' suite?'

'Of course,' he said, even though it was a lie. He hadn't had the chance to see it properly as he'd wanted to see *her*.

'Well, then. She is quite likely to be by the stables.'

Unused to being told off by his staff—other than Amin—he made his way towards the stables, hating the fact that Masoud was right. He turned the corner and immediately stepped back into the shadows.

Star was with Mavia, stroking the animal's long neck even as the mare nudged for more.

Mavia never did that. Not for anyone other than himself. Not even for Samira. What kind of spell had Star cast over the palace, making everyone fall in…

His thoughts were cut short as Star looked up and straight at him and he felt a punch to his gut.

Although she'd hidden it behind a quick blink of her eyes, he'd seen it. The pain, the loneliness. The hurt. And in an instant he remembered. What it was like to be left behind. To be sidelined. And he'd done it to her without even a second thought. He'd been so lost in his own needs—his own desperate need to plan the memorial properly, to impress his father, the country—that he'd left her behind.

He emerged from the shadows, an apology already on his lips. 'I'm—'

'Did you find what you needed?' Star interrupted. She had chosen those words carefully. Because she didn't want the other words to rush out. Words that would make her sound needy, desperate…lonely. As if she couldn't be left by herself.

Only she couldn't. Not really. Every single minute he'd been away had felt like torture. Her mind had delved into things that hurt, things she hadn't thought of for years and had no desire to think of now.

Perhaps her sisters had been right. She wasn't ready to do this on her own. Either of them would have had the necklace by now, returned to Norfolk, and they quite likely would have found the jewels. She should have stayed behind.

Would she have been as lonely in the estate in Norfolk? No. It was the pain of knowing that there were people she couldn't talk to. People she couldn't be seen by. People who, as kind and amazing as they had been to fulfil her requests each day, could deny they'd ever met her.

Shame. She'd felt shame.

Again.

'Ye—'

'I'm glad,' she said, spinning away before he could either finish the word or stop her.

Tears formed, blinding her to her path, and she dashed them from her eyes. Why couldn't she have cried *before* he'd returned? she asked herself. Why not at two in the morning when she'd not been able to sleep? Why not when the horrifying realisation had swept over her that she had filled her life with people and distractions to escape from the feeling of loneliness and shame that had scarred her when she'd visited her father's family.

'Star...'

Khalif's hand was heavy on her shoulder and he spun her round to face him.

'Who hurt you?' he asked, staring deep into her eyes.

'You did!'

He flinched, but as if he'd been braced for it. 'I know. And for that I'm sorry. But I meant...who hurt you *first*?'

She almost collapsed under the sudden ache in her stomach and heart—as if the years of pushing it down, desperately ignoring it had given the pain even more power over her.

She tried to pull out of his arms, but he wouldn't let go of her. He searched her eyes, and she let him see. She opened herself up to the hurt so that he would know and was overwhelmed by it too. He cursed and, just as her legs shook, he swept her up in his arms and she felt…protected.

She knew she should tell him to put her down, ask him where he was taking her. Instead she just let go, ignoring the tears seeping into his shirt, the way her throat ached as if she had been screaming. Perhaps she had been, just silently and for far too long.

She closed her eyes as he took her up stairs and down corridors, almost afraid to look. She didn't want to go back to her room. Didn't want him to just leave her there. A hysterical woman out of sight of his staff.

As she felt him push through a door, she inhaled the rich scent of sandalwood and lime that she associated with him and curled more tightly into his body, not embarrassed enough by her neediness to stop.

He bent beneath her and sat, and she couldn't help but tense as she expected to be offloaded, but it never happened. He continued to hold her to his chest, until her tears and breathing slowed. At some point she registered his chin resting on her head, neither heavy nor intrusive. She was encompassed by his arms, as if he'd wrapped himself around her completely, and in that moment she knew that he'd make the perfect father. Just holding her, allowing her to feel what she needed to feel. No questions—not yet anyway— no impatience or sense of frustration or distraction. As if his only purpose here was her. It was almost enough to start her tears again.

'My mum didn't hide my dad from me,' she began, for some reason not wanting him to have the wrong impression of her mother. 'She spoke about him. There were photos of him in the house and always stories—stories of how they'd met, fallen in love so quickly… She would show me the things he'd made from wood, tell me what he'd hoped for his future…for *my* future. So I always felt that he was a part of my life.'

She shrugged against his chest, her eyes unseeing of the room around her. Instead she had been transported back in time, to the little council house they'd lived in when she was younger.

'I thought that's what families were. Just children and parents. Skye didn't see much of her father after he remarried, and Summer's wasn't a part of our lives so… I didn't know to ask about grandparents, about my father's life outside of us, until school, really. That's when I became aware of grandparents. The older I got, the more I would wonder about my father's parents. What they could tell me about him. Who they were. Were they curious about me? Had they been looking for me? Mum was fairly tight-lipped about them. There had been an argument…

but she wouldn't go into the details. She just shut the conversation down whenever it came to them.'

Star sniffed a little, pulling her shawl around her and tucking herself against his side as if to ward off what came next.

'By the time I was thirteen, I had convinced myself that there had been a tragic misunderstanding between my mum and his parents. I thought if I just went to see them then somehow they'd just…'

She let out a painful breath, expelling the hope she'd once felt into the room. She shook her head in wonder at her own naivety.

'That they'd just *know*, and we'd all hug each other, and my kind, grey-haired, soft grandparents would welcome my whole family with open arms. I imagined Christmases with stockings—because that's what I thought grandparents did—and perhaps even Sundays at a house with a garden. I'd decided that they had a tiny dachshund. It was called Bobbi and it was half blind and would constantly knock into things, but we would take care of it, me and my sisters, while my grandparents cooked in the kitchen with my mother.'

She huffed out a laugh then. 'I should really have known it was a fantasy, partly because Skye always did the cooking.'

Khalif felt his stomach tighten, instinctively knowing that this story did not end well.

'I'd found their address from some letters my father had written to my mother when he'd still been living with them. There wasn't a telephone number and maybe I didn't want one. It would spoil my plan. I'd saved up enough pocket money for the train ticket, worked out that if I ditched school, I could get the bus to the station and the train from there. I copied out the map from the computer at school. I even took some flowers. Who doesn't like flowers?'

The thought of thirteen-year-old Star with a bunch of flowers travelling to see these people he already didn't like did something to him.

'I was so surprised it worked. No one stopped me, or wanted to know what I was doing out of school. I thought I had been so clever. Then I was standing in front of the red-painted door of number thirty-four College Road. I'd imagined blue, but I quite liked the red. It looked cheery,' she said.

Her voice was laced with a sarcasm he'd never heard from her before.

'I knocked, and the woman who answered looked *almost* like what I'd imagined. There were still traces of the marmalade colour hair she'd given to her son, but faded with streaks of white. Just like the way her eyes faded from an open, pleasant welcome to something almost like disdain. She called for her husband without taking her eyes off me. "I'm your granddaughter," I said. You see, I thought they hadn't realised. But she had. They did. They knew who I was.'

She took a deep breath. 'They said that they didn't have a granddaughter. They said that I was unchristian and unlawful because my parents had never married and they told me never to return.'

Khalif cursed under his breath, not that Star noticed. She seemed to be lost in her memories. 'What did you do?' He was half afraid to ask.

'I found a payphone and called home, but of course my sisters were in school and Mum was away. I left a message asking Mum to come and get me and then I waited by the bus stop.' She shook her head again, the silken strands of her hair brushing against his shirt. 'I felt like I'd let her down,' she said, running her fingers across her lips.

'Who?' Khalif asked, trying to keep the consternation from his voice.

'My mum. I knew why my parents hadn't married. It wasn't because they didn't love each other, but because they did, and they didn't need a piece of paper to prove it. I felt like I'd betrayed that somehow by visiting these people.

'I didn't realise how long I'd been sat there but when a policeman found me it was dark. He explained a bus driver had seen me on his route and been worried. They finally managed to track Mum down and they drove me home.'

It was only when she'd seen her mum and sisters, rushing from the door of their little house and sweeping her up in their arms, that Star had let the tears fall. They'd surrounded her completely with hugs and love and held her while she sobbed, the force of it shaking each and every one of them.

'The only way I was able to stop crying was when Skye began to read me my favourite story. From that day on, almost every night for an entire year, after dinner we would all sit down in the sitting room and take it in turns to read stories of love, hope, happy ever afters.' Until the memories of that awful day at her grandparents' home were buried beneath *Pride and Prejudice, Little Women, Romeo and Juliet, North and South, Sense and Sensibility, Gone with the Wind...*

'Did it make things better?' he asked, the vibrations from his voice rumbling gently into the side of her body pressed against his.

She wanted to turn her lips to his chest, but instead was content with her cheek resting there.

'It did. Losing myself in romance and happy endings was a much better thing than to lose myself in sadness, hurt and shame.'

She yawned, utterly spent and exhausted. Both the emotions of the last couple of days and the work she'd put in on the suite had drained her completely.

'Thank you,' she said, looking up at him, still encircled in his arms. 'Thank you for just listening.'

'Of course.'

He'd been about to say *Any time*, but he couldn't say it and know it might not be true. 'Shall I take you back to your room?'

She looked almost on the verge of asking a question before she seemed to think better of it, smiled, and said that she knew the way.

Long after she left, he sat in the room with her memories vivid in his imagination. To be so rejected by family was completely alien to him. He might have had a difficult relationship with his parents, but they would never cut him from their lives. They hadn't when he'd run wild through Europe and they wouldn't even if they discovered Star was carrying his child and that he would be marrying her.

He stalked the halls of the palace, returning to the suite that Star had been so consumed by. He knew that it would affect him, being in what had once been his brother's quarters, and he marched towards them, braced and ready for a fight—albeit an emotional one.

First, he opened the door to the bathroom. It had been days since he'd seen it and the breath left his lungs in surprise. All over the ceiling and down the parts of the walls that weren't covered in antique mirrored glass or the shower was an incredible night sky. A deep blue paint was interspersed with thousands of stars, ranging from the smallest dot to an intricate eight-pointed star the size of his palm. It gave the room an infinite depth and he felt as if he were standing in the middle of the cosmos. He knew that it had nothing to do with ego and everything to do with fully realising Samira's dream, and in that moment he knew he'd never forget Star's kindness as long as he lived.

He was reluctant to leave the space, but he was equally curious about what lay beneath the drop cloth covering a large area of the living space wall. His hand shook a little as he pulled it away, as if he sensed that whatever it was would be profound, but as the cloth fell away he had to cover his mouth with his hand to stop his shock from escaping into the room.

A tree wound its way up from the floor to the ceiling. Branches covered the length of the wall, the texture and detail of the bark making him want to reach out and touch it. It was only as he got closer that he saw little hand and foot holds drilled into the walls.

The girls would be able to climb it, just like Samira had climbed the tree in the palace garden. Stepping up to the wall, he felt the floor beneath his feet change to a soft mat that would protect them if they fell. Star had thought of everything. He shook his head in wonder.

'I hope you can see this, brother,' he whispered out loud. 'Samira, I know how much this would mean to you.'

Now it was up to Khalif to try and repair some of the hurt he'd caused and it came to him instantly, knowing the rightness of it by how his chest filled with excitement and his pulse pounded.

He knew just the way.

CHAPTER NINE

STAR GENTLY PADDED down the corridor to the dining room she'd been shown on that first day and never used. She hugged the midnight-blue silk kimono around her, still feeling a little vulnerable from her conversation with Khalif the day before.

'No, that will take too long,' she heard Khalif say before she'd entered the room. The smell of cardamom tea made her mouth water and the sweet pastries she was going to have to learn how to make had her stomach grumbling.

'It will have to be the Jeep... Yes... I don't care about the expense, it's worth it,' he growled. The moment he saw her in the doorway, he ended the call and put his phone on the table.

'Was that Amin?' she asked, coming into the room and sitting down where her place had been set. He poured her a cup of tea as she took a few pastries—she couldn't say which ones because she'd become lost in the way that his powerful hands gripped the thin silver arm of the teapot, and then the tiny porcelain handle of the cup.

She blushed when he actually had to say her name to get her to take the cup he was offering her.

'Yes,' he said. When she looked up at him he frowned. 'It was Amin,' he clarified.

Oh, good God, she had to get a grip of herself.

'Why did you ask?'

'You always get that tone in your voice when you speak to him,' she replied, inhaling the scent of the aromatic tea that tasted so much better here than it ever had in England.

'What tone?'

'Mmm…that *I-don't-care-what-you-think-just-do-it* tone.'

The look on his face told her that her impression had hit home.

'I don't know what you mean,' he evaded.

'Yes, you do. He irritates you,' she stated easily.

'Because he judges me,' Khalif growled.

'Probably because you're clearly irritated with him,' she replied, unable to help the smile pulling at her lips. 'You should either make peace with him or let him go.'

'And that is your professional opinion?'

'Absolutely. If you don't want it to descend into playground taunts of "He started it".'

Star could have sworn she heard him say, *But he did*, under his breath, but by the time she looked up at him he was furiously studying a mark on the table.

'How do you feel today?'

'*Still* not pregnant.'

He smiled, and her heart eased a little.

'I... I spoke to my sisters last night.' She hated the way that his body tensed, but she was thankful that he waited to hear what she had to say. 'I told them only that I might be able to get the necklace.'

'What did they say?'

'They are very happy.' It wasn't exactly a lie. They had been happy, or at least relieved. Star had intended to wait until she had the necklace in her possession, but she'd felt awkward keeping the news of it a secret. So she had told Summer that she knew where it was and hoped to have it soon. Star would have sworn she'd felt her sister's sigh against her skin as if it had whooshed through the phone speaker. Summer had mentioned something about making the meeting with the buyer easier and had then asked some bland questions about Burami, clearly forgetting that Star was now in the desert. It was a bit unlike her. Or had been unlike her three months ago...but ever since she'd returned from her midterm holiday there had been something almost distracted about her, even though she'd denied it every time Skye or Star had asked her about it.

'And actually, Skye is engaged,' Star announced, thinking of the later conversation with her older sister.

'Congratulations. What's he like?'

'I have *no* idea. I've never met him,' she replied as Khalif blinked in surprise. 'But she's happy, I can tell.' And Skye really had been, happier than Star had ever heard her. It had been strange to hear

Skye shine with the romance of her thrilling Costa Rican adventure.

It wasn't that Star wasn't happy for her, it was just that… She rubbed at her sternum, hoping to ease the tightness there. Was she jealous? Star looked at Khalif. Here she was, in the desert with a gorgeous sheikh, literally on a treasure hunt, and while it could look like the perfect romance for all the world, beneath it all, she was only here because she *might* be pregnant.

But as the days had worn on, and as Star grew closer and closer to the man she'd first met and merged that with the complexities of the man before her, as she felt her heart slowly spread and stretch, she began to suspect that she wasn't pregnant and could no longer ignore her fear that she didn't mean to him what he had come to mean to her.

'That's good, right?' Khalif asked, looking at her as if he were worried about her.

The tea nearly jerked over the rim and she had to place the delicate cup down before she lost even more of it. She knew that he was not speaking about her thoughts of him, but his words had still cut through her.

'That she's happy?' he clarified.

'Yes. Yes, of course,' Star replied, forcing a little pastry into her mouth before she could make things worse.

'Eat up,' he pressed. 'We have places to be.'

'Do we?' This really was a confusing morning.

'Where are we going? Don't we have to be back in Burami tomorrow?'

'Yes. But, in the meantime, you're being kidnapped by a handsome prince.'

Her heart soared, loving the way he'd just teased her. 'Oh, really? Where is he?' she asked, looking around the room.

'Funny,' he groused. 'Meet me by the stables. And dress comfortably.'

He probably should have asked her whether she knew how to ride *before* he'd made his plans, but the excitement and determination that had shone in her eyes was worth it. Mavia was so completely under Star's spell that he'd almost had to stop the mare from lowering to the ground for Star to mount.

If he wasn't careful, he would not have any subjects left in the country because they'd have all sworn allegiance to her.

Star had dressed as he'd asked. A long-sleeved white top and cream linen trousers were protected by a pale gold pashmina that compared unfavourably to the rich red ropes of hair that curled down her back.

But it was her smile that truly shone.

By the time he had Star on Mavia in front of him, his pulse was ready to burst. His horse didn't even complain once at the unusual extra weight, instead flicking a gaze at him from her bent head as if to demand what he was waiting for.

In truth, he was waiting to regain control of his body. He'd not counted on the way that having Star in between his legs and against his chest, or the way his arms felt wrapped around her would affect him.

She hadn't asked him a single question, he thought as he flicked Mavia's reins. She launched from the stables as if as desperate to show Star the magical wonders of the desert as he. Star's trust in him was complete. As complete as it had been the night they had spent together. It made him feel like…a king.

As Mavia galloped beneath them he relished the feeling of having Star so close, and he loosened his hold on the reins, his horse knowing their destination, having made this journey more than a thousand times, even if not in the last three years.

He cast his gaze outwards and breathed deep. He felt alive here. The stretches of endless desert a mirage, a trick she played on the weary traveller, to test their mettle, to see their true worth. There were no lies in the desert. She may not have been cruel or loving, but she was most definitely capricious.

In the back of his mind he heard his brother's laugh, urging him on, faster and faster, and it merged with the laugh from Star. He felt it in his heart, surrounded by adrenaline, excitement and all the things he hadn't felt for so long. He could feel it. The rightness of coming here. As if he had always been meant to bring her to this place.

They were so nearly there and Mavia knew it too because she found a sudden spurt of energy. They crested a dune, trails of sand billowing in their wake for no one to see, and at the pinnacle Mavia came to a stop of her own volition as if just as awed by the sight as the humans she carried. Khalif might have known every single inch of this view, but it still struck him as something incredible and precious, known only by a rare few.

He cast his eyes deep into the valley, over the large canvas tent nestled close to the trees that lined the small lake in the middle of the basin and in the distance he looked up to see the palms Star's ancestor had written of.

Star's mouth had dropped open. Her eyes raced across the image before her, sure that it was a dream. A desert mirage. But it wasn't. She could feel the heat of Khalif behind her and the pounding of Mavia's heart beneath her.

At the mouth of the tent, rich, dark red woven rugs stretched out before a large fire pit—one that was already in full flame. Golden glints and bursts of red hinted at sequin-encrusted cushions and rich deep turquoise silks covered the sand. A low-slung table with a dazzling array of drinks and food were kept cool and contained in a glass-fronted fridge. She was sure there must have been a generator somewhere discreet, but she couldn't see it. Nothing spoiled the fantasy.

The richness of what lay in front of her was almost too much to bear, so her eyes drifted to the far side of the crystal-blue water nestled within lush green vegetation to where she saw two palms crossed at the base to form an X.

Her heart missed a beat and she gasped.

She didn't dare turn around because if she looked at Khalif now, he'd know. He'd know that she'd fallen in love with him. And there, wrapped in his arms, his hands loosely holding the reins, and half convinced that he would be able to feel the beat of her heart, she almost started to shake.

Khalif urged the horse forward and they jostled from side to side with the horse's uneven but regal gait as Mavia made her way down into the basin where the oasis flourished. When they came to a stop, Khalif dismounted and she hastily swept at the moisture in her eyes, not wanting him to see how much being here meant to her.

He reached for her and took her into his arms, bringing her down from the horse, and stood her barely an inch from him. He searched her eyes in that way of his and she thought, *I want you to look at me like that for ever.* Finally, she looked away, hiding from his scrutiny, pretending to find the lake fascinating, when all she could think of was him.

'Do you know where you are?' he asked, his voice low but strong.

'This is where Hātem brought Catherine.' *Before she had to leave*, Star concluded silently, trying to surf the wave of sadness that swept over her at the thought that she might soon be leaving too. 'Why did you bring me here?'

He looked over her shoulder, the desert swallowing the sigh that escaped his lips. It was as if he needed a moment to gather himself because when he turned back to her, his eyes were fierce. His hand cupped her cheek, holding her gaze—as if she could or would ever look away from him.

'I brought you here to remind you of the family who want you. Not just your sisters and your mother. But the family who knew you would come, following in their footsteps. To remind you of the one who trusted in her people, in the women of her blood and the women bound to those she loved. It is they who have kept her secret safe, ready and waiting for you. Not for anyone else. But you.

'You have been waited upon for over one hundred and fifty years, Star Soames. That is no small thing.'

She felt his words in her soul, as if something ancient had been woken beneath the desert and was reaching for her. So when Khalif delved into the bag on his saddle and retrieved a small velvet pouch her heart didn't pulse with surprise, it vibrated with an overwhelming feel of *rightness*. As if something predestined was finally coming to conclusion.

He took a necklace so familiar to Star from the pouch and held it up for her to inspect. She pressed slightly shaking fingers against her lips. This was what they had been looking for. It was the key to so much. To the past, to her mother's future… So much rested on such a small, beautiful thing. Khalif had been right. There were subtle differences, but it could have easily been mistaken for the one that she was wearing around her neck.

'May I?'

'Of course. It is now yours,' he said with a solemnity that felt ceremonial.

Taking it from him, she made her way blindly to the silks and woven rugs. She folded her legs beneath her, and she looped the gold chain over her head and brought the two pendants together.

She knew that they should fit together—Catherine's coded message had said as much—but she didn't quite… She ran her finger over the embossed pattern on the surface of the pendant and felt something shift. Pressing down released an indented piece of silver from the bottom of the pendant. She picked up Hātem's pendant and did the same. Staring at the two pendants, she didn't quite know what to do next. They needed to…

Khalif reached over. 'May I?' He seemed as lost in the task as she and she was happy to pass him the necklaces if it meant she could spend just a moment looking at the man who had given her more than he could ever know.

He turned the pendants in his hands, twisting and turning one piece while holding the other steady, and then, as if suddenly seeing how it could be, hooked one pendant into the other.

'Oh,' Star marvelled. Together the pieces created one key, the thick gold base forming the head and the two thinner silver offshoots forming the blade—the indentations becoming the ridges and notches that would fit into a lock.

Khalif pressed against the head of the key and the silver blade retracted into the body of the pendant. 'There. You can now wear them together.'

She stared at him, shaking her head in wonder.

'You don't like it?' he asked as if confused.

'I *do*! I love it. I just… I don't think I ever imagined actually finding it.'

I don't think I ever imagined actually finding you. *Finding the man I would love for the rest of my life.*

'Are you trying to tell me that you didn't believe your search would have a happy ending? And you call yourself a romantic,' he tsked.

She tried to swallow around the lump in her throat and a smile wobbled on her lips. 'Of course I do.'

He held up the necklace. 'Would you like me to—'

'Actually…' she said, rising quickly. 'I'd like to explore,' she exclaimed brightly, sure that the overly bright response had given her away, but he kindly let her go.

She couldn't take the necklace. Not yet. Because that would be the end of her search in Duratra. She would be done and wearing the necklace, holding it complete as the key would be the end of her time here. Especially as she was almost sure that she wasn't pregnant.

Khalif went to see Mavia, made sure that she had extra treats for carrying them both here. It hadn't been a long journey and she would have all the rest she needed, as he and Star would be driving out of here tomorrow.

He could see that Star had been affected by the necklace. He had been too, not imagining for a moment how it would feel to give away something that had been worn by the women of his family for over one hundred and fifty years. In doing so, it felt as if he'd entrusted part of his family to her.

Something red flashed in his eyeline and he knew that Star had undone the long thick plait of her hair. He clenched his jaw against the need to turn and look. Instead he worked on building a fire, ignoring the way ripples of water lapped against the fertile green border of the pool.

While his imagination painted images of mermaids with flowing red tresses and mystical creatures, he unpacked the food he had brought, placing it in the cool fridges running from the almost silent generator behind the tent.

The staff from Alhafa had worked through the night to make this happen, happy to do a kindness to the woman who had brought life back to the palace. He marvelled at how quickly, readily and easily she had become their Queen. But would it make her happy? Would being royal, being a princess in a foreign land, be right for her? Becoming a spectacle for the world to investigate, judge and find wanting, no matter how perfect she was. Her life would be on display and at risk and he knew that he could not do that to someone as pure and beautiful as her.

The fire took, the crackle and burn mixing with the chirps of the cicadas and the cry of the birds that stopped at the oasis on their journey across the desert. Wind gently rustled the leaves in the trees and water rippled and in his mind's eye he could see Star in the lake, her hair splayed on the surface and her body hidden from his gaze by the distortion of the liquid, no matter how pure.

His pulse pounded in his ears, blocking out the sounds of the desert. He cursed the wood beneath his hands because it wasn't smooth, freckled skin, soft as satin. A swift inhale followed a pinprick and he looked down to find a splinter in his thumb. Frowning, he removed the sliver of wood, watching the tiny bloom of blood before pressing it to his lips.

He'd never wanted a woman like this.

And he never would again.

'What happens if I'm not pregnant?'

Her voice, a little shaky, a lot tentative, came from behind him.

'You've only told me about what happens if I am.'

Because he'd not wanted to let her go.

He cleared his throat from his emotions' tight hold. 'You will return to Norfolk. I will return to the throne.'

'And that's it?'

'That's it.'

'I'll never see you again?'

She had posed it as a question that he chose instead to take as a statement, unable to bring himself to answer. Silently he roared his fury. Everything in him wanted to reach for her, just one last time. Not damning the consequences, but fully understanding them and facing them. His mind taunted that it was a gift, this one night, more than either he or she should have ever expected, but his heart berated him. Maybe unconsciously he'd known that coming here wasn't just for her, but for him—to have this, to have *her*. He was selfish and she deserved so much more.

'Thank you for bringing me here.' The finality of her tone ate at him. It was as if she were saying goodbye.

'It was the least I could do.' He paused, knowing that his next words would open up a path neither should take, but both seemed powerless to resist. 'It may be the *only* thing I can do.'

'I understand,' she said quietly.

He spun around and pierced her with his gaze. 'Do you?' he demanded, furious with her, with himself. There wasn't anything about this that he understood.

'I do.'

It was then he took her in. Long red tresses soaked into ropes, lying flat against her skin. The long-sleeved white top almost transparent, revealing more than it concealed, pressed against her body the way he wanted to be.

His hands itched to reach for her, to take her, to pull her to him.

He was shaking his head as she took a step forward and stopped, but he caught the way she masked her hurt in an instant and he cursed. She turned to walk away, but he was up and reaching for her before she could take a second step, turning her in his arms before she could take another breath, and punishing her with a kiss—punishing them both—before he could think again. She gasped into his mouth and he took it within him, locked it away because that was how she made him feel. Shocked, awed, thrilled…

He wanted her to remember this moment for the rest of her life, because he already knew he would.

Her arms came up to his shirt, her hands fisted the cotton, pulling him to her, their passion frantic, needy and desperate.

His hands flew over her wet T-shirt, lifting and pulling to reach her skin, as if only that would soothe the burning need within him. Hand flat against the base of her spine, he pressed her into him, her taut nipples pebbling into his chest, her neck beneath his tongue and teeth, all the while her nails scratched trails of fire into his skin.

This was madness, utter madness, but neither seemed able or willing to stop.

He pulled back, long enough to let her lust filled gaze clear, having never seen anything more beautiful in his entire life. 'Star,' he warned as he took her in, pupils wide with desire, breath heaving. She looked utterly gorgeous.

Her name felt like an apology on his lips and she wanted to shout at him, yell and scream that she didn't want apologies, she wanted *this*. She wanted him. Needed him almost as much as her next breath. Before he could say another word, she pulled him to her, kissed him with all the passion she was capable of. All the surety she felt that, no matter the reality, no matter what happened tomorrow, he was the man she was supposed to love for the rest of her life.

His hands came around her waist, pressing against her hip and ass, and she lifted herself into them, wrapping her legs around his waist, glorying when she felt his erection at her core.

'Please,' she begged against his lips. 'Please, just tonight. Just this.'

He raised a hand to sweep her hair from her face, holding her there, looking into her heart and soul. 'Of course.'

That night, Star was lost in a sea of pleasure. Fingers tangled, tongues danced, her skin was alive beneath his touch. She felt a fire building deep within her, expanding and filling her until the point where she couldn't contain it any more and an explosion of the most intangible beauty scattered her being across the star-covered desert.

Again and again he broke her into pieces, only to put her back together as something new, something different, and in that moment she knew she would never be the same again.

By the time the sun's rays cut a path through the tent's awning to rest against her skin, Star was aware that Khalif was no longer there. She dressed, her clothes feeling as if they didn't quite fit, and a sense that the morning—and the day—wouldn't quite be right fell against her soul.

She found him looking out across the desert.

'What are you...?' Her voice broke a little, her throat raw from screaming her pleasure through the night-time hours.

'I was making a wish. I—'

'Don't tell me,' she rushed out. 'It won't come true,' she warned.

'I was wishing not to be a prince.'

She swallowed the emotions begging to be released. It was a wish they knew couldn't and shouldn't come true.

'You are a wonderful prince. Conscientious, careful about others and what they think, thoughtful about doing the best thing possible for the greatest number of people. You will make a good ruler. Fair, strong, determined.'

Still looking out into the desert, he quirked his lip into a wry smile. 'Why do I hear a "but"?'

Star hurt for him, shook her head, but determined to say this to him. *For* him. 'You are not being *you*. You are being the Prince you think they want.'

'I am not my own any more. I am theirs,' he said, as if trying to explain himself to someone who refused to see his truth. When in reality he was simply refusing to see hers.

'You could be the ruler you want to be, if you are willing to stand by the consequences.'

She knew how that sounded, but Star really wasn't thinking of herself. She was thinking of the man who had already begun to lose himself under the weight of the crown. 'I wish I could have seen you before.'

'What,' he scoffed, 'as the disreputable playboy?'

'No. Just the boy.'

Khalif reared back as if she had struck him. He was about to reply when the roar of a Jeep's engine cut through the desert.

They were out of time.

CHAPTER TEN

'SO, STAR'S APPOINTMENT with Maya is tomorrow?' Amin asked for the hundredth time that day. Even Khalif's other members of staff glared at the bespectacled man.

Reza leaned against the wall of the meeting room, refusing to take his eyes from Khalif, who was spending an unnecessary amount of time trying to ignore that fact.

'And you know she can't attend the event tonight?'

Khalif was going to have to see a dentist before the week was out. And Amin might be paying a visit to the doctor. He opened his mouth to speak when he felt Reza's hand on his shoulder, as if holding him back from the violence he wanted to inflict.

'I think we all understand that. In the meantime, let's take a short break before reconvening for the run-through for tonight's event.'

The quiet authority of Reza's tone had the desired effect on his staff and the opposite effect on Khalif.

'I don't need you to speak for me,' he growled.

'Of course you don't. But you also don't need a

mutiny on your hands, which is what will happen if you push your staff any harder.'

'It is no harder than I push myself.'

'You're right. It is considerably less. But that doesn't mean either is manageable.' His best friend let go of the hold on his shoulder as the last staff member left the room. 'What are you more afraid of? That she is pregnant or she isn't?'

'Does it matter? I couldn't do this to her,' he said, finally saying it out loud. 'I know what it is like to have that freedom taken away and I can't...' Khalif shook his head.

'I know the sacrifices you have—'

'Sacrifices? I changed *everything*! I *stopped* everything.' Khalif stared at his best friend in disbelief. Finally, after three years, it poured forth. 'I gave up an international business I had built from scratch, I dropped everything and came home. I buried my brother and Samira in front of the world's press. I made phone calls and shook hands within hours of their funeral... I did what I had to and would do it again. But Reza, I couldn't *breathe*, let alone grieve in the way I wanted.' And for *who* I wanted, he finally admitted to himself. 'This? It's like being in a straitjacket, folded in on yourself, cramped, confined. The expectation of everyone, the watching, the pressure. How on earth can you think I would willingly put that on someone as innocent as Star?'

Reza stared at him with deep understanding and sympathy. He placed his hand on Khalif's shoulder, the weight both comforting and steadying. He nodded once and Khalif knew that his best friend understood.

'Okay,' Reza said simply. 'Then let's talk about how this holographic presentation is going to work, because that is going to blow their minds.'

It felt strange to be back in Khalif's suite. Especially since everything that had happened between then and now had begun to feel like a dream. She was on the balcony, the late afternoon sun sinking into her skin, warming her pleasantly...but not quite enough.

She rolled her shoulders, bracing her hands against the balustrade, eyes searching the horizon. The view of the city looked a little different now that she knew out there, beyond the stretches of golden sand, the sloping dunes and hazy blue skies, was a desert palace seen only by a few and an oasis that would always be in her heart.

She glanced at the rucksack containing everything she had brought with her and one new item. She had returned the connected pendants to the velvet bag and was yet to be able to wear them, putting off the moment until she truly knew that she would be going home. The necklace now had a double chain, as if it would always acknowledge that it had needed two people to come together to make it whole.

She felt a tide of anxiety washing against her soul, back and forth like the sea. She was nervous for Khalif, knowing how much the reveal of his plans for the memorial meant to him. So much so that she'd borne the look of guilt he'd worn as he'd explained why she couldn't come to the event that night with understanding and acceptance. Both of which she truly felt. But it had hurt nonetheless.

Yet it hurt in a different way to how she had felt alone in the palace in the desert. This was not the sense of shame and rejection she had felt because of her grandparents, it was more a sense of inevitable ache. A sense of loss that was down to fate rather than intention. Where once Catherine had been forced to do her duty, now it was Khalif's turn—and Star honestly couldn't have argued against either.

He'd offered her a way that she could still see the presentation, which she would take, because it was his moment and she wouldn't take that away from him. Which was why there, on the balcony, facing the desert, she sent a prayer to Catherine and Hātem, and Faizan and Samira, to look out for him that night.

There was a knock on the door. Star had been expecting it, but it still made her jump. She turned back into the room to find Maya closing the door behind her. She smiled at Star, who braced herself.

'I was hoping you could help me with something. Do you think it's possible to take the test today and for it still to be accurate?'

Khalif flexed his jaw, hoping to relieve the ache in his cheeks from the perfunctory smiles he'd masked himself in.

Samira's father, Abbad, had been casting grim glances his way since the first guests had arrived and his wife's vacant gaze wasn't any better. The only time he'd felt himself relax was when Nadya had winked at him and run off to play hide-and-seek amongst the legs of the guests. His parents were thankfully preoccupied by small talk with dignitaries and international diplomats.

'It is a stunning design,' Reza said quietly, having stuck by his side the entire afternoon.

'I know.'

'You should be proud.'

'And she should be *here*,' he growled, his tone grating his throat.

'There are three hundred people present, the Duratrian press both inside and outside the palace, along with more than a few representatives of the international newspapers. You think that a woman with hair like the sun would go unnoticed in here?' Reza reminded him. 'Tonight is about Faizan, Samira... and you. *After* tonight,' he pressed, 'is another matter entirely.'

You are wrong, my friend, Khalif thought, no matter how much he wished it weren't the case.

Khalif stepped up to the podium and the audience grew quiet and turned to face him. He looked out across the faces he could see beneath the bright powerful glare of lighting trained on the stage. He felt the hairs on the back of his neck lift, his heartbeat stumbled and while he didn't know how, or where, Khalif knew that Star was here. He took a breath.

'Ladies and gentlemen. My family and I are honoured that you could be here tonight. For some, it may have seemed like a long time coming,' he acknowledged to the gentle murmur rippling across the guests. 'However, I truly believe that my brother and Samira deserved such consideration. The...hole they left in the lives of their family and friends is immeasurable and it was important to respect that grief. Faizan and Samira touched so many lives. They didn't just merge two families, but they brought two countries together and two beautiful princesses into this world.

'Growing up with Faizan was no mean feat,' he said, to the slight laughter of the crowd. 'He was focused, driven, bright, intelligent, compassionate. And I can see those qualities already in Nadya and Nayla. Faizan always knew what legacy he wanted to leave behind him. One of peace in the present and hope for the future. Hope not just for his people, but his planet. And Samira? She was always smiling, always ready to be the balance in disagreements, always ready to bridge the gap between her husband the Prince and the man who loved his family and his people above all else. Samira and Faizan were proud, loving and very conscious of their countries.

'She was the bridge and he the river that ran deep beneath it and that is how I, and I hope all of you, will remember them.'

He stepped back from the stage and allowed the lights to dim. The gentle hum of excitement building from the crowd momentarily stopped in awe when they saw the first images from the holographic display.

Khalif heard the words of his pre-recorded voiceover explain about the area between Duratra and

Udra that had long since been abandoned. It was a kind of no man's land where the river, coming from the Red Sea, cut between Duratra and Samira's home country.

The hologram showed images of what the country looked like now and slowly how the area would be cleared, cleaned and prepared for what was to come. Over the next few minutes, the graphics showed a bridge being built over the river between the two neighbouring countries. Beautiful plants and lush greenery developed along both sides of the banks as well as each side of the wide bridge. Oohs and aahs came from the audience as they could see the trees grow, healthy and strong and high on top of the bridge.

'There will be no cars or vehicles in the area. It will be completely pedestrianised. Wildlife will be introduced—birds, insects and eventually larger animals—all cared for by specially trained staff who will provide guided free tours for any visitor.

'It will be a sanctuary. A place for people to come and honour the memory of Faizan and Samira, and the investment in the future that was always so very important to them. It is the paradise they would have wanted for their children, and it is what their children wanted to honour and remember their parents.'

His family needed this, his country needed— *deserved*—stability, unity, cohesion and healing and he knew deep down in his bones that this would be the first step.

Khalif looked out into the audience, touched

by the overwhelming emotion he felt rising up to meet his own. Goosebumps pebbled his skin and he thought that he saw a flash of red, looking up in time to see the movement of a curtain at the balcony near the private suites on the upper level.

'Uncle Kal... Uncle Kal!'

He turned just in time to catch Nadya, who had thrown herself at him in wild abandon.

'You had the birds!' Nadya's voice was a little muffled from where her face was pressed against his stomach and she gripped his waist like a limpet. Nayla, the shyer of the two, stood with a massive grin and wide eyes showing her delight, standing with one foot tucked behind the other.

'And flowers,' he said to her, and she nodded enthusiastically.

'Will it be bright blue and pink like the hologriff?'

Kal didn't have the heart to correct her. 'Well, maybe we can speak to the designers about that. We have quite a bit to do before we get to that point.'

Over his nieces' heads, he saw his parents making their way towards him. Unease stirred briefly but then he grounded himself. He knew that he had done the right thing—not because it pleased everyone, but because he felt it in his gut. The memorial would be doing the right thing by his nieces and by Faizan and Samira.

'My son,' his mother, Hafsa, greeted him, her eyes crinkling the fine lines at the corners into fans. He wasn't sure whether it was a consequence of losing his brother, or valuing the family he did have and the love he felt for them, but his heart felt torn—between being here with his family and being with the woman upstairs. And he knew that neither deserved half a heart.

It took him an hour to extricate himself from the gala, but he couldn't have said that he'd tried too hard. He had felt it. Something in the air had shifted. A kind of knowledge, or awareness, had begun to creep over him, without him knowing specifically what it was. He just knew that he had to get to Star.

His heart was pounding as he made his way through the private areas of the palace, but his footsteps were slow and purposeful. Something inside him was roaring to get out, but he hardly made a sound. He smiled at the staff and few family members he passed, though in his mind's eye he saw only one thing…one person.

He closed the door to his suite behind him and stopped. He inhaled the scent of her on the air, wondering if that might be the last time he did so. He didn't have to look, to know that she was out on the balcony. She loved that view almost as much as he did.

He took two steps into the room and paused. Letting himself see her. The way her hair twisted in the gentle desert breeze. From this angle she stood at the balcony amongst the stars and he bit his lip to stop himself from saying something, not wanting to spoil the moment—for her or him.

She turned slightly to the side, as if sensing his presence, and wiped at something on her cheek that he didn't quite see, so caught up in the sight of her.

'What are you doing here?' she asked.

'I live here,' he said, but the joke fell flat. 'I was worried.'

'About the presentation?'

'No, that went well. Really well.' He closed the distance between them as she turned to face him fully. 'Everyone loved it.'

'Of course they did.' She smiled and his heart ached at the easy acceptance and surety ringing in her voice. 'You should probably get back,' she insisted, 'it's still early.'

'I was wrong,' he said, offering her all that he could. 'To ask you to stay here.'

'You weren't and you know it,' she replied without malice or anger. This was Star as he'd never seen her before. Regal, poised and absolutely breathtaking. And that was when he saw the necklace, the double strands of the chain on either side of the pendant making it something strangely beautiful. And instinctively he braced himself against something he felt he already knew.

Star searched his features, her eyes running over his head, shoulders, down the length of his body, consuming as much of him as she possibly could. There was no way Kal could have let her be there at the event that evening. She understood a little of that duty now. How the crowd had looked up to him, watched him, hung on every word. How they had cried and sighed their appreciation of his plans for the memorial. He had given them a focal point for their grief and the beginning of the healing process. She supposed in some way she was about to give herself the same.

'I'm—' Khalif started.

'I'm not pregnant,' she interrupted before he could say anything more.

He simply held her gaze as if he had felt it in the same way she had. When Maya had presented her with the results of the test, Star hadn't been surprised by the fact she wasn't carrying Khalif's baby, but by the extent to which she'd actually been wanting to. Not once had she let herself hope or believe because…because, she realised now, she had never wanted anything more in her life.

'Maya assured me the test was accurate.'

He closed the space between them in just two steps, drawing so close to her, only inches really. It was as if he wanted to touch her, reach for her, just as much as she wanted him to…but couldn't. Wouldn't.

In one breath, Star was lost just to the sense of him. His exhale shuddered against her cheek, before he turned to stand beside her, facing the desert. She placed her hands on the stone balcony close to his, their little fingers almost touching, but her heart knew the distance might as well have been a chasm.

Go…go now.

But she couldn't. She forced herself to stay, refusing to turn and run. She was a reader. She was a romantic. And, whether it was foolish or not, she had hope. All the things they'd experienced—an impossible meeting, ancestors torn apart by duty, families brought back together by fate. She had found Catherine's Duratra out there in the desert. Khalif had found her necklace...

'So that's it then.' His voice was rough and dark in the dusk.

She felt as if she'd conjured up the words herself. The first steps of the dance that would see them either spending the rest of their lives together or...

'Is it?'

'Star...' he warned.

'No, Khalif. It's a question I am asking you. *Is* that it then?'

She refused to look at him, even though he was staring at her hard, trying to get her to face him. But she wouldn't. Couldn't. Because he'd see. He'd see all that she wasn't quite ready for him to see.

'It's funny how people behave when they think they don't have a choice,' she said to the desert. 'It traps them, makes them feel helpless, makes them behave in ways that aren't authentic to them. Ways that aren't right for them.'

'You can't consider my life to have choices.'

'Why not?' she demanded. 'Look what you did when you realised that you had a choice for Faizan and Samira's memorial? Look at the incredibly beautiful, amazing thing you have set in motion. Do you not think that we could—'

'It's not the same. *Everyone* in my family, every heir to the throne has been in the same position,' he growled. .

'The definition of madness is doing the same

thing over and over again and expecting different results.'

'Why do you think I'm expecting different results?' He looked at her, genuinely confused. 'There were no disastrous results for my parents. And Faizan and Samira's marriage was a very happy, fruitful one.'

'But not for you. Not the hurt it caused you,' she half cried. 'Would you force this on your nieces? Would you expect them to marry for duty rather than love?'

'No! I'm doing this so that they can have that option for themselves.'

'Really? You're not doing this because it's easier than being true to yourself?'

His gaze met hers in a fiery clash, the golden flecks in his umber eyes swirling like a sandstorm. 'Star—'

But she couldn't listen to him. She had to press on. This was her last chance. Her only chance. 'Because I suppose you can't really fail if you're always trying to please everyone else. If you're being everything other people need, then it's their need that's failed, not you. And you'll never know.'

'Know what?'

'You'll never know how incredible you could be if you were just yourself.'

Her voice rang with such sincerity, such hope and such optimism he half wanted to believe it himself.

It was seductive, what she was saying. Be himself, choose her, be a great ruler. But she was wrong.

'I was myself,' he bit out angrily. 'For three years, I wined and womanised my way around Europe. Is that the kind of ruler Duratra deserves? Is that the kind of man you want?' His voice had become a shout.

'You were hurt. Your entire family condoned a marriage between your brother and your first love. Of course you acted out,' she said, desperately grasping for justifications for his terrible behaviour.

'Acted out? Is that what…?' He ground his teeth together, hating the way that her words ran through his head and heart. Her understanding, her belief in him crucified him, made a mockery of every single choice he'd made since, tearing him in half between what he so desperately wanted and what he felt he needed to do.

And he was furious. In that moment, he wanted to bring down the palace, smash and burn everything— anything to make the questions stop. So he did the only thing he could do.

'I know you think being a prince means that—'

'Don't,' she said, the single word a plea. 'Don't use that—'

'I know you think being a prince means that magical adventures await and love comes with singing birds and talking clocks,' he said, looking away from the tears brimming in her eyes. 'But it's not. It's *not*, Star,' he insisted. 'It's constantly putting the country first. It is making a marriage that is strategic and for the good of this country.'

'And there is nothing strategic about marrying me?'

'No.' He shook his head. 'There just isn't.'

'Your happiness is not strategic? It doesn't count?'

'No. It never has,' he said with the same sense of acceptance that had descended the moment he'd realised he was to take the throne.

'If you allow that feeling, that anger and resentment about Samira marrying Faizan to shape everything you do, the choices you make—'

'Don't say her...' He couldn't finish the sentence so instead he bit off his words, his tongue. It had been cruel, and he knew it. The hurt on Star's features was two red slashes on her cheeks.

'You can attack my dreams but I can't challenge your fears? Is it yourself that you're punishing by refusing to listen to your heart, or someone else? Why would you damn yourself to unhappiness?'

Why wouldn't she stop? Why was she pushing him like this?

'Is it because,' she pressed on, 'if you can have a happy marriage, if *you* can choose who you marry, then so could Faizan? Then it would mean that your wonderful, incredible brother made the wrong choice and it hurt you?'

'Wow, you're really going for it tonight, aren't you?' he scoffed bitterly, wondering what else she was going to drag him through. Because being angry with her was easier than feeling the truth of her words.

'Of course I am. My heart is on the line. My love for you. Can't you see that?'

White-hot pain slashed across his chest, a death blow that wouldn't end his life but could still stop his heart. Because only in the moments when his heart wasn't beating could he find the strength to be cruel enough to force her to go.

'Love? In two weeks?' he taunted. 'That really *is* a romance,' he said, forcing scepticism into his tone that burned all the way down. 'Then again, it's easier to fall in love when the fantasy can never live up to the reality, isn't it? You hide in your romances, preferring them to reality. But I don't have that luxury, Star.'

She looked as if she'd been struck and the only decent thing he could do was bear witness to it. He hated himself more than he ever had done before, but her words had taken hold and weren't letting go. He couldn't follow them, not now, not yet, and he greatly feared what would happen when he did. He felt like a bull, head down and ploughing forward, because anything else meant that he had to confront his feelings, her feelings.

Confront *her*. The way she was always challenging him, demanding of him, expecting him to be better when he couldn't.

'You're right. I do have choices. And I'm sorry that the one I need to make causes you pain.' His words were mechanical, forced. She knew it, he knew it, but there was also, inevitably, a truth beneath them. 'But I would make this choice every time. I choose Duratra.'

She wiped at a large, fat tear that escaped down her cheek, the action reminding him of what he'd seen when he'd first come onto the balcony. And he realised in that moment that she'd been crying before they'd talked. Before he'd said the horrible things, because she'd always known how the conversation would play out. She had known, before she'd even told him that she wasn't pregnant, what his reaction would be.

As she walked from the balcony, out of the suite and the palace, he realised then that he'd got it so terribly wrong. She was not a coward, hiding in romance. She was strong enough and brave enough to face reality. Stronger and braver than him.

The blow to his stomach and heart was doubly hard, physical and emotional, and he collapsed to the floor, his back against the cold, unyielding stone balcony that both held him up and anchored him while everything in him wanted to run after her.

CHAPTER ELEVEN

AT AROUND TWO in the morning Khalif found himself in one of the larger family suites, looking for whisky. He'd not had it in his quarters for three years. He'd not even had a drink in three years. But tonight he needed one.

He opened the door to the alcohol cabinet his father kept for visitors, retrieved the weighty cut glass tumbler and poured himself a satisfyingly large couple of inches of whisky. He swirled it around the glass as he sat, letting the peaty alcoholic scent waft up to meet him, his taste buds exploding with expectation and his conscience delaying the moment of gratification as punishment.

What had he done?

He was about to take a sip when the door to the living room opened and he looked up to find his father surveying him with something like pity.

'I haven't seen you drink since before Faizan died.'

It was on the tip of his tongue to lash out and say he'd not actually had the drink yet, but that felt churlish. Instead, he watched his father go to the cabinet and retrieve the whisky bottle and pour himself an equally large glass. 'I haven't seen you drink since...'

'Faizan's funeral?' his mother asked as she too came into the room. Both men's faces held the same look, as if they'd just been caught with their hands in a cookie jar. Never had they more appeared like father and son. 'Oh, don't be silly. If I was outraged at this, I'd have never survived the first six months as your Queen,' she teased the men in her life, leaning to press a kiss to her husband's cheek.

Bakir grinned conspiratorially at his son and took a seat in the large leather chair opposite Khalif as his wife perched on the arm.

Then the light dimmed from his eyes and Bakir took a breath. 'Faizan and Samira,' he said, raising his glass.

Khalif raised his and blinked back the sudden wetness in his eyes, swallowing his grief with the first powerful mouthful of whisky.

'Khalif, we are—'

He held his hand up to ward off his father's words but, though he paused, Bakir pressed on.

'We are so very proud of you. The memorial is...'

'Perfect,' his mother concluded, her smile watery and her eyes bright with unshed tears. She sniffed and her husband handed her a handkerchief without breaking eye contact with his son. 'Where on earth did you get the idea?' she asked.

Khalif clenched his jaw before prising the words from his conscience. 'A friend. She asked about Faizan and Samira, encouraged me to remember them. She suggested I talk to Nadya and Nayla about what they might like to have in the memorial.'

'She sounds very clever,' his mother observed.

'She is,' Khalif agreed.

'Did she encourage you to do anything else?' his father asked.

Through gritted teeth, he said, 'To be myself. To stop trying to be you or Faizan,' he confessed.

'She really *is* a wise woman,' his mother said, the smile in her voice evident. His father scoffed and Khalif's head jerked up to stare at his parents. He wanted to yell at them, to say that it wasn't a laughing matter.

'That's only because you said a very similar thing to me many years ago,' Bakir groused.

'*And* you barely listened to me,' his mother complained.

Khalif's head was swimming and it wasn't from the alcohol. 'What are you talking about? I thought you had an arranged marriage?'

Bakir cast a level gaze at his son. 'Well, a lot of work went into making it look that way, so I'm glad it was successful.'

Khalif couldn't work out whether his father was being sarcastic or ironic.

'We had met before,' his mother explained on a slightly flustered, and somewhat guilty, exhale. 'Before the engagement.'

'Your mother told me that if I couldn't orchestrate a good enough reason for us to get married, how would I ever manage to run a country? So I found a way.' Bakir shrugged. 'She challenged me then, and has each day since.'

His father stared at him intently and sighed deeply, as if not looking forward to what he was about to say. 'We all knew that you cared for Samira and she for you.'

'Cared?' Khalif almost choked, anger gripping him almost instantly.

'But we also knew that she wasn't right for you,' his father continued. 'Us, Faizan and even Samira.'

Khalif fisted the glass and clamped his jaw shut. He was furious. Not with his father but because he knew that his father was right.

'You were the younger son, Khalif. The one protected from the lessons and the rigours of royal instruction. In hindsight, that was a mistake. I…' Bakir seemed to struggle for words for the first time Khalif could remember. Finding his strength, he pressed on. 'My father taught me nothing about ruling a country, for fear that I would try to usurp him. My learning curve was steep. I didn't want…Faizan to have the same difficulties. I never thought—'

Hafsa placed her hand on her husband's and their fingers intertwined.

Khalif put the glass down on the side table, reached forward and placed his hand over theirs, joining them in their grief but also their love. He was ready to hear whatever his father had to say.

'I knew how much you wanted to be part of Faizan's lessons, but I feared the distraction. So you were given every freedom in compensation. And while you didn't want those freedoms, wouldn't have chosen them for yourself, you *did* have them. You were spoilt by that freedom—wholly unintentionally.

'No one challenged you, not even Samira. You had a special bond, no one can deny that, and we all loved her greatly. But she would have let you do anything, and you would have run roughshod over her all the while, never needing to do more, to be more, or better. You wouldn't have been good for each other.'

Khalif had braced for it and his father's words still hurt. But he couldn't deny the truth in them. All this time he had taunted Star for romanticism, but had he not done the same? Had he not fantasised the perfect, but mainly imagined, future with Samira? Had that not been the truest form of romanticism? All the while Star had questioned him, teased him about his preconceptions, challenged him to make better decisions, to follow his gut, encouraged him to make mistakes and learn from fixing them. And with that thought hope bloomed and his heart soared.

'What is that look on your face?'

'I've made a terrible mistake, Father.'

'Then why do you look so happy?'

'Because now I get to fix it,' he said, the smile lifting his lips and his heart soaring for the first time that evening.

'And how are you planning to do that?'

'Romance books. I need romance books.'

'I think he's gone mad,' his father said to his wife, looking deeply concerned. But his mother's eyes were lit with sparkles that only reminded Khalif of Star.

Star plucked at a loose thread on the long end of the pashmina she wore, her eyes sore and finally dry. She had sandwiched the phone between her ear and shoulder to leave both hands free so she could tackle the frayed cotton.

'I can be on a plane in two hours.'

'Mum, you don't drive, your bank account is pretty much empty, you hate carbon emissions more than you hate the Tories, and my plane leaves in three hours, so I'll be back in England before you would even get here.'

'Your sister said exactly the same thing,' Mariam Soames grumbled.

'It's the thought that counts, Mum. Star sounded happy?'

'Yes, she did. I'm looking forward to meeting this Chalendar. And I'm looking forward to having all my girls back in the same country and under the same roof. I don't like the idea of Summer at that house all on her own.'

Star marvelled that her mother had grown up in the sprawling, dilapidated Norfolk estate and insisted on calling it a 'house', despite the fact it had over thirty bedrooms. Star's fingers left the cotton thread and lifted to the gold ropes of the chain at her neck.

How she and her sisters had thought they would

have been able to keep the search for the missing jewels from their mother a secret, she had no idea. It had hurt to reveal Elias's manipulations to their mother, but when Skye had called them from France they'd known that it was time to tell Mariam everything. She had been as angry as much as Mariam Soames was capable of being angry with her daughters, which was about as long as it took to sigh.

'I know what you girls are trying to do—'

'We're so nearly there, Mum,' Star whispered, more of a plea than a promise. 'Skye has the map of the secret passageways, I have the key—we just need to find them now.'

'I know, Star. I just…' There was a pause on the end of the line and Star imagined her mother shifting her shawl around her shoulders. 'I've decided that I'm going to move in with Samantha for a bit.'

'Really? I thought you might want to—'

'Live with my just-beginning-to-find-their-feet, lovely and well-meaning daughters?' Mariam replied and Star couldn't help but smile at the laugh in her mother's voice.

The words *just beginning to find their feet* really struck Star. It was a little too close to what she'd hoped to achieve by coming to Duratra—to prove that she could stand on her own two feet—and Star felt as if she both had and hadn't.

'Samantha has known me for years. She's perfectly capable of putting up with me for a little longer,' Mariam said assuredly but without thought. A sob rose suddenly and shockingly in Star's chest. 'I didn't mean it like that,' her mother said.

'I know,' Star promised.

'We are going to beat this.'

'*I* know,' Star replied, forcing a smile to her lips in the hope that it would be heard in her voice. 'Actually... I was thinking about moving out of the flat and setting up somewhere on my own. Do you think that Skye would be okay with that? I mean—' Star struggled to find the words to explain her sudden need to hold onto that bit of independence she'd discovered in Duratra '—with Summer away at uni most of the year...'

Her mother sighed. 'I think that Skye will worry but, with her engagement, it's more than likely that she'll be relocating to France. If it feels right for you, my love, then we will all support you one hundred per cent.'

'I think it might scare me a little, but it's something I would like very much. I love Skye and Summer but...they need to see that I am capable of being independent.' Star sighed, all the pent-up emotion pouring from her chest in one breath. 'Mum...' she started, nervous as to the answer. 'Do you think Kal was right? Have I been hiding?'

'No, my love,' said her mother, her voice warm and reassuring. 'You haven't hidden in romances. You've been learning. Learning what you like, what you want, and what you will and won't put up with.

'Romances don't warp our expectations, they raise them. And there is nothing wrong with that. They show us that it is okay to put ourselves, our desires, at the forefront of our intentions. They show us not to be ashamed of our wants. Whether that want is emotional, practical or sexual, my love.' While cringing at her mother using words like sexual, because that was *never* going to be okay, Star knew what she meant. 'You should never have been made to feel ashamed or rejected. Not by your grandparents, nor your prince.'

'He's not my prince, Mum.'

'They should be the ones who feel shame, Star,' Mariam carried on as if Star hadn't interrupted. 'You reached out to make a connection with honesty, integrity, love and hope. They are lesser for turning you away. You are worthy of someone who reaches for you.'

Star smiled at the old family joke and she couldn't help the flood of memories overwhelming her. Khalif reaching to take her from his horse...the incredible gift of taking her to the desert, giving her a connection to Catherine that felt fated...making her feel loved and wanted by her ancestors, even if he hadn't been capable of it himself.

She allowed herself to feel that love, for her heart to swell with it as she promised to call her mother the moment she touched down in England. But as she ended the call, clutching the double-chained necklace which she kept interlocked together, she forced herself to face reality.

He had also left her alone without barely a thought and kept her hidden even when he knew he shouldn't. He had pushed her away with cruel words because it was easier than fighting his demons. And he had made her feel just as unwanted as wanted. But, despite the hurt and pain she felt, she knew he had been right.

He couldn't have chosen her any more than Catherine could have chosen Hātem, but she couldn't help but feel that there was a sense of wrongness about repeating the same decisions that had been made by their ancestors.

She glanced at the departures board, frowning when she noticed that there was a delay sign against her flight that hadn't been there two minutes ago. Everything in her wanted to go home, but she couldn't shake the feeling that her home was no longer in England.

Perhaps the desert sand had got into her blood somehow. She shook off the curious notion as she noticed a few heads turn towards the entrance of the airport. There was a rise and fall in murmurs, like the dip and swell of the sea and, while she tried to ignore it, more and more heads were turning and she began to hear audible gasps.

A group turned into a crowd and nearly forty people were now gathered near the entrance, all focusing on one point and then parting like the waves to make way for…for…

Oh, my…

The first thing she saw was Khalif, his eyes blazing with purpose and something she dared not name. Then she saw the horse. Mavia, she recognised, decked out in a saddle that had more gold and jewels on it than Star had thought possible. What on earth was he doing here on a horse?

The gold brocade *bisht* over his *thawb* was immaculate, and the *keffiyeh* around his head picked out the same gold tones, making him impossibly regal and almost too handsome for her to look at. Star focused on as many details as possible, trying to ignore the burst of hope that swelled in her heart.

Mavia lifted her head as if to say hello and Star soon found herself within metres of the incredible animal and her rider. The crowd who had at first held up their phones to capture a picture of their Prince, soon began to lower them one by one, some being nudged by a neighbour, others of their own volition, and Star could have sworn that she'd seen Amin somewhere in the midst of it.

Khalif swung ever so gracefully from Mavia and took two steps towards her before dropping to his knee, much to the gasped delight of the crowd.

'Kha—' Star clamped her mouth shut, took a moment and tried again. 'Your Highness,' she said—clearly unable to ignore the royal on bended knee right in front of her.

Once again, she felt the familiar search of his eyes across her face, her body, as if trying to take her in all at once and it not being enough. At least that was what she felt she was doing to him. Searching, hoping…waiting.

'Miss Soames,' Khalif said, loudly enough for the entire crowd to hear, 'I stepped down, trying not to look at you, as if you were a Star, yet I saw you, like a Star, without even looking.'

The words were poetic and lovely, but familiar and— She frowned. Wait, was that *Anna Karenina*? If not in full, then near enough. She opened her mouth to ask, but he pressed on.

'Because whatever our souls are made of, yours and mine are the same…' he insisted with a smile, as if confident she would recognise that as Brontë. 'Because I assure you, I was asleep, until I fell in love.'

Star couldn't stop the roll of her eyes. 'I refuse to believe that you read *War and Peace* in the last twenty-four hours, Khalif,' she chided.

'It might have been the crib notes version, but still… A very clever romance novel once said that "It is better to love wisely, no doubt: but to love foolishly is better than not to be able to love at all."'

'Thackeray,' she whispered, the goosebumps spreading from her toes to her shoulders.

'"In vain I have struggled. It will not do. My feelings will *not* be repressed. You must allow me to tell you how ardently I admire and love you."'

She couldn't smile—not yet. In spite of all the hope and all the love she felt in that moment, she needed more. '*Pride and Prejudice*? Really? Is that how you come to me? With the words of others on your tongue?' she demanded.

'No,' he replied, with no hurt or censure in his eyes, as if he'd expected her to challenge him. 'That was just to get your attention.'

'And you didn't think the horse would be enough?' she teased.

The crowds laughed a little, reminding her that they had an audience.

'Do you want to go somewhere a little more private?' she whispered to him.

'I am right where I need to be, Star Soames,' he said, his voice loud, confident and carrying, causing tears to gather in her eyes. 'And no. The horse was not enough,' Khalif said, as if all joking was done and now he wanted her to know the sincerity of his words. Of his love.

'I'm not completely sure that there will ever be enough ways for me to tell you how much I love you and why. But I'm going to try. You exploded into my life, dragging me by the arm and leading me to places I never expected.'

She blushed at the memory of how she had first encountered the Prince of Duratra, not having a single clue that he had been anything other than another tourist.

'You put your trust and faith in me from the first, though I had not earned such a gift. You experienced, in the harshest of ways, the constraints of royal life and bore them without question, without argument or censure. You taught me things I didn't know I still needed to learn and helped me to rediscover the things I knew but had forgotten. And in return I made you doubt your dreams. I will not forgive myself for that. I made you feel unwanted, and I promise never to let you feel that again. I made you feel shame by hiding you away, but *I* was the one who should have felt shame for my actions. So now I vow to you, before the people of my country, that I will spend every day for the rest of my life being worthy of you—even if you choose not to do me the honour of becoming my wife.'

Star looked down at him, bent at the knee on the floor of the airport, and still the most amazing thing she'd ever seen.

'What do you say?' he asked, and the flash of uncertainty nearly broke her heart.

'Well, I'm tempted to say that you should never ask someone to marry you in the negative, but that's only really because you asked me to challenge you.'

A gasp of consternation that sounded very much like Amin caused Khalif to smile. He smiled because it was exactly how he'd hoped Star would reply, loving that she still surprised him and kept him pushing for more, for better. Her smile was a little wobbly, but her eyes were bright, clear and full of love he felt to his very soul.

'Surely,' she said, her voice carrying without effort, 'my faith in my dreams would not have been that strong if it was shaken by one conversation? In as much as my sense of self would have to have been weak if I blamed you for making me feel unwanted or ashamed. And how could that be, when you were the one to show me that I have been looked for all my life, wanted and cared for by my family through centuries? When you were the one who has shown

me that reality can be even more romantic and wonderful than fantasy?'

She shook her head as if in wonder that he hadn't,
couldn't see what she saw in him, her love for him.
He got to his feet and reached for her, cupping her
jaw in his hands, taking what felt like his first breath
since the early hours of that morning as she rested
her head against his palm.

'Ask me again,' Star whispered, her eyes locked
with his, lit with love and a happiness that made his
chest burn.

'Will you, Star Soames, be my wife, my love, my
partner, my Queen?'

'Yes,' she said as a tear of happiness rolled down
her cheek.

'I love you so much,' he whispered so that only
she could hear.

'Good,' she replied, with a cheeky smile that made
his heart soar. 'Now, please, can you take me home?'

'To England?'

She shook her head and smiled, playing with the
strands of the necklace. 'No. To Alhafa…to the desert.'

'As you wish,' he said, his heart full of love and
peace.

'*After* we have couriered the necklace to my sisters,' Star said, with light sparkling in her eyes.

'I know just the man to do it… Amin?'

EPILOGUE

STAR STOOD ON the balcony of the suite she shared with her husband at Alhafa, gazing out at the view of the desert she would never tire of.

She could hear her husband in the shower, and the scent of eucalyptus oil was heavy on the steam escaping from the bathroom. She inhaled deeply, trying to catch it before it disappeared, loving the scent she always associated with her husband.

She blinked away the jet lag from the time difference between Duratra and the Dordogne, smiling as images from Skye's wedding to Benoit Chalendar filled her mind and heart. Her older sister had looked breathtakingly beautiful, the love she felt for her husband shining so bright it touched each and every guest. Their mother had cried through the entire ceremony, just as she had at Star's wedding, stopping only for a short while to laugh at Summer's daughter Catherine who, despite her mother's intentions, absolutely stole the show. But only for a heartbeat. And none of the sisters would have had it any differently.

The relief following her mother's successful treatment had been both shocking and surprising in its intensity. Khalif had been there and supported her through an aftershock that she had not expected, as all the fear, the hurt and pain she had kept at bay during their search for the jewels had run free only *after* they had accomplished all they had set out to do. Khalif had held her, comforted her, reassured her, soothed her and loved her through it all.

Star absentmindedly smoothed a hand over her stomach as she looked down at the sapphire wedding ring on her fourth finger of her other hand, remembering not only Khalif's proposal but her own magical wedding day six months before.

A smile lit her features and her heart as she thought of how the whole of Duratra had turned out to watch the wedding of Sheikh Khalif and his bride. Celebrations had filled the streets for days and Star had found a welcome and acceptance she could never have imagined. The love that Khalif had shown her in the year since they had first met was something wondrous to her and she thought she'd never have too much of it.

She smiled now as she remembered how protective he had been of her, especially in the first few months of their engagement and marriage. She would never forget the look of shock on Khalif's features as she'd requested Amin as her personal advisor. He had asked her again and again if she was sure, but Star had been determined. Within weeks, Amin and she had become allies and she now considered him one of her most loyal and trusted friends as he guided her through royal etiquette and protocol. And, surprising to almost everyone, she hadn't caused an international incident. *Yet*.

As another wave of tiredness hit, she yawned, despite the excitement thrumming through her veins. They were supposed to be heading into the desert with Nadya, Nayla and Khalif's parents and, although she would absolutely love to go with them, she wasn't sure she was quite up to it.

Star had been there when Khalif had revealed the suite to the twin girls, and been half deafened by their squeals of excitement and squeezed as hard as six-year-old girls could squeeze with their love and thanks. Surprising both their uncle and their grandparents, Nayla had been the first up the tree, while Nadya had had to be bribed away from the bathroom, but both loved their bedroom equally. Hafsa and Bakir's eyes had sparkled with tears of gratitude and love and Khalif had held her hand as if he would never let her go.

She heard the sound of bare feet stepping out onto the balcony and turned to see her husband, her Prince, her King, standing there with nothing but a towel wrapped low around his hips, making her instantly dizzy with desire.

He smirked as if he could read the shockingly intimate, passionate thoughts running through her mind as he walked towards her and pressed a kiss to her forehead.

'I know we're supposed to be going to the oasis, but you look exhausted.'

'Gee, thanks!' She laughed, playfully slapping him against his big broad shoulder, the secret flickering in her chest burning away the tiredness and brightening her with expectation and excitement.

'How are you feeling?' he asked, his hands burning a trail of desire down her back and over her hips. Her pulse picked up and her core throbbed with need, but she pushed that all aside for just a moment.

'Pregnant,' she said, smiling, knowing that Khalif was half distracted and it would take him a moment to—

'Wait, what?'

She looked up at him, a smile wide on her lips, loving the strong connection between them, their gazes locked, hers filled with confidence, his with wonder and disbelief.

'I'm pregnant.'

His hands went to her hips, his fingers gentle against the ever-so-slight bump, but his eyes had not left hers. His gaze searched hers in the same way he'd always done, as if awed and unbelieving that he'd found her, that she had chosen to be his and would always be his.

'I love you,' he whispered against her lips before pulling her to him and kissing her with all the love she could ever want and more. And in all the years to come, all the time they had together, she never felt anything but cherished, wanted and loved.

* * * * *

The Greek Secret
She Carries

DEDICATION

This book is for my sister, Kate.

I would not be where I am without her,

I would not be who I am without her.

Love,

always,

Xx

PROLOGUE

Last night…

THERON THIAKOS STALKED the damp London street, cursing the rain. It just never stopped. How could people live like this? he angrily asked himself, longing for the piercing heat and pure bright sun of Greece, the glittering blue sea that sparkled enough to make a person squint. The cloud-covered night gave the Mayfair street an air of mystery as he came to stand before the impossibly exclusive private members club, Victoriana.

Before him, two men stood either side of a door with such thick black gloss the paint looked like running water. The Tuscan columns supporting the portico spoke of riches and a sense of history that struck a nerve. Theron bit back a curse. This was exactly the kind of superior, expensive establishment that would appeal to Lykos's ego. Theron made to step forward when, shockingly, one of the men raised his hand to stop him.

'I'm here to see Lykos Livas,' Theron stated, not

bothering to conceal the distaste in his tone. He had neither the time nor the patience for this. The anger in him was overpowering and he wanted someone to blame. *Needed* someone to blame. And he knew just the person.

The other doorman nodded, holding the door open and gesturing Theron towards a woman wearing some sort of strange green tweed trousers that cut off at the knee and a waistcoat. Lykos had always had a flair for the dramatic, but this was so… English. *Old* English.

The immediate press of warmth that greeted him after the cold London night was a blessed relief. His mouth watered at the thought of the whisky he'd fanta-sised about for the entire drive down from the Soames estate in Norfolk where he'd left Summer standing on the stone steps, unable to face the look in her eyes as he drove away.

He'd lost everything. Absolutely everything.

Theron followed the hostess weaving her way through a surprisingly large establishment, completely decked out—as one would imagine—in furniture and furnishings from the Victorian period. And, despite the negative bent of his thoughts, he couldn't help but be impressed by the bar that stretched the entire length of the main room. Two houses, at least, must have been knocked together to create such a space.

He caught sight of his quarry, sitting at a booth of deep green leather with a woman no less exquisite than to be expected in Lykos Livas's company. Theron's gaze barely touched the brunette, his mind instead seeing rich golden hair, hazel eyes and lips that were ruby-red when full of desire and pale when devastated.

His fingers pulsed within his fist as Lykos finally turned to acknowledge him.

'This is all your fault,' Theron charged, his tone firm and bitter.

Lykos stared at him for a moment, his gaze so level Theron wondered if he'd even heard the accusation. Then he blinked that silvery gaze. 'I'd say it's good to see you but—'

'We are well beyond niceties, Lykos, so I'll say again, this is all your fault.'

'That depends on what "this" is,' Lykos said over the rim of his glass before taking a mouthful of his drink.

Inhaling a curse, Theron turned to the brunette. 'Leave us.' He hated being so cruel but he was at his wits' end.

'That is hardly necessary,' Lykos protested half-heartedly.

'It's not as if you won't find someone else to play with,' Theron said truthfully, turning his back on the girl as he looked for the hostess. 'Whisky?' She nodded and disappeared into the bar's darkness.

'True,' Lykos replied with a shoulder shrug, watching his companion leave in a huff before narrowing his eyes at Theron. 'I see you once in ten years and now you won't leave me alone?'

It was a relief to speak in his native tongue again. It had been—what?—a week since he'd left Athens and found himself in that hellhole in Norfolk. Some found the Greek language harsh, but to Theron it flowed like *tsipouro* from Volos and tasted like honey in *loukoumades*.

'This is not the time for jokes, Lykos.'

'You never did have a good sense of humour,' he groused.

Theron's drink arrived and he slipped into the now empty seat. He palmed the glass, staring at it as if he hadn't spent the last three hours wanting it.

'You'd best bring the bottle, *glykiá mou*,' Lykos said, leaning well into the server's personal space. Not that she seemed to mind. At all.

'What are you doing in London anyway?' Theron asked before challenging himself to only take a sip of the liquid he wanted to drown in.

'I like it here.'

'I don't believe you. I don't believe that any Greek worth their salt would enjoy all the...*grey*,' Theron said with such distaste it was as if the colour had taken up residence on his tongue.

'Grey? I'm not quite sure I've seen London during the daytime hours. Is it that bad?' Lykos asked, appearing to sincerely ponder it.

'Yes. But Norfolk is worse.'

Lykos's silver eyes narrowed and Theron's dark gaze held the challenge. 'Is that so?' Lykos asked.

'It is. They've even named a paint after it.'

'What, Norfolk?'

'Yes. It's grey.'

Lykos sniggered into his glass, before sobering and then sighing. 'What did you do?'

Theron clenched his jaw at the accusation. For just a moment it had been like it had always been between them. The banter flowing freely from the bone-deep knowledge of each other. But that was before Lykos had walked away from their friendship.

'If you're looking for absolution,' Lykos warned, 'you've come to the wrong damn place,' he went on before eyeing up the bottle of Glenglassaugh the waitress had placed on the table as if he wasn't sure he wanted to waste such good alcohol on Theron.

Theron shook his head, frustrated with the man who'd once been like a brother to him. 'I don't need absolution. I need to know why you called me a week ago.' Theron knew with absolute certainty that he was involved in all this somehow, but he needed to hear it from Lykos.

'To taunt you, of course,' Lykos said with a smile that had more than likely charmed women right out of their underwear. 'When your holiday fling turns up at my door—'

'Watch your mouth,' Theron growled.

'Ooh, touchy.' Watching Theron from the corner of his eye, Lykos continued. 'When the lovely Ms Soames arrived at my door trying to offload a fifteen-million-pound estate in the country for a third of the market value, I just wanted to brag. I've always wanted a castle.'

'It's not a castle.'

'Oh?'

'And it's rundown. There are holes in the walls and it's freezing. All the time. And the damp...' Theron threw his hands in the air as if in despair.

'Oh, well, that wasn't in the sales pitch. Is that why you're here? To talk me out of buying the estate?'

Theron thought about it for a moment too long. 'Buy the estate,' he said tiredly. 'And it's worth the market value, Lykos. Don't take advantage of a vulnerable woman.'

Lykos slammed his glass down on the table, ignoring the stares it drew from the other guests, his eyes shards of ice but the burn in them white-hot. 'There's a line, Theron, and you are skating dangerously close to it.'

Theron wanted to bite back, wanted the anger Lykos threatened. His pulse pounded and he welcomed it, his breath audible now as his lungs worked hard. They stared at each other, while Theron waged an internal war and Lykos waited to see what he would do.

Gritting his teeth, Theron decided it was better to leave than to cause a scene and got to his feet.

'Oh, sit down before you break down,' Lykos bit out.

Theron stared at the doorway long enough to realise that he didn't have anywhere else to go.

'Break down?' he asked.

'I can practically feel the tears from here. Drink that,' Lykos said, passing him a large measure of whisky, 'before you start weeping all over the place. *Then* have the kindness to leave before you scare off the rest of tonight's entertainment.'

'You're a real piece of work, you know that?'

'Theron, as hard as this is to believe, I really don't care what got your knickers in a twist.'

'You would have once.'

'And you chose Kyros,' Lykos growled.

'No,' Theron shot back. '*You* left.'

'And you could have come.'

'And how would that have repaid the man who gave us *everything*?' Theron demanded.

'That was always your problem. What could ever be equal compensation for what he did for us? What could you give him that would repay such a thing?'

Theron turned away from the demand in his oldest friend's gaze and stared into the whisky, trying to ignore the feeling that he might have finally found something worthy of such a debt.

His heart.

And his child.

'Fine,' huffed Lykos. 'You may explain, if it will take that look off your face.'

Summer paced before the fire in the Little Library. Back and forth, back and forth as her eyes went from wet to dry, red to pale. But her heart ached as if she'd never stopped crying.

This room had become her sanctuary in the last two months, every inch of it as familiar to her as if she'd lived here all her life. But instead of seeing books that would make the British Library jealous, she saw eyes, dark like coals, making her shiver from the heat. Eyes that had laid her bare, exposed her soul. Her heart pulsed and her core throbbed as if taunting her, reminding her of the night before, as he'd thrust into her so deep and so deliciously she *still* ached from the pleasure. She turned and paced back past the fireplace where flames danced joyously as if there was nothing wrong, as if her world hadn't just shattered into a million pieces.

She brushed her hair back from her face. Six months ago she had been a naïve third-year geophysics student whose only worry was how to pay her sisters back for working all hours to pay for her to go to university. And now?

She was pregnant.

And yet she couldn't afford to think about it. She couldn't think about Theron Thiakos or even her father, Kyros. Now she *had* to think about her mother and sisters. About finishing the treasure hunt she, Star and Skye had been sent on by the grandfather they'd never met. The task? To find the Soames diamonds, hidden over one hundred and fifty years ago by their great-great-great-grandmother from her abusive husband. Clues had been found, coded messages translated, and her sisters had travelled the world to track down the elements needed to find the jewels.

It had been easy to hide her baby bump three weeks ago, when Skye had flown first to Costa Rica and then to France to locate the map of secret passageways that led throughout the Norfolk estate. And Star had been so full of romance when she had left for Duratra in the Middle East, searching for the one-of-a-kind key made by joining two separate necklaces that her sister had missed all signs of Summer's pregnancy too.

Meeting the terms of the will, she had been forced to stay behind. She had scoured their great-great-great-grandmother's journals, searching for clues about exactly *where* Catherine had hidden her family's jewels, but hadn't been able to find any. But if they did find the jewels, the sisters would have met the terms of their inheritance and be able to sell the estate in order to pay for their mother's lifesaving medical treatment. That was *all* that mattered right now. The jewels. Her mother's health. She couldn't think of anything else.

Especially not a man with eyes as dark as obsidian and a heart protected by granite. A granite, she thought with a sob, she'd hoped to have chipped. She placed her hand over the crest of her bump, reassuring both herself and their baby that they'd be okay.

'It will all work out in the end,' she whispered. 'It's what Auntie Star is always saying. And Great-Great-Great-Grandmother Catherine? Trust, love and faith,' Summer assured her child, wiping away the last of her tears.

The sound of the ancient doorbell ricocheted throughout the sprawling estate that looked—at least on the outside—like Downton Abbey. On the inside? It could have inspired Dickens. For five generations the men of the Soames line had let the estate go to ruin, fruitlessly looking for the Soames diamonds. And the last, their grandfather, in his madness had been driven to knocking great holes in the walls. The irony was how close he had actually come to finding them.

Summer took a deep breath, swept another reassuring hand over her belly and whispered, 'It's time to meet your aunties.'

Summer opened the front door and was instantly

pulled into a tangle of arms that squashed and hugged and she didn't need to see her sisters' faces to know she was *home*. It didn't matter where they were in the world, as long as they were together. Summer breathed them in. She had missed them so much.

'Oh my God, it's so good to see you,' Star rushed out in one breath. 'And oh my God, we have so much to tell you, and oh my... *God, what is that?*'

Summer found herself thrust back as Star stared wide-eyed at her stomach. Over her shoulder, Skye's delighted smile followed Star's gaze down to Summer's waist and her eyes sparked with shock.

'Surprise!' Summer called weakly just before she burst into tears again.

As if the spell had been broken, Summer was instantly pulled back into her sisters' loving embrace and given soothing declarations of support and reassurance. Unfortunately, this only made her cry harder, until Skye took charge and guided them off the steps and into the estate.

They held her all the way to the Little Library, Skye on one side, Star on the other, words of love filling the cold damp estate and easing Summer's hurt just a little. Once they had seen her settled in the large wingback chair, Skye put another log on the fire and ordered Star to make a cup of herbal tea from the kettle they'd set up in the library almost two months ago.

Skye crouched down and levelled her gaze at Summer. 'Are you okay?'

Summer nodded, blushing furiously now that the crying had once again stopped.

'Is the baby okay?' Star asked from behind her sister.

Summer nodded again, her hand soothing over the crest of her bump, and when she looked back up she saw the most beautiful smiles on her sisters' faces—joy lighting their eyes, pure and bright. Summer sniffed and Star passed her a tissue, keeping one back for herself and wiping at her eyes. Summer smiled as she could see Skye trying to suppress an eye-roll at their romantic middle sister.

'Can I ask—?'

'I don't want to talk about it. Now you're here—'

'Summer,' Star chided.

'I don't,' she replied, shaking her head resolutely. 'Besides, we have to find the jewels.'

'But I thought you found the jewels?'

'I haven't actually seen them. I was waiting for you both.'

As if quickly weighing up the importance of things, Skye seemed to come to a decision. 'The diamonds aren't going to disappear overnight,' she insisted gently. 'They can wait. *You* are more important right now. And we're not going anywhere until you tell us what's going on,' she said firmly.

The kettle reached boiling point and clicked off, all the sisters' gazes called to it, and a sudden silence blanketed the room until Star laughed. 'Okay, let's have some tea, take stock and, you know, breathe.'

Skye and Summer shared a look.

'Okay, who are you and what have you done with Star?' Skye demanded.

Star smiled. 'We have a *lot* to catch up on.'

And for just a moment they enjoyed the silence, enjoyed being back together again, reunited after the longest time away from each other. Then, as Star made the tea, Skye told them about her fiancé Benoit and the cottage in the Dordogne they had been staying in for the last few weeks. Star asked a few questions before telling her own tale about the oasis the Prince of Duratra had whisked her away to before his ostentatious proposal and how much she wished she had some *qatayef* to share with them as they had their tea. It was as if they sensed that Summer needed time just to let the heavy emotions settle. Warmth finally seeped into her skin and wrapped around her heart and finally both Star and Skye looked at her expectantly.

'I don't know where to begin.' Summer shrugged helplessly.

'At the beginning, of course,' Star replied, as if she were talking to her primary school class.

Summer took a deep breath, the words rushing out on a single exhale. 'I found my dad.'

'Wait…what?' Skye asked, clearly not expecting that to be where Summer's story began.

'In Greece. I found my father.'

'But I thought Mum didn't know his name?' said Star, frowning. 'Which was why she could never find…' She trailed off, as if suddenly understanding.

'Oh, no,' Skye said. 'Really? She knew the whole time?'

Summer nodded, the ache of all those missed years, of all the questions unanswered for so long, that missing part of her… She understood *now* why her mother had done what she'd done but, with a child growing within her, she knew that she couldn't have made the same choice.

'Why didn't you tell us?' Skye asked gently.

'I didn't want you to think badly of her. *I* didn't want to think badly of her.' Summer shook her head, trying to find the words to explain why she'd hoarded that information, hoarded that hurt from her half-sisters. Skye's father had started another family after he and Mariam broke up, Star's father had died tragically when she was just months old. But Kyros? He was *her* father and a part of her feared they wouldn't understand the need she'd felt to meet him. The need in her to connect with a man she'd never met. And perhaps beneath that, deep down, the thing she hadn't been able to admit… that if he rejected her then she wouldn't have to tell them. No one would have to know.

'I… I wanted to meet him first,' Summer said.

'And did you?'

CHAPTER ONE

Five months ago...

YOU CAN DO THIS, Summer told herself as she stepped out of the air-conditioned arrivals hall in Athens and was hit by a bank of heat that nearly knocked her back. Looking out at the wide road and the bus stop, she squinted as the sun bounced off the pale concrete floor.

She stared at the instructions from her hotel—a hotel that was within walking distance of Kyros Agyros's office building—and after gazing longingly at the line of taxis she steeled herself and found the ticket machine that thankfully had an English language button.

Less than five euros and ten minutes later she was on the bus, with half her mind on the stop announcements and half a mind on her father. An ache bloomed in her heart, one that had been there ever since she'd found the photo of her parents tucked away in the attic amongst all the old albums and family documents. Mariam had always told her that she'd never known her father's last name.

Oh, she'd told Summer many other things—that his name was Kyros, that, just like her, he had a little mole on his collarbone. That he'd made her laugh, made her believe in love again, even through her grief, and, despite how brief it had been, they'd had a wonderful, magical relationship. And Summer had never doubted it. Until, when looking for her passport, she'd instead found a picture of her mother staring deep into the eyes of a handsome man—and on the back, written in her mother's handwriting, the name Kyros Agyros.

Her already shaky foundations had been rocked by the secret Mariam had kept from her and, no matter how much she wanted to ask her mum about it, she couldn't. Because Mariam Soames was ill. Very ill. Words like stage three and cancer sent tremors through her and Summer dashed away a tear that threatened to fall. So no. She couldn't ask her mum about why she'd lied about knowing her father's identity. So that only left her one other option.

'Syntagma Square,' a robotic voice announced, and Summer grabbed her large rucksack and made it off the bus just in time.

She had planned to find her hotel first. It was, according to the guide, less than a ten-minute walk south of the square. But when she turned and saw the Parliament building behind her, she lost her breath on a gasp. On the opposite side of a wide road, white columns gleamed against the burnt yellow brickwork and towered magnificently over the square. Behind her, steps led down to a fountain where kids were playing and screaming and splashing water at each other.

Off to the side were rows and rows of canopied tables and chairs, the scent of coffee hitting her all the way to where she stood.

In an instant she was filled with something she could hardly explain. Her geophysics professors and fellow students certainly would have laughed if she'd tried to explain it to them, but her heart swelled and she was brimming with something warm and thick and sweet. This was part of her culture, her heritage, her identity.

She walked across the length of the square, taking it all in. The heat, the people, the colour, the noise—it was so different to what she was used to. She was about to try and find the road that her hotel was on when she followed the sleek lines of a gleaming office building into the sky, shocked to see a bright red illuminated sign bearing her father's name.

She'd known his office was near here, but…an entire building? Her heart started to race and she rubbed her suddenly damp palms on her trousers, resenting the physical manifestation of a hormonal shift in adrenaline and cortisol. As if in defiance, Summer hitched her rucksack higher onto her shoulder and pushed her way through the circular doorway into a large atrium.

Instantly she found herself gawking as she looked up at the ceiling that reached thirty storeys up, feeling a strange sense of vertigo. The press of the air conditioning cooled the sweat slicking her skin and she resisted the urge to shiver. Summer looked to the reception desk where a beautiful dark-haired woman was waiting, her smile a slash of bright red lipstick.

'May I help you?' she said in perfect English as she approached, without Summer even having to do the awkward *Do you speak...?* dance.

Summer bit her lip, releasing it only when she finally had the courage to utter the words, 'I would like to see Mr Agyros, please.'

The receptionist hit her keyboard with a few furious strokes. 'I see, and do you have an appointment?'

'Unfortunately, no. Could you tell him that... Mariam Soames would like to see him?'

The receptionist looked at Summer, a little confused. 'I'm afraid that won't be possible.'

'I'm sorry, I know I don't have an appointment but it really is quite urgent that I speak to him.'

'I *appreciate* that, but it's not possible because he's not here. He is away with family.'

Family. The word sliced through Summer and, although she knew it was just a word, knew Kyros Agyros would have a family, it hurt unaccountably. He was supposed to be here. She'd done her research.

Her expression must have betrayed her because the receptionist was looking at her as if worried. 'Is there someone else I can put you in contact with?'

'No, thank you,' Summer said, shaking her head. 'Do you know when he'll be back?'

'I'm not at liberty to say,' the receptionist said, not unkindly.

Summer left the building feeling utterly shocked. She'd checked—he was supposed to be at a conference here in Athens according to several press releases and two different websites.

Back out on the street, the wave of heat made her feel nauseous and she sank onto the stone wall surrounding the building, trying to ease the seesawing motion the world seemed to suddenly take on. She felt so *lost*. She had wasted almost her entire savings on this trip. Savings that she'd planned to use to pay back her sisters. So *foolish*. Did she really think that… what—she'd come all the way here, head into his office, introduce herself and he'd welcome her like the long-lost daughter he'd always wanted?

The online research she'd done on Kyros had shown a lifetime of financial success stories and philanthropic endeavours, but very little about the man himself. He seemed to have kept himself out of the public eye as much as possible and the few articles she'd found indicated that he protected his privacy with two things: ruthlessness and a man called Theron Thiakos.

And as she looked up at the entrance to the building the man himself emerged from the revolving doors and Summer put her hand to the stone to steady herself. He stopped a few feet from the building to take a call. There, in the middle of the pavement, he seemed utterly heedless of the people having to swerve around him, an innate authority signalling his superiority.

She had seen pictures. Vague impressions of dark hair and formidable expressions, but at the time her attention had been on her father. Now, as she took in the entirety of Theron Thiakos, Summer lost her breath, as if the full Technicolor image was too much for her brain to handle.

Angles. Sharp, clean angles she wanted to trace with the palm of her hand. That was what Summer saw first. The wedge of his shoulders, the slant of a determined brow, the sharp cheekbones and the slash of his lips. They made her want to touch. She'd *never* felt like that before. She shook her head and tried to appraise him clinically, like the scientist she was.

He was tall, at least six foot.

Sleek. Fine.

She frowned at the useless descriptors, but they wouldn't stop coming.

Dark. Brooding.

She slowed her breathing, hoping it would help calm her erratic pulse, forcing her online research to mind. Thiakos was only six years older than her and, at twenty-eight, he had achieved a status and security that some could only dream of. He had graduated from a *very* prestigious school that counted the children of princes and diplomats amongst its alumni.

Elite.

Summer bit her lip at the rising heat on her cheeks.

After excelling in his national service with the Greek armed forces, staying for longer than the allotted time period, he had walked straight into a high-level position in Agyros's company before branching out with his own security company. Agyros had been Thiakos's first contract, but was by no means his only client. But nothing in her research of Theron Thiakos had prepared her for…*him.*

She looked down at her hands and noticed that they were fisted against her trousers, before shaking them out. By the time she looked up she couldn't see him any more. Panic rushed through her as suddenly what felt like her only connection to her father had disappeared.

The receptionist hadn't been able to tell her when her father would be back, but Theron Thiakos might.

She jumped up, blood rushing to her head as if she'd been holding her breath, and ran across the road, ignoring the blaring of car horns behind her. Careening round a corner, she caught sight of him again and the wave of relief that struck her was so powerful she sagged against the nearby building. Forcing her legs to move again, she took measured breaths, trying to slow the pulse raging in her ears, and focused her gaze squarely on his back. Her eyes tripped along the inches of his very broad shoulders and danced downward to lean hips and...

The sound of a laugh cut through her thoughts and, although it was still early, she noticed that all around them bars and cafés were bustling with people and animated conversation, the air electric and infectious. Everyone looked glamorous and sophisticated, bright and colourful and Summer felt the opposite of her namesake in black cropped chinos and a white and black striped boatneck top.

But she had learned a long time ago not to draw attention to herself. Each of the Soames girls had. It wasn't the 'done thing' to have children by three different fathers and, while no one had said anything to their faces, the whispers and drawn curtains and judgement was evident from parents, teachers and neighbours alike.

And then choosing to study science? Worse, a subject like geophysics. The first and only time she'd worn anything remotely bright to class it was as if she'd thrown potassium into water. God only knew what would happen if she'd dared to wear make-up. Or—heaven forbid—a *skirt*.

Theron Thiakos turned into a bar on the corner. Large windows had been folded back like a concertina and people spilled onto the outside seating area. It was like everything Summer had encountered so far, colourful and riotous. She watched as he was greeted by a group of friends, shaking hands and kissing cheeks, and she barely resisted the urge to rub at her own tingling cheek.

'Good evening, are you looking for a table?'

Summer's focus on Theron was such that the waiter had to repeat his question before she realised he was speaking to *her*.

'Yes.' The word jerked out of her before she could change her mind.

'Theron, what are you doing here?'

It was the second time someone had asked him the same question and, unsurprisingly, his response was the same. A tight smile reminded them that not only was he their boss and the owner of the hugely successful international company they worked for but that he didn't have to explain himself to anyone. As expected, the person who had asked the question scurried off into the crowd.

He was here precisely because he didn't want to be. It was good for him to keep himself *and* his staff on their toes. But as he accepted a drink from the waiter he couldn't block out the conversation he'd had with Kyros's niece that morning.

It's just family. I'm sure you understand.

Just family.

Family.

Four hours ago, Theron had ensured an irritated Kyros boarded the boat kept docked at Piraeus, which took him away to the 'surprise' family gathering that the Agyros clan had organised. It had been pitched as a celebration, but it was so close to the first anniversary of Althaia's death that neither man had been fooled. Kyros had left to commemorate the loss of his wife and Theron hadn't been invited.

He had watched the boat sail out from the harbour, ignoring the devastating ache deep within and instead feeding the belief that he was better off alone. Repeating that thought like a mantra in his mind, he tuned back in to the sounds of the bar. Over the low hum of voices, glass shattered, a woman screamed in delight and a man laughed. His head snapped up.

It was the tone of their laughter that gripped him. It poked and prodded at a memory from Theron's childhood—from the orphanage in the days before he'd met Kyros. From before his life had changed irrevocably. It was snide, conspiratorial, mean and it cut him like a knife.

He turned to search out the source of the laughter amongst the bar's patrons. Noticing the two younger men standing on the brink of the outdoor seating area, he followed their gaze towards a blonde rolling her shoulder as if working out a tight muscle.

His gaze stuttered over her and a sudden rush of incendiary heat poured over him. A heat that felt without beginning or end, but one most definitely with her at its focal point. She glowed, a golden halo of hair, her skin warm like the first blush of life and her lips...the kind of fresh luscious red that money couldn't buy. Hungrily, he consumed what he could see of her, gorging himself so quickly he could only take in broad strokes. He almost stepped back to sever the power of his reaction.

He forced his gaze back to the two men and it was clear. She was their intended target.

Picking up his drink, Theron pulled out his phone as if checking an email and slowly closed in on the men.

'I bet you one hundred euros that she'll spend tonight in my bed.'

'Her? Why?'

'Why not?'

All three men turned to look at her as she thanked the waiter in English and the second guy grinned. 'Two hundred says she'll be in mine.'

'Three hundred with photos,' the first said with a leer that made Theron see red.

He forced himself to loosen his grip or he'd break

his mobile. And he'd much rather break something of theirs.

He watched as the first guy made his approach, the way they tag-teamed it made Theron fear just how many times this had happened before. Surreptitiously, he took photos of both the men before putting his phone away, looking up to check the girl's reaction. They had chosen her because she was on her own, English, a tourist, a *target*.

The word ricocheted through him, bouncing off different memories from the past. In those first few months in the orphanage, he had seemed like a target to the other kids too. But he had learned and paid attention and used everything available to him so that no one considered him a target ever again. Him or those he cared about.

Through the haze of his thoughts, he felt her eyes on him, pulling him back to the present, and an unholy need exploded into being deep within him, like a punch to his gut. She held his gaze as if she was there with him, standing in the eye of the storm of need, and it was an experience unlike any he'd ever had.

And then one of the men moved between them, cutting off Theron's line of sight and taking a seat at her table. By the time he could see her again, she was smiling, her face open and curious and wholly unaware of the danger she was in. Theron rejected any further prevarication.

'Darling,' he called loudly in English as he made his way towards her table, his purpose in reaching her quite clear. A few heads at surrounding tables turned to him and as she looked up her eyes widened to near comical proportions—only there was nothing funny about the gold and green that glittered in her hazel eyes. It was such a sight he nearly stopped. But didn't.

'Sorry I'm late—forgive me?' he asked as he rounded the table and placed a kiss on her head. He felt her flinch beneath him, but he didn't give her the time to question what was going on. 'You have company?'

'Mr Thiakos,' said the first man, half rising out of his chair—to greet him or run away, it seemed the man himself wasn't sure. It wasn't unusual for strangers to recognise him, and in this instance it would make things considerably easier.

Theron held his hand out and when the man reached his out, Theron's grip would have crushed walnuts. The second man in the chair beside him rose and Theron placed his other hand heavily down on the man's shoulder and pushed him back into his seat.

'Gentlemen,' he all but snarled. To the outsider they looked like a group of friends meeting for a drink, but the undertone was as dangerous as a riptide. 'Allow me to explain,' he said in rapid Greek. 'I overheard your little *bet*.' The guy beside him jerked beneath his hand, but Theron simply held him in place. 'Now, as you can imagine, the man who wins this bet, who takes this lovely young woman to bed, will have to contend with me. Or not? I suppose, then, it could be said that *I* will win this bet, no?'

The first man paled considerably, and Theron waved off the verbal fountain of apologies that streamed forth. 'The money?' he demanded. The man's eyes flashed with anger, but Theron had seen and been worse. He simply nodded, forestalling any further objection.

The first guy reached for his pocket and pulled out two hundred euros as the second guy did the same.

'I believe it was three hundred. I have *photos*,' he said, offering his phone and displaying their images, the threat clear. After a reckless moment of deliberation, each man finally handed over three hundred euros and left.

Theron watched them until he was sure they were gone and turned back to find the blonde watching *him*. Again. As someone used to being the observer, it was a novel experience.

'Theron Thiakos,' he said, holding out a much gentler hand in greeting, wondering if she had any idea how close she'd come to a very dangerous situation.

She looked up at him with huge wide hazel eyes, not once glancing at the six hundred euros on the table. She reached out her hand and, as it slipped into his, the smooth skin gliding against his flashed the most indecent images into his head.

'Summer,' she said by way of introduction.

Heat. Warmth. The feeling of the sun against his skin.

It wasn't her name that conjured such impressions. It was *her*. He needed to leave. Theron nodded to the money on the table. 'That's yours,' he said and got up to leave.

'Why?'

It was the way she asked. As if it was completely

foreign to her that she would be given something for nothing. 'It was a con,' he bit out.

'I don't understand.'

'They had a bet as to which one could sleep with you tonight.'

The colour ran from her face, leaving her looking pale and shocked.

'They were being perfectly nice,' she said in the way that people did when they didn't want to believe they were victims.

'And take the photos to prove it,' he explained.

'And the money? That you took off them?' she demanded as if she wanted to see all the workings of what had just happened before she could believe him.

'They'll only learn if it hits them where it hurts.'

And if Theron delivered the photos to his investigative team to see if there would be enough evidence to take to the police. This probably wasn't their first time. He had turned away and was about to leave, determined not to give her another thought, when he heard what she said next.

'Thank you,' she said, sounding a little unsure if that was what she meant.

Against his will, he turned back to her. He came from a world where *thank you* was a forgotten word and the conclusion of business was the payment of an invoice. But she was looking at him as if he sat on a white horse and had just slayed a dragon. And he didn't think *anyone* had looked at him like that before.

Before he could leave, a waiter arrived with three drinks, oblivious to the disappearance of two of his customers, mainly because he was eyeing the pile of banknotes on the table. Theron resumed his seat and waited for the server to leave.

He gathered up the money and passed it to *Summer*. Her name in his mind did things that he didn't want to look at too closely.

'Please. Put this away before you draw even more unwanted attention.'

She took the handful of notes from him, blinking as if only now realising just how much it was. 'I can't take—'

'You can,' he said firmly.

The dim lighting made it impossible to tell, but he thought she might have blushed when his fingers met hers. The women he encountered didn't blush. Oh, he would leave them flushed. And panting. But...blushing spoke of innocence. An innocence he shouldn't even be in the proximity of.

'He knew you?' she asked, as if finally processing the events that had happened. 'He *recognised* you,' she said, a statement this time.

He shrugged off her apparent realisation of his notoriety, instead finding focus once again in her features. Her thoughts had furrowed her brow, drawing his attention to a nose that was distinctly 'button-like'. From there it was impossibly easy to drop his gaze to her lips and he was forced to stifle the sound of his swift inhalation.

Her lips looked swollen, as if recently kissed and thoroughly so. It wasn't a pout, and it wasn't the exaggerated bee-stung puff that silly people paid ridiculous

amounts for. It was a natural fullness that he wanted
to bite down gently on. There wasn't a slick of lipstick
on them, yet their colour was as rich a red as his favourite Limniona. He could almost taste the wine on
his tongue, the scent of the herbs and cinnamon spice
in the air about them.

'What are you doing here?' His question surprised
them both and for the first time in a long time he felt
the white-hot sting of embarrassment. Never before had
he shown such a shocking disregard for self-control
as to give voice to what definitely should have been a
passing thought.

'I'm... I was supposed to be meeting someone.'

Her answer pierced the haze she had plunged his
mind into. 'Oh, my apologies,' he said, frowning. He
wasn't used to misreading situations, given that his
career depended on it. 'I'll—'

'Oh, no, it's not like that,' she said, the words rushing out just like the hand she placed on his forearm.
'I... Family. I was supposed to be meeting family, but
he's not here.'

Summer was quite aware that she was staring, but she
couldn't help herself. And it had absolutely nothing
to do with whether Theron Thiakos had access to her
father, and everything to do with the fact that she had
never seen anyone like him before.

He was impossibly good-looking. Carelessly so.
Although his body was angled away from her as if he
was desperate to leave, he seemed as unable to break
the strange connection between them as she was.

Which was why she noticed the minute tremor that rippled beneath the surface of him when she had mentioned family. To some he might have appeared relaxed, but there was a tension formed deep within him and she didn't need a seismograph to know it. He reminded her of dolerite, the rock formed from pressurised molten lava.

'You are on your own?' He didn't seem to like the idea.

'In Greece? Yes,' she confirmed.

He turned back to his friends, his gaze snagging on the exit to the bar and then back to her, and something in her curled as she realised he didn't want to be there. With her. Shame. Embarrassment. Frustration?

She looked down as she saw him press a business card along the table with his index finger.

'Just in case you get into trouble.'

'I won't need it,' Summer said, no matter how desperate she was to accept the link to him, to her father.

He smiled, a painfully civil press of his lips that she felt around her heart. 'Maybe, maybe not. But take it so I will be able to sleep tonight.'

And with that he disappeared.

For a moment she sat, stunned, watching him leave. And only then did she realise she hadn't asked him when her father might return.

CHAPTER TWO

SUMMER HAD BEEN awake for a while without realising it. Staring up at the ceiling, her mind had continued to play out her dreams from sleeping into waking. And if it had just been a matter of images she might have been able to shake off the strange fantasies that had rolled out through the night hours. But it was the feel of them that had shaken her.

She could have sworn on the Bible that she knew the weight of his hand on her thigh, the press of his lips against her neck, the warmth of his body against hers, the safety she felt within his arms. A safety, a presence that made her unaccountably sad. The kind of deep sadness that felt familiar, that felt *old*.

Loneliness.

She realised it with a sense of confusion. She blinked at the ceiling and then approached it with a rationality that she was known for. Clearly it had more to do with missing Kyros Agyros than Theron and any such emotional reaction was surely understandable. Perhaps it was because she was in Athens alone that made it seem more…powerful.

She blinked back the threat of tears and threw herself into the shower, making plans as she washed the entirety of last night from her hair.

She didn't know when Kyros might return from wherever he was, but she had to hope that it would be before she left in a week's time. She decided to pass by the Agyros building later that afternoon and if there was a different receptionist she would try her luck again. If he hadn't returned in three days, then she would *have* to call Theron and somehow force the conversation onto her father. Until then she wanted to see as much of her heritage as possible.

After breakfast she left the hotel and decided just to walk. The streets ranged from hidden cobbled passageways littered with coffee tables, fuchsia bougainvillea and old men playing backgammon, to wide city streets that stretched for blocks and shops with expensive fashion labels and jewellery.

She wondered what her father was doing now. Was he still here in Athens? Or had he left for some other part of the world just at the exact moment she'd arrived looking for him? She tried to imagine what it might have been like to grow up here and was pierced by a sharp prick of guilt. She would never exchange what she'd had growing up with Skye and Star and her mother. Whenever she thought of Mariam her mind skittered over itself. As if she wasn't able or ready to think about how she had lied to her.

It hadn't taken much research to discover that Kyros had been married to a woman called Althaia. She had died twelve months ago and Summer had felt a strange grief on behalf of a father she had never met for a woman she had never known. They had married before Summer was born, so clearly her father and mother must have had an affair. Summer didn't know what to think about that, but wondered if it was why Mariam had never told her the name of her father.

She went to buy a bottle of water at a kiosk, pulled out her wallet and felt her eyes widen at the sight of the six hundred euros from the night before that she had completely forgotten.

Should she give it to the police? She took the change from the man at the kiosk and clamped her bag a little more tightly under her arm as she took a sip from the bottle of water. It wasn't exactly stolen though. She bit her lip and frowned. The thought of spending it made her feel a little hot around her neck—as if it were wrong. Yes, she could use it to pay for her flights or the hotel, or even a little treat, but it made her stomach squirm.

She and her sisters had always been frugal with money. They'd had to be. Mariam had provided love and security but not always consistency and over the years all three sisters had been there to fill in the gaps. But in the last few years Skye had worked as a secretary for a local builder and Star as a teaching assistant at the local primary, sharing a flat so they could help pay for the expensive tuition fees for Summer's geophysics degree. And she was determined that when she graduated and got her dream job she'd be able to give back to them.

Summer's part-time job meant that she had *some*

savings so the lure of ill-gotten gains waned considerably. And only when she saw the animal shelter on the corner did her heart ease a little and she knew what she had to do. Five minutes later and six hundred euros lighter she felt *good*. For the first time since leaving her father's office she felt...*happier*.

She passed beneath a bright white and yellow awning, absentmindedly looking at the display in the window, and stopped, staring at the most beautiful yellow dress she'd ever seen. The long-sleeved ankle-length dress was deceptively simple and utterly elegant. A button-lined deep V-neck reached tantalisingly low and hugged the torso, flaring out at the legs and making it eminently cooler than what she was currently wearing. The design was pretty but it was the colour that really caught Summer, the kind of bright sunny yellow she'd always been told that blondes could never wear. *Should* never wear.

Beyond her reflection, she saw a woman smiling at her and beckoning her into the shop. Summer was about to shake her head regretfully when she saw herself meeting her father in a dress like that. Looking beautiful and accomplished. And not like...*her* as she was now. Crumpled old clothes in muted colours. *Invisible* colours.

She did have her savings...

You can't, she told herself.

Unbidden, Theron's voice from the night before replied, insistent and final.

You can.

* * *

All morning Theron had stared at the Parthenon from his office window when he should have been answering emails, phone calls, running last month's figures or doing *anything* but thinking of an English girl waiting for her family.

He could blame it on the fact that he hadn't been with a woman for nearly eighteen months, but that would only be a half truth. Ever since he'd bought the apartment at Althaia's insistence, he'd not been able to bring a woman back there. Before her death, Althaia had asked him to stop living in the short-term rentals that had made up most of his adult life thus far. Beneath that had been the silent censure about his short-term pastimes of the female variety, but she'd been too kind to call him on it.

Stability. Kyros and Althaia had always known how important it was to him. How it was more than a desire, but a need in a life that could very much have gone the wrong way, like so many others in the orphanage had. For just a moment, a memory of the first night in that place slipped through his defences and his entire body turned to stone. In a heartbeat he'd shut it down but that tension still held in his shoulders, in his jaw.

It will be good for you, she'd said.

All the while Althaia had been trying to give him stability, knowing that her death would rob him of it. She'd even tried to get him to reach out to Lykos, but that had been a step too far.

As he looked up the hill once again, he cursed. He

needed coffee. Despite his assurance that he would only sleep well if she took his number, his dreams had been fevered images of Summer wrapped in his sheets, heated, flushed and utterly debauched. And as frustrating as those images were, he much preferred them to thoughts of the past.

Stalking from his office, he ignored the confused look of his assistant, blanked the question from his second-in-command and went for the stairs instead of the elevator, hoping to work off the nervous tension thrumming through his veins. Theron took them two at a time, his sense of urgency gaining rather than decreasing with the action.

He burst onto the pavement, sending a couple of pedestrians scattering, and made his way to the best coffee cart in the whole of Athens. He caught the eye of the mean old man who worked the cart every day of the year, rain, shine and even the occasional snow. He'd had the same coffee here every day for ten years and the old goat still growled, 'What do you want?' at him every time. It might have had something to do with how he and Lykos had once stolen a whole tray of muffins from his cart and, although he was fifteen years and several million euros away from the kid he'd once been, Theron had the sneaking suspicion that the vendor remembered it.

The rich smell of chocolatey coffee hit him and soothed this strange aimless fury unsettling him. He rolled out his shoulders and waited at one of the cheap metal tables that despite its apparent frailty—much like the coffee vendor—had somehow lasted the test of time.

His fingertips tapped out an impatient tattoo on the table top. The old man was mean, but he didn't usually make Theron wait. He turned just as the most incredible flash of yellow caught his eye. He fought against it, he tried *so* hard not to look, but the impression of supple curves outlined in gold was seared immediately and indelibly into his mind. The woman had her back to him, affording him an exquisite—if illicit—view of the way the material caressed the sweep of her backside and swayed gently as she leaned towards the coffee vendor, who looked as if he'd just fallen in love.

Theron couldn't *not* trace the arch of her spine and wonder whether the space between her shoulder blades would fit his outstretched palm perfectly. Blonde tendrils had been swept up to reveal a neck pink from the sun, but no less tempting to his lips and tongue.

She looked around too quickly for him to turn away and his gaze crashed into a gold-flecked hazel stare that instantly widened with surprise. A surprise he felt himself, down to his very soul. Her name sounded in his mind as if he hadn't already thought it a hundred times that day. But his name on her lips sent a surge of fire through his blood.

Her footsteps faltered and she came to a stop in the middle of the tables, staring at him while Theron sat there, hypnotised by the sight of her, so beautiful he felt changed by it.

Finally, he stood, pulling himself to his full height. 'Summer.'

She looked back to the coffee vendor, who shooed her in Theron's direction explaining in broken English that he'd bring her coffee over. Looking decidedly uncomfortable, she picked her way through the tables, the sway of the yellow material he wanted to feel beneath his fingertips gently billowing in her wake.

'I didn't know that you'd…'

'My office is just round the corner.'

'Of course.' The moment she said it she blushed and he couldn't quite fathom why she would think that his office would *of course* be round the corner.

She stood beside the chair he had offered her, looking at him in that way she did, until the vendor arrived with his coffee and her frappe. Theron ignored the side-eyed glare from the old man that warned him implicitly not to upset the nice English lady, and waited for Summer to sit.

He looked out to the street, but even the cars and tourists couldn't wipe the sight of the deceptively provocative V of her dress from his mind. As he turned back, he caught her averting her eyes and smiled at this strange dance happening between them.

'So. What do you do?' she asked, biting her lip immediately after the last word was out of her mouth.

And then he registered her question with slight surprise. It had been a while since someone had not known who he was, what he did. Had not known him to be joined at the hip with Kyros. It was novel.

'Security,' he replied, his natural disinclination to talk about himself cutting his words short.

'Financial?' she asked, a slight pink to her cheeks.

'No.'

The light seemed to dim from her eyes a little and he silently cursed. He was so unfamiliar with flirting. Was that what he was doing? In the past it had seemed much easier, the women more knowing and determined and he just as willing to go along with the simple sexual exchange. He had the suspicion that there was nothing simple about Summer.

'What have you done today?' he asked and she seemed relieved.

'I went to the Acropolis today. It was...' she shook her head, her eyes lit with excitement and pleasure '...incredible. The sense of history there is quite amazing. And the way that the underlying rock formations have developed...' She trailed off, biting her lip as if to stop herself from continuing.

'Yes?'

'Mmm?' she replied, as if asking a question.

'The underlying rock formations?'

'Oh, shall I continue?' she asked, surprised.

He couldn't help but laugh a little. 'Are you in the habit of pausing mid-sentence and changing the subject?'

'Well, yes, actually,' she answered honestly. 'Usually when I start to talk about rock formations, people's eyes glaze over,' she said, sweeping a loose corn-coloured tendril back behind her ear.

'Are my eyes glazed over?' he asked and held his breath as she leaned forward across the table to look more closely at his eyes, squinting and assessing and smiling as if he'd delighted her somehow.

'No,' she replied, trying and failing to contain a gentle laugh.

He gestured for her to continue, picked up his coffee and sat back in his chair to listen to her talk on, of all things, rock formations.

'It's actually quite interesting really, because the limestone capping the Acropolis—the ground on which the Parthenon is built—is Cretaceous Age Tourkovounia Formation. But the layer beneath that, the Athens Schist, is from nearly thirty million years *after*. So the upper rock layer is older than the lower, which is a perversion of the principle of superposition.'

He nearly choked on his coffee at the way she said perversion and he felt like a naughty schoolboy. He didn't think he'd *ever* felt like that, even when he had been at school.

'And because the schist is more susceptible to weathering than the upper layer of limestone, it's being nibbled away over time from the sides. But essentially it's an erosional remnant of a much larger…'

'Larger…?'

'Thrust sheet,' she said, blushing, and as much as he tried, he really couldn't help the smile that pulled at his mouth. 'I'm sorry, I should shut up,' she concluded.

'Why?' he asked, genuinely intrigued why she would regret something that brought her to life in such a way—even if he'd been amused by her accidental double-entendre. 'This is your work?'

'I'm a geophysics student. It's the study and analysis of the physical properties of the earth and space around it.'

'And your interest is in...' He had never had to work so hard to get a woman to talk to him. Instinctively, without question, he knew Althaia would have loved her.

'Well, most people go into oceanography, but I'm quite interested in engineering.' She shrugged helplessly. 'It's—' her eyes sparkled '—it's fascinating to me, but boring to most people.'

He frowned. He might not have understood all of it but her enthusiasm and expertise had been electrifying. 'Boring or intimidating?' he asked.

'Well,' she said, giving it that same kind of focused consideration he was beginning to appreciate about her, 'perhaps it's just harder to relate to,' she said, shrugging. 'Or to talk about,' she concluded.

'Or they're just not taking the time to understand why it's important to you?'

Summer's mind went completely blank. No one outside her course could relate to it and while her sisters loved her greatly and made obliging sounds and supportive gestures, they didn't know *why* it was important to her. It was something she'd never really told a soul. But the way that Theron was looking at her... expectant and...and...as if he were challenging her not to disappoint.

'I never knew my father.' His eyes flashed for a second, as if surprised at the direction of the conversation. 'It...it made me feel less...tethered. As if I wasn't quite sure of the ground beneath my feet. I have a wonderful mother and two incredible sisters, but there was something about having half of my history, my identity, hidden that made me need to know that everything around me is…'

'Safe,' he finished for her.

'Yes.'

He nodded. And for just a second she thought he understood. That he knew that feeling too.

'What you do is important,' he stated and the ferocity shining in his eyes painted her skin in sparkles, the assurance of his words vibrated in her chest, making her feel glorious. But then he blinked and it was too late to ask him about the hurt she had seen beneath the burn in his eyes. He had covered it so quickly, if she hadn't been so used to observing and recording she might have missed it. 'Everyone in Greece knows that.'

She linked his two statements and made the connection. 'Of course. Your earthquakes here are—'

'Almost daily.' He seemed dismissive.

Summer nodded, feeling a little less shiny. She had waited so long to find someone who was impressed by what she did, but when it had happened, when Theron had said those things, all she'd wanted was for him to be impressed by *her*.

She leaned back in her chair, trying to shift away from the gravitational field that seemed to pull her to him. She took off the straw's paper wrapping and plunged it into the coffee the vendor had assured her she'd like. The moment the cool, sweet, creamy coffee exploded on her tongue she couldn't help but moan. In her peripheral vision she saw Theron's jaw clench and pulse. Perhaps he believed that iced coffee was for children, she thought, but she didn't care. It was delightful.

He checked a watch that could only be described as obscenely expensive and glanced at her quickly, as if checking it was safe to do so. 'You've eaten?'

The question caught her as slightly strange. As if he didn't quite care, but wanted to make sure that she was looking after herself. She was tempted to lie, but found herself shaking her head when he returned his eyes to hers.

Then a gaze that had been distracted, as if he'd been at war with something in his thoughts, cleared and the creases at his eyes softened. 'Would you have dinner with me?'

Her mind skittered to a halt, quickly running over the last few moments. She might not be well versed in dating, but had he intended 'You've eaten?' to be an invitation? She couldn't help but smile a little at the discomfort he was hiding fairly well as she kept him waiting. A hundred reasons to refuse ran through her mind against the one that connected him to Kyros. But that wasn't the reason she placed her hand in his.

It was a little awkward at first as they made their way out of the square, past cafés and bars, weaving between pedestrians, but after a few minutes it eased and became comfortable. And then comfortable became something warmer, softer…something intangible that Summer couldn't explain or quantify, but could most definitely *feel*. She smiled and when she turned to see him casting a glance her way, the hint of something soft curling the corner of his lip, she felt it in her chest. A thud. A beat. A pulse.

When he asked, she explained a little about her family, what it was like to grow up in the New Forest, focusing on her siblings rather than her mother. The ache in her chest from the hurt and confusion over her mother's lies a bruise she gently protected. Theron was now talking about the way the different areas in Athens had changed over the years, and she wondered what he would think if she told him about Kyros. Her conscience stirred, warned her that by not telling him the truth, not telling him why she was there, she was lying to him. But, for the first time in her life, Summer ignored the rationality of her mind and followed the beat of her heart.

The sun was low in the sky by the time she saw the first glimmering shimmer of the sea. And soon they were walking along a pathway that bordered the thin strip of sand between them and the sea, towards a small white-fronted building with blue and white checked tablecloths.

'Is this where you bring all the girls?' she asked, forcing her tone to be light, but genuinely curious.

'No, I've never brought a woman here,' he said, looking as surprised by the answer as she was.

He was greeted like royalty by the staff and customers, who he waved off good-naturedly, and eventually they were led to an outdoor area where lines of fairy lights created an illuminated canopy above. She sat in the chair that Theron had pulled out for her and, before she could even take a breath, a carafe of wine had been placed beside large glasses of iced water. The waiter said something to Theron in Greek before leaving.

'You're hungry,' Theron determined.

'Starving,' she confessed. And within minutes nearly ten different plates had filled the table. Some she recognised, some she didn't, all smelling absolutely divine. Not knowing where to start, she followed Theron as, plate by plate, he dipped some of the gorgeous warm pitta into each dish.

He hardly ate a thing, while Summer seemed to taste and test everything, returning to ones that she liked in order but leaving her favourite until last—the one that made her eyes drift closed and her shoulders lower as if finally relaxing.

All afternoon he'd known that he should put her in a taxi and send her back to her hotel. But then she'd say something to make him laugh and he honestly couldn't remember the last time that had happened. Or she'd ask a question and the next thing he knew it was an hour later. Or she'd look at him in a way that convinced him she was the most innocent person he'd ever met. Everything was there on her face, each new delight, concern, question, joy, desire...

'Thank you,' she said, putting the fork down, her gaze low and her smile small but satisfied. 'So, why here?' she asked.

'The food is the best in Athens,' Theron said, speaking God's honest truth. It was also about two miles from the orphanage he'd grown up in and would probably still be leaving out food for the kids had he and

Kyros not funded a soup kitchen two corners over eight years ago.

'You must have been coming here a long time.'

'I have,' he confirmed, watching her look around at the humble restaurant in awe.

He speared some of the *xtapodi*—his favourite dish—and was just about to open his mouth when she asked, 'Did you come here with your family?'

The sharp sting cut him from head to toe. He hadn't expected it. He usually didn't get this far in conversation with anyone, let alone a woman. He blinked to wipe the haze from his eyes, mind and heart. 'No,' he said, trying to find his way back to the present. 'They died when I was five.'

Her eyes flashed to his, a sudden fierceness in her gaze as if she could personally hold back his grief, standing between him and it. Her sympathy was active, alive and pulsing and it shocked him to his core.

'I'm so sorry for your loss.' Even her condolence was defiant almost, rather than the muted sadness he'd had from others.

'It was years ago,' he dismissed and as she held his gaze something fresh came into his mind.

It was twelve months ago.

His eyes widened in shock. The sudden, completely unbidden realisation that Althaia's death had hit him just as hard as that of his parents gutted his heart. He mentally shook his head and excused himself from the table. As he stalked out towards the rear of the restaurant, he ordered himself to get a grip. When he got back to the table he'd send her on her way. He couldn't be around her. She prised things from him he usually kept locked tight. And he didn't have to be told how innocent she was. She'd blushed at the word thrust, for God's sake. He should send her home and head back into town and find someone to lose himself in.

Summer felt a presence coming towards the table, but instinctively knew it wasn't Theron.

'Good evening.'

She looked up to find a man even taller than Theron standing at a respectable distance away, as if not wanting to interrupt.

'Lykos Livas,' he said, holding out his hand for her to take. 'I'm an associate of Theron's. I hope you don't mind,' he said, placing his free hand on his heart in a gesture she was sure would have charmed a large percentage of the population. It might have worked on her too, if her mind wasn't already on *another* handsome Greek man. Her mind and her heart.

'It is sacrilege to allow a woman as beautiful as you to be here on your own,' he concluded.

The sheer ridiculousness of the line made her laugh and, to her surprise, rather than being offended, Lykos Livas seemed strangely pleased.

'Does that usually work?' she couldn't help but ask.

'Yes, actually,' he declared.

'Tourists?'

'Always,' he affirmed happily.

Summer shook his hand and felt…nothing. Not the tingles that shot up her arm every time Theron accidentally brushed her hand. Not the heart pounding, breathless feeling in her chest when she caught him looking at her that echoed deep within her until she felt as if she might explode.

'So, you work with Theron? With Kyros?' Summer asked, trying not to flinch as she said her father's name.

Lykos's silvery gaze sparkled as he held her gaze for a little too long. 'No,' he finally replied with a deadly smile. 'My millions are my own.' He looked behind him as if checking for Theron and reached into his jacket. He handed her his card. 'Just in case you ever need anything.'

'Why would I—?' she said, taking his card and, before she could stop him, he had swept up her hand, bowed and pressed his lips to the air just above her skin in a kiss right out of one of Star's historical romances.

'It was nice to meet you, Ms Soames,' he intoned and vanished as quickly as he had appeared.

Summer was still staring after his retreating form when Theron stalked over to the table with such fury she reared back.

'What did he say to you?' Theron demanded.

'What?'

'Livas. What did he say?'

'Nothing,' she said, folding Lykos's card in her palm. 'He just asked if I was alone. When I said no, he left.'

Theron stared at her, then threw some money onto the table. 'And the kiss?'

'What kiss?'

CHAPTER THREE

THERON KNEW HE was overreacting, knew absolutely one hundred per cent that he had regressed several millennia into caveman behaviour, but he couldn't help it. His blood rushed in his veins, pounded in his ears, and his inner voice had howled out the word *mine* the moment he'd seen Lykos bent over her hand.

He hadn't seen Lykos for ten years and Theron hated that his first reaction had been one of joy. And then he'd remembered. The way that Lykos had left, the argument they'd had, the demand Lykos had made. The betrayal he'd felt. He hadn't even been there for Althaia's funeral.

'He didn't kiss me—my hand, I mean.'

'I know what I saw.'

'Or you saw what he wanted you to see,' Summer replied, watching him closely. 'And, even if he had, it was just a kiss,' she said with a shrug.

'Just a kiss?' Theron demanded, horrified. 'There is no such thing as *just a kiss*,' he said, wondering what inept individuals she had been kissing to say such a thing.

And then she blushed and looked down at the table. And he knew. *None.*

How was it possible? This beautiful, vibrant, incredible woman and no one had kissed her? He stared at her as she tried to gather herself, understanding that she was embarrassed, and glared off into the ocean to give her a moment's privacy.

He cursed himself mentally. He'd known she was different from the women he had associated with in the past, but this? This was an innocence that should be well beyond his reach.

Coffee was placed on the table along with plates of baklava and Theron wavered. He desperately wanted to leave, return Summer to her hotel and never look back. But he couldn't leave her looking like that.

'He likes you,' he said to her. When Summer raised eyes full of questions, he explained. 'The owner. He only ever gives out one piece,' he said, pointing to the two squares of baklava on her plate.

His answer took away some of the hurt in her eyes and he was thankful. But he still marvelled at her innocence. How she could—

'The town I grew up in is quite judgemental and, my sisters and I, we have…we have different fathers. So…' she shrugged, as if that would make all the preconceptions, judgement and sadness he imagined she must have battled as a child just disappear '…for the most part people avoided us.'

'For the most part?'

She frowned, making him want to smooth away the little furrow in her brow. 'When I was about thirteen, a boy—*the* boy—at school asked to meet me after class.' She smiled sadly at herself as if she should have known better. 'I overheard his friends talking about it. How they wanted to see if I was just like my mother.'

Theron clenched his fists under the table, feeling the anger he'd banked ignite instantly, her experience with bullies and teasing melding a little with some of his own. The fights he'd had, before Lykos.

'I left him waiting and ignored him and his friends for the rest of the year.'

He tried to let go of it—the anger—the way she seemed to have done.

'It was easier to stay away from boys like that. And at uni the guys on my course... Well, they tend to be more interested in...'

'Igneous rock formations?' he asked, thinking of her studies.

She laughed, as if it was funny that she had so little experience of receiving attention, and his heart broke a little. 'Yes. Exactly,' she affirmed.

He nodded. 'Eat your baklava,' he commanded.

'Yes, sir,' she replied with a smile.

From the first mouthful of the sweet, nutty, sticky dessert she had fallen instantly in love. And through every subsequent bite Theron had sat back in his chair, sipping at his coffee, never once taking his eyes off her.

At first it had made her self-conscious. Her forkfuls had been small, dainty and her eyes low on the table. But then she had lost herself in the tastes and textures of each mouthful, caught herself stifling a moan of sheer delight and risked a glance at Theron, who seemed almost carved from stone. Almost, because there was nothing inert about his eyes. They flashed, sparked, flared, flickered... There was such movement in them she could look at them for ever. She felt them graze over her face, her shoulders, her hands where they picked up the fork, her chest when she sucked in a breath, her neck when she leaned forward to take a sip of coffee, her lips when her tongue smoothed over a drop of syrup. Every single action made her aware of her heart beating in her chest and the low pulse between her legs. Something was building within her, a yearning, a need, and she felt as if she might jump out of her own skin if it wasn't let loose. She might never have experienced it, but she knew exactly what it was. She put her fork down, giving up on the unfinished dessert because that wasn't the kind of hunger she felt now.

She knew it. And so did he.

Theron reached across the table and picked up her hand. He brought it towards him and her heart shifted. He cradled it within his palm, the pad of his thumb smoothing imaginary lines on the back of her hand as if slowly, inch by inch, he was erasing the memory of one man and imprinting himself in its place.

He lowered his head and she felt sparks ricochet in the air between his lips and her skin, the vibrations getting quicker and quicker until her heart felt as if it might burst from her chest. As his lips pressed against her skin, her heart missed a beat, her fingers curled in his palm, tightening around his hand and her thighs pulled together. She bit her lip and felt unaccountably angry when he finally released the press of his lips and looked up at her.

Just a kiss?

He had proved her wrong. They both knew it, but in doing so he'd opened a door that she'd never walked through before, never wanted to before. And now… now she feared he might close that door before she'd even tried.

Now *she* was angry. With him because she knew Theron wanted to walk away. With her father for not being there. Angry for him and for the loss of his parents. Angry with her mother for being ill. With everything *not* going to plan.

She lurched up from the table, startling him and the other customers with the scratch of the chair legs against the floor, and turned, running down the stairs and out onto the walkway illuminated solely by the light of the moon.

She called herself all the different kinds of fool she could think of. How had she let this happen? She pressed the back of her hand against her lips, as if somehow she could superimpose his kiss onto her mouth. But it only left an aching emptiness inside that hurt even more now she knew what it was like to feel filled with need and desire. Her breath sobbed against her hand and she tried to hold in the tears that wanted to be let free.

She drew to a halt, staring out at the inky black sea merging with the night, wishing for something she couldn't put words to. Fingers wrapped gently around her wrist and pulled her round and when she refused to look up into the dark expressive eyes she knew would be there, a finger hooked her chin and tilted her face to his. Eyes flickered back and forth over her face, as if trying to read thoughts that were incoherent even to her. She felt as if he were turning the pages of her mind, reading the words of her heart: desire, need, desperation, sadness, fear, yearning, permission, consent. It was there, all of it, and she just wanted him to—

He moved so slowly she thought she'd imagined it at first. She'd expected him to crush her to him, like the romances her sister Star was always swooning over. But he didn't. And somehow it was so much *more*.

She was sick with want and it took her a moment to realise it wasn't just her that felt that way. He reached up to brush a lock of hair back behind her ear, his fingers shaking ever so slightly. The moment he noticed it he clenched his fist and looked at her accusingly, as if demanding to know what she was doing to him.

Before he could take it back or change his mind, Summer closed the imperceptible distance between their lips—a space that felt like a heartbeat between before and after and...

Oh...

That was what it was like.

She'd expected his lips to feel firm and a little cool perhaps, but they were soft and so warm and sent fireworks shooting through her entire body. It was such a shock that her mouth opened on a gasp just as he began to kiss her back and the feel of his tongue gently pressing against the curve of her top lip made her breath hitch and her hands curl and, before she knew it, she had risen up onto her toes and pressed herself against the length of him and leaned into everything she was feeling.

But it was nothing compared to what she felt when he took over the kiss.

He'd given her a chance to explore, to feel, to touch, slide and press her way through it. And then he moved. His hand cradled her neck as his fingers threaded through her hair, sending the band holding it in place flying and the tendrils of her long hair falling down her back.

His other hand cupped her jaw, angling her head and her mouth in the most perfect way. Her chest rose to meet his, wanting to feel him against her, skin to skin—needing to. She reached up to clutch the lapels of his jacket, pulling them closer together. His hand slipped from her neck to her back, his fingers stretching between her shoulder blades, and she felt him sigh.

He pulled back from the kiss and pressed his forehead to hers, their rushed breathing buffeting the air between them.

This was it. This was the moment he would leave. Summer's fingers clenched reflexively. She swallowed the hurt she felt already.

'I should take you back to your hotel.'

'Should you?'

'Summer—'

Unwelcome nausea swelled in her stomach, her inner voice already howling at what he was taking away from her.

'Is this the bit where you tell me that I'm too innocent to know what I want?' she demanded. He pulled back, searching her face, and she raged at him for underestimating her. For denying her something she could see that he wanted too. 'The bit where you tell me that you're not good enough for me?'

His eyes darkened, whether in defiance or defence, she couldn't tell. And then he let her go, turned back onto the walkway and began to disappear into the night. Summer clenched her jaw, all the feelings within her bubbling up to the surface, hot, angry and aching.

'You're not that much older than me, you know,' she called after him. 'And…and…' He paused, as if wanting to hear what she was going to say. 'And you were a virgin once too!' she yelled, shocked by her own audacity.

He spun round and ducked slightly, as if to avoid the words, and closed the distance between them in seconds. '*Éleos*, will you keep your voice down?' he growled, casting wary glares left and right. He looked like an angry schoolboy, a dark curl having fallen onto his forehead and a ruddy streak on either cheek. It was comical, the laugh rising up in her chest cutting through the darker emotions from just moments before.

'Are you blushing? Was it the word virgin?' she demanded, incredulous.

'Oh, for the love of—'

He kissed her then, the way she'd thought he might but could never have expected. The crush of his lips, his body dominating hers, overpowering her and it was incredible. It was all she could do to hold onto him and not be swept away into the sea.

'You're going to ruin me, aren't you?' he asked between kisses.

'Isn't it supposed to be the other way round?' she asked, the breathlessness of her voice causing his pupils to flare. She loved being able to see the reaction in him, to know that she was the cause.

'Come with me?' he asked.

The drive they took back to his apartment was short but interminable. Nothing was said, but it was far from silent. Sitting beside her in the back seat, Theron watched her for the entire journey, his eyes conveying more than words could as they touched every part of her in a caress that she could feel. It stoked an arousal within her so strong, so pure, and the curve of his lips told her that he knew *exactly* what he was doing. Was purposely doing. And Summer gave up any concerns or embarrassment, his clear desire of her as sure a thing as she'd ever known.

He paid the driver and led her through the foyer and into the elevator, up to his apartment, and gestured for her to pass the threshold first. All the while her eyes were unseeing and her senses heightened.

He stalked her through his apartment. He hadn't turned on the lights, so only the glow of the moonlight pouring in through the glass walls spanning the length of his corner apartment illuminated her path. She was breathless with delight and dizzy with need, adrenaline coursing through her veins making her pulse trip.

The gleam in his eyes told her he felt it too. Fed from it even. Summer kicked her shoes off and into the corner of the living area as she rounded the sofa and her jaw dropped as Theron simply stepped up onto the cushions and over the back, reaching for her, but she twisted and spun away from his hold with a laugh.

She reached out to the door frame of another room and paused on the threshold as she realised it was his bedroom. Her heart pounded in her chest as she felt him behind her. He leant against the frame, his hand just inches above hers, the warmth from his body crashing against hers in waves as she took in the sight of the large bed. The throbbing of her heart radiated outwards through her entire body and she was filled with desire and need.

'We don't have to do anything you don't—'

She turned and kissed him. To stop his words, to stop the awkwardness she feared was replacing the delighted fizz from mere moments ago. She felt the curve of his lips through the kiss and he gently pulled away, softening his retreat. She couldn't quite explain the writhing emotions twisting in her because it wasn't that she was unsure, it was as if she felt embarrassed by it, even though rationally she knew she shouldn't be.

'Summer, consent is an important conversation to have,' he said, his words whispered into her ear, brushing against her neck and filling her with want. 'It's not embarrassing. It's respectful. You have as much control in this as me, and if you want to spend the entire evening making love I will. And if you want me to stop I will.' He shrugged as if it were that simple.

Summer turned, touched so deeply by his words, his assurance not only sweeping aside the awkwardness she'd felt but making her want him more, making her feel protected and cared for in a way that was somehow more than just moments before. She knew then she'd never regret tonight.

'This is something I want very much,' she said, reaching up to cup his jaw. 'And something I've only ever wanted with you. So, I do want you to stop…' she said, Theron's nod swift and sure against her palm, '…*talking*,' she finished and pulled him to her in a kiss that took him only a second to take over.

His hands settled over Summer's body, reaching for her waist and lifting her up above him so that her hair fell about them. He locked his arms around her thighs and walked them back to the bed, turning so that when they fell he was beneath her, cushioning her as she became a tangled mess of laughter and legs and arms that turned into kisses and sighs and touches that made his heart soar in a way he couldn't remember ever having felt.

'You are so beautiful,' he said, reaching up to tuck a long blonde tendril behind her ear so he could see the golden flecks in her hazel eyes. 'You should always be in this colour.'

She bit her lip as if embarrassed by his observation, but the blush on her cheeks, the widening of her eyes… He'd pay her compliments until she got used to them, until she welcomed each and every one of them as her due.

He reached for the zip he'd noticed at the side of the dress and slowly pulled it down, his fingers impatient, dipping between the opening and casting circles over smooth skin. She was exquisite. Every touch new, every taste incredible, and if this was ruin then he would go to it willingly and gladly.

She shrugged out of the top of her dress, her arms slipping through the material while holding it to her chest. He could see her nerves but he could also see her desire, her determination and when she let the top go, revealing herself to him, it made him feel so damn honoured. She bent down at the same time as he reached up towards her and they met in an axis point of pleasure and need, and as she rocked against him his pulse roared and his heart leapt.

His arms wrapped around her waist and he pulled her beneath him, drawing the dress down her hips and away from her ankles. He made quick work of his own clothes, hating to leave her even for that short time, but the way her eyes flashed and flickered all over his body was worth every second.

It was as if she were studying and analysing every inch of him and he let her, beginning to understand that it was part of her process, working through variables and collecting data. He retrieved the condom from his wallet, tore across the seal and rolled the latex over himself, her hot eyes not leaving him for a second, turning him on even more.

He placed his hands on her thighs, gently sweeping caresses inch by inch towards the apex of her legs. 'This may hurt.' She nodded, her expression serious, understanding that it wasn't his intention to. 'And know that I will stop at any time. Any, okay? Nothing is too late, or too far.'

She nodded again and he almost groaned out loud. The look in her eyes was his undoing. He leaned forward and pressed open-mouthed kisses to her neck. 'I need to hear you say it, *agápi mou*,' he whispered.

'Yes, Theron. Yes. Please… I want…' she trailed off and the yearning in her hazel gaze exploded like starbursts '…everything,' she finished, as if confused by her own desires. He wanted that for her. He wanted to scoop up the world and give it to her.

He kissed along her collarbone, his gaze snaring on a mole about two inches from her clavicle. He pressed his thumb over it, something jarring in his mind, before she shifted beneath him, beckoning his touch to the valley between her breasts. He kissed back up the long column of her neck and positioned himself between her legs. He longed to taste her, but this wasn't about his wants. He trailed his hand over her thigh and between her legs the evidence of her need, the slickness dampening the curls made his heart stop.

He bit his lip, grounding the need for control with every ounce of his intent, and as he locked his longing gaze on hers he slowly pressed into her, consuming her gasp with a kiss. He held himself still as she tensed, her eyes flaring wide with the shock, and his eyes held only regret and hope that it would pass for her quickly. She blinked slowly, breathing through it, her body beginning to relax around his. He pressed kisses against her skin, showered her in words he had no hope of her understanding, and slowly began to move within her. Bit by bit her body began to move with his, her thighs hitching around his hips, her ankles crossing behind him, pressing him closer to her, and his heart began to pound. He braced himself, his hands either side of her on the mattress, his muscles beginning to shake as he fought to control the desire that was spinning out of his reach. As if Summer felt it too, her sighs became cries of pleasure, urging him to some impossible point. Sweat-slicked and on a knife's edge, he held them at the absolute pinnacle until her release urged his own and, together, they fell deep into the night.

Summer woke the next morning encircled in Theron's arms and decided there was no better feeling than that. A blush heated her cheeks at the way he had drawn from her a pleasure she'd never known existed. She ducked beneath the covers, hiding the smile that felt private yet utterly full of joy behind the cotton. It felt… magical to be with Theron here, in this way.

But, as wonderful as it was, she knew she'd not be able to get back to sleep, so she slipped out from under his arm, tiptoed to the bathroom and turned on the shower. She threw a look in the mirror, wondering who the beautiful woman staring back at her was. The one with pink cheeks, bright eyes and thoroughly kissed lips.

Ducking beneath the powerful spray of the water, she wondered what they might do today. Maybe Theron could take her to somewhere only he knew.

Maybe, she thought, she could tell him about Kyros. It was crazy to think that she could trust him with her body, but not that…

Theron was still asleep when she came out, so she grabbed a shirt from his closet, her dress now completely crumpled on the floor, and quietly stepped out of the room. She went to the kitchen and spied a very fancy coffee machine that only took her fifteen minutes of opening drawers, pressing buttons, cursing under her breath and one hair pull to produce a decent espresso.

She took the cup over to the large window that led onto a beautiful balcony, staring at the way the sun swept up from the sea, casting the sky in orange and yellow hues that had her so mesmerised she didn't hear the key in the door before it was too late.

She spun round, nearly spilling the coffee over the borrowed shirt, and stared.

'Theron!' yelled the man with shocking white hair, deeply tanned, lined skin and a scowl. 'Theron?'

Summer didn't recognise the rest because it was in Greek, but she certainly recognised the man. It was her father. Two steps brought Kyros Agyros into the apartment enough to see her standing by the window and close enough to break her heart.

The look he cast her was barely a sneer, the distaste in the gaze he raked over her cut her deeply and brought a sheen to her eyes that she feared might fall down her cheeks. Turning her back to him, she bit her lip so hard from trying not to cry out, she tasted blood. Her breath shuddered out of her lungs as she heard Theron emerge from the room, throwing back to Kyros whatever response was needed. She tried to tell herself that her father didn't know, that she didn't feel mortified, humiliated or shaken, but she couldn't.

Summer held her breath through the short exchange and let it go only when Kyros had left the apartment. But something had changed. Something irrevocable. She turned, blinking away the sheen, to find Theron standing there in his trousers from last night and nothing else. He was staring at her and, no matter how much she tried to hide it, he'd seen enough.

'Care to explain to me what that was about?' he demanded, doing up the button above his trouser zip without taking his eyes off her.

'I don't know—'

'Don't lie to me.' His voice might not have been a shout, but the tone was cold and harsh in a way she'd have thought impossible after last night.

'It's hard to explain,' she replied, suddenly realising how it might look to Theron. She'd thought she'd have time. Time to explain herself.

'You are articulate and intelligent. Try.'

Summer breathed deeply. 'He's my father.'

Every single emotion that had been shining in his eyes was immediately blanked. He uttered what could only be a curse and sent a glare her way. 'Don't be ridiculous,' he all but spat.

'He is,' she insisted. 'I—'

He threw up a hand, cutting her off before she could explain. 'Of all the schemes and lies you could have told to have me even *half* believing you?' His gaze

was frigid, disgusted and horribly like the one Kyros
had spared her. He shook his head. 'No. That is the
one that would *never* work. Kyros was absolutely one
hundred per cent committed to his wife and family. I
know this to be true. I have seen it with my own eyes.'
His accent grew thicker and heavier the more vehe-
ment he became. 'So, what, this was a shakedown?'
he demanded.

'No!' Summer cried, appalled at how he'd inter-
preted the situation.

'A money-making scheme? Coming here after his
wife's death—'

'I didn't—'

'And sex with me was—what? A perk? An in?'
Theron yelled, before slamming his mouth shut as if
to prevent anything worse from coming out. Not that
Summer could even begin to imagine what that might
be.

'Did you know who I was?'

Shock pooled the blood in her stomach, leaving her
face cold. 'Theron—'

'That first night in the bar. Did you know who I
was?' he said, taking one step towards her and then
holding himself back.

The anger, the betrayal, the pain. She could see it.
Familiar as it was to the way she had felt when she'd
discovered her mother had lied to her about her father. Regret and hurt washed over her in a tidal wave,
threatening to pull her under.

'I tell you what,' he said, sniffing and walking past
her to the coffee machine. 'I'll give you fifteen minutes

to get out. And that is purely a *professional* courtesy. You were incredibly convincing last night, *agápi mou*, I must say. I am man enough to admit I fell for it,' he said, his back to her, before turning and clapping his hands together slowly.

'Well done. Now get out.'

Last night...

The noise of the bar in Mayfair cut through the haze of anger that Theron felt as if it were only yesterday rather than five months ago.

Lykos cursed. 'That was low, Theron. And, coming from me, that's saying something,' he said, disgust heavy in the air between them.

Theron felt the thick slide of shame in his gut and he took a mouthful of whisky to drown it out, not sure that it was any better than the rage he'd felt burning a hole in his heart when she'd left his apartment in Piraeus five months ago. Or the devastation he'd experienced four hours ago when she'd stood on the steps of an estate in Norfolk, staring at him in the rear-view mirror.

'I thought she was trying to get to—'

'Your precious Kyros. I know,' Lykos said as if tired of repeating himself.

'It's my job!' Theron growled.

'You keep telling yourself that.'

'What's that supposed to mean?' Theron demanded furiously.

'It means that you've always put him on a pedestal.

You've idolised him. And you'd do anything for him, no matter what it cost you. And that's not the way to live a life, Theron.'

'He stayed. Not even *you* did that,' Theron accused.

'I asked you to come with me, Theron. You made your choice. Do us both a favour, be a big boy and live with it, okay?'

'I want you to tell me what Kyros did that was *so* bad that it erased all the money, time and effort he chose to pour into us? He gave us somewhere safe from looking over our shoulder every two minutes, he gave us an education, somewhere with food we didn't have to steal.' Theron stared at Lykos, searching his features for something other than anger and disdain—searching for a trace of the man he'd grown up with, the man he'd once called brother. Before he had left him without a second glance. 'All I know is that one day you were working for him, and the next you were telling me you were going to leave. What happened? What did he ask you to do?'

But Lykos just shook his head, holding and hoarding his secrets, as he always had. He signalled to the waitress and turned back to Theron. 'So let me guess. Summer left your apartment and you went back to work as if nothing had happened, right? Did you even tell Kyros?' Lykos asked.

'What, that I had let some con artist into my bed? That as the owner of the company he uses for security, I had nearly left him open to that?'

Theron felt Lykos's silvery glare through the darkness of the bar. 'And you didn't suspect anything beyond that?'

'I didn't think of her at all,' Theron lied. 'Until you called.'

'Here,' Star eased the cup from Summer's shaking grasp, put it on the floor and took her hands in her own. 'I'm so sorry that happened to you. That you shared something so special with Theron and that he didn't believe you…'

'I'm calling Benoit. We'll do a background check on him or something. Find a way to—'

'It's okay,' Summer interrupted with a watery smile and a sad laugh. 'I'm not finished yet.' Star reached for a couple of blankets as Skye threw another log on the fire and they settled in. 'I went back to uni, not telling anyone about what happened in Greece. I thought it would be better if I forgot the whole thing and I decided I never wanted to see my father again.'

'Oh, no, Summer, you can't hold that one moment against him. I'm sure there was something else going on,' Star said, ever hopeful, always loving.

She shrugged. 'I couldn't forget the disdain in his eyes. He barely even looked at me. And what proof did I have, really? A name, a photograph, the story of a matching mole?'

'There are DNA tests that we could get,' Star offered.

'Well, that wasn't the test I ended up doing back then,' Summer confessed, remembering sitting on the bathroom floor of her room in the university halls, her back against the door and her knees pulled up to her chest, numb with shock, staring at the little blue tick.

She'd thought it was the flu. She'd felt rundown, achy, nauseous. It could have been any number of things. And then one of the guys in her class had made a stupid joke about nausea and pregnancy and, as she'd stood there smiling while everyone laughed, she'd been doing the maths. She'd been working out just when her last period had been and her world had morphed into something she barely recognised.

She'd bought a pregnancy test immediately after class and taken it the moment she'd got back to her room. Waiting for the results, she'd wanted to call her sisters…but also hadn't. She'd thought about calling Theron, but his slow clap had rung in her ears as the seconds passed. She'd left his apartment that day, eyes blinded by hot tears and cheeks stained red by hurt and guilt.

Guilt because he'd been right. She had lied to him, she had intended to use him to find out about her father. But that had been before Theron had looked at her and she'd felt *seen*. So to have that taken away when he'd refused to believe or even hear her about her father had felt like an eclipse. A sudden absence of light. And ever since she'd left Greece there had been an ache in her heart that she'd tried to blame on the disappointment of meeting her father, but she'd known that was a lie.

And in that instant she'd made a promise to her unborn child. Never would they feel rejection. Never would they feel the shame and confusion and sadness that she had experienced. And, sitting on the cold laminate floor as the blue cross had appeared, something had stirred deep within. A maternal instinct she'd never known she had. It was fierce and true and surer than anything she'd ever felt before. And it had only grown bit by bit each day since. There had not even been a second when Summer considered anything but having her child. But that didn't mean it hadn't plunged her into a state of worry and confusion.

'And within days of finding out, we were told that the NHS were unable to offer Mum's cancer treatment, Elias died and we came here for his funeral. And then, when his will dictated the search for the Soames diamonds…'

'Did you call Theron?'

'I wanted to. But I was pretty sure he'd want a paternity test and I didn't want to risk any harm to the baby. He thought the worst of me already, so I was going to wait.'

'Going to?'

'It didn't quite work out like that.'

CHAPTER FOUR

Six days ago...

THERON FISTED HIS HANDS in his trouser pockets and stared up at the Acropolis, thinking of hazel eyes, blonde hair and a yellow dress. His notoriously lethal focus had drifted in the last few months and Kyros had noticed. Theron had felt a wave of guilt each time he'd avoided the older man's probing questions. Guilt and shame that he'd been taken in by such a con. But each night as he reran the events of that morning through his mind, he came back to the same question. Summer had admitted that she'd known who he was with the same open expression as when she'd insisted Kyros was her father. An open honesty that had bewitched him from the first moment.

Had she been telling the truth?

It had driven him mad in the days and weeks following. And more times than he'd care to admit, he'd been on the verge of asking Kyros about it. About her. About whether Kyros had cheated on his wife while she'd been on her sickbed. The thought made him more furious than he'd been in years. But still, he couldn't risk it. Kyros was everything to him. He'd given Kyros his word, his loyalty, and in return Kyros had given him stability, security and a home. Theron owed Kyros that trust.

A knock on the office door cut through his thoughts, causing him to turn.

'I'm sorry, Mr Thiakos, you didn't answer your…' His secretary appeared, red-cheeked, reluctant to call him on his ineptitude. 'Mr Livas on line two for you. Would you like me to tell him you're not available?'

Lykos hadn't been in this building for nearly ten years but his reputation still stalked the halls. Theron frowned, something swift and sharp twisting in his side. Whatever it was, it couldn't be good. He picked up the phone.

'What do you want?' Theron demanded as his secretary retreated from the room.

'Lykos! Great to hear from you after all these years! You well? I *am*, thank you, Theron. And how are you? Oh, can't complain. Can't complain.' Lykos performed his one-man show through the earpiece replete with intonations worthy of an Oscar.

'Really? This is what you waste my time with?' Theron bit back angrily.

'Is it so surprising that I might want to check in on my oldest and bestest friend?' Lykos's saccharine tone made Theron's teeth ache.

'Given that it would be the first time in nearly ten years? Yes,' Theron admitted.

'Well, I've just been presented with an interesting business opportunity but… I don't know, there's something about it…'

'You're worse than a cat with a mouse. Stop toying with me and spit it out.'

'But where's the fun in that?'

'About as much fun as me hanging up on you,' warned Theron, preparing to do just that.

'Wait!'

Theron didn't say anything.

'It's a business opportunity in Norfolk.'

'You're in America?' Theron asked, confused.

'No, Norfolk, England. An acquaintance of ours brought it to me.'

'We don't have mutual acquaintances,' he growled, his voice one hundred per cent sure, but his mind flashed onto Summer looking up as Lykos bent over her hand. How had he forgotten that?

'Oh. My mistake. I must have been confused.'

'Stop being coy. You don't get confused,' Theron bit, a dangerous edge to his voice now.

'Small, blonde. Very pretty—positively *radiant*. Must say, fits her name perfectly.'

Theron gripped the phone. 'What is she doing with you?' he demanded, shocked by the phosphoric fury burning in his veins.

'Get your mind out of the gutter. It was a business proposition,' Lykos replied, distaste heavy in his tone.

'And you never mix business with pleasure?' Theron scoffed.

'Oh, all the time,' Lykos replied easily. 'I just don't mix *my* pleasure with *yours*.'

Theron breathed his heartbeat into submission. 'Has she mentioned Kyros?'

'Not once. Why?' Lykos replied.

'Are you sure?'

'It's possible that it slipped my mind,' he taunted.

'What was the business?'

'She has a twelve-million-pound estate in Norfolk she wants to sell for a third of that value.'

Theron cursed. 'She's a student. Where the hell would she get an estate from?'

'If you want to know, go ask her. Though might I suggest, before you go in there bashing down the front door—'

'No,' Theron interrupted, the sudden need to find out exactly what was going on, intoxicating. 'I don't know what the hell you're getting out of this, but I know you have an angle here somewhere. So, no, you can't suggest a thing. I'm going to get to the bottom of this *right now*. And you will *not* buy that estate,' Theron commanded.

Less than twenty-four hours later, as Theron put the rental car into park, he told himself that his pulse was pounding because of the near miss with a scaffolding lorry, *not* because Summer Soames was hiding somewhere inside the estate in front of him. What was her angle here? Had she moved on from Kyros? Was she now targeting Lykos? He could have her.

No!

Everything in him roared denial at the bitterly careless thought. He could lie and claim not to have dreamed about her every night since she'd left his bed. He could try to tell himself that he'd put her out of his mind as the money-grabbing con artist he'd accused her of being, instead of remembering the devastation in her eyes that morning, first with Kyros and then with him. But he wouldn't lie to himself about how much he'd wanted her with every single fibre of his being since that morning.

So, no. Lykos couldn't *have her*. Because Theron wasn't done with her yet. He needed to know what she was doing and whether it had anything to do with the man he would protect with his life if need be.

His shoes crunched on the gravel as he got out of the car. He had to crane his neck to take in the sprawling building, little more than a dark outline against the dusk. In the evening's gloom it was clear the estate was in need of some serious repair, but it was still a thing of beauty, faded or otherwise. There was a sense of something more, though, tugging at him, drawing him closer…but he shook the silliness out of his head as he took the steps two at a time, reaching the semi-circular dais at the top in front of a very large wooden door.

He pounded on it, wondering whether he had a hope in hell of her hearing it. As the minutes ticked by, Theron became increasingly frustrated. He stepped back off the steps and peered up at windows caked in grime and cobwebs. He frowned. The building looked deserted. Abandoned. Anything could happen here and no one would know. An icy tendril wound its way up his spine and he was worried. Worried about Summer. The suddenly frantic beat of his heart infected his thoughts and his mind quickly became a jumble so that when the door opened and he saw Summer standing there it took him a moment to breathe.

And he forgot. Forgot about Kyros and about her insane accusation. He forgot the anger that had so cleverly laid over the hurt. The ache that she'd fooled him. That she'd used him. And instead he just took her in.

A wave of relief washed over him, and a feeling he barely recognised and dared not name was left on the shore of his heart. Summer's eyes widened in recognition, and for just a second he thought he might have seen something like hope spark in her eyes.

As if tethered to her he approached her with one step. And then another. And another until somehow he was within an inch of her and his hands were reaching to frame her face and his mouth was claiming hers and he felt as if he was *home*.

A moan sounded on the air between them and he couldn't be sure if it had been hers or his. Her lips tasted of honey and opened beneath his and a shocking heat unfurled within him, his heart in his mouth and realisation on his tongue. He'd been lying to himself for months. He'd not put her out of his mind, he'd kept her there, the memories of her locked away, and the moment that he'd seen her again they were all unleashed. This was what he'd needed, just so he could breathe, he thought as he pulled her flush against his body and…stopped.

He opened his eyes to find hers staring at him, shock and something horrifyingly like fear sparking to life in them. He pulled back and reached out at the same time, his hand unerringly finding the curve, not of her stomach but a bump. Just about the right size for a…

Summer closed her eyes. It had taken her only seconds to consume the sight of him. The thick wave of hair, so dark it looked velvety, the stubble on his jaw, the breadth of his shoulders, the way his forearms corded beneath rolled-up shirtsleeves—everything about him made her want to touch. Her breathing hitched and she felt utterly betrayed by her body as it throbbed and pulsed just at the sight of him. And the thread of hope she'd barely admitted to herself during the last weeks and months sprang to life. But when he'd reached for her, hopes, fears and fantasies had disappeared and she'd melted into him as if nothing else mattered.

She'd forgotten. That was the power he had over her. For just a second of madness, she'd forgotten. Until Theron had reared back, the look of shock on his features indelibly marked across her heart.

'No.'

The word severed the spell he'd cast over her, bringing her back to reality with a painful jolt. She was surprised that it hurt so much. His denial. It wasn't as if she hadn't expected it. Neither could she blame him— she'd had that moment too. The moment when in less than a heartbeat her mind had travelled through infinite possibilities and futures, all twisting and turning out of reach in light of the shocking fact that she was now going to be a parent. But she'd also seen futures in which their child was the most precious, beautiful part of her life.

But the look in his eyes—the one he was trying so desperately to mask—was all too familiar to her and just as painful as it had been in Greece. That moment of rejection, that feeling, compounded by her father's dismissal, fired a kiln that forged steel within her. She would not subject her child to that now or ever.

'You are pregnant?'

'Yes,' she said, waiting for some kind of indication that he had realised that he was a father. But where once she had marvelled at his impenetrable, stone-like qualities, now it just felt cruel. As if it made her even more conscious of their differences. She felt soft and sore and emotional and he seemed hard, cold, tough and it made her hurt even more. What kind of father would he be for their child?

'What are you doing here?' she asked, her thoughts making her voice a whisper.

Theron blinked, looking around as if he didn't know how to answer that question. He went to say something and had to clear his throat. 'Lykos…'

Summer rolled her eyes. She should have known the Greek billionaire friend of Theron's wouldn't have kept his mouth shut. Not that she'd had much of a choice. It wasn't as if as a geophysics student she knew *that* many billionaires. And when she and her sisters had realised they would need to sell the Soames estate, and sell it quickly, Summer had remembered what Lykos Livas had said when he'd handed over his card. *Just in case you ever need anything.* Lykos had been there for her when she'd needed it, not Theron. Not the man who had tossed her from his apartment in such a cruel way.

Hurt fired her fury as she focused back on Theron, who was staring at her stomach. 'I don't have time for this,' she said around his silence. 'I don't have time for *you*. You can go,' she dismissed, her heart breaking as she turned blindly down a hallway, not caring where she went.

'I'm not going anywhere.' The tone of Theron's voice was all the warning she got before he pulled her round to face him and in an instant she was overwhelmed with the memory of the first time he'd kissed her. She looked up just in time to see the flare of his pupils as if he too was lost in the same thought. But then he blinked and once again she was shut out and the icy-cold stare he levelled at her made her shiver.

'Ask me,' she demanded.

For a second he looked confused. 'Ask you what?'

Summer shook her head, blinking furiously, praying that she could get through this before the tears came. She looked up at him, her heart breaking. 'Ask me if it's yours.'

Shock slashed angry red marks across his cheeks and gutted his chest. That was what it felt like. As if everything inside him had been scooped out and exposed.

He was more certain that she was pregnant with his child than anything he'd ever known in his entire life. The question hadn't even crossed his mind, let alone formed into a sentence, and the thought that she'd believe he'd question such a thing burned his soul.

You were incredibly convincing last night, agápi mou, I must say. I am man enough to admit I fell for it.

This time the slow clap that echoed in his mind was for him and him alone.

Of course, she had doubted he would believe her. What on earth had he done to make her think otherwise?

'Summer—'

'Ask me,' she repeated, her voice raised this time but stronger.

'No.' The word clawed against his throat.

She cocked her head to the side and his heart pounded. He knew where this was going and he wanted to stop it. He wasn't prepared for this.

'Why not?'

'Because I don't have to.' He knew that wouldn't be enough and that she'd be right to demand more. Because he saw it now. She'd had the same look on her face the morning of the argument. 'Because I know.'

'Know what? That if I said it was yours that I'd be telling the truth?'

He nodded, shame, anger, guilt making him nauseous.

'I want to hear you say it,' she said, her voice trembling.

He gritted his teeth. It was the least she deserved and, if he had his way, the first of everything. 'I believe you.'

He cursed mentally, knowing the truth of it. Knowing that the child was his, but more than that—Summer was Kyros's child. She had been telling the truth the day he'd kicked her out of his apartment, treating her no better than a...

He fisted his hands. He didn't want to know, but the question was burning a hole in his empty chest. 'Were you going to tell me?' He couldn't look at her as he asked the question. He didn't want to see what her expressive features betrayed.

But she was hell-bent on making him work for his answer. It was only when he met her gaze that she responded.

'After. When a DNA test would have been safe.' Her eyes told him that she'd wanted to lie, wanted to say never, but she wasn't like that. Why hadn't he seen that then? Why hadn't he believed her?

A phone ringing in the distance cut through the moment. Summer looked behind her and then back to him. 'I have to get that.'

'We will talk about this,' he warned.

'Fine. But... I just... I need to get that.'

She disappeared into the bowels of the building before he could argue and suddenly Theron felt dizzy. He turned, with no idea where he was going, just knowing that he needed to get back outside. The corridors were too dark, the house too damp, empty... It was lifeless and he couldn't breathe. Bursting through a door that led out from the back of the house, he bent over, his hands on his knees, pulling air into his lungs.

Had he missed it? The mole on her collarbone? No. He remembered putting his thumb over it, remembered the strange sense of recognition stirring within him. Something sure and strong tightened in his gut. Kyros had the same mole. He was proud of the strange family trait. Every Agyros had it. Theron remembered it, because once as a teenager Lykos had found him trying to draw one on his clavicle and mocked him mercilessly for it.

Theé mou. How could she be Kyros's daughter? The old man had been faithfully married to his wife—his incredibly sick wife—hadn't he? Theron had never known Kyros to leave her side. He'd never spent a night away from her, never had anything but love in his words and actions towards her.

But Theron had only known him for fifteen years. Perhaps something had happened before that? Summer was, what…early twenties?

Early twenties and pregnant. He tried to cast his mind back to that night. How many times had they made love? How many times had they used protection? That he couldn't quite remember was damning enough. He'd been utterly mindless in his desire for her.

A desire that hadn't been misguided. He'd thought himself a fool for thinking her so pure and so bright that night. But he'd *not* been wrong. He hadn't misread her, been fooled or tricked. Summer was absolutely all of the things he'd thought and wanted that night.

He pulled himself up and tried to fill his lungs with oxygen, but he feared they'd never fill again. He was going to be a father. Something primal, instinctive roared to life within him. A possessive, determined, living need welled inside him with such ferocity it almost scared him.

Was this what his own father had felt? And his mother? Had his birth been planned or, as with him and Summer, had the pregnancy been a shock, a surprise?

He had no one to ask these questions, no one to tell him about his parents, their relationship, their lives, their hardships. Both Kyros and Althaia had tried to help him find someone who was connected to his life, but they hadn't been able to find anyone who had known his parents.

And now he was going to be a parent himself. The vow didn't even form words in his head before he felt it in his heart. His child would *never* have questions about their heritage. His child would never feel the losses that he had experienced. It would never want for a single thing. And instinctively he knew Summer would feel the same. It was there in her determination, her challenge to him.

Ask me.

It had been as much a demand as it had been a test. One he had already failed.

There was only one possible way forward now.

Summer found him sitting on the old stone steps at the back of the house, shrouded by the night. She'd hung up after talking with Star, who had left Duratra and headed into the desert to find the second half of the key to wherever and whatever held the family's missing diamonds. A part of Summer quivered with fear that Star might not find it, and that she herself might not find this hidden location where her great-

great-great-grandmother had placed the family heir-loom. And without the diamonds they wouldn't meet the terms of their grandfather's will and be able to sell the estate to Lykos, so that they could pay for their mother's treatment.

The other part was trembling because of a certain Greek magnate staring into the sky, looking as if he had no plans to leave.

I believe you.

If he'd said it immediately, freely even, she might not have trusted him. But he'd said it as if it had cost him something and she couldn't understand what that might be.

Kyros was absolutely one hundred per cent committed to his wife and family. I know this to be true. I have seen it with my own eyes.

'What is my father to you?' Summer had been so busy putting the pieces together that she'd spoken before she'd thought. And the look in his eyes when his gaze rose to meet hers made her wish she hadn't.

The tangle of hurt, resentment, love, protection... all these emotions knitted together in his eyes.

'Everything,' he replied, turning back to look up at the stars. 'I still...'

She flinched, knowing that words of disbelief would have finished that sentence.

'I do believe you,' he said, as if he'd felt rather than seen her hurt. 'It's just *hard*. I've known him since I was twelve.'

And I've never known him, she thought as something twisted in her heart.

'He gave me everything that I have today and I would do anything for him.' He said it simply, easily, like floating on water, but she felt the words like a stone, weighing and pressing him down. Maybe he couldn't see it.

'What happened? How...?' He asked as if she held the answer to understanding a shocking mystery.

'I don't know. I was hoping to ask him.'

'And...your mother? What does she say?'

'I can't ask her,' she replied past the hurt in her chest.

'Why not? Surely she'd—'

'She's not well,' Summer said, cutting him off, the stubborn jut to her jaw putting an end to his line of questioning. His eyes softened, and she didn't want to see it. Things had been much easier when he'd been an ocean away and ignorant. She'd hardly thought of him at all.

Liar.

'Does she know about the baby?' he asked quietly as if, without being told, he knew that darkness stalked the fringes of their conversation. Loss. And possibly worse.

'No.'

He nodded once. 'Well, we can stay here until you're ready.'

'Ready for what?' she asked, not quite sure what he was talking about.

'To return to Greece.'

'Why would I return to Greece?'

She couldn't understand why he was looking at her as if she had lost her mind, or memory, or something.

'Because that is where we'll live.'

'What?' she demanded, heat creeping up her neck and twisting in her belly.

'When we're married.'

'What?' she said, louder this time.

Theron's hands were cold and he felt as if he'd swallowed stones. He clenched his jaw, stifling the desperation he felt lest it show in his tone when he next spoke. He was used to people simply doing what he said. Managing his business like an army. It was how he'd achieved what he had in such a short time. Supreme self-confidence and determination. But Summer was like a live wire, twisting and turning, and he never knew what she would do next.

'We will marry,' he announced and this time she laughed.

'No.'

'What do you mean, no?' he demanded, shocked by her response.

'What do you mean, we will marry?'

'Well—' he frowned, confused '—exactly that.'

'Yeah. Me too. So *no*.'

Theron frowned. Opened his mouth. Closed it again. He'd not foreseen this. He stood up, feeling that he needed the height advantage, and regretted it as she seemed intuitively to know he'd done so on purpose. He realised this the moment she took two steps back to meet him at eye level.

'I don't know you,' she growled softly.

'I hardly think that matters,' he replied, mentally batting away how much her statement had hurt.

'Really?' she demanded. 'What *does* matter then?'

'That you have my name and my protection,' he insisted.

'I'm happy with my name, Theron, and I don't need your protection.'

Her response was so damn reasonable, when he felt anything but. He wanted to shout, to yell, to roar against this strange sense of everything he'd never known he'd wanted slowly slipping through his fingers. He tried to get himself under control before he made things worse, but Summer seemed to be one step ahead of him at every turn.

'Look,' she said, striving for a calm that felt impossibly out of reach. 'Clearly we have to talk, but it's late. Why don't you go and come back tomorrow, or…?'

'Never? Would you prefer that?' he demanded, cursing himself and his own anger when he saw her eyes flare in defiance. She made him so…*emotional*. He took a breath. 'I'm not going anywhere,' he explained, keeping his tone as calm as possible.

'You can't stay here,' Summer replied with a shake of her head.

'It's not as if there aren't any free rooms,' he pointed out.

She held his gaze for a moment, an explosion of wicked sparks in her eyes. 'By all means, take your pick.'

She'd known, he realised half an hour later, as he lay down on a dusty mattress that was sure to give him allergies in a room that probably hadn't been heated for one hundred years. She'd done it on purpose, leaving the choice to him, knowing there was literally no good option. This was the sixth room he'd tried and he was too exhausted to care any more.

The wind howled down an empty fireplace and reduced the room's temperature by another degree or two. It was definitely the least he deserved and if there was more, Theron swore to himself and his unborn child, then he'd do whatever it took. Because they were now—whether Summer liked it or not—his family.

CHAPTER FIVE

THERE WAS SOMETHING in the walls. Theron didn't believe in ghosts, yet he would have sworn that he'd heard footsteps. But when he'd stuck his head into the corridor it had been empty. And then, after returning from the most unpleasantly cold shower he'd had in at least ten years, he'd thought there was someone actually in the room, even though it was obviously empty.

He threw his trousers on and rubbed his hair dry with a towel, thinking back over last night. The way he'd reacted, the way he'd demanded she marry him…

An explosion crashed through the estate and adrenaline instantly drenched his body as he ran towards the sound.

'Summer!' His heart pounding, he tried to figure out where the sound had come from, searching left and right. 'Summer!' he yelled again. He cursed in Greek and careened around a corner to find a slowly dissipating cloud of dust. In the middle of it was Summer, dressed in jeans, a jumper stretched over her belly, dust in her hair and on her face, coughing.

'What the hell is going on?' he demanded, striding forward, grasping her arm and pulling her from what looked suspiciously like a giant hole in the wall.

Summer sucked in huge lungfuls of air and shook her head, sending little bits of centuries-old plaster flying. She coughed once more, fanning her watery eyes and then looked up at him, her eyes seeming to clear.

'Are you okay?' she asked.

'Me?'

'Yes. You've gone quite pale,' she stated before marching off, patting down her clothing as she went.

'Stop!' he commanded, regretting it the instant she turned with a raised eyebrow. 'Don't give me that look,' he growled. 'You emerge from a *hole in the wall* as if it were nothing, and I don't have a right to know what's going on?'

'A right? No. You don't have a *right*. But if you would *like* to know, you could change your tone, lower your voice and ask nicely. *That* might work.'

He stared after her for a moment, floored. Althaia had been the one and only woman to put him in his place and he couldn't shake the feeling that she would have definitely been on Summer's side.

'Can we start again?' he called after her.

He could have sworn he heard a huff of laughter.

Summer rested her head against the tiled wall of the shower as water rushed over her head, neck and shoulders. She'd done her best to keep the surprise from her face as Theron had found her emerging from the hole in the wall. She'd been on her way back from searching the last of the secret tunnels in the east wing when

she'd caught her shoulder on a bit of protruding bat-
tening which had knocked her centre of gravity and
she'd fallen against the hole already there from Elias's
search and it had collapsed. She'd managed not to fall,
but the mess it had created was impressive.

She eased out the kink in that same shoulder as
she reviewed her progress. So, the jewels weren't hidden in the east wing's secret passageways. Summer
had now thoroughly searched all of them. The ones
around the main section of the building appeared to
be more functional, serving as shortcuts through the
building, which left just the secret passageways in the
west wing.

She had the map from Skye, could only hope that
Star was close to retrieving the key...but none of it
would matter if she couldn't locate where Catherine
had hidden the jewels.

But the look in Theron's eyes kept bursting in on
her thought processes. Unwanted but determined—
just like the man himself. He'd been worried about
her—because she hadn't missed that. She couldn't
have missed it. It had shone from his—admittedly
angry—eyes, but the worry was what had pinned her
heart.

He'd stayed last night, which was more than she'd
expected of him. He hadn't browbeaten her, ridiculed
her or threatened her last night. Not that she'd expected
that of him—or at least not what she knew of him from
their time in Greece before he'd kicked her out.

She sighed in defeat. She owed him an explanation
at least and, in all likelihood, a lot more. But before

she could change her mind, she turned off the shower, dressed and went to find him.

He was looking out of the large library window, his profile outlined by morning sun, the rest of him cast in shadow. His profile made her heart soar inexplicably. She hadn't realised how lonely she'd felt in the last few weeks in the estate on her own. But, if she were honest with herself, she'd felt it ever since returning from Greece. There was something about Theron that had made her feel…seen. Briefly, at least.

He turned and for just a moment she felt the burn of his gaze, the power he had to simply light up her body as if she were hackmanite, left to glow in the dark even in his absence. And then he blinked and she shivered.

'It's a long story,' she said, half hoping he'd tell her to skip to the end.

'I have time. And breakfast,' he said, pointing to the table, where fruit, toast and tea were all gathered. Her stomach growled at the sight and she realised she'd forgotten to eat that morning. He smiled wryly, snared an apple before taking a seat.

She sat in the opposite chair, swept her legs up under her and picked at the buttery toast. 'Just before I went to Greece, Mum had been diagnosed with stage three cancer. We were waiting to hear back on the treatment plans.'

'Summer, I… I'm so sorry.'

She nodded, gritting her teeth against the wave of nausea that always came when she thought of her mum's illness. It swept at her ankles and feet, threatening to topple her sense of up and down. But, strangely, Theron's words anchored her. Their sincerity surprised her and touched her. 'Thank you.'

'Is that why you were looking for Kyros?' he asked.

Her stomach churned, making the nausea acidic. She pressed a hand against her sternum to hold it back. 'I didn't…it wasn't like that.' She shook her head, fearful that he believed she was trying to replace one parent with another. 'Kyros wasn't a backup or—'

'Summer.' His tone was firm but gentle. 'That is not what I meant. At all. I know that's not what you were looking for.' The way he said it, the current that swirled beneath his tone, pushed back the ache just enough for her to feel thankful that he didn't think the worst of her. She breathed, but it was full of sadness as she remembered the fresh hurt laid over the rejection of both Theron and her father.

'When I came back from Greece, we found out that the treatment Mum needed couldn't be offered.'

'Why not?'

'Different areas in the UK have different access to certain treatments. We didn't live in the right area for the treatment she needs.' She shook her shoulders free of the tendrils of hurt and fear that still reached for her now. And if she concentrated she could hear the tick-tock of time running out. Every time she thought of her mother, the illness, it prompted a wave of helpless fear that made her need to find the jewels feel like claws scratching at her ankles.

'That's…' the look on Theron's face was incredulous '…barbaric.'

She nodded, agreeing with him completely. 'Just over two months ago, Skye got a call informing us that our grandfather had passed away. We never knew him,' she said quickly, forestalling his sympathy, 'and I don't think I would have wanted to. He clearly wasn't a pleasant man, having cut his daughter from his life and financial support. Still, he left me and my sisters the estate and everything in it—on one condition. That we find the Soames diamonds that have been missing for over one hundred and fifty years. No one searching for them had discovered their hiding place in all that time.'

'But you have?'

'Sort of.' She nodded. 'We uncovered a collection of journals, a photograph and a necklace hidden here in the library. In the journals was a coded message, explaining that our great-great-great-grandmother had hidden the jewels from her undeserving husband after her marriage.'

'In the walls…?'

Summer couldn't help but laugh. She supposed it did sound a little crazy. It was, after all, a one hundred and fifty-year-old treasure hunt. 'The estate suffered some fire damage in the mid to late eighteen-hundreds and was rebuilt by a French architect named Benoit Chalendar.'

Theron frowned. 'As in Chalendar Enterprises?'

'Mm-hmm. He put in a secret recess behind the shelves over there,' she said, pointing behind him. 'And also built secret passageways behind the walls here in the estate for Catherine Soames's amusement. They turned out to be a sanctuary for her. And somewhere within the passageways is a room, or a box, where the diamonds have been kept safely locked away.'

'So, you have the key?'

'I *think* so,' she said, desperately hoping that to be the case. 'Star is in Duratra now and says that she knows where the necklace is.'

'What does a necklace have to do—?'

Summer scrunched her nose, realising she was telling this all wrong. 'Sorry. The necklace we found here in the library interlocks with a necklace that the royal family of Duratra have been protecting. Together, they form the key to where the diamonds are.'

He frowned, as if mostly keeping up. 'So you have a map of the tunnels, the key is nearly here, but you don't know *where* in the passageways the diamonds are locked?'

Summer nodded.

'And you won't inherit the estate if you don't find the diamonds?'

She nodded again.

'But if you find the diamonds, inherit the estate, then you can sell it to Lykos, so that you can...pay for your mother's treatment,' he concluded, understanding finally dawning in his eyes.

'Exactly.'

'Summer, I can give you that money,' Theron insisted.

She bit her lip and shook her head. 'In exchange for?'

'What? No, there would be no strings,' he said. For

a moment he appeared offended that she had thought such a thing. But he'd said it as if he actually believed it.

'Oh, so maybe when we have a disagreement about me having a home birth—'

'A home birth?' he choked.

'Or the name of our child, or where I live with our child, or—'

'We *will* be getting married.'

'Or *whether* we marry… Theron, if I take your money for my mother's treatment it will always be there. We are going to be parents together. We are going to look after a baby, a child, a teenager and a young adult. We *have* to be equals in this. I could not spend the rest of our lives in your debt.'

It was probably the only thing she could say to cut through the fog of his indignation and incomprehension. Because Theron knew the weight of such a debt. He felt it every single day. Even now, thinking of Kyros, he felt the hot ache of guilt. Coming to England had been the first time Theron had ever lied to him. A new client. The words had stuck in his throat when he'd lied to the man who had given him so much that no repayment could ever be compensation enough. Theron should have never kept this—kept *her*—from him.

'I will stand for nothing less, Theron.'

'You shouldn't,' he agreed, swearing to himself that he would never do such a thing to her. The pride he felt seeing her determination, seeing the spark of golden fire in her hazel eyes, was bewitching. In that moment he knew that she would be fierce as a mother, protective, sure and powerful. It humbled him.

And then it scared him. What kind of father would he be if his first act had been to cast out the mother of his child and accuse her of…? His heart pounded in his chest and he clenched his fists, trying to refocus himself as a cold sweat broke out at his neck.

'How long have you been searching the tunnels?' He forced the words out, trying to distract himself.

'Skye sent pictures of the map about a month ago.'

He cursed, his mind moving from himself to her in a heartbeat. 'You've been searching these tunnels on your own for a month?'

'We're all doing our bit,' she said defensively. 'Skye is in France with Benoit—they're figuring out a few things through the engagement and Star is in Duratra trying to get the key back from Sheikh Khalif Al Azhar. And I'm supposed to find the jewels, except I can't.'

She sounded so lost he wanted to help. Needed to.

'How did you find the map and the key?' he asked, genuinely curious.

'There were coded messages in the journal entries we discovered, and the last message said, *You will find them when the map and the key are brought together.* Which is fine, but we don't have the time to wait. If the diamonds are here then I *should* be able to find them. Yet I've been through the passageways and the journals and I can't see where they might be hidden.

Catherine writes so much about faith and love and truth, and *trust*, but...'

'That is not quite your area of expertise? Because you like touching and knowing and understanding?'

She looked up at him as if surprised that he recognised that about her, but then his words incited a different understanding. Her cheeks heated, raising his own temperature, the pulse of desire catching and flashing the entire length of his body.

Mine.

But it was more than desire. It was more than recognising someone as sexually compatible. This time it was primal, animalistic. He'd never felt anything so powerful in his entire life. She was his and carrying his child. The cry of possession, loud, insistent and undeniable, tolled through his entire body.

The fierceness of it scared him. Because already to want that much, to need it...it was spinning out of his control and he was *never* out of control. He'd never been out of control. Before her. He drew in a lungful of air to stop the way the ground seemed to shimmer beneath his feet.

'Let's get out of here,' he said, rising as he spoke, surprising them both. His skin itched and he felt half suffocated by his thoughts and by this estate.

'That wasn't my fault,' Theron growled, wondering how quickly he could book a dental appointment back home. His molars were getting a pounding from the clench of his jaw.

Beside him in the car, Summer slowly exhaled.

'That was most *definitely* your fault. You're too far out in the road.'

'What road? It's little more than a dirt track,' he replied, outraged.

'Do you want me to drive?' she asked, not wholly sarcastically.

Theron actually *felt* the look of utter disbelief on his features and tried to ignore the way she bit her lip to stop herself from smiling.

Following the satnav directions on the postcode he'd plugged in, he tried not to become distracted by the slashes of verdant green stretching along the horizon in ways he'd never seen before. But from the corner of his eye he could see Summer's fingers twisting in her lap.

'I want to apologise.' The words fell from his lips urgently, before he could change his mind.

Summer flicked a confused glance at him. 'What for?'

It was a valid question. There were quite a number of options. He saw her bite her lip just before he returned his eyes to the road.

'The way I…behaved,' he said, the words twisting, hot, guilty and painful, in his gut. 'The way I treated you in Greece.' He shook his head. 'Sorry doesn't change it, but I am very and truly sorry.'

He felt the press of her gaze against his skin, checking the road before turning to look at her, hoping that she saw the truth of his words. But it cost him dearly, because he saw the depth of her hurt from that day. He turned back to the road only after she nodded.

'Where are we going?' Summer asked after a few minutes. 'Only I don't like being away from the estate too long.'

Theron paused for a beat. 'When was the last time you actually left the estate?'

She pressed her lips together and looked out of the window. Clearly she hadn't left. He frowned. From what she had said, they had arrived for the funeral nearly two months ago and her sisters had left nearly one month ago. All that time with nothing but searching for the diamonds to distract her from her worry about her mother.

Waiting for the inevitable, hoping for a miracle.

He knew that feeling well. It had been written on his soul during the days he'd spent with Kyros beside Althaia's bedside in the hospital room as the monitors beeped down to a flat line. Theron had hurt with Kyros, cried with him, paced with him and held both his and Althaia's hands. He'd realised in that hospital room that Kyros and Althaia had been in his life longer than his own parents had. The love he had borne witness to in those weeks, and over the years, had made it so hard for him to believe what Summer had told him in Greece.

How ironic then that as he looked at Summer now he suddenly saw Kyros in her. It wasn't the mole on her collarbone or the shape of her face. It was her eyes. The way that she faced the future with a sense of inevitability. As if braced for hurt.

He remembered that feeling. Waiting for the next blow, emotional or physical, it didn't matter. He'd had to cut himself off from feelings, he'd had to embrace a numbing to live through that and he didn't want Summer to experience that. He wouldn't let that happen.

He turned off the main road and cut down a track, wincing as the car's suspension took a pounding. Perhaps he should have rented a four-wheel drive.

He was focused so hard on the road and the car that he hadn't looked further until he heard Summer gasp. Having grown up in Piraeus, practically on the beach, Theron was faintly dismissive of her reaction to what was presumably a small strip of blue. Until he looked up.

'Oh.'

The car rolled to a stop and they stared out at the incredible stretch of sand and the ribbon of blue bisecting the horizon. It was as if he were looking at an optical illusion. Both far and near, impossibly wide yet completely attainable. It made him feel small, as if he were the tiniest speck of sand in the universe.

Summer got out of the car and he followed, watching her eyes grow round with awe and surprise. 'It's beautiful,' she exclaimed as she pulled her coat around her, walking towards the path to the sea.

The wind whipped across his face as he followed her, drawn to her like the tide was to the land. The pulse of the sea had been like an echo of his heartbeat; it was the most constant thing in his life. To hear the crash of waves on a quiet day brought him peace. The same kind of peace, he realised now, that he'd felt in Summer's company that night back in Greece.

As the pathway opened up to the beach, the stretch

of sand before them was endless. They drew to a stop and unaccountably his fingers found hers, their palms touching and easing the tension in his chest for the first time since the day before. The sun was warm on his face, taking a little of the sting out of the wind's bite, and he closed his eyes for just a moment.

Unbidden, the memory of his mother's laugh came to him on the wind. The press of her lips to his cheek, the warming of his heart, something soft that he couldn't quite place…and then it was gone. He breathed through the hurt, forcing himself forward towards the water. He felt Summer's gaze on his skin and he resisted the urge to reach up and capture it, to hold it there.

'You like the sea,' she observed.

He nodded. 'Lykos and I spent nearly every evening at the beach. We'd sneak out of the orphanage after lights out and just sit there. The sea, the stars… My father was a fisherman and being out there, I felt…' he sighed '…connected, I suppose.' He could feel her silent questions pressing against him and owed her that much at least. 'I was five when they died. The earthquake, it was a six point zero,' he said, shaking his head. 'Devastating. It killed over one hundred and forty people and injured thousands.' He no longer saw the sea, the English horizon.

The sound of the tide became a roar, a rumble, the shift of the sand beneath his feet became a tremor. His heartbeat pounded in his ears. In his mind he put his arm out to the doorframe to brace himself. He was screaming for his mother, for his father. They were on the other side of the house. He was all alone and tears were blurring his vision, the whole room was shaking. Where were his parents? Then he saw him—his father, he was coming to get him, his mother following just behind. They were coming for him and they would all be okay. He wouldn't be alone and...

Theron clenched his jaw against the hot press of tears against the backs of his eyes, refusing to let them fall. He focused on the sound of the waves, their gentle sweep across the sand somehow making it easier for him to speak the hurt of his past, as if it took his words and brought them back changed. 'A ceiling beam came down on top of my father and caught my mother. She died later in hospital.'

'Theron—'

He squeezed Summer's hand gently. He knew. He felt her sympathy. 'I was taken to an orphanage. Neither of my parents had family, so that was where I ended up. And where I met Lykos,' Theron said, shaking his head, unable to help the smile pulling at his lips. 'He was... I had lost my family, but I found a brother,' he said, realising just how hard the last ten years had been without him. Even though it still felt as if Lykos was in his head sometimes.

'But when I met him in Greece you seemed more like business acquaintances.'

'We had a falling out,' Theron stated.

'Did it have something to do with my father?' she asked.

Theron kept his features neutral, even though the mention of her father still twisted a knife. Theron should have called Kyros last night. He was torn between loyalty to the man who had been like a father to him and the woman who carried his child.

'Yes,' he said, finally answering her question about Lykos but reluctant to delve into it further.

'How did you meet Kyros?' Summer asked, as if sensing he wasn't going to say any more.

'He found us running scams on the streets. We were picking pockets, raising hell, the usual wayward stuff,' he said, a smile pulling at his lips. They were some of the best memories he had. 'Lykos had picked his pocket, but when he saw the photo in it he said we had to give it back.

'The photo was of him and his wife dancing.' It was only later, when Theron had met Althaia and realised how badly the multiple sclerosis had ravaged her body, that he'd realised the significance of the photo. Kyros eventually told him it was the last time they had danced. 'He wanted to reward us for returning it to him. Lykos,' he said, smiling broadly at the memory of the then fifteen-year-old's audacity, 'demanded one hundred euros. Kyros laughed, insisted that he wanted to give us something much more valuable than that.

'He paid for our education at one of the most exclusive schools in Athens and promised us that if we graduated then we would come and work with him.'

Theron looked out at the endless sea, marvelling at what an incredible gift they'd been given—the opportunity to be more than a statistic, a failure. They hadn't been stupid, even then he and Lykos had known. Life half on the streets, half in the orphanage, little education or hope even after that…it didn't paint a pretty picture. For all that life had been fun with Lykos, it also had nights full of terror, days full of worry—where was the next beating going to come from, where was the next meal…? Life hadn't existed past that.

'We stayed at the orphanage, but went to a good school. It was a little rough at the beginning—a few kids trying it on—but Lykos put a stop to that immediately. It helped that he was a couple of years older and a hell of a lot bigger. Kyros putting us in that school got us off the streets, gave us an education we would never have had. On Sundays we'd go round to Kyros's house for dinner. He'd ask us what we were learning, how our week had been, and he'd tell us about his business. We didn't realise, but even then he was preparing us to work for him.'

'And Althaia?'

Theron looked at Summer. Her hazel eyes had dimmed, the green clearer in them than ever. She'd lost some of the colour he liked seeing so much in her cheeks and for the first time he wondered how Summer would have felt about the woman her father had chosen to be with.

CHAPTER SIX

'SHE JOINED US on the days when she could. Which wasn't often,' Theron said, squinting in the bright sunshine piercing the blue-grey sky that seemed to blanket everything. 'The form of MS she had affects a small amount of people, but the symptoms were difficult and devastating. She was bed-bound for the last two years of her life and constantly battling infections and the slow deterioration of her body.'

Summer's heart hurt for them all and what they'd been through. 'What was she like?' she asked, half wanting to know, half not.

'She was...loving, kind.' He shrugged. 'As interested in us as Kyros was, but often distracted and in pain. Her diagnosis was progressive and it made things very hard for her. Hard for them both.'

Summer wondered if that was why Kyros had strayed—to have one moment outside of the impossible heartbreak he faced. She wondered whether her mother had known, and couldn't quite work out how she felt about it, hating the idea that one thing in her mother's past could change the way Summer saw her. She shook her head, her heart hurting.

'So you both went to work for Kyros when you finished school?' she asked, half changing the subject.

'Yes. For a while.'

Summer frowned, sensing his hesitancy but not the reason why.

Theron took a breath. 'Lykos was two years older than me, so he had gone to work for Kyros before I joined the company. But when I was eighteen, Lykos turned up and told me he was leaving.'

'Why?' she asked.

'I don't know.' Summer didn't know whether he'd realised his hand had tightened around hers, but she soothed her thumb over the back of his hand and his grip loosened. 'He never told me. We had an argument and…we have only spoken once since that day.'

His jaw was clenched so hard that Summer could see the flare of his muscle. She thought he was done, but he surprised her by carrying on.

'He wouldn't tell me why he was leaving, but he wanted me to go with him. I said that we couldn't. That we'd promised to work with him after school. Lykos accused me of choosing Kyros over him and… I couldn't deny it.'

He turned to her, his eyes filled with hurt and pain, warring with that decision all over again.

'I remember every word he said. "It's not real, you know. This little family you've created in your mind from Sunday dinners with Kyros and Althaia. You'll never be part of their real family. You'll be the dog that they feed scraps to for the rest of your life. Because you'll never find a way to repay that debt of yours, will you? *I'm* your family, not them. Come with me".'

'I'm sure he didn't mean it,' Summer said.

'He did,' Theron said, looking out at the sea, the stoicism in his expression heartbreaking for her to see. 'But all I knew was that I had somewhere I felt safe. Somewhere I felt I belonged.' He turned to Summer and she knew, even if he didn't say it. With Kyros he'd found a home. A family. 'I owe Kyros my life. I know what happened to some of the boys at the orphanage. I know what some of them did, what they had to do and where they ended up because of it.'

He lifted the veil holding back his feelings then and she could see it. See it all. The honesty, the fear that it could have been him, the dread of truly horrible things that she could barely conceive of. She might not have had Kyros in her life, but she'd had her mother, her sisters, a roof over her head and a sense of constant security. She understood the awfulness of his childhood, the shock of losing his parents, of being placed in an orphanage—and then being presented with what Kyros was offering. She could see so clearly how impossible it would have been for Theron to have left with Lykos.

'My debt to him will never be repaid.'

Something inside her curled in on itself, as if it recognised something final, something horribly conclusive. She pushed past it to try to see what he wanted her to see.

'Is that why you sent me away in Greece? Because you were trying to pay your debt?' she asked.

'I am in charge of his security. Summer, you're not the first person to claim to be the illegitimate child of a very rich man.'

'He looked right at me—'

'Summer—' he said, as if about to defend him.

'He looked at me and saw nothing.' The words hurt as they poured out of her, her throat thickening with pain.

Theron took a breath. 'He doesn't know about you,' he said simply, with horrifying ease. 'He's not looking for you in young women around him because he doesn't *know* to look. If you were to take a DNA test you could prove it to him. It's a mouth swab. It won't hurt the baby.'

'But it could hurt *me*!' she cried, remembering the pain she'd felt when he'd dismissed her with a glance. *Or you*, she thought, already beginning to see how precarious his position was with Kyros. If she proved herself to be Kyros's child, she couldn't see how that could be any kind of good for Theron. Not with how things stood.

That thought, that realisation, made her frown. 'Is that why you proposed?' Nausea swirled in her stomach.

'Is what why I proposed?'

'Because I'm his daughter. Because—' she shook her head '—I can't imagine how getting your mentor's illegitimate daughter pregnant with an illegitimate child would go down particularly well.'

'I proposed because family is everything. I learned that from him. I cannot allow you to have our child, unmarried.'

'My mother was unmarried when she had me, so don't you dare—'

He held his hands up in surrender.

She shook her head in disgust. 'Kyros might have taught you about family, but my mother taught me about love. And love isn't a debt you can repay.' Her heart ached, her soul felt heavy and her tongue thick with grief. 'Don't ask me again to marry you,' she ordered, before storming off down the beach.

He'd felt it. For just a moment, the softening between them. He'd hardly dared to ease into it, a softness that felt both strange but familiar. Like a half-forgotten song. Until she'd asked why he'd proposed.

Love isn't a debt you can repay.

Her words had echoed in the silence of the journey back to the estate and it felt as if they were eroding his foundations—the very things that he'd clung to for security for all these years. He searched his heart and had to admit the truth. There had been a part of him that sought to appease a future he could see on the horizon. A reckoning with Kyros that he'd perhaps always sensed coming in one form or another.

But it wasn't the only truth. And that was the thing that scared him the most.

After their return he had spent a couple of hours in the room he'd taken as his, answering work emails, concluding business with one client and reassuring another, before going to look for Summer.

As he rounded the corner to the kitchen, she was drawing various ingredients from the fridge that he registered with disgust.

'What is that?' he demanded.

'Dinner.'

'It is no such thing,' he replied, taking steps towards the monstrous selection of food she had gathered together. She turned on him, and had to lean back to peer up at him. He hadn't intended to get so close that he could smell the faint traces of salt and sea air still clinging to her clothes and skin. But he wouldn't retreat. Couldn't.

'There is nothing wrong with a cheese sandwich,' she said defiantly.

'"Dinner" is supposed to be *hot*. And it should most definitely have a vegetable in there somewhere.'

'Fine. Cheese and tomato then,' she snarked. Only he wished she hadn't, because the gold flecks in her eyes sparkled and danced when she did.

'Tomatoes are a fruit,' he dismissed. She had to step back as he went to the fridge to see what there was and sighed heavily. 'Is this an English thing?' he demanded.

'What?'

'A horrible relationship with food.'

'No. It's just that…well…' He turned to find her looking uncomfortably at the floor and he bit his tongue. He hadn't meant to shame her. 'Skye cooked.

For us,' she clarified, 'when we were growing up. She always cooked.'

'Mariam can't cook?' he asked, more gently this time.

'She can. Actually, she's a great cook,' Summer said, her shoulders tensing slightly at the mention of her mother. 'It's just that…she was a bit scatty when it came to mealtimes. She'd always be lost in a sunset, or her yoga or…like, right now, she's focused on her candle magic and…' She trailed off and Theron hoped to God the confusion he felt wasn't on his face this time.

'You've done it again.'

'Done what?' she asked.

'You've stopped mid-sentence.'

'Oh, well, I was expecting some kind of commentary on candle magic.'

Theron frowned. It might not be his thing, but who was he to judge? Althaia had insisted on reading his coffee grains whenever he had visited on a Sunday morning. 'Nope. I don't have any. But I'm curious how you and science fit with such a free spirit.'

'Not easily,' Summer said, and he wondered if she was aware of the tension in her voice. 'I sometimes felt too serious for her, but I always felt loved.'

He doubted that she realised how much she defended her mother to him. As if it was important to her that he thought well of Mariam. He gestured for her to take a seat as he finally figured out what he could do with the limited ingredients in the fridge, pulling the potatoes out before he went looking for a pan.

'You cook?' she asked.

'Yes,' he stated.

'I thought you'd be more of a restaurant kind of guy,' she said, shrugging.

He smirked. 'I do that too, but…' He sighed. 'Althaia taught me. On Sundays, when we'd visit, she'd teach me a new recipe and we'd eat it together. *Not like that*,' he echoed, his hand coming down in the air in a cutting movement. *'Like this,'* he said, smiling as he repeated the gesture at Althaia's 'correct' angle. But then he remembered the days she hadn't been able to help so much. She'd sat in the corner of the kitchen, rattling off directions like an army general.

'I'm sorry,' Summer said, and he frowned. 'She clearly meant a lot to you.'

He nodded and poured boiling water over the potatoes and then pulled flour down from the shelf.

'What are we having?' she asked, eyeing the potatoes and flour suspiciously.

'*Gnocchi.*'

'Really?' she asked incredulously. 'You're just *whipping up* some *gnocchi*?'

'Yes,' he replied, and a touch of pride flashed through him as the gold in her eyes sparkled.

He opened his mouth to ask the question that had snared in his mind earlier, but he hesitated, reluctant to broach it. And he wouldn't have if he hadn't thought that Summer needed it. Her mother was important to her and, whatever was holding her back, she would never forgive herself if anything happened while she held onto that hurt.

'Why are you angry with her?' he asked gently.

'Who?'

'Your mother.'

'I'm not.'

Theron just managed to stop himself from contradicting her, choosing instead to wait her out.

Summer pressed her lips together and stared at her hands until her shoulders sagged ever so slightly.

'She told me she didn't know who my father was.'

Summer watched as he filled the pan with water and put it on the lit stove. He was waiting for more, she recognised that in him now. Waiting for her to say what she needed. She liked that about him. It would make him a good father, she realised with a jolt that hurt her heart a little as she realised just how much she'd missed.

'Mum told me that they'd met, that the time they'd shared had been magical, but that they hadn't exchanged names, so she'd never been able to tell him about me. Over the years there might be slight variations, a few extra details, or some that changed. But it had always been an almost mystical holiday romance. As if it had been outside of time and incredibly special, but entirely contained within that bubble.

'But that was a lie. She could have reached out to him. Even if Kyros was married, even if it was difficult, even if he'd said he didn't want anything to do with me,' she said, the words rushing out on a shaky breath, 'I would have preferred that to...'

'To?' he nudged gently.

'To growing up searching every face, every person,

for the thing that I felt I was missing. Not knowing, it was a physical pain for me. An ache for something I couldn't even name.'

A sense of security—was that what a father gave? Summer wondered. A template for how men should behave, how they should treat her as a woman? Was *that* what she'd missed? A safe haven, somewhere to turn, no matter how hard or bad or difficult things got? She loved her mother fiercely and with her whole heart, but keeping her father from her had hurt her and shaped her in ways Mariam could never have realised.

And in that moment, in that half breath between that thought and her next, she realised something that would change her life irrevocably. She could never do that to her child. No matter what happened between her and Theron, no matter what, her child would know their father. They would be a part of each other's lives if she had to move heaven and earth to make it happen.

She looked up and blinked back a shimmer of tears as Theron's gaze searched hers as if he wondered where her thoughts had taken her. She shook thoughts of her child from her head, memories of her own childhood in her heart. Now wasn't the time for that conversation with Theron. There was so much more to speak of first. She bit her lip and looked out of the kitchen window at the night sky beyond.

'So yes, absolutely, growing up without a father hurt. But it was a hurt that I had made peace with. Until I found the photo.'

Theron put down the pan and walked to where she sat.

'Before then, it wasn't anyone's fault. It was a horrible *absence*. But finding the photo… She'd lied to me and I can't even tell her that I know. She betrayed me and I have so much… I'm so *angry*.'

He reached her on the first sob of breath and pulled her out of the chair on the second. 'Oh, God,' she half cried. 'What if we don't find the diamonds? What if Mum doesn't get the treatment and what if I am still angry with her when she…?'

She couldn't bring herself to even say the words.

Theron held out his hand. 'I'd like to show you something.'

Summer followed Theron as he led her down a hallway and through a door to the garden that had become devastatingly overgrown. In a strange way it reminded her of the roses around Sleeping Beauty's castle.

The evening air was surprisingly warm and the sky was a blanket of stars, shockingly bright and clear. The sight of it burned away some of her anger, but not enough. She could still feel it roiling, barely a millimetre beneath the surface. She hated it. She wasn't this person. She was practical, not emotional. Logical, not irrational. But ever since her mother's diagnosis, ever since the discovery of her father's identity, ever since *Theron*, she'd been behaving completely out of character.

She inhaled the scent of honeysuckle and frowned. She'd not seen the beautiful fragrant plant out here. In the dark, Theron seemed to be looking around.

'Neighbours are quite far away?'

'Yes. Why?' she asked, very confused now.

'Good. No one will hear you.'

'You get how that sounds, right?' she asked, unsure whether to laugh or back away.

He looked at her in all seriousness and then a smile broke out across his face, lighting his eyes and making him look his age for the first time since she'd met him. 'Yes. That's the point. You are going to scream.'

'Okay, enough with the psycho talk,' she said, turning back, before he caught her arm to stop her.

'No. I'm serious. All this anger. You're going to scream it out.'

Summer stared up at him, finally understanding what he wanted. 'I don't think—'

Theron sighed. 'That's the point. You *do* think. You think far too much. Screaming? It's visceral, it comes from here,' he said, pressing his hand to her diaphragm, just above the round of her stomach. There was a slight pause, a flare in his eyes, before he masked it. 'You need to let it out because it's damaging. So, scream.'

Summer was so tempted. She could imagine it. How it might feel to release all the emotions bottled up inside her. But she was embarrassed. She'd sound stupid, she'd probably get it wrong, and she'd look—

Every thought stopped as a thunderous bellow cut through the night sky. She turned to Theron, eyes wide and shocked.

'That's how you do it. Your turn.'

She frowned, still unsure.

'Hold on,' he said, placing his hands over his ears

as if he understood her concern, as silly as it might be. 'Go.'

She huffed out a laugh, but he didn't move, just waited for her to get on and do it. Finally, she took a deep breath, looked out across the mass of brambles and stars…and *screamed*.

She winced through the first awkward second or two, but then it rushed out of her, gaining power and volume just at the end.

'*Naí*. Good. Again,' Theron commanded.

Her heart pounding and the pressure in her head and chest beginning to flow, she screamed again, the sound, the anger, the tension, the constant fear she'd been holding in, all purged from her body in one long howl. She nearly choked when she heard Theron join her.

Her blood fizzed in her veins and there was a lightness in her chest that she hadn't felt since Greece. 'People are going to think we're crazy,' she said, laughing.

'That's okay.'

She looked up at him, outlined by the stars in the night sky, his eyes blazing more fiercely than the moon. And then she remembered. That night on the beach. She'd tried to force it from her mind because of the intensity of the feelings, the emotions it brought. Her fingers itched to reach up and brush the stray lock of hair that had fallen across his brow.

Because she wanted to see him. All of him. She wanted so damn much. But she was scared. And that was why she turned back to look out across the garden.

'Was it Lykos who taught you that?'

There was a beat of silence before he answered.

'No. It was Kyros.'

And suddenly it hurt. Hurt that her father had given him this...*thing*, had spent years with Theron, while she'd had nothing. It made her feel mean and angry all over again. But most of all it made her sad.

Once again, he stopped her before she could turn to leave. His hand was at her wrist, a gentle clasp that she could have easily broken, but didn't. Couldn't because of the way she felt alive beneath his touch.

'I remember a similar feeling,' he said, his voice quiet but breathing sincere emotion into the night air between them, 'to the one you described. That anger. At the world, at my parents for dying, at Lykos for leaving. It's as familiar to me as the blood in my veins. And if Kyros hadn't intervened, things might have been very different. But he did.

'Do you think it's possible,' he asked, looking down at her, as if trying to read the eyes she kept hidden from his gaze, 'that Kyros taught me, all those years ago, so that I might be here with you now, showing you?'

The idea behind his words, the intent, was all too much. She felt like a raw nerve, exposed and vulnerable, and she wanted to feel powerful. She wanted to feel confident—all the things she had embraced the night she'd spent with him in Greece. And, before she could stop herself, she reached for him, her hands threaded through his hair, clasped at his neck, pulling him down towards her, and when his lips finally met hers it was as if she could breathe again for the first time.

For just a moment he didn't move and she thought he would pull back, feared that he would leave her breathless and wanting. And then he groaned helplessly against her lips as he deepened the kiss, thrusting his tongue into her mouth at the same time as pulling her against his body and everything in her exploded. Open kisses, tangled tongues and pounding heartbeats were all Summer knew for blissful endless moments that rolled into each other.

She breathed in the scent of him, salt from the sea mixing with honeysuckle and cedar. His hand settled between her shoulder blades and the other swept up her side, perilously close to her breast, but not close enough. Her nipples tightened in anticipation, in need and then—

The harsh, bright ring of the doorbell cut through the night.

Theron reared back, dark slashes of crimson on his cheeks, matching—she was sure—those on her own, his hungry gaze consuming hers until the doorbell rang again and he stepped back. Summer hugged her arms around her body, pulling the edges of her shawl around her shoulders before turning away from the look of…what, regret? Frustration? She didn't want to know.

Hurrying down the corridors, she called that she was coming to whoever it could be at the door at this time of night. The doorbell rang again, spiking her adrenaline for some reason, the urgency of it scratching against her delicate nerves.

She pulled open the door, the heat she felt from Theron hovering in the dark corridor behind her giving her a sense of safety.

A small, bespectacled man stood blinking up at her, frowning as if she were not what he'd expected. Behind him was a long sleek town car with three dark-suited men who, at the sight of Theron looming behind her, came to stand tall, puffing out their chests as if to meet power with power.

She refocused on the man in front of her.

'Ms Summer Soames?'

'Yes.'

'Can I see some identification?'

'Why?'

He inhaled, as if frustrated by her response. 'What I have is—I've been told—of great importance to you and your family and I will not give it into the wrong hands,' he said, his voice imperious. 'It is from Ms Star Soames. I have brought it all the way, in person, from—'

'Duratra! It's the necklace!' Summer cried, making the bespectacled man wince, the suited men around the car start, and Theron draw one step closer. 'Don't go anywhere! Don't move! Theron, please make sure—'

'They don't leave. Got it,' he said as she disappeared into the bowels of the house to retrieve her wallet.

She ran, the whole time her pulse racing, but never as wildly as it had when Theron had kissed her.

It was the key. It was here. Finally.

So why did her thoughts keep veering back to the kiss? Why did she stop in the middle of the corridor to bite her lip where his lips had touched, to try and hold that sense of him to her, instead of rushing to retrieve her identification? Her breath juddered in her chest and she put her hand half out to steady herself. But then she steeled her spine.

It was the key. It was here and she needed it. Now.

She returned to the front of the house with her passport and showed it to the man, who bowed low and when he righted himself presented her with a package as solemnly as if it were a crown jewel.

The man eyed Theron suspiciously, then snapped his fingers and he and the suited men disappeared into the car, which turned in a slow arc before grinding down the gravel path away from the estate.

Last night...

Lykos howled with laughter. 'I still can't believe you took a convertible to Norfolk. Even *I'm* not that ridiculous.'

'The English can't drive. It was not my fault.'

'You keep telling yourself that,' Lykos said with a smirk on his lips. 'Drink up.'

Theron took the last mouthful of his whisky and pulled on his jacket as Lykos palmed an obscene number of notes off to a very happy-looking waitress. As he shrugged into the sleeves of his coat, he could have sworn he still smelt the salt of the North Sea.

'You remembered it wrong, by the way. *You* saw the photo and forced me to agree that we should give it back,' Lykos stated as they stepped out of Victoriana onto the wet pavement, throwing his collar up against the rain, ignoring the man with an umbrella and stalking towards the sleek town car waiting for them.

Theron stood on the steps, staring not at Lykos, holding the door open for him, or the black cabs and yellow lights of London, but the way Summer had run off into the house after receiving the package from Duratra, her focus so all-consuming.

'Look, get in the car, don't get in the car. Not my concern. Whatever you're going to do, do it,' Lykos said, sliding into the back of the car, leaving the door open.

He got in and closed the door, turning to Lykos, scanning his phone for something.

'There's nothing wrong with my memory,' Theron said.

'I ought to sue you for misrepresentation.'

Theron waved him off. After a while he couldn't help himself. 'What are you doing?'

'Looking for that *gnocchi* recipe,' Lykos answered, eyes still glued to the screen. 'Since you clearly turned into a domestic goddess—'

Theron reached for the nearest thing, which happened to be a rather creased newspaper, and threw it at him.

Lykos caught it without looking up, a smirk across his lips.

As they made their way through the city at night, the faint glow of Lykos's screen illuminating the back of the car, Theron spared a brief thought for what Lykos had been doing all these years. Because of his job, Theron had access to as much information on people as he'd ever want. But he'd never looked Lykos up.

'Okay, fine,' his old friend said, putting away his phone just as they pulled to a stop. 'Right, I've got it. Maps, secret passageways, hidden jewels, treasure hunt. Blah, blah, blah.'

'I'm beginning to think you're more interested in me and Summer.'

'No idea what you're talking about,' Lykos hotly denied. 'My only interest is in whether I can get my hands on that castle or not.'

'It's an *estate*,' Theron growled, getting out of the car and staring up at the building it had pulled up in front of. He frowned. He had expected to find Lykos staying in some sleek and impossibly expensive penthouse. And while this definitely ticked the impossibly expensive box, the Regency terrace in a tree-lined road in the heart of Knightsbridge was altogether something *other*. He looked from the house to Lykos and back to the house again as his old friend passed through the wrought iron gate, pressed his thumb against an electronic keypad and pushed open the front door.

'But it *was* the necklace from Duratra, right?' Lykos asked, not bothering to look back as he stalked into the living area, tossed his suit jacket on a chair and went straight to a drinks cabinet to pour himself a whisky. Belatedly, he turned, gesturing to Theron, who nodded and accepted the glass Lykos then gave him.

'Yes, it was the necklace.'

CHAPTER SEVEN

Three days ago...

THERON PACED THE tiled floor of the kitchen.

That kiss.

It had been just like the one on the beach in Piraeus. It had knocked him off his feet and made him lose his mind. Only it hadn't been enough. Not nearly enough. He knew *exactly* what would have happened if they hadn't been interrupted. His body did too and was still clamouring for it. Needy for it.

He shook his head in swift denial of his thoughts and his body. He needed to get a grip and put it to the back of his mind. Summer and her sisters had been searching for the jewels non-stop for nearly two whole months. Dancing to the tune of some now dead relative in order to save their mother. She now had within her grasp the ability to help save her mother's life.

What would he have done for such a chance?

Anything. The answer was swift and sure.

He could see in an instant how nothing would be conceivable for Summer until she found the diamonds.

No thinking about the future, no decision, nothing. Her mother's health and her and her sisters' ability to secure it would have, and clearly had, eclipsed all else.

But there would come a time when they would have to sit down and talk—about their future, their child's future and what that would look like. And before they could do that he needed to know what *he* thought, what *he* wanted it to be.

His mind flashed back, not to Sunday dinners with Kyros and Althaia, not laughing with Lykos on the beach, terrorising tourists and local vendors for money and food, but to sitting in his mother's lap in a room he could barely remember, hands clasped around her neck, cheek to chest, feeling nothing but safe, nothing but love.

That was home. That was what a parent gave a child—what *he* wanted to give *his* child.

But could he give that to Summer?

The sound of water bubbling over the edge of the pan drew him back to the *gnocchi*. Seeing that they were ready, he tossed the potato dumplings into the frying pan with the sauce and finished with salt and pepper, before dividing them between two plates. He found a tray from somewhere and put the plates, some water and cutlery onto the tray and took a deep breath before heading to the library.

As he'd expected, Theron found Summer hunched over the small table where she'd gathered all the journals, her hand resting on the necklace's velvet pouch while the index finger of her other hand traced the handwritten instalments in leather-bound journals that looked exactly what they were: decades old.

He turned on the overhead light, causing Summer to momentarily sit up, blink, and then go back to the journals. Her concentration was fierce and impressive—it must be, to study what she did, to think the way she did—but he worried about the toll it took on her. He placed the food on the table beside her and took his to the chair by the fire.

Over the next few hours Theron came and went and Summer barely moved. He took away the plates, washed up, added logs to the fire, looked at the rows of books on the shelves, but none of the titles caught his eye.

He frowned, looking over at one of the journals Summer had discarded and snagged it from the table without her noticing. Gently, delicately, he fingered the pages, frowning at the tightly curled cursive handwriting, passing dates that spanned months through the late eighteen-hundreds. Unable to resist, he turned to the final page.

I have heard it said that life is lived forwards, yet only to be understood backwards. I believe I know a little of that.

Theron recognised the Kierkegaard quote as one of his favourites, marvelling at how forward-thinking Catherine had been. And then he smiled, realising that he shouldn't be surprised. The Soames women were impressive, and his heart warmed with the hope that their child might be a girl to carry on those same indomitable traits.

Finally, he turned back to Summer, just to watch her. She had fallen asleep, her arm folded beneath her head and her hair falling free, the flames from the fire flickering over the golden rope-like twists. She made his heart expand. He couldn't understand it. Couldn't explain it. But she did.

He stood, rolled his shoulders. Everything was about to change. And he needed to change with it or risk losing everything. He walked over to the table, reluctant to wake her. Beyond the curve of her neck, he could see the map of the estate with the details of the secret passageways that ran just behind the hallways.

The map itself was a thing of beauty. Over one hundred and fifty years old, the detail was incredible. A filigree border surrounded the map and in the light of the fire it looked as if there were two pale gold lines leading down towards the map of the estate, but they stopped just before there was a sense of where they might lead. He peered over Summer's shoulder at the necklace. It was a strange design with two chains. He'd never seen anything like it. He remembered Summer telling him how the two necklaces would fit together to form a key, but it was still a beautiful piece of jewellery.

Then another set of faint gold lines caught his eye and he traced them with his fingertips and smiled. If he were to place the necklace chains along the four gold starter lines, then the pendant would come to rest in the north-west of the estate. He smiled to himself, feeling a deep satisfaction, which he tempered. Whether he had just found the location of the diamonds or not, Summer needed to rest. They would not disappear by the morning.

'Summer?' he whispered gently. He rubbed her shoulder, not wanting to disturb her too much. She shifted in her seat, the hold of sleep strong, and he gently pulled out the chair. Reaching down, he placed an arm beneath her legs and lifted her into his arms. Her eyes fluttered briefly but closed immediately and she leaned against his chest trustingly.

For a moment he stood in the library, Summer in his arms, and felt humbled. And then he turned into the corridors that would take him towards her room and, pushing open the door with his foot, walked to her bed and placed her gently onto the mattress. But as he went to stand, he noticed she had fisted his shirt in her hand. He tried to loosen her fingers, but instinctively he knew that she would wake. And then she'd probably yell at him for taking her away from her search for the diamonds. To avoid such a thing, he toed off his shoes and lay beside her on the bed.

As if sensing his capitulation, she crept closer and pressed into his side. The fine material of his shirt and the thick material of her cardigan were not enough to stop him from feeling the press of her chest against his side, the heat of her body and the scent of cinnamon and spice that he wanted to drown in. He took swift and harsh control of his body before it could spin out of control. He didn't care how much his body wanted or needed, *craved* hers, Summer needed sleep. And it was then that he felt it, stronger than anything he'd felt with Kyros. The bone-deep knowledge that he would protect Summer from anything and everything.

Summer opened her eyes, her fist clenched around an invisible tether she'd felt all through her dreams. It had been like an anchor to something safe, something secure, and she didn't think she'd ever felt peace like it. She opened her hand and smoothed the sheets next to her, frowning slightly at the indentation but deciding that she must have turned in her sleep.

She looked at the clock and started. Nine a.m.! It was *nine*! Suddenly yesterday came crashing through her memories like strobe lighting but all jumbled out of order. The kiss, the beach, the necklace, the library.

Her heart pounded in her chest, her mind torn between the kiss and the necklace.

Necklace first, she decided and threw off the covers, surprised to find herself still in yesterday's clothes.

Swinging her legs over the side of the bed, she shrugged out of the cardigan, pulled her T-shirt over her head. Shower now? Shower later? If she was going into the secret passageways she might as well shower later, she decided, standing up and tugging at the clasp of her bra at her back.

She yelped as Theron rounded the corner and she grabbed the blanket, covering herself as he stepped into the room, frowning at her as if she were behaving strangely.

'I brought you…' Theron trailed off as he stared at her beneath a very furrowed brow. She was behaving like a child, she knew it, but she was practically top-less. 'You know I have seen you naked before, right?' he asked, as if trying to keep a laugh from escaping.

'That was before.'

'Before?'

'Before...*everything*,' she said, unable to quite ex-press the magnitude of *beforeness* that had changed since they'd spent that life-changing night together.

'Right,' he said, as if it were normal for her to be so inarticulate. 'So, I brought you breakfast and—'

'Okay, you can leave it there. And go,' she said, inching her shoulders beneath the blanket and closing her eyes against the state of her room. It was a mess. She'd never had a man in her room before—even if it wasn't technically *her* room but simply the room she was staying in—and there Theron was, and she was so embarrassed.

Why wouldn't he just leave?

'Actually,' he tried again, 'I—'

'Theron, *please*?'

'Please what?' he asked, unable to hide a laugh of incredulity. 'I have brought you breakfast and I have something important to tell you and you act like I'm beneath consideration or...or...' He trailed off, strug-gling to find the word.

'I've never had a man in my room before, okay? And it's weird. The room's a mess, and I'm embar-rassed, and I don't even remember how I got here last night, and—'

'Summer? Breathe.' He locked his eyes onto hers, as if specifically *not* looking around her room, and she did as he asked. Breathed. 'Here is some break-fast. I want you to eat it before I show you something.'

'Can I get changed first?' She thought she saw the ghost of a smile curl the edges of his lips, but he nodded so she couldn't see it. She waited, but he stayed there. 'Turn around?' she asked.

'Really?'

'Yes!'

He laughed again, but did as she asked and turned around. She waited a second, as if he might still turn back and catch her in her underwear, but he didn't so she dropped the blanket and grabbed for her clothes. She was being silly because he'd certainly seen more of her the night they'd spent together in Greece. But she felt different now. Her body was different. She reached the wardrobe and grabbed a pair of trousers that she wouldn't mind getting dirty and a shirt so old it felt like silk on her skin. It was cream and pretty and she loved it.

Theron was whispering but she couldn't make out the words.

'What was that?' she asked, slipping her hands through the arms of the shirt.

'You don't want to know.'

'I do, or I wouldn't have asked,' she corrected.

'I said, "Please no more grey…please no more grey".'

Summer pulled up short. 'No more grey?' she repeated.

Theron turned and she sent him a glare, but not before she saw his eyes snag on the yellow dress hanging in the wardrobe, next to a vivid green one from the same shop. A look of deep longing passed over his features. It was so strong Summer blushed, as memories of the dress, how he had taken it from her body, what he had done to her crashed through the mental barriers she'd placed around that night.

'You shouldn't wear any more grey. Or black.' He shook his head, as if awkward. 'You should always dress in colour,' he said, nodding to the two dresses in the wardrobe. 'I'll be in the library.'

With that he turned on his heel and disappeared, all trace of his gentle laughter gone.

Biting her lip, Summer made her way into the library after eating the toast he'd brought her. Okay, one piece, but it counted, she told herself. She wasn't quite sure what to make of what he'd said about her clothes. If she was honest with herself, she knew they needed to have a proper conversation about exactly what kind of relationship they had and would have in the future. But all that could wait. The diamonds—her mother's health? That *couldn't*.

He was leaning over the table she had sat at last night, studying the map, and she had a sudden image, half memory, half wish, of him behind her, the heat of his skin against hers, as if they had been cheek to cheek. Unconsciously, she raised her hand to her face and he looked up, something passing across his gaze, making her drop her hand. His eyes went to the scarf, back to her face and down to the map without a word.

Awkwardness. She hadn't felt it before…before the kiss.

'So you've searched the east wing and you don't think it's in the central secret passageways?' he asked, still not looking at her.

'Yes. But, even so, there must be one final clue to the precise location because the secret passageways stretch for miles.'

'Well, I think you're right. And I think I know what it is.'

'What?' she demanded, rushing to the table, staring at the map and the necklace that seemed strangely placed over it.

'Can you see these faint gold lines?' he asked, nudging one of the four gold chains attached to the interlocked pendant. Summer nodded as she saw the finest of gold lines on the map. 'If you line up the chains with the lines then the pendant hangs, not in the centre of the map as you might expect, but here, amongst the west wing secret passageways.'

She leaned over to where he pointed, trying to focus through the scent of cedar from his aftershave, making her lick her lips. He pointed to where the pendant hung. The block handle of the key formed by the two intertwined necklaces created a large rectangular hole through which the chains threaded, allowing the entire key to sit flat against the map. However, the rectangular shape also had a circular cut-out, showing a small and very specific section of the map.

Summer moved the necklace out of the way to see where on the map it had pointed to, but there was nothing there. She tried again, but still she couldn't see anything but the secret passageways that had always been on the map.

She threw up her hands in frustration. 'There's nothing there!'

'With all the hidden journals, the secret maps and the far-flung corners of the world that your sisters have had to travel to, I hardly believe there would be a giant "X marks the spot".'

He was so calmly rational about the whole thing she wanted to scream.

'You've read Catherine's journals a million times. She must have said something in them about the final part of the treasure hunt.'

'It's not a treasure hunt.'

'It kind of is.'

She huffed herself into a chair, wondering why she was fighting this so hard.

'Summer?' Theron asked, coming to crouch in front of her. 'After all the searching and all the stress of the last two months, it's completely understandable to fear that it might all come to nothing.'

Summer angrily wiped at the tear that told them both he was right. She clenched her jaw against the threat of any more tears. 'I'm not this person, Theron. I am rational, deductive, sure.'

'And why is it not okay to be the opposite of those things?' he asked gently. 'Why can't you be all those things *and*...this?'

'Because I'm not the emotional one. That's Star. And Skye's the one in control. So...'

'So, then you are the best of both,' Theron announced as if it were as simple as that. She looked at him and wondered how he could see her as the best of anything. She'd been nothing but trouble since she'd entered his life and couldn't see how she'd be anything less for the rest of it. 'In the meantime, I can't believe that your great-great-great-grandmother would be so meticulous as to plan all this for it to completely fall apart at the end.'

'You can't?'

'No, I have faith.'

Summer huffed out a slightly teary laugh. 'Faith... *Faith!*' she yelled, springing up from the chair and grabbing the journal with the last entry in it.

'Where is it, where is it...yes! Here. Listen. *Faith that all will be well and, most importantly, faith that you will find not just what I have left for you, but what you truly need. For the thing about faith is that while it cannot be seen, it can be felt.* You're right. Faith in what cannot be seen!'

Summer placed the necklace back over the map as Theron had done and carefully made a pen mark in the space in the necklace's ball. She gently swept the necklace out of the way and laughed, rolling her eyes at herself. 'Of course,' she groaned. 'Look,' she said, beckoning Theron to the map.

'What? I don't... Wait, is that—?'

'Catherine's room. It's in the secret passageway just behind Catherine's room.'

She stared up at him, not realising how close they'd become and for the first time not caring. Her heart was soaring with excitement, her pulse racing, and she swept her arms around him and clung on for dear life. Hope, relief, shock and excitement all warred within her and Summer rode out the storm in his embrace.

Theron was sure he could be forgiven for expecting a sliding bookcase or a vase on a table that swung open, rather than the hole in the wall, with fine wooden slats and bits of plaster crumbling onto the floor.

He wanted Summer wearing a face mask. *He* wanted a face mask. There would be at least a century's worth of dust in these passageways, surely. He followed the shadowy outline of Summer created by the beam of her torch as she made her way along the narrow corridor constructed within the walls of the house. The design was ingenious and the construction infallible. He wondered at Catherine, who had made all this happen, and was beginning to think it wise not to underestimate the Soames women.

Summer was trailing her hand against the wall when she came to a stop, and Theron had to pull up quickly to prevent himself from crashing into her. She ran her hand back and forth along the wall on the opposite side of the corridor, frowning, until her eyes widened in shock.

'What is it?' he whispered, not quite sure *why* he was whispering.

'Here, feel this.' She grabbed his hand and he ignored the burn he felt from her touch. It was a heat that his body welcomed, and his heart struggled with.

Spreading his fingers beneath hers, she gently pressed them against the wall and he felt it.

The metal rectangle with a small impression where a key might go. Even he felt a childlike glee at the thought that they might have found the hidden treasure.

'You've found it!' he exclaimed.

She bit her lip, but failed to disguise the smile of pure joy spreading across her features. '*We* found it.' She produced the key and placed it into the lock. The metal slid into place as if it had been used only yesterday. He inhaled in expectation and then...

Nothing. Summer didn't turn the key.

'Summer?'

She leaned forward, pressing her forehead against the door. 'My sisters should be here for this.' She shook her head against the door. 'I can't... I need to wait for them.'

Theron understood. *Family.* He knew why that couldn't be him for Summer, not in this. Star and Skye had gone on this journey with her. It was as much their right as Summer's.

But it didn't stop the twist of hurt slice his heart.

He reached up to where her hand still held the key in the lock and pulled it gently back, taking the key from her loose fingers and hanging the necklace around her neck.

'It's time for you to call them home then,' he said.

CHAPTER EIGHT

SUMMER WANTED TO bottle what she was feeling. She didn't think she'd ever been so excited. Here in this half place where she knew where the diamonds were but hadn't yet seen them. She was on the brink of infinite possibilities and anything and everything she'd ever wanted could happen. Her mother healthy and well, her sisters back with her, she even felt for just a second that she might want to meet her father. That perhaps somehow, being with Theron, they could smooth over old hurts and together they could create something beautiful for the future. She could pinch herself.

There was something about the way that Theron had said she should call her sisters back *home*. Until that moment, the estate had been in the way. It had concealed the one thing they needed to truly help their mother. It had been broken, dusty, old, damp, full of her grandfather's ugliness and his father's, and his grandfather's—Anthony Soames. The man who had married his unwilling cousin for the estate and some jewels, abused her terribly and been miserable until the day he died. There was so much sadness and anger and neglect in this estate.

But there was also Catherine. And Benoit with his secret passages, and even Sheikh Hātem, who Catherine had met in Duratra, had become as much a part of the fabric of the estate as his family had been integral to finding the diamonds. So this time, as she walked through the corridors, instead of the gloom and darkness, she saw the beams of soft sunlight through hazy windows, she saw the potential that was there, just beneath the surface of dust and chaos.

She shook her head. Renovating and repairing the damage to this estate would cost millions and take years. But, even as she discarded the completely impossible idea, her imagination soared as she picked and discarded various styles or materials that could restore the series of problems in the east wing. Her mind jumped ahead to wonder whether Skye's fiancé might be interested and able to help. Then she laughed, wondering what incredible fantastical decoration Star would delve into, what inspiration she would return from the desert with... And in a heartbeat an impression of the estate, restored beyond its former glory to something that honoured both Catherine's history and the Soames sisters' futures, formed in her mind like a miraculous mirage and a longing so deep, so hard took root.

She paused, peering down one of the hallways, and could have sworn she heard the faint echo of children's laughter. She placed a hand over her bump and just for a moment let herself imagine what it might be like to raise her child here. With Theron.

And she could. She could see it so clearly, feel it so powerfully, it made her heart hurt. And it scared her because she'd never wanted anything more in her life.

She found Theron sitting at a table in the garden, leaning back in a chair, his face turned up towards the sun, his features relaxed, and he looked, for the first time, his twenty-eight years. He inclined his head just a little towards her and she realised that was his way of telling her he knew she was there.

She took the seat beside him. 'Do you miss it?' she couldn't help but ask. 'The sun. Greece,' she clarified.

'God, yes. I don't know how you do it. It's…*unhealthy*.'

The laugh tumbled out of her. She was not in the least offended by his over-exaggerated negativity towards England, or Norfolk. It was playful, the teasing. Not mean or cruel. And the idea of him not being able to withstand a bit of English weather was exactly that: laughable. Because there was something incredibly strong, immovable about him. She had—back in Greece—compared him to dolerite and now she realised how fitting that was.

Its powerfully strong properties were what made it so suitable in protective barriers and construction. That was what she felt about Theron. That, no matter what, he would protect her. Perhaps whether she wanted that protection or not.

'So how does it feel?' he asked, cutting through her

thoughts. 'To have found a treasure that's been hidden for over one hundred and fifty years?'

Summer smiled, her heart soaring once again. 'Incredible. But knowing that we'll be able to sell the estate and pay for our mother's treatment is...' She shook her head, trying to find the words that could express the relief, the joy, the hope... 'I know it's not a guarantee that the treatment will work, or that she'll be okay, but it feels as if we've won half the battle at least,' she said truthfully. Although she couldn't quite explain why the thought of selling the estate dimmed her joy a little.

'Catherine Soames must have been a very impressive woman,' Theron mused. 'I can't imagine the thought, determination, the...'

'Faith?' Summer asked as she smiled at him.

'Faith,' he acknowledged with a nod, 'to plan something like this. It must have taken years.'

'I don't know what I'm going to be doing in five years, let alone...' Summer's careless words trailed off and her smile fell as she realised that she would have a four-year-old child. That *they* would have a four-year-old child. She swallowed. She knew they needed to talk about this, but until now she'd been so focused on the diamonds, her mother, even Kyros... Had she thrown them all up as excuses to stop this very conversation? 'I didn't plan for this,' she said, trying to explain.

'I know,' Theron said, looking intently at his hands.

'No, I mean... I had *plans*. Always. Skye was the one who looked after us, Star was the dreamer, the romantic, and I was the one who was going to get *the job*. The one who would make sure we were all going to be okay. Financially.' Summer squinted and it had nothing to do with the gentle sun's rays and everything to do with trying to pierce the shrouds of time to a point when she'd *not* had plans. 'My *plan* was to go to university. Take my fourth year abroad. Finish my degree and find a job in the environmental engineering sector. Get settled. Save money. Look after Mum and the girls.' Summer took a breath, wondering how many years she'd clung to that plan. Nearly ten, maybe? 'And then everything started to fall apart when I found out about Kyros. I deviated from my plan and went to Greece and…' she broke off, laughing bitterly '…and he wasn't there. And then, when he was…' Her heart hurt so much at the memory of his dismissal. She'd never felt such rejection. Until Theron had said what he'd then said. She tried to close the door on that hurt.

She now understood why he'd behaved the way he had. Theron had thought she was a threat to Kyros— the man who had been more of a father to him than he'd had the chance to be to her. And she also had to face the fact that she could have stayed. She *could* have. Theron hadn't the power to kick her out of Greece. Her plan had gone wrong and she'd left because it had been easier than staying and confronting her father.

'The point is,' she pressed on, 'I was making plans. And now I'm not. Because they don't work and I'm not sure what to do any more.' She slowly exhaled the breath that had built in her chest and wondered if any-thing she'd said had made sense.

Theron held her gaze when she looked at him. It was open, accepting and understanding. And suddenly she didn't want it. She didn't want his understanding. She wanted him to tell her what to do.

'Plans are not *wants*. Plans are what we do to get what we want. So, until you know what you want, you can't make a plan. What do you want?' he asked.

'I want you to tell me what you want,' she hedged.

Theron smiled ruefully and narrowed his eyes as if considering what to say. 'I want you and our child to be safe and happy.' But he said it in a way that sounded sad. As if he was separate from it. And in that moment Summer didn't have the courage to challenge him on it.

So, what did she want?

The answer was there, beating in her heart. She wanted the strong, patient, protective man who had not laughed at her mother's esoteric leanings, who had not dismissed her job or her interest, who was stubborn and sometimes sulked like a teenager, but who felt so deeply he didn't always have the words to describe it.

But something was holding him back. And until he was able to face that, Summer felt a little too vul-nerable to voice the truth in her heart. So instead she thought of what she wanted for their child and the an-swer flew from her lips.

'I want you to be there. I want you to be all the things that my father wasn't or couldn't be. I don't want our child to hurt the way that I hurt, to feel the inability or yearning that I felt. I want them to know who their parents are and be absolutely sure that they are safe. That they are loved. So,' she said, taking a breath, 'I need you to promise that you'll be there.'

When she looked back up at Theron she noticed that his hands were fisted and his knuckles were white, his mouth was a fine tight line, and her heart broke a little. She felt foolish for speaking so freely, but knew that her words had been right and true and she would stand by them for her child.

He nodded once. But to let her know that he'd heard her or in agreement, she couldn't tell. And then he was gone. Just like that. As if he'd never really been sitting there.

Theron paced the length of his room, passing the empty fireplace and unseeing of the dust and damp that had horrified him on his first night here. He felt as if creatures were crawling up his body, scratching against his skin, and he couldn't stop it.

I want you to be there.

She'd had no idea what she'd said, how her words had poked and prodded at the open wound in his heart. He clenched his jaw at the sudden rush of memories, all piling in on each other. Lykos walking away from him, the loss of Althaia, Kyros leaving him behind as he left for the island without him. As if he'd never been a part of the Agyros family. His hand fisted and he wanted to lash out. To punch something. To have a physical pain that would be easier to bear than the chaotically sprawling emotions he couldn't seem to control.

I want you to be all the things that my father wasn't or couldn't be.

He looked at his phone, staring at the five missed calls from Kyros. Theron dropped down onto the mattress and put his head into his hands. Summer still held so much hurt from not knowing Kyros. And what of Kyros? He couldn't imagine what pain it would cause him to have been kept away from his child for so long. He couldn't put it off any more. He had to call Kyros, no matter what it cost him.

Even as he picked up his mobile, Theron couldn't shake the feeling that everything was about to go horribly wrong, just when he needed it to be right.

An hour later Theron stalked through the halls of the estate, knowing that he had to find Summer but feeling utterly out of control. He wanted a tether. He needed her. She had anchored him since the first time he'd seen her. Pulled at his unconscious like a magnet. From the first time he'd got up to leave and sat back down, he'd felt as if he was constantly returning to her, would always return to her, somehow.

She wasn't in the kitchen, or the library. The garden looked empty and he hoped that she wasn't in the secret passageways again. He was about to go back to the upper floors when he thought he heard something being dragged across the floor. It was faint, but there. He followed the strange sound. Whatever it was seemed heavy, which worried Theron. Summer had a habit of biting off more than she could chew.

He turned down a corridor he'd not visited before,

running parallel to the back of the house, seemingly all the way to the other side. The sound finally began to grow louder and the end of the corridor began to throb with light, firing his curiosity. Treading softly, he made his way towards the light, peering around the corner, hoping to remain hidden, but what he saw made his jaw drop.

A floor of aged white and blue tiles stretched down the centre of a large glass-roofed structure attached to the main house. At the far end two thin-paned glass doors were thrown open to the setting sun and in between were huge, deep forest-green plants of all shapes and sizes. Thick, broad leaves bent open like palms, thin, spindly, pale green tendrils coiled and curled, and some kind of climber hung beneath the peeling white ironwork of the ceiling, through which the sun shone beams of dappled light back onto the ornate floor.

'What is this place?' he wondered out loud as he passed into the glass chamber.

'It's the orangery. As the only place utterly ignored by our grandfather, it has—unsurprisingly—thrived,' Summer replied from behind him.

He turned to find Summer hauling an impossibly large sack of compost across the floor. 'What on earth are you doing?'

She peered up at him, huffing a long blonde tendril from her eyes. 'Making a roast dinner. What does it look like I'm doing?'

She was angry. She had every right to be, he knew that, but he felt it too. Anger, frustration. The sense that everything he wanted was right there within his grasp...but not quite.

'You shouldn't be trying to move that,' he declared over his chain of thoughts.

'I *moved* it. I wasn't *trying*.'

Theron suppressed a growl. 'You don't have to do it all yourself, you know.'

'You don't get to do that,' she said, dropping her hold on the enormous plastic bag of compost and rounding on him. 'You don't get to come here, out of nowhere, and suddenly be everything.'

'Be everything?' he asked, the anger in Summer's tone igniting his own.

'I meant be every*where*,' she lied badly. She stepped towards him. 'You might find this hard to believe, but I was fine without you.'

'Yeah?' Theron demanded, taking a step towards her, closing the distance between them like pieces on a chessboard. 'Well, so was I,' he gritted through his teeth, the lie like iron on his tongue, with the realisation that he'd not been even remotely fine until meeting her, even as his mind scrabbled to take the thought back. And that vulnerability, that weakness only angered him more.

His eyes caught hers, the golden sparks firing against the green evidence of her own internal war. And then, as if static electricity arced between them, linking them, drawing them together, he couldn't fight it any more.

They moved together at the same time, lips crashing, hands reaching and curling, hearts beating, breath hitching, caught and held. All of it, he wanted to hold all of it—Summer, their child, the past and the future, in one single breath. To consume it and keep it safe for ever.

She moved against him, her hands reaching around his neck, holding him to her as if worried he would stop. She was like fire, twisting and turning in his arms, and he Prometheus, as if he'd stolen her from the gods themselves and he couldn't help but fear what his punishment would be.

But when she opened her mouth to his, when her tongue thrust against his, all thoughts were lost to sensation. Her fingers moved from curling in his hair to his chest, one hand pulling and the other pressing as if she couldn't tell what she wanted more.

Theron had no such confusion. He wanted everything. The thought roared through his veins, beating like a drum in his chest. He placed his hand at her back, fitting it between her shoulder blades, loving how he could stretch his palm between them, pressing her against him, feeling her chest and thighs against his.

His other hand slipped beneath her shirt and the moment his skin touched hers his heart missed a beat. He thought he felt her gasp against his mouth as his fingers swept around her waist to her stomach, and when his palm pressed against the gentle slope of her abdomen he paused. Gently, she pulled back and gazed up at him—a moment of calm in the madness. A moment just for them that healed a hurt he wasn't sure he'd known was there. But, as they gazed at each other, peace turned to hunger, turned to need, and desire became impossible to resist.

Summer inhaled once swiftly, her eyes inflamed, and she drew him back into her kiss.

She tugged at his jumper, dragging it from him as he tore at the buttons of her shirt. Her hands went to the button on his trousers and his went to her thighs and he lifted her up into his arms. He swallowed the squeak of surprise with his kiss and drew her up his chest, the friction sending enough sparks to consume them both. She shifted endlessly in his arms, and he could have held her there for eternity, but he wanted to touch, to taste, to tease. He backed towards the chaise longue he'd seen—the ancient piece of furniture fitting the faded dignity of the room and completely at odds with what he wanted to do to Summer. He wanted her indecent, he wanted her incandescent, he needed her as mindless with pleasure as he was every time he touched her.

He wanted to hear her scream his name and know that no other man would be able to do that for her. He wanted... The backs of his legs met the cushion of the lounger and he sat, bringing her with him, the air knocked out of their lungs at the impact.

He groaned out loud, not from the fall but from the exquisite pleasure of having her in his arms again. He felt completely lost to her, his heartbeat racing, an urgency in him that he couldn't quite account for. As if time was running out for them and he greedily wanted everything he could take, every memory he could make. It was as if Summer could feel it too. He could sense it in the way she searched his gaze, the way she held onto him so tightly, the desperation that seemed to make their hearts beat together.

Summer had never felt anything like this. As if all the want and need she'd tried to deny had boiled up and escaped and was now coursing through her veins. She was drunk on lust and she felt out of control, as if she honestly didn't know what she would do next. She wasn't this person, she was considered, rational, calm, but right now she was mindless, incoherent and wild. Here in this beautiful orangery, with deep green plants curling up to the ceiling, she felt elemental.

The thought struck her and stuck.

Elemental.

It was as if the word unlocked something within her that freed her from any further doubt, debate, any last vestige that would stop her from doing and taking what she wanted. It was just like it had been that first time in Greece. There was some strange alchemy between her and Theron that seemed to alter her DNA. And that change, that new element that rose within her filled her so completely it took over with the power of a crashing wave.

She pulled back from his hold and slipped her arms from the now damaged shirt, from where he had pulled it apart and sent the buttons flying. Her eyes were on his as his gaze scoured every inch of her skin, flicking back to her every other second as if making sure she was still there. That it wasn't all a dream. She knew how he felt.

She reached for the clasp of her bra and released it, her heart soaring at Theron's swift inhalation and the slash of crimson on his cheeks at the sight of her. She felt glorious. She felt beautiful and womanly and empowered all at the same time. Backing up off the chaise longue, she undid the buttons of her jeans and pushed them from her hips, kicking them out to the side with her bare feet.

He bit his lip and clenched his fists as if he was trying to restrain himself from reaching for her and she loved that she wasn't alone in the madness. Her thumbs hooked in the waistband of her high leg briefs and the gold in his eyes flared. In a second he was half off the sofa, his hands pressing against hers stopping her as she was about to draw them down her thighs.

He looked up at her from a half crouch and her breath caught in her lungs. She felt worshipped. He batted her hands gently aside and slowly, inch by inch, drew the cotton down her thighs. The intimacy of it was overwhelming. As her legs began to tremble he placed a supporting hand against her hip, his fingers sweeping around, and once again she felt cared for and desired at the same time—a combination she'd never experienced before.

She stepped out of her briefs and Theron tucked them into his pocket as if they were something too precious to kick to one side. There she was, naked and vulnerable, while he was dressed only in his dark trousers, the button at the waist she'd undone what felt like hours before.

He gazed up at her as if he were more than happy

to stay there at her feet for as long as she could ever wish it, but that stirring of need, that impatient desire unwound thick and fast in her chest and she reached to pull him up.

When he reached his full height she had to crane her neck to look up at him to take him in, to understand what arcane language their bodies were using to communicate. She wanted to spend the rest of her life learning it, using it and exploring it. She barely had time to register that thought when he swept her up in his arms and took her back to the chaise longue, laying her gently down on it.

He looked at her as if he couldn't get enough. His gaze covered every inch of her and she smiled at the errant thought that he might even turn her over and inspect her back too. The thought brought a blush to her cheeks, one that his keen gaze didn't miss. He opened his mouth as if he was about to ask her, but then shook his head as if he forgot what he'd intended, lost in the sight of her, his eyes glazed with the same desire and lust that she felt coursing through her body. Rather than the frantic desperation of moments before, the thick heavy thump of need pulsing in her veins became slow and languorous, as if they had both been hypnotised by the same thing.

He leaned back on his heels and reached for her foot, picking it up gently and bending to place kisses along the arch. Unconsciously, she pulled her leg back slightly, the sensation driving a laugh from her lungs and drawing him towards her and exposing her in a way that caught her breath. His hands swept up her thigh, his kisses following, open-mouthed and deliciously decadent as her heart thundered in her chest and he gently pressed her thigh to the side.

Her back arched off the mattress the moment his tongue pressed against her, and her hand fisted over her mouth to prevent herself from crying out. She had barely caught her breath when another long sweep of his tongue drove the oxygen from her lungs and her back into the air once again. She cursed, unable to stop herself, and she swore she could tell that he was smiling.

He pressed gently against her pelvis, angling himself and her into a position that allowed him to—

Her mind completely blanked. She couldn't have said what he did, she didn't know, other than it was amazing and incomprehensible and in the space of a heartbeat she was completely overcome by an orgasm that she felt broken by.

She came back round to the feel of gentle kisses around her abdomen, something about them bringing a sweet tear to her eye that she dashed away before Theron could see.

Eventually, as if reluctantly, the kisses began to move up her body, along her ribcage, Theron's head gently nudging at her side, causing her to shift onto her side so that he could slip behind her and place more kisses on her shoulder blades as his hands wound around her protectively.

The hot humidity of the orangery was the absolutely perfect temperature to be there naked in his arms. Her heart felt light, happy but scared, as if this moment was precious only because it might not last.

She felt his forehead lean against her shoulder.

'I don't have a condom,' he said, his tone regretful but not more than that.

She sighed, unable to help the smile curving her lips. 'I think it's a bit late for that, Theron.'

There was a pause before he replied. 'There is no risk from me. I have not been with anyone since you.'

She swallowed, realising the thought of risk hadn't crossed her mind. Even in this, she marvelled, he was protecting her. 'Me too. I...' Her words trailed off as his fingers entwined with hers, reassuring, loving even. She turned back to look at him, his gaze burning bright and intense. And, just like that, want and desire ignited in a firestorm and she reached for him, knowing he was the only thing that would quench her need.

They made love until the stars disappeared from the night sky and the sun peered at them from over the horizon. A gentle yellow glow filled the glass-walled room, warming the jasmine until its perfumed scent filled the air. Summer pulled the large throw Theron had found at some point during the night over her shoulders and burrowed deeper into his embrace. She thought he was asleep, but a new tension filled his form, an energy that ignited her own and for a moment she indulged in it. A moment where heady desire, expectation and promise were just there in the next heartbeat, if she could only—

In the distance she could hear the ring of Theron's

mobile and they stilled, holding their breath, as if instinctively they both knew.

Knew that something was about to happen that would change everything.

CHAPTER NINE

THERON WAS WAITING in her room for her when she came out of the shower. Her steps faltered when she saw his broad shoulders outlined by the early morning sun. He appeared to be looking out of the window, but she was half convinced it was to protect her modesty.

'You should wear the green dress,' he stated without looking at her.

And in an instant the fury that she'd banked with cool water from the shower reignited. 'Calling Kyros was bad enough. You don't get to tell me what to wear too,' she threw at him.

Theron's shadowy outline bowed his head. 'He needed to know.'

'Will you always put his needs before mine? Before yours?'

Frustration bloomed over anger like a watercolour painting. They had just been getting somewhere. There were things they still needed to say. But now Kyros was twenty minutes away her thoughts had completely scattered.

'You sound like Lykos.' Theron's tone was dark, but not bitter or resentful.

Summer felt seasick. She just wasn't sure what she should be feeling, where her allegiance should be. With Mariam? Her father? Or the father of her child? The man she knew she was falling in love with. Nerves tickled her soul.

What if Kyros didn't like her? What if he became angry with her mother? What if she didn't like him? Theron clearly respected him, loved him even—he'd cared for his wife throughout her illness and part adopted two teenage tearaways. So he couldn't be *bad*.

But she couldn't shake the feeling that meeting her father would cost Theron something. Cost *them* something. No matter what happened, it would definitely alter his relationship with the man who had been like a father to him for longer than his own parents were alive. And Theron had still made the call to Kyros.

For her, she realised. It was a sacrifice he'd made. For her.

'Theron—'

The sound of a car on the gravel drive turned both their heads towards the window.

'He's here,' Theron announced needlessly, and he looked back at her before leaving. 'The green dress. You will look beautiful in it.'

Theron made it to the doorway as the sleek racing-green Jeep pulled to a stop in front of the stone steps. He felt numb. As if he'd gone into shock ahead of some great trauma, as if protecting himself from what would come.

Kyros stepped out of the vehicle and straightened his tie. Despite the fact that his hair and beard were shocking white, they were thick and vital. No one ever mistook Kyros for a weak old man. At full height they stood shoulder to shoulder and, despite the immense power he wielded, Kyros had always been quick to laugh and his heart was huge.

But it was a heart that, once wounded, rarely recovered and when Kyros looked Theron straight in the eye, Theron knew. Any hope he might have entertained that they could survive this, that their relationship would survive, was gone.

Kyros looked at the house and for a fleeting moment he seemed scared, before he returned his steely gaze to Theron.

Theron opened his mouth to speak but was cut off.

'We will speak later. My daughter?' Kyros demanded, wanting to know she was here.

Theron nodded, but before he took Kyros inside he needed to know. Theron forced the words out through clenched teeth. 'She is pregnant.'

Kyros's steely gaze turned glacial. 'Yours?'

'Naí.'

With nothing left to say, Theron led Kyros into the house. Summer had said that she'd be in the library and each step towards her felt inexplicably as if it were taking him away from her. He had to put a hand out to steady himself, vertigo hitting him as if he'd entered an Escher painting.

* * *

Summer had hastily slipped into the green dress and pinned her hair up, let it down and put it back up again in the time since Theron had left her room. She was in the library now, finally deciding on hair up because she was so hot and flustered she needed it off her neck. To stop herself from pacing she'd sat in the chair, but the moment she heard footsteps in the corridor she lurched up, her hands clasped before her.

Suddenly she wanted to cry. But she fisted her hands, ordering herself to be strong. She was aware that two men stood in the doorway, yet she only had eyes for one. Kyros—her father—looked so familiar she had to sit down. Kyros covered the room in strides as if worried that she was unwell, his arm at her side, ready to support her, which she gratefully took.

'I'm sorry,' she said, embarrassed by her reaction.

'There is *nothing* that you could be sorry for.' His reply was strong and sincere, his eyes wide as if he just couldn't look at her long enough. She knew the feeling because it was exactly how she felt. He pulled up a seat so he could hold her hand. '*I* am the one who is sorry and I cannot even begin to ask for your forgiveness. I only hope that you believe I truly did not know of your existence.'

Summer smiled through a watery gaze that hungrily consumed every single inch of the man who had fathered her, yet not been her father. 'I know. Mum always said that you didn't know.' She pressed her lips together at the mention of her mother. She didn't miss the way that Kyros's blue gaze sparked, but not with anger, something more like surprise before it was quickly mastered.

'We have so much to talk about,' Kyros insisted, pulling his chair closer to hers.

'We have time,' Summer said, a slight pinprick of hurt cutting deep at her heart, wondering whether the same could be said for her mother. She couldn't stop staring at him. Her eyes raked over him, wondering that he was really there. Wondering at this strange sense of connection she felt branded into her heart in an instant.

'Your mother, Mariam. How is she?' Kyros asked in a way that made Summer think he already knew. Summer turned to the doorway, wanting to see if Theron had said anything, but he wasn't there.

She frowned, but returned her attention to Kyros and took a deep breath. 'She is not well.' Her father seemed to clench his jaw, as if bracing himself. 'But we are soon going to be able to get her the treatment she needs.'

'We?'

'Yes,' Summer said, her smile wide and full of love. 'Me and my sisters.'

Kyros nodded. 'You have sisters. That is good. You have…' he seemed to search for the words '…you have had a good life?' he asked tentatively.

'Yes. So very good,' she said sincerely and reassuringly. 'I never blamed you. Mum made it very clear that you would have moved heaven and earth if you'd known about me. But…' Summer hesitated, not wanting to paint her mother in a bad light '…she…she told me that she didn't know your full name and how to find you.'

Confusion passed into realisation in her father's gaze and a nod that reminded her of Theron seemed to conclude his thoughts.

'I would like to tell you how we met,' he began. 'I don't want to…contradict or say anything your mother wouldn't want you to know, but… I want to be honest,' he said, shrugging into the words as if feeling his own way through this strange situation.

Summer nodded and as they huddled together he explained how he had met Mariam Soames.

'I was on one of the islands. I had gone there by myself in order to figure some things out. My wife, Althaia—I loved her greatly. We had been together since we were sixteen and twice that many years later our love was still strong. It was a soft, gentle kind of love, but one that was unbreakable.' His eyes misted for a moment and Summer put her hand on his. 'We had just found out her diagnosis and our world had been shattered. Althaia had asked me to leave to give us both some time to process how we felt.

'I was…devastated. Selfish. Hurt. Angry,' Kyros admitted, shaking his head at himself. 'Your mother, Mariam. She…burst into my life at that moment and, somehow, took it all away. Before I even knew her name, I—' He clenched his jaw, seemingly to stop himself from saying more. 'I told your mother. Everything. About Althaia and her diagnosis, our marriage. She told me about the loss of the partner that she was still grieving, about her daughters and the love she felt for them. She was so…bright and fierce. She was like a whirlwind and I couldn't help but be drawn in. Somehow, together, we found more than solace in each other, and I need you to know that what we shared…it was incredibly special to me.' Summer looked at him as his gaze clouded with memories and unspoken moments, before it cleared enough for him to carry on. 'We agreed, nothing more than that one week together, but it's important that you know it changed my life.

'The moment I returned home I told my wife about Mariam. Althaia's understanding was as surprising to me as my short time with Mariam. Althaia understood the kind of love we shared was different and that the future we would have was not for a moment what anyone could ever imagine or choose. But I did. Each and every day, I chose that life and her love and I would do it again in a heartbeat. But it was your mother who helped me make that choice.'

He gazed at her with watery eyes, the sincerity and truth shining in them warming her through.

'Mari and I—'

'Mari?'

He smiled, as if embarrassed by the name he had given her mother. '*Mariam*—' he stressed for her benefit '—and I knew that what we shared, even for that brief moment, was special but could not be. I had Althaia, she had her daughters… We felt as if it had been a gift of sorts. One that we could carry within us for ever, but not something to be revisited.

'I thought at one point…' He trailed off and Summer searched his face for a conclusion, until Kyros shook his head and any possible ending away. He sighed deeply. 'But I am here now. And so are you!' The exclamation lifted his features from darker memories and she thought she recognised some of herself in him once again. She lifted her hand to sweep aside a tendril of blonde hair that had fallen from the band and Kyros's eyes caught on her collarbone. 'Oh.'

She immediately pressed her hand over it, protectively rather than secretively.

'You have the family birthmark?' He laughed, surprised and pleased.

'Yes. It was how I first realised you were my...' The word, so strange and unused, sat on her tongue.

'Father. Yes, Summer. I am your father.'

She had waited her entire life for those words, half convinced she'd never hear them, never feel this bond that welled up between them, surrounding them, binding them together, and tears brimmed in her eyes.

'You were in Thiakos's apartment. Five months ago?'

'Yes.'

'I...' His head hung down. 'I am ashamed. I did not know who you were. An urgent business deal had brought me back from the island and I—'

'Please. You don't have to explain. What happened with Theron—'

'No. Let's not discuss that now. I will deal with him later.' Summer frowned, worried, but not wanting to contradict or push things with Kyros when things were so fresh and new. He took her hands in his and held them tight. 'There is so much I want to tell you. So much history you have back home in Greece. Perhaps, when things are settled, you could come and visit.'

'I'd like that very much,' she replied, feeling a wetness against her cheek that he reached up to brush away. His hand paused and he looked to her, seeking permission, and when she nodded his thumb swept away the tear and she leaned into his palm as if it had always been there.

Theron looked out across the impossibly flat Norfolk horizon that seemed incredible to him. It gave the sky so much space that it seemed further away than ever, so untouchable that it made his chest hurt.

He was unused to the silence and it was unnerving. It gave rise to too many thoughts—thoughts that were on the future now. Summer had her father. When she and her sisters found the Soames diamonds and sold the estate, Summer would be more than financially secure. She had their love and support. She would be protected by them, her family. And Kyros would make sure that she never wanted for a single thing.

But not him.

Because he couldn't give her the one thing she wanted. It ate at his soul, scratched and lashed out like a living thing, breathing fire and burning everything it touched.

I want you to be there.

Bitter breath fell from his lips. He hadn't even been there for Kyros. He'd lied to the old man, kept him from his daughter. He had taken her virginity and kicked her out of his life as if she were less than nothing. And now she was pregnant.

Theron fisted his hands, impatient for Kyros to return, because he knew what was coming. He'd seen it when the old man had looked at him as if he were a stranger. Family meant everything to Kyros. And he was not part of Kyros's family.

She is your family.

He rejected the thought that sounded far too much like Althaia, making his heart hurt all the more. He felt torn between the absolute desire, a need so powerful it rocked his foundations, to be there for Summer. With her and their child. But he couldn't. He couldn't make that promise. Even the thought of it tore his heart, his pulse pounding, a cold sweat tickling his neck.

The breath left his lungs, burning as it did, as he thought of what he would miss. Watching Summer grow big and round with their child. The quick change of her temper, from ridiculous anger to tears, to a laugh so pure it healed everything. The way she'd look at the world as if everything was wondrous and worth study, worth investigation. He'd miss the moment of her success when she was able to find the jewels with her sisters. The moment that her mother would receive the treatment she needed, and the moment Summer realised that it had worked. That it had all been worth it. In his mind's eye, Theron saw her future, full of love and laughter and sunshine. And he wasn't in it.

She had everything she needed now. Her father. Her mother. The diamonds. There was nothing for him to give her other than promises he couldn't keep.

The sound of the Jeep's engine firing drew Theron back to the present and he looked up to find Kyros standing at the top of the stone steps.

'She's incredible,' Kyros said, as if in wonder at his daughter.

'She is,' Theron agreed.

'I looked for her mother once.'

Theron frowned in confusion.

Kyros sighed. 'I…thought you might have known because of Lykos, but this surprises you?'

'I had no idea. I didn't…' He clenched his jaw, hating the words he forced from his lips. 'I didn't believe her. When she first told me.'

Kyros nodded, looking out over the estate's long driveway, squinting in the sun. And, without another word, he got into the Jeep and drove away.

Summer was looking for Theron. Meeting her father had been beyond anything she could have imagined. It had healed a part of her that had ached since first finding the photo and soothed a part of her that had hurt for years.

She had just got off the phone with her mother and felt strangely as if everything was falling into place. Mariam had been shocked, yes, but Summer hadn't missed the hope and the yearning in her mother's voice. As if she still thought of Kyros, still cared for him. Mariam had been desperate to explain that she had kept Kyros's identity secret out of respect for his wife. It had been her decision to embark on that affair and she had hated the thought of Summer or Al-

thaia suffering because of it. And even though she'd
hated lying to Summer she had honoured the promise
she had made to him. Mariam told her that she had
always intended to tell her one day, but somehow that
day had just got further and further away. She'd pep-
pered Summer with questions about Kyros, and was
startled by her response.

'He will be in England for a while and I was hoping that you would come up to Norfolk. We have some
news and I would like you and Kyros to be part of that.'

Her mother had agreed instantly, but Summer had
been distracted because she'd seen Theron through the
window, looking out at her father's car driving away.

As she turned towards the estate's entrance Summer
decided that she didn't want to be like her parents—two
people who clearly had strong feelings for each other
but had missed so much. She was happy that Kyros had
stayed with Althaia, that the love they'd shared had accepted and moved beyond his affair with her mother. But
the thought of that lost time was like a pull on her heart.

She didn't want that with Theron. She didn't want
to miss another minute with him. Because, even when
they were arguing, he seemed to understand her. Even
when he teased her, he taught her something about
herself. And it was more than that…it was *him*. She
wanted to know *him*. She wanted to help soothe the
hurts she felt were just beneath the surface. His inse-
curity about his place with Kyros, the loss of his relationship with a man who was still like a brother to
him even after ten years of silence—and the deepest
pain of the loss of his parents. She wanted to help him

heal. She wanted him to see what she saw in him. She wanted him to see…how much she loved him.

She drew to a stop, her hand covering her mouth in shock. *She loved him.*

The man who yelled at her for trying to drag compost across the floor, the man whose eyes didn't glaze over when she talked about her work, who could see how important her independence was, who understood her need to be responsible and accountable to and for herself. The man who had brought her to dizzying heights of pleasure, the man who was the father of her unborn child. He had asked her to marry him once and she had said no. But now it was all she could think of.

She burst through the front doors of the house, hoping that he would still be standing where she had seen him from the window, but he wasn't. She turned, looking out to the road, her heart thumping with the need to see him, to tell him. Not just about what had happened with her father, but her feelings for him. Her love.

She was teary from happiness and she couldn't wait to share it with Theron. He had brought this to her. He had brought her father to her and given her hope and a sense of more than she could ever imagine.

A little voice in her head told her to slow down, to hold back, to pull back from the edge, when all she wanted to do was hurl herself over it with blind faith and love. Maybe her head had been turned by Catherine's journals, a treasure hunt and what she secretly believed was a reunited love between her parents, but all this…*happiness*…she didn't think she'd felt it before.

Theron was at the table they had sat at yesterday and, when he saw her, his eyes raked over her hotly as if he'd never seen anything more beautiful and she felt so utterly precious. Until he blinked and the look was gone. She frowned, rubbing her arms against the sudden bite to the westerly wind, and her steps slowed as she approached. It was as if a cloud had passed over the sun and she resisted the urge to shiver.

He sat there, unmoving, as if he were cut from a piece of dark marble, eyes watching her in one long gaze, taking her in completely. She halted on the other side of the table, suddenly uncomfortable. She could see his jaw flexing from here.

'Theron—'

'How was it?' he pressed out through teeth she was sure were clenched.

She looked about the garden, trying to find signs for why it felt as if everything was strange all of a sudden. Off-kilter, as if she were in a dark, twisted, kaleidoscope version of her world.

'It was…amazing,' she hedged, not able or willing to lie. 'He…is beyond what I'd hoped. He wants to see Mum,' she admitted, unable to prevent the hope in her voice. 'And I can't thank you enough. For calling him. Bringing him here,' she said, hoping that the sincerity in her voice, the truth of it would penetrate this strange, hard outer shell he seemed to have retreated behind. Her stomach twisted as she realised that something bad must have happened between him and Kyros.

'Theron, did something—'

'It's good. That he wants to see your mother.'

She frowned at his responses, his actions, all just a little delayed. She felt out of step with him in a way that she'd never done before. Giving up all pretence, she rushed round the table and went to him, kneeling on the floor, her hands reaching for his, uncaring of how desperate or needy she might look.

'Theron, in the last week...' She struggled to find the words. His lack of response, the way he looked at her as if he couldn't comprehend her behaviour, was awful in comparison to how she'd always felt understood by him. She huffed out a breath, shook her head a little and said, 'Theron, ask me to marry you again.' The smile pulling at her lips, the sparkle she could feel in her eyes hung on a heartbeat. And as if she could sense him withdrawing even in her silence, she leant upwards, reaching for him, and pressed kisses against firm, unyielding lips.

It was then that she realised her heart was already breaking. It had cracked just a little each minute since she'd seen him sitting at the table. And still she kissed him. Again and again, hoping that he'd open beneath her. Wishing that he'd let her in.

Finally, he reached up to her hands to pull them free from his neck and leaned away from her, that dark hollow look in his eyes. And this time she wasn't able to prevent the shiver that trembled through her body.

'Ask me to marry you,' she whispered. 'Please, just—'

'No, Summer.'

And her heart shattered.

'Why?' she asked, not quite sure she wanted to know the answer.

'I could ask the same question,' he said, his tone devoid of emotion. She stood up and frowned at him, stepping away from him, wondering why the sun she felt against her skin wasn't warming her.

'What?' she asked. 'Why I want you to ask me to marry you?' He nodded. 'Because I...' The words felt silly now. Strange. Even though in her heart she knew it was the truth, saying them to him now when he was being like this felt wrong. 'I want us to be a family,' she replied eventually.

Her stomach dropped as she looked at his face, and she knew somehow that she'd said absolutely the wrong thing. But, before she could take it back, Theron stood from the chair and turned his back on her as if unable to look at her any more. The ground beneath her feet shifted and Summer couldn't work out what had happened. When had everything gone so wrong?

'You have a family, Summer. Your sisters, your mother... Kyros.'

'Is that what this is about? My father?'

Theron took her question and turned it in his mind. Was it about Kyros? It might have started out like that, trying to protect Kyros from Summer and then to protect the old man from Theron's own mistake.

Liar. You were protecting yourself then, just like you are now.

No!

Theron knew how much growing up without Kyros

had hurt Summer, he knew what she wanted, what she needed. Stability, safety, security...she'd asked him to make that promise and he just couldn't. A part of him knew that he was being irrational, but the feral part, the animal instinct was flooding him with the need to flee. It felt visceral and all-consuming and he shook with the effort to fight it.

I want us to be a family.

He'd wanted that for so long. For ever. But he couldn't... Images of his parents' fear-filled eyes, of Althaia's, full of pain, of Lykos's hurt and anger, turning away from him, and his heart turned in on itself.

'No,' he said, having to clear his throat, finding the strength for what he needed to do. 'This has nothing to do with Kyros,' he said, turning to hold her gaze, surprised at the numbness settling over his body. 'You have what you need now, Summer. You have the diamonds, your mother will receive her treatment and you will be supported by your family. Kyros will ensure that none of you will want for anything ever again.'

'But I want *you*,' she said, her words bouncing off the barriers around his heart. 'I *love* you.' A distant part of him recognised the panic, the hurt flooding her expressive features, but that numbness was too strong. 'Can't you see that?'

'You can't see love,' he retorted.

'Neither can you see faith,' she returned instantly.

'So you think you love me? In a matter of days?' he scoffed, wondering at his own cruelty.

'In a matter of *moments*,' she replied determinedly.

As if somehow his dismissal of her had only made her stronger. 'From the moment I saw you I—'

He shook his head, the act cutting her off mid-sentence. He was glad. He didn't want to hear the rest of what she had to say. He knew instinctively that he would bring out those words to torture himself in years to come. When he thought of her. When he thought of their child.

Would his child feel the same sense of loss as Summer had done? As he himself had done? The ground beneath his feet jerked, but he ignored it. No. She and Kyros would make sure that the child wanted for nothing, including love.

As if her thoughts began to follow the same path as his, her hands flew to her stomach as if to protect it from their words. Their hurt.

She looked up at him, her eyes watery but glinting with something else. Something fearfully like understanding.

'I think…' she said, her breath shuddering through her words as if she were fighting to say them. 'I think…' she tried again '…that you are scared.' His scoff gave her pause, but she pressed on. 'I think that you have experienced great loss and hurt over the years and that…that the idea of family is terrifying to you.'

'Summer—' he warned.

'I think that this family is something you want so much that it terrifies you.'

He turned away, unable to look at the truth shining in her eyes as she spoke. From over his shoulder, he heard her words.

'So I don't need a promise from you that you'll be there for me. I'm promising to be here for you.'

He took a step away from her, the anguish in his heart so severe that he feared he'd never recover.

'I will *always* be here for you,' she said as he took a second step and a third. And just as he reached the car he could have sworn that he heard her say, 'I love you.'

'Oh, Summer, when did this happen?' Skye asked.

Summer held back a sob and looked at her hands. 'A couple of hours ago.'

'Oh, hun!' Star cried, pulling her into a hug that Skye quickly added herself to.

Summer let herself sink into her sisters' embrace for a moment, indulging in their comfort. She'd meant what she'd said to him. She did have faith that he would come back to her. That he loved her. But there, in their arms, she allowed herself to accept the possibility that he might not be able to overcome the traumas of his past.

'You're sure he's going to come back?' Skye asked and Summer nodded, blinking away the tears.

'And if he doesn't?' Star tentatively asked.

'Then we will be fine,' Summer insisted, pulling her head up from the hug to speak and lock eyes with her sisters. 'Mum raised us all on her own. And I have you both. And we'll find these damned diamonds and sell the estate to Lykos and Mum can be receiving treatment as quickly as the beginning of next week. And then—*then* I can make a plan.'

'What about uni?' Star asked, her eyes glistening with sympathetic tears.

'I'll take a few years' sabbatical,' Summer replied, her own eyes glistening. Not with regret, but determination. 'This is the twenty-first century, and I can and will have my child, my education *and* my dream job.'

After a beat, her sisters sent up squeals of delight and cheered, Star started to dance and when Skye turned to watch her, laughing, Summer allowed herself just a moment of hurt that Theron wasn't there to witness her family's joy for her. Because now the ache in her heart wasn't just for herself, it was for him. It was for the damage done by his childhood that held him back from being all that he could be, feeling all that he could feel.

As she looked up at her sisters, celebrating her pregnancy, the culmination of their journey to find the Soames diamonds, their heritage, their mother's future health and the love that had inspired it all, Summer felt and saw the richness of life. She understood why Catherine had protected the jewels from a husband who would most likely have sold them. She understood too how Catherine had embraced the love she had felt for Benoit and Hātem, despite the heartache. How she had used it to give her the strength she'd needed in her marriage and her motherhood. Summer looked around the room and felt the Soames heritage rise up, as if generations of Soames women were here to witness and celebrate yet another of their line.

She allowed a tear at the thought of having to sell the estate to roll down her cheek—she would give it that—

knowing that she would take their heritage with them forward into their new future, with their mother's health secured and her sisters' happiness assured.

'Let's do it,' she announced.

Skye frowned. 'Do what?'

'Find the diamonds!'

'What, now?' Star asked. 'It's five-thirty in the morning,' she replied as if Summer had lost her mind.

'We've been talking all night?' Summer asked, shocked.

'Yes!' Star and Skye announced together, laughing.

'I'm so sorry,' Summer said, thinking of how tired they would all be.

'Don't be,' Skye said. 'It's been a while since we stayed up like that. I've missed it.'

'And I've missed you,' Summer said, looking between Skye and Star. 'The last couple of years, it's felt a little like we've all been drifting apart.' She'd been scared to say it, but breathed a sigh of relief as she saw on their faces that her sisters felt the same way. She reached for their hands, a smile of joy pulling at her lips. 'And now you're going to be living in France, and you in Duratra… Everything's changing,' she said, her voice soft with wonder. 'But that's okay. We don't always have to have a plan, we don't always have to see our path. Sometimes, we just need a bit of faith.'

This time Star laughed. 'Who are *you* and what have you done with Summer?' she demanded.

'I am your sister,' she said, the tears welling once again. 'And I'm going to need both of you to help me so much in the next few years.'

'Whatever you need,' said Star.

'Whenever you need it,' said Skye.

Staring into the flames of the fireplace in Lykos's London townhouse, Theron bowed his head, his fists clenched against the pain that still rocked his body from Kyros's dismissal of him from his life. From his own personal exile from Summer's life. But this time, instead of fighting it, he chose to feed the anger instead. The fury coursing through his veins at what had happened after and at what had happened so many years before collided, and he glared up at Lykos.

'You knew,' Theron growled.

Lykos's silvery gaze narrowed ever so slightly before he nodded firmly, confirming the accusation.

'You knew that Kyros had an illegitimate child—*Summer*—and that is why you left all those years ago?'

Lykos looked away, as if debating how to handle him.

'No, I'm done, Lykos. No more evasions, no more lies or witty rebukes. No more. I want the truth. All of it.'

Lykos turned his steely gaze on Theron, the anger burning like phosphorous in his eyes. 'You want the truth? Fine. When I was nineteen, Kyros asked me to go looking for Mariam Soames. He didn't tell me why, but I wasn't stupid. A Greek billionaire tycoon looking for a young Englishwoman and all he had was a faded photo?' Lykos got up out of his chair and stalked over to the window, the sun beginning to rise across the London skyline. 'He had betrayed Althaia! He had betrayed his family!' Lykos raged.

Theron might have flinched but his own anger was simmering. 'So you discovered Summer's existence, and what—just abandoned them?'

'No. Over the years, I have checked up on them. Made sure they were okay.'

'Really? So, Mariam Soames' stage three cancer diagnosis just slipped through the gaps then?' Theron demanded. 'The way that Summer constantly worries about money, about paying her sisters back for all they have sacrificed for her to attend university?' Theron spat before rising out of his chair to face Lykos. 'A girl who thinks that spending one hundred euros on a dress for herself is an extravagance she doesn't deserve, Lykos. You've drunk more than that this evening alone!'

'I didn't know about the cancer,' Lykos roared back. 'I'm going to buy the estate!'

Theron shook his head in disgust. 'Were you? Why did you call me, Lykos? The truth this time.'

'I recognised her, that night in the restaurant. I knew who she was. But what I didn't recognise was the way you looked at her. Because I've *never* seen you look at a woman like that. And I know—or I *thought* I knew—how you would feel if she were pregnant.'

'What do you mean, *thought* you knew?'

'I believe it's time for you to tell me just what the hell you think you're doing here with me instead of being with *her*,' Lykos spat disdainfully. Theron could see it as Lykos paced back and forth in front of the fireplace—the anger that he had been keeping at bay all evening.

'What is it to you?' Theron demanded, wanting it. Relishing it.

In the blink of an eye, Lykos spun round, grabbed Theron by the shirt collar and shoved him up against the wall. 'You walked away from them!' he roared, the fury in his eyes blazing as strongly as the hot coals in Theron's gut. 'You know where we came from and you *walked away*?'

Theron shoved both palms into Lykos's chest, pushing him back, but not as far as he'd have liked. 'Yes!' he roared back, stepping forward and closing the space he'd just created between them. His blood pounded in his veins, his hands fists already and desperate for a fight, for the sting of physical pain to overshadow the emotional wound that he'd opened up in himself and he feared would never heal.

'How dare you?' Lykos growled.

Theron shoved again and the look on Lykos's face was thunderous. But also knowing.

'What does it matter to you, Lykos?' he demanded.

'Because your parents *died*, Theron. But mine left. They—as you have done—*chose* to leave.' The disgust written on his face was so much worse than his anger. 'And you have *no* idea what that feels like.'

'No? Like when *you* chose to leave?'

'I asked you to come with me. *You* chose *him*.'

'I chose family, Lykos. I chose Althaia and Kyros. And…' Theron clenched his jaw, a wave of grief hitting him hard and threatening to pull him under '…you didn't even come to the funeral.' His eyes felt hot and wet and he had to turn away.

'I was there.' Lykos's words were a low whisper. 'I was there, Theron. I just…didn't come close enough for you to see. How could you think I wouldn't be?'

'Because everyone leaves, Lykos. Everyone. My parents, you, Althaia. And when Summer asked me to promise to be there—to give her the one thing her father had not been able to give her… I just couldn't. I've hurt enough. It's easier to let her go.'

'So she was right. You are scared? Theron—' Lykos started, but Theron interrupted, not wanting to hear what his friend had to say.

'No. I'm done. With the lot of you,' Theron said, turning away and grabbing his suit jacket.

'Then you are not the man I thought you were,' Lykos accused.

Theron paused. Jaw clenched, hands fisted, all that anger and hurt so very close to the surface.

'I called you because I knew she was pregnant. I called you because I knew how much you cared for her and I knew how much you would love both her and your child. But love isn't anything without faith. And I was hoping she'd have taught you that.'

'Faith?'

The words so familiar, bound up in a one-hundred-and-fifty-year-old treasure hunt that had nothing to do with him, struck a chord and held him still.

'Faith that it's worth it. Faith that her love for you is more powerful than the hurt that you *might* feel,' Lykos demanded.

While faith can't be seen, it can be felt.

Theron shook the words from his memory.

'And you love her?'

'Yes, of course,' he admitted, his head bowed.

'Then you are a fool and you don't deserve her at all.'

Theron rounded on Lykos, fury spreading through his chest.

'No,' Lykos pressed. 'You don't get to have it both ways. You can't love her and turn your back on her and your child because you're scared, Theron. Be better than my parents. Be better than me, dammit, and I swear…if I have to say one more soppy thing to get you to realise that you need to go back and fight for her, I'll kill you myself,' he finished, angrily throwing his hands into the air and turning to pour himself another drink.

Theron couldn't help the laugh that launched from his chest, cutting through the tension and the anger. It cracked something within him, letting something free. Something powerful, strong, bright and healing.

'I'm not joking, Theron. If you tell anyone what I've just said, I'll hunt you down,' Lykos threatened, pointing at him with his whisky glass. 'Sit down,' he ordered.

'Why?'

'Because you need a plan.'

'A plan?'

'Do I have to do everything for you, brother? To win her back, of course.'

* * *

The sisters crept through the tunnel, Summer in the lead, jumping at every little sound, and laughing at themselves.

'Why is this so creepy?' Star asked in a whisper.

'Why are you whispering?' Skye asked, also in a whisper.

Summer felt the childlike giggle rumble in her chest. She felt drunk. Drunk on love and excitement— all the more sweet for the underlying ache that felt as if it would always be there until Theron came back to her.

If.

No. She wouldn't think like that.

She held the key in one hand and the torch in the other and came to a stop, her sisters stumbling a little.

'Aren't we on the other side of Catherine's bedroom?'

'Yup,' Summer confirmed with a smile.

'All this time!'

Skye shushed Star as Summer found the lock and retrieved the key. The last time she'd been here was with Theron. He had been so close she had felt—

'Summer?'

'Sorry.' Summer shook the memories from her head and pushed the key and turned, this time gently pressing against a door that swung inward as easily as if it had been used only yesterday. She cast a glance to her sisters and, holding out her hand for Skye, who held out her hand for Star, they made their way through the door.

The torch illuminated a room large enough for them

all to stand, albeit slightly hunched. There were shelves
on the walls lined with books that Star was instantly
drawn to, and Skye's torch beam passed thoroughly
over every inch of the room as if properly inventorying
the space. But Summer was drawn to a table beneath
a once-white dustsheet and when she gingerly lifted
the sheet she saw three velvet-covered boxes on it.

'Summer?'

She removed the sheet and her sisters huddled
around as Summer lifted the first box, the smallest of
the three. At her sisters' encouraging nods she raised
the lid and in the torch's beam three diamonds sparkled so much that she had to blink. Perched between
the folds was the most beautiful ring she'd ever seen,
pristinely preserved and absolutely breathtaking. All
the sisters lost their breath simultaneously. Gingerly,
Skye reached for the second box and Star the third, as
Summer placed the torch on the floor facing up to il-
luminate the small space better. Star's box was deeper
and narrow, and when she lifted the lid she gasped at
the sight of the large diamond in the centre of an exquisitely detailed diadem. And when Skye opened the
box she held to reveal a stunning necklace the rush of
air from her lungs drew the gazes of her sisters and
they each sighed, as if stunned by the sheer opulence
and beauty that Catherine had hidden away.

A longing rose in Summer's chest, a want that rivalled the way she felt about Theron, but different.
Sadder. She would love to have kept these pieces. Not
because of their financial value but their emotional
one. It was as if each of the sisters was taking a mo-

ment, remembering the journeys that had brought them here. All they'd wanted was to fund their mother's treatment, and now they would be able to do that.

But Summer had sensed a change in her siblings. Their journeys had done more than bring them here. They had changed, and not because of the men they'd met and now loved, but because of the women they had become. Women who were worthy of this inheritance, as Catherine had known they would be. And it was there, in a secret room created by their great-great-great-grandmother, she felt as if something had been righted in the world, felt the sigh of relief that came when something had found its true home.

She allowed that feeling to fill her, even as she knew that within hours, after meeting Mr Beamish, the estate lawyer, she would be arranging for the sale of the estate, and it hurt. A layer added over the ache caused by Theron. Summer knew that it would likely get worse in the weeks to come, that hurt and pain, if he didn't return to her as she'd hoped. But for the moment she focused on the plan. Even if his voice whispered in her ear.

Plans are not wants. What do you want?

Summer wanted him. She wanted this. She wanted the future that she could see just beyond her reach. And with a hand around the curve of her bump, she wondered if she had the faith to make something magical happen.

CHAPTER TEN

FOUR HOURS LATER and the world looked impossibly different. Summer's head was spinning at the shocking plans she had put into motion. Her sisters looked at her, eyes wide, round but utterly thrilled.

'Are you sure you want to do this?'

Summer was so tempted to shake her head. She was terrified but also excited, as if she were on a roller coaster and never wanted to get off. So she nodded, quickly and surely. 'Yes. I am.'

'You're crazy,' Skye whispered in awe. 'But I love it.'

'Good. Because I'm going to need Benoit's help. And lots of it!'

'Duratra has incredible metalworkers. They made the necklace. I'm sure that they could help too.'

'I would *love* that, Star. I think Catherine would have too,' Summer said, the press of tears, happy ones for now, against the backs of her eyes.

They were in the office where Skye, Star and Summer's journey had started just under two months ago. Of all the rooms and corridors Summer had searched, she'd never come back to this one, knowing that the hard-faced portrait of Elias Soames sent shivers down her spine every time she caught sight of it. But somehow, at that moment, it felt poignant, *right*, that they had come full circle to end where it had all begun.

Summer sat between her sisters as Mr Beamish imperiously scrawled on the paperwork—a witness following his every signature—seemingly thankful that the whole sorry mess of the Elias Soames estate was soon to be behind him. Star peered over her shoulder at the room off to the side, where Mariam Soames and Kyros Agyros had been sequestered for the last hour.

'Do you think they're okay?' Star asked.

'He's very handsome, your father,' Skye said with a smile.

'They have a *lot* of catching up to do,' Summer said, her heart warming.

'Did you see the way she looked at him?' Skye asked. *Fireworks*, she mouthed and Star let out a snort.

'Even though it's Mum, that's still a bit—'

The door to the room opened and all three sisters squeaked and turned away as if naughty schoolgirls being caught out. Mariam Soames was blushing like one herself, and the twinkle in Kyros's eyes was something magical to Summer.

'And that concludes our business, I believe,' Mr Beamish announced, calling their attention back to him. 'The estate, the entail, all yours now that you've found the Soames diamonds.' Summer felt a sigh of relief, no longer expecting someone to magically appear and snatch it all away from them. 'Congratulations. I hope that—' he broke off, looking around at the dark, damaged house with barely concealed disgust '—you are happy here.'

The girls couldn't help but laugh as he hightailed it out of the estate with his assistant and the witness as quickly as humanly possible.

'And you are sure that this is something you want to do?' Kyros asked his daughter, everyone seeming to hold their breath.

'Absolutely,' Summer replied resolutely. 'I—*we*—couldn't be doing this without you, though. And we can't thank you enough.' Her sisters' agreement rose in the air, but Kyros seemed to shake them off, the swift jerk of his head reminding her bruised heart of Theron.

Mariam Soames looked to Kyros. 'But after Althaia…'

Summer could sense it—her mother's sadness, guilt even, about Kyros caring for another sick lover.

'It is the least I can do,' Kyros said, taking her hand in his and gazing into her eyes, 'and the least I want to do. The treatment will start the day after tomorrow and I will be there with you every second of it. And when you beat it, you will come with me to Greece and recuperate in the sun, on my island.'

Star's eyes bugged out. 'He owns an island?' she whispered, and Summer smiled.

'You own a country,' Skye chided.

'Well, not *own* and not *yet*,' she replied, fanning herself as if the thought was suddenly quite overwhelming.

'And I own an estate,' Summer said in wonder as her sisters looked at her with joy and excitement for her.

'Yeah, you do,' Skye said, gently bumping her shoulder against Summer's shoulder.

It unfurled within her, this sense of rightness and excitement. She would restore the building using the latest and safest technologies and ensure that Catherine's heritage, *their* heritage, would stand for a very, very long time.

Once again, she could have sworn she heard the sound of a child's laughter disappearing into the estate, and, whether it was prescient of the future or an echo of the past, Summer felt comforted by it. A gift, given to her by her ancestors.

The sound of wheels on gravel drew the group's attention to the windows.

'I'd hoped Beamish had left,' Skye said, failing to suppress the shiver of dislike that ran through her body.

'He must have forgotten something,' Summer said, standing from her seat.

'I'll go,' Star offered.

'That's okay,' Summer said, stretching out the slight ache across her shoulders. 'I'm sure I'll only be a moment.' She left the room before there could be any more protests. It was a strange feeling, but after weeks on her own in the estate, with her parents and her sisters here it suddenly felt crowded, a little claustrophobic even. A part of her wanted to be alone, to feel all the things that had happened to her in the last twenty-four hours. If she thought about it too hard her head started to spin.

The sound of the car grew closer and closer as she reached the front of the house and she pulled open the door in time to see a black behemoth pull to a stop. It looked like something from the army.

She frowned, a little worried now, as the passenger door opened and she heard the tail-end of an argument in heavily accented English, 'At least it's better than a convertible!'

The slam of the door drew her attention to the tall form stepping down from the beast of a car, long legs easily reaching the distance to the ground and turning on the gravel. From the handmade shoes to the expensive superfine wool trousers moulding powerful thighs, the leather belt at lean hips she had clung to, the broad expanse of chest that made her pulse trip, she knew every inch of the father of her child and would never tire of seeing him, even if he had shattered her heart.

The sensuality of his lips was inflamed by the determined slant to them, the flare in his gaze as he drew to a sudden halt, seeing her standing in the doorway at the top of the stone steps. For moments they just stood and stared, as if gorging on the sight of each other.

They both moved at the same time, starting towards each other and stopping again.

'*Gia ónoma tou Theó...*' Summer shot a glance over Theron's shoulder to see Lykos Livas standing against the monstrous vehicle with his arms crossed over his chest and an almost childlike look of irritation on his features. Summer had to suppress a smile, guessing at the translation from the obvious impatience in Lykos's voice.

Then she saw him flinch as Lykos looked over her shoulder, and she turned to find her father and mother standing behind her with her sisters off to the side. Lykos and Kyros stared each other down, before Lykos purposely cut his gaze away.

Summer frowned, wondering what had happened there but knowing that was a story for another time. Paying no more attention to them, her gaze hungrily returned to Theron. Hope bloomed in her heart and she gazed into his eyes, knowing that something was different. She'd been waiting for the shutters to come down to mask his feelings, but they didn't and she began to believe that they might never come down again.

He opened his mouth as if to speak, then stopped. She moved a step forward as he did and then stopped again.

'I love you,' he said, and her legs trembled. 'There are things I was supposed to say. A *plan*. But… I love you.'

She couldn't help but laugh gently as she repeated the words he'd once said. 'Plans are not wants.'

'I *want* you,' he said helplessly. 'With every single fibre of my being. I want you. I always have. You need to know that. But now, and for ever, I want to *be* with you. To hear you laugh, to help you cry, to be the vent for your anger, your frustration. I want to argue with you, I want to make up with you, I want to care for you, protect you, grow old with you. I just… I want to love you and be loved by you. Any plan, now or in the future, will always be for you and our child. Whether I'm with you in the same room, house or even country. Whether—' he paused, as if swallowing some deep emotion '—you want me or not.'

Her love-filled gaze cleared enough to see his sincerity, but his words brought back the memories of their argument and, despite the joy she felt at his declaration… it wasn't enough. She needed it and their child needed it. 'What changed?' she asked, shrugging helplessly.

Theron stood to his full height, never once taking his eyes from her, drawing strength from the earth beneath him to say what he needed to say, desperately hoping that Summer would know the truth of his words.

'I left because I was scared,' he said, his throat thick with emotion, the shame and hurt filling his chest. 'You asked me to be there for our child,' he said, stopping himself from explaining why. He cast a glance to where Kyros stood beside an older version of Summer and two younger women who could only be her sisters. He refused to shame either Mariam or Kyros for their choices, but he knew Summer would know the depth of her request. 'And I…that terrified me. You were right.' He shook his head, hating the way his heart trembled in his chest. 'I've lost so much family. My parents, my brother,' he said, casting a look back to Lykos, who raised a wry eyebrow. Smiling slightly, Theron realised that Lykos would always be his family. He knew the hand that Lykos had played in this, in leading him to Summer, guiding him back to where he needed to be.

He took a breath and thought of the other person he had loved and lost. 'Althaia,' he said, unable to meet Kyros's gaze. 'The thought of losing you, the thought of anything happening to you or our child... I couldn't bear it. I still can't. But even just a night without you was more painful than anything I've experienced,' he pressed on truthfully. 'And if there's even a chance that you'd consider letting me prove to you how much I love you, then please tell me. Give me hope.'

The sheen in her eyes told him there might be, but he would settle for nothing less than her words. Her heart. Even if it took him a lifetime. Behind him Lykos cleared his throat and he suddenly remembered.

'No matter what happens, though, I want you to know that the estate is yours.' He watched as her brow furrowed in confusion and he silently cursed himself. He was messing this up. 'I've spoken to Lykos and I will buy the estate.'

She stared at him, her thoughts hidden from him. 'It's not for sale,' she said quietly.

'What? You didn't find the jewels?' he demanded, shocked, a thousand fears going through his mind at once.

'We did,' Summer said, her head tilted to the side, a smile pulling at her lips. He was distracted for just a second until her words penetrated.

'But your mother's treatment?'

'I am handling that,' Kyros announced from the steps behind Summer, his arm around the woman who Summer resembled so very much. When Theron looked at Kyros this time, there wasn't disappointment or rejection, there was pride, love and a determined glint that warned Theron not to mess this up. He felt it. A blessing. One that he would never take for granted. He turned back to Summer, trying to read her gaze.

'So you're keeping the estate?' Theron asked, instinctively knowing how much she would like that.

'I still want a castle!' Lykos groused in the background, pulling smiles from both Theron and Summer almost against their will.

Summer nodded. 'Benoit and Skye will help with the redesign and Star and Khalif will arrange for help from Duratra on the large amount of metalwork I'd like done. I want to put my studies to use on the renovations.'

There was more to it, Theron knew. He could see it burning in her gaze. 'You have a plan,' he said, knowing instinctively that it would be marvellous.

'But I also have a want,' she whispered, stepping closer to him, a spark of something deliciously wicked in her eyes.

A tendril of hope unfurled in his heart and heat soaked into his bones. 'Tell me,' he demanded.

'I want you to ask me to marry you,' she said, closing the distance between them to inches.

He searched her gaze, the sparkle in her eyes, the mischief, the promise.

And his heart crashed.

He pressed his forehead against hers as an ache of sad frustration coursed through his body. 'I don't have a ring. We left London at six-thirty in the morning. I…' he bit back a curse '…I want to do it properly. I want to give you everything you deserve,' he said, his voice rough with emotion.

She bent her head back, her hazel eyes sparkling with gold. 'Is that all?' she said with a smile, though what she could possibly find to smile about he had no idea. Until she looked back to her sisters, the taller one he imagined was Skye, who smiled broadly and threw something small towards Summer, who caught it and presented it to him.

'It's perhaps a bit unorthodox, but I think Catherine would approve,' Summer said, passing him the small ring-shaped box.

'The Soames diamonds?' he asked, and she nodded, her eyes and heart seeming as full as his own felt.

He took the velvet box, warm from her touch, in his palm and pressed it against his heart. But he wanted one last thing. He would propose no matter what, but this felt right. Felt just.

He looked up to where Summer's family had gathered by the front door of the estate, catching Kyros's eye first, then Mariam's.

'Ms Soames, Kyros, I would very much like to ask for your daughter's hand in marriage. I want you to know that I will protect her and our child unconditionally, I will love her and our child unconditionally, and I will—'

'We get the idea, Theron,' Lykos said, rolling his hand as if to say get on with it. The smaller sister with red hair hid a laugh behind her hand and the older one bit her lip as if to stop herself from smiling. The love and happiness shining from Mariam was one of the purest things Theron had ever seen. She looked up to Kyros and back to him and nodded.

'You have my blessing, *yié mou*,' Kyros said, the words *my son* miraculous to hear after all these years.

And then absolutely nothing could have pulled him away from Summer.

He took her hand in his and slowly bent to one knee, unfeeling of the bite of gravel through his trousers. Wonder and awe coursed through his body as he looked up at the woman who made him feel complete. Whole. The woman he would spend the rest of his life loving to distraction.

And there, surrounded by people bonded by blood or by choice, he knew *this* was his family: Summer and their child and the people who loved and cared for them, all brought together by Catherine and the Soames diamonds. Wetness pressed against his eyes as he looked up at the love of his life. 'Would you, Summer Soames, do me the greatest honour and be my wife, my confidante, my love, my family, my *home*?'

'Yes,' Summer said as tears rolled down her cheeks and her sisters screamed and yelled, and even Lykos seemed to clear his throat of emotion. 'Yes, I will,' she said, pulling him up from the ground and bringing him into a kiss that branded his soul as hers.

'I love you,' she whispered between presses of her lips. 'I will always love you,' she promised and Theron knew that, no matter what happened in the future, the love that he felt in that moment would fuel the rest of their lives.

EPILOGUE

Five years later...

SUMMER WAS JUST finishing her journal entry. She'd been hurrying to get it done in time, looking as the clock ticked down the minutes until—

'Mummy! Mummy? Where are you?'

Right on time, she heard Katy's not so dulcet tones calling for her, even as a smile full of love pulled at her mouth. Theron always tried to keep their mischievous daughter occupied in the kitchen for at least half an hour after dinner so that Summer could have this time, knowing how important her journalling was to her.

Quickly she put down the journal, turned off the light, closed the door to the secret room, slipped through the passageway and back into the master bedroom just before Katy burst into the room.

'Mummy, where are—' Katy descended into a fit of giggles as she realised she'd been shouting when Summer was standing right there.

'Mummy, that's naughty,' she accused. It was Summer's daughter's latest delight. Although Catherine was the name on their daughter's birth certificate, they had called her Katy from day one.

'What's naughty, sweetpea?' she asked.

'*You* are!'

'*I* am? *I* am?' Summer demanded, all mock outrage as she chased her daughter with tickle fingers and they both ended up in a hysterical heap on the bed. She didn't think that there was anything more pure, more beautiful than the sound of her daughter, out of breath from laughter.

Summer pushed a dark curl from her daughter's forehead, so happy that she had her father's deep dark eyes. But the sparkle? That was *all* Soames.

'Where are my girls?' Theron's voice boomed into the room.

'Here, Daddy. Mummy's being naughty again,' Katy said, bursting into laughter as Summer's quick tickles found her.

'Oh, really?' Theron demanded as he came into the room, staring down at them with a glint in his eye that Katy was thankfully far too young to recognise. He smiled and Summer felt it in her heart.

Summer didn't know how, but he was able to do this thing where he'd look at her and time would just *stop*. She'd feel an infinity of love in an instant and knew that she could never want for anything more.

He sighed, before checking his watch, as if he'd felt it too. His eyes widened and then he pulled a grimace. 'Katy, we have to get dressed. The others are going to be here in twenty minutes.'

Katy scrabbled up on the bed and started jumping up and down, crying, 'The others are coming!'

Even as Summer put her hand out, just in case, Theron was by the bed in an instant, plucking his daughter from the air mid-jump.

'Come on, my love. You have your new dress to—'

The scream of delight from their daughter was so loud it could have burst his eardrums but he didn't flinch, didn't loosen his hold even for a second. Cradling her to him, Theron bent over the bed, Katy now giggling at being horizontal, and kissed Summer quickly but lovingly and took their daughter off to get ready for the day.

Summer watched them go until she checked the time and jumped off the bed and threw herself into the shower. Fifteen minutes later, she was showered, dry and opening the wardrobe door, marvelling at the array of colour that was on display. She passed the teals, the beautiful bright yellows and the verdant greens. There was only one colour to be worn today.

As she came down the stairs, the beautiful scarlet silk swirled around her calves, matching the red stilettos she knew that her husband would appreciate, even if she didn't last the *full* day in them. Her fingers tripped over the red velvet ribbon Katy had insisted should wrap around the banister, and the scent of pine trees and spiced orange rose up from the lower floor. Everywhere she looked was sparkles of tinsel, rich green foliage and deep red velvet. Theron, apparently, loved Christmas as much as their daughter.

An impossibly tall spruce stood proudly in the hallway to greet every member of the family as they arrived. Giant red bows, little silver bows and American candy canes hung from the boughs while sparkling cream lights twinkled between the fronds. There was a giant silver urn on the side table with mulled wine and glasses ready for their guests.

Summer inhaled deeply and rolled her shoulders free of any stiffness, relishing the excitement and anticipation of the day ahead. In the last few years it had become her favourite part of the year because it was the one time that everyone was guaranteed to gather together. At any other point, they were spread as far and wide as Greece, Duratra, France, Costa Rica and wherever else Skye could entice Benoit to wander.

But everyone came home for Christmas.

Although Kyros hadn't been happy about it, Summer and Theron had waited until Katy was three years old before marrying. By that point, Skye had married Benoit exactly a year on from his proposal in a gorgeous outdoor wedding in France, the Soames diamond necklace as her something old. And no one had minded one bit when little Katy had burst into beautiful laughter as the priest had asked for anyone to 'speak now or forever hold your peace'.

Star had married Khalif in a stunning ceremony in Duratra's capital, where the celebrations had lasted for days and Katy had been treated like a little princess and loved every minute of it. Star had worn the Soames diadem and the interlocked necklace in honour of both Catherine and Hâtem. The joining of the two families felt fated.

But Summer's wedding to Theron had been a little closer to home.

Two years ago today, Summer had walked down these very same stairs in a wedding dress of oyster-coloured silk. The design had been similar to that of the yellow dress she had bought all those years ago in Athens. And although everyone proclaimed her to be the most beautiful bride they'd ever seen, she only had eyes for Theron.

In front of their families, those of blood and those of friendship, Summer had sworn to love her husband for eternity and a day and Theron had promised to be by her side and never leave. The glint in his eye as he'd finally made the promise that had terrified him so much was more than Summer could have ever asked for.

In a mixture of Greek and English, wreaths and rings, their love had been celebrated and cemented in the estate in Norfolk that had been in her family for hundreds of years, and Summer couldn't shake the feeling that Catherine had been watching over them that day.

Before she could round the corner, Theron appeared at the bottom of the stairs and Summer couldn't help the burst of arousal from deep within her at the sight of her husband dressed in a suit that fitted him to perfection.

As if he were feeling the same way, his eyes flashed for just a moment before he blinked. But while the intensity in his gaze had been banked, in the last five years and all their years to come his thoughts and feelings were never hidden from her again.

To her surprise, he bent to one knee.

'What are you doing?'

'Asking you to marry me.'

'But—' she broke off to laugh '—we're already married,' she said as she drew closer and closer to him.

'I know. I just want to be able to promise you that I'll never leave your side in front of our family and friends as many times as possible.'

'We don't need a lavish ceremony just for that.'

'*Just* for that?' he demanded in the same way he'd once demanded what 'just a kiss' was supposed to mean. 'If I want, I will have a hundred ceremonies to tell you how much I love you and to make unending promises to the most beautiful wife a man has ever had.'

'Theron, don't let Lykos hear you say that, or he'll be offering a *thousand* ceremonies to his wife.'

Theron laughed, standing to his full height. 'I still can't quite believe that he actually ended up with a castle,' he said, fitting her to his side and placing his hand between her shoulder blades as he liked to do. He guided her to a stop and took her hand in his, pulling her round to face him.

He slowly inched forward, his lips hovering a hair's breadth from hers, pleasure and anticipation rising within her as she held onto the tease, waiting to see which one of them broke first this time.

The moment was broken by the peal of the doorbell.

Theron smiled and whispered, 'You owe me a

kiss,' into her ear before he turned and braced himself against the screams of her sisters and nieces as they rushed the couple with hugs, laughter and love. Through the chaos Summer saw Benoit following through the entrance, talking to Khalif about the incredible memorial project for his brother and sister-in-law and she couldn't help the tendril of professional curiosity getting the better of her. Theron caught her eye and understood her desire, enticing her sisters and nieces away to meet Katy, so that she could catch up on how the bridge and conservation area between two kingdoms in the Middle East was coming along.

Before long, Katy came running to find her and pull her back to the living room, where piles and piles of presents were being unloaded to her mounting horror.

'I thought we said only one present each,' Summer said, feeling a little worried.

Star laughed gently. 'We did. And we stuck to it. But we wanted to take some gifts to the children's ward at Norfolk and Norwich Hospital. The boys are going to take the girls there this afternoon.'

Understanding dawned in her eyes and she nodded, feeling a spread of love for the generosity they were able to share, but also the tug of a promise they had made when Mariam had first started her treatment.

Five years on and Mariam had received the all-clear and was officially cancer-free. The celebration planned for that evening, after Mariam and Kyros flew in from Greece, would be incredible. But no less important than the personal moment the sisters had planned for that afternoon.

Over a leisurely late brunch, that Skye argued with Theron was more lunch, and Lykos, who had arrived with his wife, rolled his eyes and complained about, saying the English didn't know anything about food, which Theron wholly agreed with, Summer felt love for her family rise up around her and fill the house completely.

In her wildest dreams she couldn't have imagined such a future. And it was all thanks to Catherine Soames. She caught her sisters' eyes and, as if they all felt and thought the same way, they quietly excused themselves from the table. Their husbands, understanding, kept the children distracted and soon Summer heard the entire group getting into their respective cars and heading out to the hospital for the family tradition that had started the year after Skye's little girl had spent a terrifying three months in hospital over Christmas. She could see that Skye was torn, wanting to go with them, and Summer put a hand on her arm for comfort.

'It's okay,' Skye insisted. 'There will be plenty more years for that. *This* is something I want to do.'

'It's something we all want to do,' insisted Star, and Summer led them to a section of wood panelling beside the master bedroom that they hadn't seen before. 'Wait…what…?'

Summer smiled and shrugged mischievously. 'Well, we were renovating so many of the areas and I thought that just because they were secret passageways doesn't mean they have to be *grim* passageways.'

Skye's eyes grew round, staring at the panelling

and finally seeing the faint impression of a secret door. 'You didn't! Benoit didn't say anything,' she chided.

'We wanted it to be a surprise,' Summer replied.

'Naughty,' Star teased.

'You're the second person who's said that to me today,' she said, confused. 'I don't think I'm naughty at all.'

Skye made a face and Summer gently nudged her with her shoulder.

Star looked up impatiently. 'Well, what are we waiting for?'

Summer laughed. 'You.'

'Me?'

'Yes. The key.'

'But that's for the… Wait. Oh, Summer!'

She smiled as Star produced the key and found the lock on a door that looked like part of the mahogany panelling beside the master bedroom.

The key slipped in as if it had been used only the day before. Which it hadn't. Summer had a secret entrance from the master bedroom to Catherine's hidden room, but she'd wanted separate access for her sisters whenever they wanted to use it.

The door opened to a gently lit corridor, grained wooden flooring and smooth plastered walls. The corridor wrapped around the bedroom and all the way to the small room Catherine had hidden the Soames diamonds in. A room which had also undergone a bit of a transformation.

Skye and Star looked around, wide-eyed, at the little room that now contained shelves and three chairs and was cosy and beautiful.

'This room is now separate from the rest of the secret passageways,' Summer explained. 'We thought that the girls might enjoy being able to use the other passageways when we're ready to show them. The renovations have made them safe and secure and I have promised Theron a thousand times that they won't get lost in them,' she assured her sisters. 'But this room is separate and can only be accessed by us. For the moment.'

Skye and Star nodded. 'It's perfect,' they said together, each taking a seat in one of the chairs.

'Have you brought them?' Summer asked.

The girls produced little velvet boxes and placed them on the table in between them. Star had brought the diadem she had worn on her wedding day, Skye the necklace and, with a little bit of a heart-wrench, Summer twisted the beautiful engagement ring from her finger, before replacing her wedding ring.

For the last five years, Summer and her sisters had been talking about the idea of returning the Soames diamonds and Catherine's journals to the secret room that had kept them safe for so many years. Unaccountably, each of the sisters felt strongly that it was the right thing to do and had decided to leave their own journals and letters for future generations of Soames women.

For a while the sisters talked, caught up, shared the stories of their lives, laughed, cried and loved, until a text from Theron announced their return. The women placed the Soames diamonds in a box on the shelf next to Catherine's journals, and their own diaries. In the years to come, those shelves would become full with the writings from generations of Soames women, each telling their own story of adversity and triumph, loss, but most of all love.

But, for now, Skye, Star and Summer left the room, locking it behind them and returning to their families, ready and waiting for Mariam and Kyros's arrival.

Later that night, as Summer got ready for bed, Theron came out of the bathroom, a towel slung low on his hips and drying his hair with another, and she marvelled at just how handsome her husband was. Not once had their attraction dimmed, even through their occasional arguments and their even more occasional hurts, and Summer wanted her husband with the same ferocity as she had on the beach at Piraeus that first time.

Theron's gaze flickered from her eyes to her ring finger and back again.

'I'm sorry, I should have said—'

He smiled, knowing and loving, the look in his eyes cutting her off mid-sentence. 'You didn't need to, *agápi mou*,' he said, kneeling on the bed, tossing the towel back into the bathroom and reaching into the drawer of his bedside table. He produced a small white box she'd not seen before. 'I know. I see you. And I love you. More than anything in the world, Summer Soames. I am the proudest man alive that you chose me and I will spend every day being worthy of it.'

Love bloomed in Summer's heart, strong, powerful, fierce and determined. He opened the box to reveal a stunning diamond engagement ring. It was different to the Soames diamond she had worn, but it was just as special to Summer.

Before reaching for it, she placed her hand on her husband's. 'Five years ago I went to Greece, looking for a part of me that I knew was missing. A part that had felt missing my entire life. And there, in Athens, I found it. Not Kyros, not my father. But you, Theron Thiakos. You are the other half of me and you will always have me and my heart, in yours.'

That night they made love until the sun crested on the horizon and not one of their family minded that they missed breakfast. Apart from Lykos, who grumbled about it for the rest of the day.

* * * * *

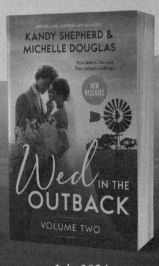

Subscribe and fall in love with a Mills & Boon series today!

You'll be among the first to read stories delivered to your door monthly and enjoy great savings.

WE
SIMPLY
LOVE
ROMANCE